**Blood made it real.
Everyone understands blood,
especially the blood of children . . .**

Cheering reached a hysterical pitch as the blond and beautiful Queen of England stepped out with a wave and a smile.

Walking beside her was the heir apparent, the next Prince of Wales.

Over the crowd's expectant hush, Madog heard the deep-throated crump of a distant explosion, then a shattering roar of glass and steel.

Now! Madog shivered. Now they were committed.

On every side the spectators were dropping to the pavement in an eerie silence, punctuated only by the soft thumps of falling bodies. A gray-suited palace security man flung himself over the Queen.

Bullets started to zing. Madog froze. No violence, that was their agreement.

Suddenly everything was changed. . . .

MERLIN'S WEB

S. W. MAYSE

AVON BOOKS ◆ NEW YORK

AVON BOOKS
A division of
The Hearst Corporation
105 Madison Avenue
New York, New York 10016

First Avon Books Printing: July 1989

AVON TRADEMARK REG. U.S. PAT. OFF. AND IN OTHER COUNTRIES, MARCA
REGISTRADA, HECHO EN U.S.A.

Printed in the U.S.A.

K-R 10 9 8 7 6 5 4 3 2 1

For Arthur Mayse
Gwae ny wna da a'e dyuyd.
Great sorrow, not to do good when opportunity comes.
—*The Heledd Poetry,* C. A.D. 850

Several people were generous with information that made it possible to write this book. It would be inappropriate to name them, but I thank them all.

AUTHOR'S NOTE

Nationalist groups are active in Wales. Most have a pacifist philosophy and work quietly by legal means to further Welsh language, culture, and political independence. A few extremists resort to bombing, arson, and other property destruction.

The existence of such groups prompted me to write this novel. The people, organizations, and incidents in the book, however, have no foundation whatsoever in reality. *Merlin's Web* is wholly a work of fiction.

S.M.

A PRONUNCIATION GUIDE

Welsh almost always puts emphasis on a word's second-to-last syllable. If you can't sound the LL, sometimes called the "hissing L," substitute an L sound. Y is a vowel and may be pronounced UH or EE or soft I, depending on its place in the word. DD is pronounced as TH in "then." F is pronounced V. Most other consonants are hard: C as in "cat," G as in "goat."

Here are some approximate pronunciations:

Gwyn—rhymes with pin

Ceridwen—Cer-ID-wen—soft vowels; roll the R

Madog—MA-dog—soft vowels

Sion—pronounced "shon"

Elen—EL-en—pronounced much like Ellen in English

Gareth—GAR-eth, rhymes with "marath-on"

Mair—pronounced "mire"—roll the R

Llanfyllin—Llan-FYLL-in—soft vowels

Dolgellau—Dol-GELL-eye

Aberystwyth—Ab-er-YST-wyth—soft vowels

Tywyn—TY-wyn—pronounced Tuh-win

1

Without tourists, the seaside resort of Tywyn was almost as desolate as it had been fourteen centuries earlier when a wild-eyed Welsh saint founded his monastery there. A December wind, full of fresh malice from the Irish Sea, whined inland from the harbour and across the famous esplanade. By one in the morning the high street's narrow houses were dark and still. An hour later, a quartet of the boys from the Tywyn rugby club blundered out of the Red Dragon's back door. They stumbled past the inn's privy in their beer fug and pissed instead into the austerely pruned front rose bed of Brynawel, elderly Mrs. Jones's house, and with a collective sigh of satisfaction stumbled homeward. The quiet of winter night again descended on Tywyn.

One solitary and unseen figure worked on. "All through the night." Maudlin song. Corgi hummed it and carefully moulded the plastic around a second concrete piling, this one under the school office. Easy as shaping a child's play dough, even in the dark. Pleasing thought. Corgi worked with smooth confidence, a product of the best training.

Nearly dawn. Not yet time to worry about daylight or someone walking a dog across the school playing-field. The fat Welsh constable Corgi had watched yesterday, helmet strap cutting deep between second and third chins, was asleep in his neat bungalow with the immaculate garden, on call. There would be no call. Tywyn was a quiet little town. Its native Welsh, the few still clinging to their bleak hills, were a dull, spineless herd, Corgi thought, their hands extended for English coins. The retired English bureaucrats and sleek hoteliers rarely called on the police. Never, yet, had they called on the bomb squad.

One last concrete piling under the school. Corgi ran his fingertips around its top, feeling the roughness and air bubbles out of sight under the wall skirting. No building inspector would bother to crouch down there with a torch. Besides, a few air holes in concrete wouldn't collapse a class-room wing. But they did make a fine rough surface to hold explosives.

Corgi, humming the syrupy tune, stroked the plastic into shape. It felt dead, slightly rubbery, like a cooling body. In the same inexplicable way, it was disappointing. Alive, people were full of possibilities for pleasure or pain. Not afterwards. Afterwards there was only debris, which looked random to the uninitiated; to the explosives expert's trained eye it revealed charges detonated with maximum structural damage.

Corgi placed the detonators, linked them, and checked over the workmanship. Flawless. Tools in the suitcase. In the unlikely event of a search, the fat constable would find only a tourist's new Marks and Spencer weekend wardrobe, passport, camera, silver cigarette lighter engraved "Deepest gratitude, M." "Yes, of course, my Aunt Mary," was the indignant answer. Who would be crazy enough, in smug seaside Wales, to substitute Moammar al-Qaddafi?

Corgi—colleagues had bestowed the name long ago—slipped the gloves from strong fingers and smoothed them side by side in the suitcase. Two detached hands, like the last time in Beirut. Or was it Athens? Corgi pulled off the Balaclava and shook out hair limp with sweat. The sea wind sidled across the school playing-field and Corgi shivered, picking up the case. Highly professional work. It would have taken the locals hours longer, and they probably would have detonated themselves into red tatters like several earlier Welsh activists. "All through the night." Perhaps there was something to be said for the song. Oppression's night is ending, welcome the glorious crimson dawn. Not Corgi's tune, but some clients sang in that key.

After a brisk walk, Corgi locked the suitcase in the boot of the stolen car and strolled on past the bus shelter. Month-old London newspapers scrabbled back and forth in the wind. The graffiti were in English. *Queen*. *West Brom Rules OK*. *Living Dead*. And the usual obscenities. Just in sight past the corner, the high street looked half-occupied. A few shops were boarded up, even in this tourist town. Tywyn's natives were mostly on the dole in Manchester, while freshly scrubbed English university graduates fought for work behind Welsh shop counters. Jobs were scarce. The explosives expert yawned theatrically into the growing daylight. No one in view. No one had noticed. Corgi idled, contemplating work well done, until lights went on behind fly-specked windows in a café across the street.

Breakfast was tasteless, offering small reward for a night's service to this soggy little country that England was edging deeper into economic oblivion. The waitress chattered on, across the grain of the radio's country and western music.

"She's an angel. She wanted to be Joseph or a shepherd, but I told her it's time she learnt to be ladylike. That's what I told her."

Corgi let her rattle on while he prodded the watery orange eggs. What did they feed the hens? Human waste, probably, in this backwater. Quarter to nine. Time to settle the bill.

"She's been driving me mad with her rehearsals, and now I'll be there tonight to see the play too. Thank goodness it's the last day before the Christmas holidays."

Corgi frowned. Last day before the Christmas holidays?

That idiot from the Welsh nationalist group had said there were three days left. It was a sheer accident that Corgi had chosen today. Amateurs. Needed lessons from the ground up, but too high-minded to ask the Provos for instruction. They'd learn.

Five minutes to nine. Corgi's fingers had only the slightest tremor when they drew out a filterless Gitane and the lighter.

"Ta, love." The waitress scooped up the money and shuffled off to the cash register.

Corgi walked out of the café and flicked the lighter, the smallest detonator he'd yet tried. A full-bodied explosion rocked the town. Glass sprayed into shops. Back in the café a woman screamed and kept on screaming. Corgi, a startled tourist, joined the handful of people hurrying by. Beyond the dirty park and the housing estate billowed a cloud of thick grey smoke. A fire engine clanked past towards the school. Rain started to fall.

The explosives expert stopped at the edge of the playing-field, surveying the destruction. The explosion had taken out the entire class-room wing, as planned; enough remained to eliminate any question of a faulty heating system or whatever excuse the police would use to dismiss the blast. A few key people would recognize the precise and masterly explosives placement. That was Corgi's secondary objective.

Flames probed up into the dirty smoke, and a group of adults were held off, choking and shielding their faces against the heat. No one was alive in there now, the explosives expert could have told them, but they would still insist on going through the motions of heroic rescue. Corgi saw crimson splashed against one standing wall, and three small bundles of rags crumpled at its foot, extruding long red ropes of intestines. Sad. That was Corgi's first objective. Or his client's, at least.

Blood made it real. Everyone understood blood, especially the blood of children.

The client hadn't enough vision to understand that. Take

out the Trawsfynydd power grid, were the orders, or fall back on a television transmitter mast. But the locals had already done both—often, if incompetently. What was the point? Corgi saw an opportunity for more effective strategy. No one would ignore this bombing. The worse the damage, the more it smashed the foundations of society. And that had its merit.

A knot of about twenty young children clung together on the pavement in unnatural silence, momentarily forgotten in the adults' ludicrous flapping at the flames. A few children clutched plastic lunch boxes, and one had dropped a white garment on the wet ground. Corgi remembered the waitress's daughter, the nativity angel. How much would the waitress care if one of those distasteful bundles were her kid? Would she be angry enough to react, or would she just snivel about God's will? The girl also would grow up to be a stupid woman shambling around a dirty café in a dying town, unless Corgi had spared her this fate.

The driver of a delivery van ran up and tugged Corgi's sleeve, gabbling in an unknown language. Corgi adopted an expression of shocked incomprehension.

One of the children broke into querulous weeping, then several started in; the sound set Corgi's teeth edge to edge. Someone ought to shut them up.

Quarter past nine. Time to move out. The explosives expert gave a shake of the head, miming grief or bemusement to anyone who might be watching, and walked away, limping slightly. It was the old training injury he received in the Libyan camp where American CIA burnouts and British SAS graduates instructed those with ambitions concerning national liberation movements. Rain and cold always stiffened the bad leg, and the rain here was bitter.

2

Peter Holt slouched near the monitor screen as the Tywyn videotape played yet again. Even on a day's visit to London, using a borrowed monitor at BBC television news in Wood Lane, he couldn't let it alone. The BBC had aired only a thirty-second clip of the erratic hand-held footage with the brief school-explosion story three weeks ago. They were fortunate to have even that; BBC Wales's mobile unit had hurried from setting up for a Theatre Clwyd performance at Dolgellau to the Tywyn school. Peter turned off the sound and leaned forward, frowning, to watch.

The devastation was awesomely thorough. It looked as though a giant fist had smashed down into a child's balsawood model building. A standing wall on the right must be part of the second class-room wing. In the centre, behind a knot of firemen, double entry doors sagged drunkenly on their hinges. Only the collapse pattern of the classroom wing showed its original size. Then there were three talking heads on the tape, local people reluctantly voicing their dismay at the accident. After that the cameraman panned along the other class-room wing, where the kids' bodies were huddled at the foot of the wall. Two shabbily dressed young men thrust themselves determinedly inframe from the left towards the cameraman, their faces contorted angrily with shouting. Peter's Welsh was not

6

colloquial, but he'd picked out "English ghouls" clearly enough on the sound. The BBC man edged right and kept on taping the bodies until the footage fragmented into a confusion of hands across the lens, a raised fist, and finally a dizzying blur as the locals threw the cameraman to the ground. Then to black.

That was it. Seven minutes, forty seconds of useless hand-held footage—which Peter Holt had played twenty-odd times in search of the clues that must be there. For a minute he stared on at the blank grey screen, seeing only the reflection of his own long, supposedly earnest face. Absently, he combed a hand through his thinning brown hair. Even through the screen's distortion his face looked anxious; it had looked that way since April, when he had been carpeted over the Welsh-extremists story and bounced back onto the street as gormless Harry Price's number-two man on BBC Wales's news desk in Cardiff.

They'd called him all the way to London just for his annual review, finished an hour ago. The panel of four BBC Pooh-Bahs—that in itself boded no good for what was usually a routine business—made it perfectly clear that he was a hair's breadth from getting the sack. They had icily informed him that he would be granted no salary increment this year.

Peter thumbed the reverse button on the monitor. There was nothing to add, no sudden insight. He was wasting his time. He crossed the borrowed office to the computer terminal and called up his weekend assignment on the terminal's video screen, a story on the Allt Valley Dam protest scheduled for Saturday. Undeb Cymru Fydd and the other nationalist associations were planning to bus two thousand into Cardiff for the march and demonstration—they said. Peter Holt, after four years in BBC Wales, had learned to divide any Undeb estimate of the size of a crowd by exaggeration and apathy and middle-class self-importance. His arithmetic reduced two thousand people to five hundred at best. He scanned the map of North Wales, found the Allt Valley, and followed the projected high-water line

over the villages of Llanallt and Hafoty. The rally to protest the decayed hamlets' drowning would start a rash of
painted slogans, Welsh Nationalist ranting in the Commons, and clumsy minor vandalism. Then, nothing. The
whole thing would be forgotten.

Back in the seventies Wales had stirred restlessly like a
battered old dragon, then it had nodded off to sleep. Now
it stirred again. Or was this the death rattle? All the English problems—rocketing unemployment, street violence,
police crack-downs, the National Front, curfews, the es-
calating Japanese and West German purchase of anti-
quated industry—rippled into Wales and mingled
unhealthily with the old language issue. Inevitably, Peter's
thoughts drifted from the Allt Valley Dam towards other
nationalist concerns.

He killed the protest story from the screen and called
up library files on Undeb Cymru Fydd activities and the
old debates on home rule and Welsh television. He was
doing it again, getting obsessive about another Welsh story,
as though the last big one hadn't already cost him seniority
and salary. Exorcising it the only way he knew, Peter
pulled out his yellow newsprint pad—a BBC economy
measure—and went over his notes about Tywyn.

Police claimed the Tywyn explosion was a boiler mal-
function. So why did the Liverpool bomb squad arrive by
helicopter within an hour? In a school only two years old
was a faulty heating system likely? Most of all, why would
a boiler explosion leave the school's central boiler room
standing but demolish a class-room wing? It added up to
a bomb: not one of the cottage-burners' home-made Mo-
lotov cocktails but a highly complex bomb.

Ysgol Gymraeg Tywyn was the Welsh-language school.
Who would destroy it on a school morning? No Welsh
extremist group. They wouldn't murder kids who could be
family. Peter had learned never to underestimate the Welsh
sense of kinship. He reckoned the Welsh could attach
names to three-quarters of the bombings and burnings, but
they never would. Family was family. The Welsh bickered

interminably among themselves, but when it came to English police and Welsh suspects, Wales became a single close-mouthed clan. At first he'd thought the two young men who attacked the camera crew in Tywyn must have been involved somehow; then he realized they were simply protecting their own.

The nationalists stridently denied responsibility. A generation ago, Welsh activists had routinely destroyed government property and turned themselves in to police. But this generation bombed television transmitters, burned cottages, and hurled paint bombs at the King and Queen. Now the Royals didn't even venture into Wales. If not the Welsh groups, then who? The bombing carried earmarks of the Provos, the Libyans, someone like that. But the Provos never mucked about in Wales, perhaps out of deference to the Celtic cousins, and the others would scarcely bother. Libya had long since cooled down over the Yanks' idiotic bombing of Tripoli from an English air base. Peter glanced at his notepad and found he had scrawled it deep enough to tear the cheap newsprint. Who?

Professionals.

Peter thought of the children, murdered in cold blood. The kids standing behind the police cordon were about Andrea's age, and, as his seven-year-old daughter still sometimes did, one little girl had a thumb thrust in her mouth as a solace against the terror. Belfast in mid-Wales. That prospect *was* terror.

Peter's exorcism was a failure. Nothing added up. But he couldn't shake his hunch, bolstered by mutterings from his dependable Welsh contacts, that something big was on the books for Wales. Was Tywyn the start?

Peter considered his lost seniority, his maintenance and support payments, and McKinley's promise that any further muck-raking would cost him his job. He considered prudence and decided to file it under C for cowardice. A good reporter couldn't afford it. He straightened his tie and picked up his thumbed-over notepad. It was properly Harry Price's decision, but Harry would dither for months and forget it. Peter headed down the hall to the executive manager.

Gwyn leaned against the clammy brick wall and listened to the echoing drip of water. The place smelled of mould. Like a prison. He pressed the heels of his hands hard into his eyes. When he dropped his arms to his sides, the blackness was merely grey.

The grey was broken by a slash of dingy yellow as the door at the end of the corridor swung open on its single hinge. Briefly the light outlined the masonry rubble scattered the length of the hallway. Decay set in quickly. This had been an annex of London's Tate Gallery only a year ago, before the Provisional IRA expressed their final criticism of the arts.

A man shuffled through the doorway, dragging a plastic sack and mumbling inaudibly. Hell-fire. The last thing Gwyn needed was a scavenger prying around. The rest of the team would be along anytime. It was an idiotic place to meet, he realized now, but it was near their destination. And he liked the symbolism. He watched the tramp scuffle and stoop along the littered corridor, turning over boards and chunks of plaster. He was singing tunelessly under his breath. Gwyn pushed himself flat against the damp wall and wondered what to do about the old wretch.

The derelict looked up suddenly, grunted, and picked his way over. Would telling him to leave bring an outcry?

"Go find your own, mate," the tramp croaked out of the gloom. He didn't sound as old as he looked, hunched in his army-surplus trench coat with the watch cap pulled low over his brow. "This 'ere's mine. Has been for months."

"I'm not in your way," said Gwyn. What now? Giving him money might attract all his seedy friends, the victims of a decaying bourgeois society.

"Stealing."

"You have nothing I want to steal, I can tell you." He

eyed the door. The others would arrive to find him debating territorial rights with a derelict.

"All the same. Stealing from the poor."

"I don't own anything." *Including my soul.* "And I don't want to."

"Property is theft," agreed the derelict.

Mouthy devil. It was his luck to get a Marxist tramp. "Friend, if I had the price of a meal I'd give you it. But then I wouldn't be here, would I?"

"Meeting someone, are you? Turning tricks. On my turf."

"Are you mad? Look—"

The tramp straightened, grinning, and one gold tooth gleamed dully. *"Paid a phoeni, machgen."*

Gwyn struggled to take it in stride. "What do you mean, don't worry? You're late. And stick to Welsh. You have less of an American accent."

Madog Nilsson sketched a casual salute. "Where are the others?"

"Coming. I wanted to talk to you before they get here." Gwyn and Madog had four hours to talk, driving in from Cardiff before dawn, but it took Gwyn more than four hours to overcome his revulsion for what they would do today and the compromises he'd had to make to do it—not the least of these were Madog and his cursed technology.

"Maybe you should stay out of it," Gwyn added. "You've done all you can. We're grateful." True, but it stuck in his throat. Everything about Nilsson stuck in his throat and had for three months. His privilege, his military slang, his juvenile antics. Gwyn knew his resentment was small and mean, which only deepened it. If only he could work alone, take it all on his own head. . . .

Madog looked at him in the gloom. "All right."

"Good." He'd expected an argument. No, he'd wanted an argument, wanted to hear answers to all the questions he hadn't steeled himself to ask.

"You don't trust me," said Madog.

Gwyn looked away, down the shattered corridor.

"Mostly I deal in binary choices," the American said. "Black or white. It's one or the other when you program a computer. But on an operation like this you can have both."

"What the devil are you talking about?" Gwyn asked, knowing too well.

"Compromise. Think of it in terms of benefit versus cost. I supply certain resources. You keep quiet about my involvement."

"Sometimes I can't tell the cost from the benefit."

"You and quite a few others."

"I have blood on my hands."

"He screwed up."

"I should have been there. I could have prevented it."

"I had a buddy used to call that a J.C. complex."

Excusing evil was itself an evil act. Gwyn wouldn't give it a foothold. But his questions were still unanswered, indeed unspoken, when the ruined door let in another silent figure.

Ten minutes later all but one had arrived, distinguishable only by voice in the dim light. Gwyn took their reports one by one. John, or Sion as he was calling himself these days, was boastful and excited about Etifed's contribution of a safe house. Elen, the girl from Cadwyn, gave Gwyn her bedroom-eyes treatment along with the report on transport. Raffael offered a crisp run-down on the weapons and schedule.

"Special devices?"

"All ready," said Madog. "But if you don't need me. . . ."

"Wait one moment," said Raffael smoothly. "We are much too late to make changes. You will be there."

Madog looked from the Italian to Gwyn, perhaps wondering who to listen to. Raffael smiled.

"Madog?" Gwyn side-stepped the decision. He didn't want to forfeit Nilsson's resources just to assert control over Raffael, and he didn't want to back down. "Can you contribute anything further?"

"Maybe. Like if you run into any problems with the remote."

"Very well," said Gwyn.

The American had the sense to say nothing.

"I want to know where Nora is," demanded Elen snottily. If she thought she'd bought special privileges, she would learn her error. "Is she backing out?"

"If she fingers us, it'll be the last time she fingers anyone," said Sion, an empty promise if ever there was one.

Raffael adjusted the silk scarf at his throat. "Nora will join us. Have no fear."

Thank God it was only for an hour. Gwyn didn't think he could take the lot of them much longer than sixty consecutive minutes. But, as the Yank pointed out, you had to compromise.

Contortions in the back seat of a car, for God's sake, parked in an alley for anyone to walk by.

Nora was wrapped around him humping like a mink. Irish crumpet, Corgi learned early, was deadly one way or another. Rather push his pecker into a nestful of scorpions, unless there was a bloody good reason. Eventually Nora climbed off.

"You're better with plastics."

Corgi gathered the kinky black hair at the nape of her neck into a fistful, pulling her head back hard. She closed her eyes. Of course, she would like that. Bitch. He released her.

"Big plans, I hear." He zipped up.

"You had your slice at Christmas," Nora said, pulling up her jeans. "It's our turn."

"Soon?"

She smirked. "Turn on your telly tonight."

Corgi smiled. It was big, it was related to the Tywyn job, she was in on it, and it was today. But where? He'd have to fly a kite.

"Beautiful," he said. She preened, thinking he meant

her. Vanity was boundless. "Hope you enjoy North Wales."

"Fuck off. I told you it's ours. Besides, it's here. Drum up your own business."

Corgi needed no encouragement in that department. "All the best," he wished her genially. "Trust you'll beat the clock."

Thomas McKinley looked at Peter owlishly over a desk the size of an aircraft carrier, lost in an expanse of pale blue broadloom. If he put anywhere near the effort into program content that he put into furnishing his office. . . . Peter, assuming a stance of easy confidence, asked for a film crew and time to delve out the story.

"I find your request rather unreasonable, Holt, in view of your regular assignments." McKinley folded his hands deliberately on the desk top. Their backs were hairy right down to the first finger joint. McKinley's hard little eyes were set under lowering black eyebrows. "You can scarcely claim BBC Wales lacks staff who are competent to uncover such a story, if it exists." He placed the slightest stress on "competent."

Peter nodded too vigorously. "But since I'm familiar with the background and with some of the groups who may be involved—"

"Yes, you are, aren't you?" McKinley couldn't pass up that opportunity.

MI5 and a coterie of obscure civil servants had swarmed over Peter last April, demanding his sources for the story on a threatened new rash of Welsh property destruction. Peter knew he was ethically right to protect his contacts. McKinley, an accountant who had strayed over to the production side on the strength of his tight bookkeeping, knew he had been personally embarrassed by government gentlemen who accused Peter Holt of abetting criminal acts.

"Yes, I am. It's my job." Peter tried to sound self-assured. Instead, he sounded belligerent.

"You'd better run through your background." McKinley glanced at his watch. "I'm leaving for an appointment in ten minutes."

And so is your sloe-eyed secretary, by coincidence? Peter sat on the edge of a chair and started ticking off points on his fingers.

"Undeb Cymru Fydd, the nationalist group," Peter said.

McKinley bridled at the sound of Welsh. Even Peter's Cardiff night classes in the language, at his own expense, had aroused the executive manager's suspicion.

Peter explained, "Undeb Cymru Fydd means the Union of Future Wales. You've probably seen their posters and rallies. Their symbol is a golden sun with all the rays interlaced together."

"Always howling about cultural genocide? The cottage-burners?" McKinley tapped his fingers audibly on his desk top.

"That's them. Future Wales made a fund-raising tour through America three months ago. At first their entry to the States was refused, and they broadcast their appeal from Canada. They raised a lot of sympathy for what they call their oppression by the English. You know how that line always appeals to the Yanks. The grapevine also says they collected a hundred thousand pounds from sentimental third-generation Welsh-Americans."

"Surely that has nothing to do with—"

"Terrorism costs money. Also, one of their top people took a touring holiday in south-east Algeria last summer." Peter had no intention of naming Gwyn Davies, his best contact, now, after stubbornly refusing to identify the dramatically televised silhouette in April.

"Now really, Holt, I don't see any possible connection."

Peter shoved on with the news-hungry determination that always made accountants nervous.

"South-east Algeria is a wasteland. There's nothing in it but the Libyan border, which is easy to cross unnoticed. In Libya there are several state-run terrorist training camps. Apparently most of them are for third-world dissidents. A couple are for European urban guerrillas. The same fellow who took his summer holiday in Algeria spent a long weekend in Catalonia, chatting up the ETA, the Basque terrorists.

"Another thing. Welsh nationalists may recently have made new overtures to the Provisional IRA, who fouled their own nest so thoroughly in Ulster they're looking for new targets in England. Backing their Welsh colleagues could help them recover some of their lost credibility. That means backing Future Wales, or Cadwyn, or Etifed."

"Who the devil are they?" McKinley was shifting around restlessly in his chair.

"Cadwyn—The Chain—has been doing a lot of cottage-burnings and ham-fisted small bombings. Most of the members seem to be college students. Etifed—that means Heritage—wants to set up a protected Welsh-speaking region like the Gaeltacht in Ireland. With taxpayers' money, of course."

McKinley snorted. "Come to the point."

"All my sources, and everything I've seen recently in Wales, point to big trouble. That explosion at Tywyn looks like a skilled bombing by an established terrorist group. It could be the first step towards serious terrorism in Wales. A bombing campaign, I reckon. They're not organized enough yet for anything fancy."

"In other words, you want the Corporation to send you wandering around Wales looking for this vague threat, which you can't describe or give me any evidence for?"

"What I want is—"

"What you want is trouble. These aren't the days of the Falklands War, Holt, when we used to broadcast any sensational story. Things have changed. We don't embarrass the government just for the fun of it. We show some responsibility."

Hardly accurate. Peter remembered the virulent censorship slapped on the Falklands shoot up, except in the Welsh-language press, which had cheered on *Y Malvinas* and the Argentines. Many Welsh served in the Argentine forces, their families having emigrated at the turn of the century to a Patagonian Utopia; it was not the first time Welsh soldiers faced each other at gunpoint in the uniforms of two different foreign powers.

McKinley got to his feet and tugged his pin-striped waistcoat down over his paunch. Peter wondered what the secretary saw in him. Free lunches, probably, or maybe a raise. She wouldn't get it. McKinley was a notorious budget pincher.

"Frankly, I think this is all imagination. The Welsh have been settling down nicely for years. They themselves voted against home rule in 1979." McKinley started for the door.

"What about a crew, and some time?" Holt demanded, jumping to his feet.

"No crew. Continue your present assignments. And I warn you, Holt, the Corporation will not stand for more public embarrassment on your behalf."

McKinley vanished into the corridor of the Television Centre, leaving Peter gazing glumly across the plush office. He stretched his long legs on the pale blue carpet and folded his arms, contemplating ways to film without a film crew.

LONDON/JANUARY 12/1040

Madog Nilsson lifted his limited-edition Seiko Voiceprint to his ear. Ten-forty, the tinny electronic voice announced. No messages. He shut off the New York Stock Exchange index. He'd consulted the watch a moment earlier, but nothing had registered. There were times when his thoughts arrived at a slick emptiness that deflected all new information. It was too late to admit now that he was perilously close to terror. He slipped a hand inside his jacket to touch the narrow triangle of glass black stone he wore around his neck. Obsidian.

"Time?" demanded Gwyn Davies in his mother tongue.

"Twenty to eleven."

"Where's the bloody vans, then?" Davies muttered, fingering his theatrical-supply beard. He was looking along the Kensington street from their spot near the kindergarten's front doors.

Madog said nothing. He'd arranged the stolen credit cards and forged the rental signatures. That didn't mean he knew what kind of traffic the drivers had encountered. Everything in London came to a standstill when the royal family made an appearance, though so few things happened in this country he couldn't see how they could slow down noticeably. He shrugged. Madog knew how to keep his nose clean and button his lip. He'd been doing it since they left Cardiff before dawn—so Gwyn Davies would have no inexplicable overnight absence—he'd done it at the meeting at the Tate, and he would keep on doing it until they got back over the Severn Bridge tonight.

Madog glanced over his shoulder at the kindergarten and was startled for a second by the tallish guy with sun-streaked brown hair and a Malibu tan who stared back at him. Getting pretty flaky when he jumped at his own reflection. Davies looked pissed off as usual, all keyed up, ready to cut and run. Madog did his best not to think about having to cut and run. He glanced along the building. The spectacular new structure yelled money and privilege. A single storey at the front rose backward in a glassed pyramid containing a tropical arboretum and enclosed playground for the children of the ruling élite. The rest of the country couldn't afford bread and cheese; this school had imported orange and avocado trees growing inside and a staff of gardeners to check each one for leaf blight. A stately pleasure dome. Never mind that. The important thing was the pyramid construction of the building. No palace security could use the upper storeys to oversee the street. They'd have to settle for other buildings nearby, a considerable disadvantage.

Madog shoved the hair out of his eyes, listened to his watch again, thrust his hands in his pockets and took them out again. The uniforms that identified them as the kindergarten's hired security guards fitted poorly, but it was only for an hour. Davies's eyes slid over him and away. Madog could guess what the Undeb man was thinking: the American with his expensive toys. Voice-synthesizer computerized watch, holo camera, space-fabric clothes with New York designer labels, some of them priced higher than Gwyn Davies's monthly salary as a Welsh Department lecturer at the University College of Wales, Aberystwyth. On this enterprise he was a poor cousin. Madog Nilsson was not poor by San Juan County standards, though, let alone Welsh standards. Ever since Boeing got the space-shuttle contracts, things had been booming for Seattle and the Pacific north-west. Especially for Caradoc Nilsson Aeronautics Incorporated. What does it matter? Madog asked once. I'm committed, same as you. It doesn't matter, Davies had agreed. But his sullen dark eyes betrayed his lie.

A gleam of red and yellow caught Madog's attention. The first van rounded the corner towards the kindergarten's loading bay. A second, identical van followed it into the alley, where they would unload trays of *petits fours* and pastries for the kitchen. Who was going to argue if unexpected goodies arrived? The palace might have laid them on. It wasn't every day that the Queen opened a girlfriend's flashy new kindergarten in Kensington. Meanwhile three extra caterers' assistants would be killing time in the kitchen and making small talk with the cooks, unless the Scotland Yard spooks rose out of their lethargy to throw them out. Palace security would soon have other worries anyway, if Nora's people kept their word about a diversion. The Provisional IRA team made Madog's skin crawl, but at least they were professional. Maybe that was the trouble. They were too professional.

Spectators jostled against the hurdles and the stolid backs of the London bobbies. Madog scanned in both directions for the third van, then spotted it two streets away, approaching slowly along the crowd-lined street. The cin-

ematographer was braced in the sliding side door, getting
his wide shots of waving, laughing people. Probably two-
thirds of these people were unemployed and on the dole,
but they still turned out in herds to cheer the royal family.
The red-and-yellow van halted behind the BBC mobile studio, in its assigned place opposite the kindergarten doors,
still filming under the suspicious eyes of the police cordon.

"Time?" snapped Davies.

"Ten minutes."

Madog wondered if speaking Welsh was the best idea,
here and now, but said nothing. It wasn't worth an earful
of nationalist sulphur and brimstone from Gwyn Davies.
He rubbed his palms on the sleazy flannel of the security-
guard uniform.

Davies turned on the small radio, which looked like a
Walkman, in his breast pocket and fitted the plug into his
ear. Other people were doing the same, following the
street-by-street broadcast of the royal limousines' approach. Davies frowned under the unkempt dark hair that
fell forward over his face. Suddenly Madog heard him
catch his breath. The whole operation's success depended
on whatever Davies was hearing right now on that ear-
plug. Long before Davies's small satisfied nod, Madog
had his answer. Clearly audible over the crowd's expectant
hush, they heard the deep-throated crump of a distant explosion, then a shattering roar of glass and steel in the
area the royal party had just travelled through. Then Madog heard or imagined a faint staccato burst of gun-fire
from the Provisional IRA diversion team's high-velocity
Armalites.

So far, so good. If it came off, it was winner take all. If
it didn't—Madog couldn't help thinking about it—the spe-
cials still might not be able to round up all the spectators
for interrogation. Davies's team wasn't yet fully committed
to this operation. They might get away. Only an hour, he
had to endure this for only an hour. Then it would all be
over.

"What is it?"

"What's happening?"

Someone tapped Davies on the shoulder, seeing his radio, but he shook his head impatiently. An elderly man in a bowler turned his own radio up full, pulling in mostly static.

People surged forward towards the hurdles, perhaps sensing they also could be in danger. The bobbies locked hands and leaned back against the flexing hurdles, then a police supervisor ran down the cordon shouting for every second man. They stepped out calmly in a phalanx and marched off towards their ranked cars. Just as Madog hoped, a carload of plain-clothes security men screeched off in the same direction. Davies pressed the signal button on the radio, one of Madog's scorned but useful gadgets. Across the street the cinematographer removed his headset and disappeared into the dark recess of the van.

"—explosion, and there now appears to be an exchange of gun-fire in the vicinity of the American embassy—" The old man's radio blared. "The Queen and her party halted briefly but are now proceeding to their engagement at the opening—"

It might actually work, Madog thought. By sundown tonight, they could have their home-rule concessions and ransom squeezed out of the English government. And by tomorrow he could be on a beach somewhere, sipping chilled wine. Only an hour.

A great wave of cheering swept along the street from their left, and the first royal limousine's sleek black prow slid into view between motorcycle outriders. Davies glanced across the street at the stationary van and made his move.

"Make way, 'ere, sir. Got to get the door," Gwyn Davies said in an authoritative tone.

A bobby obligingly stepped aside for the two security guards and Davies and Madog took up their positions on either side of the elegant brass-and-glass doors.

Now. Madog shivered. Now they were committed.

Plain-clothes men leaped out of the first and third limousines and opened the rear door of the second. Then they formed into a wall of grey suits, heads swivelling in every direction like robots. The cheering reached a hysterical pitch as the blonde and beautiful Queen of England stepped out with her customary wave and smile. Another young woman in a well-tailored suit, shorter, with dark blonde hair twisted into a severe bun, followed the Queen out of the car. Miss Jean Douglass was the royal nanny. Walking beside her and clutching the famous stuffed-mouse doll, which the Queen Mother was said to detest, was the heir apparent, the next Prince of Wales.

Across the street, the cinematographer sprawled on the van roof, getting every possible inch of footage as the Prince skipped at his nanny's side. Together they walked along the cordon shaking hands with people over the hurdles, chatting. It was the Queen's golden touch to a T. At least she was predictable. The spectators roared their delight, leaned from windows, stood on each others' shoulders. The cooks and teachers and caterers' assistants inside crowded to the front doors, craning for a glimpse of royalty. Madog, instead, watched the red-and-yellow van.

Davies touched his signal button. The van door slid further open and out stepped a man and a woman laden with camera equipment. The light-haired man took a moment to throw the end of his white scarf back over the shoulder of his suede jacket, preening. The woman with long kinky black hair, his assistant, followed a step behind. Everyone was still watching the Queen's party, except one plainclothes man who nodded at the press pass the photographer flourished.

"Jeannie!" The photographer called out cheerfully in a faintly foreign accent, keeping his distance in the middle of the street. "Over here, sweetheart!"

The blonde nanny glanced sidelong at the Queen, who was smiling brilliantly as she escaped the clutch of an emaciated pensioner. Then Jean Douglass drew the little boy closer and turned him. The photographer flung himself down on one knee as his assistant thrust another camera at him. He kept up a stream of chatter to the heir apparent. The Prince smiled at the man with the camera, his mother's kid in every way, Madog observed through a race of adrenaline. The child lifted his free hand to wave—it couldn't have been better if planned—and the fuzzy stuffed mouse dropped from under his arm onto the road. Jean Douglass stooped, but the grinning photographer reached the toy first.

Madog swivelled to look into the kindergarten. Inside, through the smoked-glass front windows, he saw the eager staff slowly drop one by one to the floor. If there was any sound, the crowd's laughter and cheers drowned it. Davies nodded and pulled a compact handful from each uniform pocket. Madog did the same, silently chanting the well-rehearsed instructions. Left hand, release pin. Right hand, release pin. Left hand, gas mask. He could do it in his sleep. He hurled the first gas grenade to his right, the second one as far as he could lob it across the street. Then he clapped the gas mask to his face and started to run. Davies was already out in the street, and three others burst through the kindergarten doors in gas masks.

On every side the spectators were dropping to the pavement in an eerie silence punctuated only by the soft thumps of falling bodies, handbags, and shoes. A grey-suited palace security man flung himself over the Queen as they both folded. The kid and his nanny lay crumpled in the street. The photographer, his gas mask now in place, took the unconscious woman under the armpits and backed towards the van, while his female assistant grabbed the heir apparent. She turned, lifted her gas mask for a moment, and leaned to spit on the unconscious Queen.

Around the corner hurtled the other two identical vans. The team neared the open door of the photographer's van. Davies pelted after them. Madog crouched for the abandoned mouse doll. It might keep the kid amused through a hectic afternoon. Then it would be over. No more of Nora, no more of Raffael and Davies and the rest. Only an hour. Maybe two.

Bullets started to zing, probably from upper storeys far-ther along the street where palace security had stationed themselves. As the kidnappers wrestled the nanny and the kid into the van, a few security men appeared, running full tilt down the street. The photographer leaned out of the van door, Beretta pistol in his hand, and fired three shots. Chips kicked up in the street around the agents, who hurled themselves towards the nearest doorway. Blanks didn't chip paving. Madog froze. No violence, that was their agreement. Suddenly everything was changed.

Madog Nilsson stood alone in the street.

3

Madog came to his senses as the van started forward and its side door began to slide shut. He leaped towards the van and got a precarious hold on the door opening as the van accelerated. He clung desperately while the driver rocked around a corner on two wheels. The other two identical vans stayed close behind, but at the second turn they split, each heading at breakneck speed in the agreed direction. A police siren started up, but veered off after one of the other vans.

As the van slowed to take the next corner, Madog hurled himself inside. He struck the far wall and dropped to the floor, dazed, nose bleeding inside the gas mask and hands numb from gripping the door handle for dear life. He sat up unsteadily, afraid he would vomit. Through his haze of shock, he saw shop fronts blurring past the shoulder of the skinny kid who was driving.

"Keep down, arse-hole," Nora snapped from the passenger seat. "You're not on a sightseeing tour."

She glanced for Raffael's approval, but their photographer was intent on the woman and child huddled on the van floor. Nora shrugged and returned to staring sullenly out the windscreen.

Madog crouched down against the wall and looked around at the others. No one paid any attention to the

Provo woman. The roly-poly little English guy who called himself Sion ap Huw had a glazed expression. Elen, the red-haired girl from Cadwyn, was watching her idol Gwyn Davies as she peeled out of her caterer's smock. Davies tossed his theatrical beard and black-rimmed glasses into a corner, ignoring both the girl and Madog.

They replaced the public-works barriers at the entrance to the parking garage in Chelsea and parked three levels underground. There they abandoned the red-and-yellow van in exchange for a weathered grey plumber's van stolen an hour ago by one of Nora's Provos; its driver was sleeping off a shot of sodium pentathol in an alley. They leaped into action, tearing off the sweaty guard's uniforms and throwing them in the van. Madog endured Nora's sneer at his flak vest when he buttoned his denim shirt over it. Sion changed the license plates.

For fifteen minutes they listened to the fleet of sirens heading towards Kensington and the muffled grunts of the garage attendant trussed like a Thanksgiving turkey in his cubby-hole. Madog went to check him once and saw that his morning's handiwork was still doing the trick. The man would stay tied and gagged for a while yet, and he was in no danger of suffocating.

Finally Davies motioned them to carry the Prince and his nurse into the grimy back of the second vehicle. Madog tossed the stuffed mouse in after them. Their driver pulled on the plumber's safety hat. He drove the van cautiously up the ramp and out of the garage into hopelessly tangled Chelsea traffic.

Slowly, edging across the flow of cars, they headed north and east. The driver pulled to the side once as another dozen police cars brayed past at top speed towards Kensington, blue lights flashing. With any luck, the confusion there and at the Provo bomb site would keep them off the scent long enough. The other two vans would be far away by now, and if they were taken, the drivers knew only that Cadwyn, their Welsh nationalist group, had required their services for an afternoon. Even the authorities' considerable expertise at torture would extract nothing further.

As they reached the garish streets of Soho, Jean Douglass began to stir. The little boy was still deep under, breathing heavily and irregularly. Raffael took off his white silk scarf and used it to stroke the nanny's forehead as she moaned and rolled into a foetal curl.

"Very bad stuff. The gas is very hard on the lungs," he confided to Davies. "We must be careful with these people. They are going to be very precious to us." Raffael smiled with a gleam of flawless white teeth. "You have the vaporizer?"

He was a hell of a lot more careful with these two, Madog thought, than he had been when he was blazing away at the palace security men back there. But at least Raffael hadn't hit anyone—he hoped. Uneasily, Madog dismissed the thought.

"At the flat," Davies answered Raffael. "Everything's there."

The driver slid the van through the back streets and alleys of Holborn. A few more police cars and an armoured carrier passed them heading west as they left the business district and travelled on through drab terrace houses. Every cop in Greater London must be converging on Kensington by now. Already they'd be scattering to throw up road-blocks.

"Left here," ordered Sion, coming into his own. The flat was Etifed's contribution. Almost everything else was Undeb's. After Davies's fall speaking tour for Undeb Cymru Fydd, lush green dollars harvested from American wallets made everything possible. Madog knew. A lot of them were his.

"Another left—down the lane."

An orange cat cringed out of their path as they drove slowly into a narrow alley, deep in shadow between crumbling three-storey apartment blocks. The grey van almost scraped brick on either side. Tenements, Madog would call them. Their afternoon's hide-out lay upstairs, Sion announced, self-satisfied as an estate agent showing off new luxury suites. Level with a rusty iron door, the driver braked. Sion slid open the side door to let them file inside, invisible from farther than a foot away. Raffael crouched by Jean Douglass, shaking his head in sympathy as she moaned towards consciousness. He motioned Davies to carry her in as Elen took the kid. Nora, squeezed behind the front seat, was arguing with the driver and Sion.

"I told you, he hides the van in the abandoned warehouse in the next street."

"But it'll take him too long—"

"Do you want to give us away? It's too obvious if we leave it here." She fixed Sion in her unblinking stare, forcing his eyes to drop.

Raffael came forward smiling and put a hand on the driver's shoulder. "Good job. But Nora is correct. Get it into the warehouse and join us at the flat. Make sure you're not followed."

Sion disappeared into the building, still flushed from Nora's assault. When the last of them was inside, the plumber's van drove off.

Trudging past dustbins and up groaning stairs to the third floor, Madog brought up the rear with the kid's stuffed-mouse doll.

The apartment was a dingy hole-in-the-wall, one room with a crusted window. Raffael and Nora quickly checked it out, then waved everyone in and shut the door softly. The nanny and the kid were deposited carefully on the sprung sofa in one corner.

Madog swiped the back of his hand across his forehead, catching his breath. Davies pulled down the tattered blind and turned to face the room, hands clasped stuffily behind his back as though he were going to deliver one of his Aberystwyth lectures on the grammatical evolution of the Welsh language. Madog sat through one class the week after they flew in together from New York, something about poetic vocabularies of the fourteenth century. After ten minutes, he was pinching himself to stay awake. Gwyn

was a bright man with a misplaced sense of morality, full
of hell-fire rhetoric about the autonomy of Wales. He
looked older and acted younger than thirty-seven. That
didn't seem to bother Elen. Of course Wales was short of
young men, thought Madog. They emigrated in droves.
Those who couldn't escape that way joined the English
armed forces at convenient recruiting posts in the deepest
sink-holes of Welsh unemployment. They went to Northern Ireland to help the English suppress another Celtic
nation. Sometimes the Irish sent them home in boxes. No
doubt the English danced on the graves.

"Now." The Undeb leader looked around at them.
"Now we make our phone call."

Raffael nodded graciously, still playing teacher to Da-
vies's student. Madog wasn't sure whose orders brought
Raffael here. Why would the Rome column get involved?
Did that mean Tripoli sent him? Madog wondered why
Gwyn thought Raffael would be useful.

"You all know the plan." Davies kept his voice low.
"We negotiate our demands with the English government.
They won't be too reluctant since we've got their precious
heir apparent. When the BBC broadcasts the government's
concessions for a free Wales, and we have the million
pounds in our Paddington drop, Sion brings the other van
around. We drop the kid and the nanny in North London.
Then we split up. Raffi and Nora ride the coach to Heath-
row and catch their planes. Sion and Elen take the train
to Dover, cross to Bourgogne, and spend a week in
Vannes. Madog and I return to Cardiff tonight. Any questions?"

Madog looked around. No one responded. Davies held
up another of Madog's gadgets—a palm-sized, black-
plastic square with a small key-pad and speaker grille—a
quiet custom job from Madog's family business, electronics division.

"This device permits us to tap into the phone in Camden Town that's set up for our call, scramble it, and relay

it. We can carry on our negotiations with no risk of being traced. Are all of you clear?''

Everybody nodded agreement, but the air rang with tension as though someone had plugged in an overpowered ionizer. Davies scanned their faces a last time, then straddled a wooden chair and tapped out the code on his remote. Silently, Madog and the others watched him hit the last number and wait.

"It works! The line's ringing." A moment later, he spoke loudly in an exaggerated Welsh accent. "Operator, listen carefully now. We have kidnapped your English Prince to bring crucial Welsh concerns to the attention of the English throne and government. If our demands are met, the heir apparent and his nurse will be released unharmed. You had better let me speak with someone in command. Right away."

The pause lasted about a minute.

"I have nothing to say to the metropolitan police. Get off the line."

A shorter pause.

"My name is none of your business. Who are you? What's your rank? Why should I talk with you? Quickly!" Davies demanded in his stagy accent, frowning with concentration. "That will do. I'll tell my comrades."

They watched him, expectant. It was working. Davies addressed the others with his receiver uncovered to pick up his words.

"Major Grenvile, military intelligence. That means MI5, internal. The fools think Wales is part of England."

"How does he sound?" snapped Nora.

Davies shrugged, but aloud he said, "The usual English jackboot. But if he doesn't act helpful he won't ever see the kid again." To the phone, he said, "Here are our demands—" There was an interruption, and Davies laughed softly.

"Dw i'n deud wrtha'chdi, y diawl, dim y chdi sy'n deud wrtha i. You understand that speaking this language of yours is unpleasant, and I tend to forget it when I'm upset.

If you want co-operation, shut your mouth and listen. You want the kid and his nurse back. Let's have an exchange. We want home rule for Wales. We want a million pounds cash, dropped at Paddington Station. We want a billion pounds to pump into Welsh industry before you starve us off the face of the earth in your current attempt at genocide. And we want full-time Welsh-language television everywhere in the country as your lying government promised years ago.''

An impressive list. Madog saw Raffael smiling faintly at the floor between his expensive boots. So he didn't take it seriously—neither did Madog, entirely. Or Gwyn. This morning as they drove from Cardiff they'd agreed that the four demands were just, but that the government was unlikely to meet them in full.

The million pounds cash was Madog's suggestion. They didn't expect it, didn't really care much about it, although of course they could put it to good use if it materialized. A billion pounds to bolster dying Welsh industry was even less likely, unfortunately, since it was a modest demand considering the arterial haemorrhage of wealth flowing out of Welsh industry and into English pockets for the last four hundred years.

Home rule and Welsh-language television they did care about, passionately, and they expected to buy them with the boy's return. Together these would cost hundreds of thousand of pounds for the next few years, maybe more, but a duplicitous government could extract this sum from taxpayers' pockets with less difficulty than they could a known quantity of hard cash. It was an old game. Gwyn Davies knew the rules—Madog had made sure of that—as any government knew the rules. And the ball was now in play.

Davies listened again.

"Talk reasonably? That's what we're doing. Now, go and fetch what we need, and you can have your snivelling English Prince. I'll call back in an hour.'' He signed off.

After that, there wasn't much to say. All they had to do was wait.

LONDON/JANUARY 12/1230

"It should not last so long," Raffael admitted quietly to Davies, with a nod towards the couch. A hissing cloud of steam from the vaporizer enveloped the restless woman and the motionless child. "But these Soviet arms—" He set an elegant hand on the Undeb president's shoulder and shrugged. "Once we had a shipment of fuses that detonated as soon as they were set. We lost two good people."

"What about after-effects?" Davies asked.

"None, if we are lucky." Raffael hesitated, but said no more.

Lucky? Madog watched their faces uneasily. Raffael was as slick as an actor, even looked like one. Madog didn't have much time for bland, charming people. If Raffael wanted to call the shots he shouldn't be depending on luck when it came to people's lives.

Elen, the red-haired Cadwyn girl, spoke up in Welsh. "She's awakening."

All heads turned to watch the nanny groan and pull herself up on the couch. Her eyes were bloodshot in a chalky face. Jean Douglass drank the water Elen fetched and was violently sick into the bowl they had ready.

"Where are we?" Jean Douglass made an effort to stand, retched dry, and sat down again shakily. She bent over the unconscious child, then focused groggily on Raffael. "You said—last night—a photograph of the Prince. What—?"

Raffael smiled. "Yes. I have my photograph of the Prince. We have borrowed the boy for an hour. Did I forget to tell you about that? Then you will both be returned unharmed."

"Dear God. Who are you?" The nanny managed to stand this time, swaying. "What do you want? Everyone will be worried sick about the Prince! Let us go."

"Very soon, Jeannie." Raffael smiled gently and steadied the nanny with a hand on her shoulder. She sank abruptly to the couch. "But first we will be certain that everything is arranged."

"They'll never pay the ransom. They'll never give in to terrorists!"

Nora crossed the cheap linoleum in three strides and slapped Jean Douglass across the face, hard and open-palmed. The nanny gasped and her blue eyes sprang wide open. They stared at each other, the woman on the couch with dark blonde hair fallen in strands to the collar of her impeccable grey worsted suit, and blue-jeaned Nora with her black eyes narrowed.

"Keep your filthy tongue to yourself, you hear me? The terrorists all work for your government and your decadent ruling class. Don't the poor boys in the Maze Prison know it better than me? And you murder them one by one."

Jean Douglass drew herself straighter and said, "That's exactly what you are. Terrorists."

Gwyn Davies frowned at Raffael, who led Nora away by the elbow. From the far wall, she lit a Gitane and watched the nanny.

Davies crouched on his heels beside the couch. "How do you feel, Miss Douglass? We worried about ill effects from the gas."

The royal nanny was leaning over the Prince's unmoving shape, fingers on his small wrist. She looked up uncertainly at Davies. "His pulse is irregular and his breathing is laboured. Can you give him anything?"

Madog, watching their conversation, wondered about Raffael's advice not to bother using disguises, since people without police records don't have to worry about identification. Or maybe they should have kept the woman blindfolded. It was too late to worry about it now.

"We can move the vaporizer closer to help him breathe," said Davies. "We have sedatives. I don't think they would be a good idea."

Jean Douglass shook her head, preoccupied, then glanced at Davies. "You're Welsh?"

"Yes."

"Whatever it is you want, don't you know you'll gain nothing this way?"

She picked up the little boy and set him on her lap, with his golden head lolling against her worsted shoulder. He might have been asleep, except for his noisy and uneven breathing. The mouse doll that Madog had placed carefully on the couch lay upside-down, forgotten.

"From the English government, this is the only way we'll get anything," Davies answered. "Do you think we haven't tried other ways?"

"You won't achieve a thing by endangering the life of an innocent child," said the royal nanny sharply.

Davies got abruptly to his feet and walked back to the wooden chair where he'd left the remote. He dialled. This time they crowded in to hear the distant voice of Major Grenvile.

"—sympathize with what you're trying to achieve," said the negotiator's miniaturized voice. "You know Welsh home rule has been under serious discussion in the Home Office and in the Commons. Everyone recognizes the severity of Welsh unemployment and industry closures. The government has been striving to overcome technical difficulties to present fulltime Welsh television to all areas on Channel Four. I personally believe you've taken an important step. I want to do everything I can to aid you—"

"Trying to win your confidence," murmured Raffael. Davies nodded.

"—problems here with the bureaucracy. Some of these people are rather fixed in their ideas about meeting the demands of, ah, people like yourself. I can't just hand you a million pounds and home rule. It's going to take a little time. What about the Prince and Miss Douglass? Are they injured?"

Davies glanced at Raffael, who shook his head. Davies turned back to the remote. "Miss Douglass and the boy are unharmed," he answered, "as you'll see for your-selves as soon as you meet our demands. Drop the non-sense about the bureaucracy. You can get the prime minister's approval in half an hour for everything we ask. If your superiors get difficult about meeting the demands of Welsh freedom fighters, remember, all we want is jus-tice. We've waited too long already for what's ours by right. I'll call you in thirty minutes. Don't bother to try tracing this line—you can't. And don't push your luck, Grenvile."

Davies jammed the off button and looked around the room. "Another half hour. No more."

"Quick," Nora hissed from the window, where she held the dirty green roll blind open slightly at one side. "Look down there."

Madog peered over the others' shoulders. He saw a mili-tary armoured carrier skewed across the narrow street; the skinny Cadwyn youth, their driver, braced both hands against the carrier's side while a policeman frisked him. All around, silently blinking their roof lights, were mili-tary police and metropolitan police cars. Raffael swore gutturally.

Nora released the blind and leaned against the wall. Her eyes looked like black pits in her white face.

"Raffi," she said, "these fools aren't competent to run a holiday camp. We'd better get out while we can."

Raffael said something in German.

"If we're trapped here," she exploded, "the SAS or bloody Scotland Yard will blow the place open. In thirty seconds we'll all be dead, except the two Brits."

"Wait a minute," said Davies, and took her arm above the elbow. "We appreciate the car bomb. Your part of the deal is—"

Nora jerked free. From her oversize shoulder bag, she pulled a gun, a light sixteen-gauge shotgun with a short-ened barrel and stock, and pointed it at the Undeb leader. Davies folded his arms across his chest. Madog took an involuntary step forward. If Davies pulled the Browning he wore under his leather jacket . . .

Nora, trapped in her threatening stance, showed her teeth like a cornered dog. They stood frozen for what seemed to Madog like an hour. Then Raffael stepped between them, smiling.

"Haste makes waste, no? Let us see what happens."

Madog stepped back, touching the piece of obsidian through his shirt.

Raffael lifted the edge of the blind and put his eye to the splinter of overcast daylight. Madog craned and saw their driver flattened against the carrier inside a tight circle of plain-clothes men and soldiers with automatic rifles. All the weapons were trained on him, and he was talking over his shoulder. He moved one hand enough to point southwest—back towards Kensington. His captors pushed him headlong into the back seat of an unmarked car and drove away.

An officer ordered the others into five or six squads. They sprinted down to the far end of the street and began to enter other apartment buildings.

Raffael turned back into the room. "They're searching. We must leave."

"But they've got one of our people," Sion said nervously.

"There's nothing we can do about that," Davies told him. His calm appeared only marginally frayed by Nora's challenge, Madog was glad to see. "Leave and go where?" Davies asked Raffael.

"It's never going to work. Surely you've lost your minds, carrying on like this," said Jean Douglass firmly, holding the unconscious child straddled on her hip. "Let us go before there's serious trouble."

"Shut up, Brit bitch!" Nora turned to Raffael. "We need transport."

Raffael nodded casually. His gaze travelled around, dismissed sweating Sion and Elen, whose eyes were huge in her pallid face, bypassed Madog, and came to a halt on Davies. "Someone must—"

"Not Gwyn," interrupted Madog. Raffael and Nora made him edgy. Who knew what they might get up to if they were left to talk to Grenvile? Or decide what to do next? "Gwyn's got to negotiate with the cops. I'll get that little plumber's van. Meet me at the alley door in three minutes."

Raffael shrugged, but Madog was already through the door.

Peter Holt counted his misgivings over vile coffee in the BBC cafeteria. He could eat on the noon express to Cardiff, though British Rail's food was immeasurably worse than the cafeteria's, and costlier. The Corporation took a dim view of non-managerial expense accounts. He dropped his plastic cup in the waste bin as the news director hurled his twenty stone into the room.

"Holt! You're on assignment," he roared and pounded back down the hall. No explanation.

"Paying my hotel bill for the night?" Peter called after him. The threat of having to pay expenses put an end to many BBC schemes.

"Christ, yes! Emergency."

"What emergency?" demanded Peter, unimpressed.

"Your bloody Welsh just attacked the Queen! And the kid's missing!"

Dismayed, Peter stopped dead in the corridor. It was unimaginable, a national disaster. There'd been nothing on that scale since Earl Mountbatten's murder. But then he succumbed to a slow sunrise of vindication. The idiots had actually done it, and done it proper. He hustled down the corridor after the retreating news editor.

"When was it? Where, London? How did they manage it?"

Peter absorbed the terse answers as he followed, already considering the Welsh angle. What would this do to the interminable talk about a Welsh parliament, the first since 1404? What were they saying in Cardiff and Aberystwyth? What about the hundred thousand Welsh in London? Isolate a few key Welsh MPs and Home Office spokesmen, then pick up man-in-the-street clips. A to-camera intro in front of a Welsh shop that sold tweed trinkets and toy sheep.

The news director had other ideas. "Price is on it in Cardiff, and we have crews out with the Scotland Yard field teams and the military. We can't get into COBRA."

"COBRA?" Peter frowned.

"Cabinet office briefing room. The secretary of state's probably called in fifty-odd staff and advisers by now. Never mind that. You talk to the metropolitan police at New Scotland Yard. Their palace security branch supplies bodyguards to the royal family. Sweet-talk a story out of the anchor operation or the technical-support people or military intelligence. They'll be advising the police."

"Military intelligence won't talk to me, not after that Welsh-extremist story."

"Convince them, or hustle your arse back to Cardiff. Now move it."

"Right." Scotland Yard and MI5. Exactly, Peter thought sourly, where his name was dirt.

By the time his taxi deposited him near the silver-lettered revolving New Scotland Yard sign in Victoria Street, radio bulletins had brought him up-to-date. The Queen was recovering from the effects of a gas grenade but her eldest son, the heir apparent to the British throne, was indeed missing with his nurse.

The Provisional IRA had already taken responsibility for the car bomb that had devastated Grosvenor Square. Provos co-operating with the Welsh? It was definitely an escalation from their occasional pan-Celtic fantasies. Police were rounding up all London's known Welsh nationalists for questioning. Peter heard the reports. Believing them was another matter. How could the Welsh, even with Irish help, pull off anything so tidy?

At one o'clock, with his small tape recorder in his

topcoat pocket, Peter edged into the standing-room-only crowd of reporters and photographers in a sterile fluorescent-lit waiting room. It was a remarkably silent gathering. Soon Peter learned why.

Herded into this anteroom, the press were barred from the action. Every fifteen minutes a dapper little police spokesman, the sort of creature the Yanks called a flack, popped out of an inner door with an information release. Before each manifestation, the newsmen had money riding on his word count. An *Express* photographer collected once on her guess of thirty-one words. Sweet bugger all.

There had to be a way to find out what was happening. Peter shoved his way through to the front. At half-past two he got his chance. The instant the door opened, Peter thrust his business card into the spokesman's hand. On the back Peter had scrawled, "Speak Welsh. Know Welsh nat. leaders. Glad to help."

The little man merely blinked and delivered his announcement that there was as yet no suggestion the Prince and Miss Douglass had been harmed.

But in two minutes the flack was at the door again.

"Mr. Holt? Come this way."

Peter followed, leaving a mutter of resentment behind.

The room was a technician's paradise, banked with computer mainframes and terminals, videotape monitors, wall speakers, infra-red screens, image enhancers, and telemetry and transmitting equipment. Peter was able to identify that much; the rest was a chrome-and-plastic battalion of unknown devices. The ceiling lights were dimmed, creating a twilight over the electronic sorcerer's cave.

After the terrorists' second call and through the slow afternoon, he had plenty of time to study it all, from a distance. The first time he approached a wall of flickering monitor screens and digital read-outs, he was turned away by a young man with an impassive face and a vaguely military uniform. Peter continued to watch the monitors from across the room, catching glimpses of aerial sequences, city street corners, activity, mainly empty rooms; the images were probably relayed from the military's electronic surveillance headquarters at Cheltenham. Peter thought one room was at the Cardiff headquarters of Plaid Cymru, the Welsh Nationalist Party. Another, he thought, was the dingy Aberystwyth office of Undeb Cymru Fydd, the Union of Future Wales. He waited, drawing tighter and tighter triangles on his newsprint. BBC would need something from him soon.

Around four, one of the clay-faced military types showed Peter into the inner sanctum, a glass-walled office in a corner of the larger room. Inside, he found a disagreement in progress between a handful of men and women in metropolitan police uniform and several others in neutral civilian dress. One man Peter recognized as the Scotland Yard commissioner, the head of London's metropolitan police. All very courteous, but their voices sounded uncompromising and flat in the small room's dead soundproofed air. A grey man introduced himself to Peter as chief of Scotland Yard's palace security division, mentioned the names of a few of his colleagues, and carried on his defence.

"New Scotland Yard will remain headquarters for the operation. Any negotiations or search can be directed most efficiently here."

"That doesn't give metropolitan police sole jurisdiction," said a wiry man in his forties. His rusty hair fell over his corduroy collar, too long for police regulations. He had small light-blue eyes and an aggressive chin. Identified only as Fox, he looked more like bulldog or terrier. Fox wasn't his name, Peter realized, but a game name or code name. He was SAS.

"Nor does it give jurisdiction elsewhere, Lieutenant-Colonel," said the palace security chief. "While we gratefully acknowledge the advice of Special Air Services personnel and other military observers, for the moment this is a metropolitan police matter. Let us do our utmost to ensure a successful conclusion before we consider a transfer of jurisdiction.''

"Of course, sir." Fox smiled. "And please bear in mind that should there be any reason to alter our approach, Special Air Services will provide experienced negotiators." Fox's eyes fixed on another man in civilian dress, whose own gaze slid away uneasily.

Major Robert Grenvile, Peter recalled from the introductions, was an MI5 hostage negotiator. His fair hair was whitening prematurely over a domed forehead and smooth, round face. Grenvile wore the same grey suit and gimlet-eyed vigilance as the palace security types. Apart from that, he looked like the kind of bloke who believed in energy-efficient housing and donations to Oxfam. Sincere. But Peter, a connoisseur of job stress, noted a nervous tic under the negotiator's right eye. He looked worried. Peter wondered how much of that could be attributed to the crisis, and how much to the apparent hostility of the SAS officer.

The palace security chief summarized, "Jurisdiction remains with Scotland Yard, and this office remains operation headquarters. Questions?''

"With all respect, sir," said a brash voice. It was the observer from 10 Downing Street, a three-piece pin-stripe among the neutral suits. "How secure is palace security? We can all recall several unfortunate incidents a few years ago. Madmen dropping in to visit royal bedrooms. The royal family guarded by flaming gays, if you'll pardon the term, sir, with notorious connections.''

No one laughed, though Major Grenvile's tic danced.

"Entirely secure," said the palace security chief curtly.

Forestalling another debate on his force's competence, Peter reckoned. This security gathering was a walk-through display of tribal hostilities. It reminded Peter of the Welsh activist groups on the rare occasions they got together.

"Negotiation is our present concern," Fox reminded, reasserting his own claim.

Grenvile cleared his throat, unsuccessfully, and rasped, "You're all familiar with the phases of classic hostage negotiation. First, establish contact with the terrorists. We've done that. Second, establish trust and good faith. We've scarcely had time to build any rapport, but that will be our next aim. Third, make whatever minor concessions will keep them happy—food and so on. Finally, make arrangements for the return of the Prince and Miss Douglass."

He was hoarse when he finished. Peter diagnosed laryngitis, or too much shouting, which seemed out of character, or stage fright. But in a hostage negotiator?

"Very concise, Major," said Fox. "What if these terrorists didn't read the handbook?" On the strength of nods and one misplaced laugh, the SAS officer continued. "The national policy on terrorism, as I recall, discourages any yielding of concessions."

"Surrender or die, in other words," Grenvile said huskily. "But we're discussing the survival of a young child who is incapable of defending himself or escaping his captors, a child who is next in succession to the British throne. We'll yield whatever concessions we must to save the Prince's life, although certainly the national policy is—"

"Just as long as we bear that in mind," said Fox. "Now, where do we stand?"

Grenvile swallowed air, and whatever retort he might have made. "We've had no success yet in tracing the first two phone calls. They're late with the third call, which could mean they're in trouble. We may have them already. If not, there will certainly be another call. That next call is our opportunity to build a relationship with the terrorists, probe their weaknesses, and delay their demands until we can pin-point their location."

"What's the search pattern?" someone asked.

The palace security chief went to the wall map and used his silver fountain pen to point out sector after sector of metropolitan London. City police from all divisions were carrying out the building and traffic search in co-operation with military intelligence and military police. Peter tried to calculate exactly how complete the co-operation would be. The various agencies were infamous for their bitter rivalry.

The man finished his briefing, "The switchboard is getting hundreds of telephone offers of volunteer assistance. At present, we see no need to use civilians."

"How professional are these terrorists?" a military observer asked.

"They appear to have advanced electronics, powerful weaponry, and a good number of people at their disposal. But their actions and demands seem to be ill-planned. We may find, once we get down to serious negotiation, that they don't care a great deal about their stated political aims."

"What do they want, then?"

"Money, perhaps. It often comes down to simple greed." The chief tucked his silver pen in his breast pocket and stepped away from the wall map.

"Should we have someone negotiate with these people in Welsh?" asked a fortyish woman, tweed-suited, with upswept auburn hair. Her voice was quiet, cultured, and mid-Atlantic. What was an American doing here? Peter frowned and cast back to the brief introduction. Some kind of professor.

"Excellent question, Dr. Chernicki." Grenvile sent her a quick smile. "Two native Welsh-speakers will join us within an hour. Mr. Holt, whom you may recognize from BBC news broadcasts, is with us now and speaks the language—"

Fox, his eyes on the Scotland Yard commissioners, broke in. "With all respect, sir, should we be discussing our strategies with the press?"

"Mr. Holt has offered to help, Lieutenant-Colonel," the commissioner said mildly, recognizing the territorial imperative.

"Unfortunately, the gunman hasn't spoken much Welsh," Grenvile added.

"Gunman?" demanded the SAS man. "Terrorist."

"Gunman as long as we're negotiating with him," Grenvile corrected and murmured into a handset. Across the outer room, a uniformed woman nodded.

They heard the taped first telephone call, crisp as though the Welshman spoke from Grenvile's elbow.

Dw i'n deud wrtha' chdi, y diawl, dim y chdi sy'n deud wrtha i," the terrorist warned them again. *"You understand—"*

Major Grenvile nodded, and the technician shut off the tape.

"Bloody unpronounceable double Dutch, that language. Worse than Polish," the pin-striped observer from the PM's office muttered, oblivious to Dr. Chernicki's arctic stare.

"One or two sentences—that's not much to go on," said Fox.

"Quite true," Grenvile confessed. "Mr. Holt, our translators haven't yet arrived. Can you tell us what the man said?"

"He said, 'I'm telling you, you devil, it's not you who's telling me.' "

"I see. And can you tell us anything about the man himself?"

Peter looked around, uncomfortable. "A native speaker, I think. It would have been easier to identify his region a generation ago. Television's had a homogenizing effect. And so have all the Welsh-language courses people are taking."

A glance at their faces warned him to say no more. Not here. After the MI5 reprimand over his program this spring, he didn't want any more notes in his dossier. In this company, speaking Welsh was considered suspiciously close to having Welsh nationalist sympathies.

"Strictly guessing," Peter ventured on, "I'd say he's young, probably educated. He doesn't sound like a coal valleys boy."

"In any case, in answer to your question, Dr. Chernicki, we are willing to try a Welsh speaker," Grenvile told the American woman, "depending largely on the next call. If I can build sufficient rapport and the terrorists seem co-operative, there should be no need. If not. . . . Are you willing to lend a hand, Mr. Holt?"

"I offered to help. That's why I'm here," Peter reminded him. "But bear in mind they'll probably recognize my voice. I'm just a learner, and there aren't many Welsh-speakers from Lancashire."

The prime minister's observer laughed heartily. Bigot. It was the same London-the-centre-of-the-universe attitude that had arranged Peter's transfer to Cardiff; two amusingly provincial regions, Wales and the North of England, had thus been disposed of in one neat solution.

"We accept that," Grenvile said, as though Peter had made an apology. "This is what you'll try—"

The lengthy briefing that followed seemed to Peter a profound statement of the obvious. Any news director who dawdled like this wouldn't last long.

"Done," he agreed, defying their jargon with a one-word answer. What he wanted now was to absorb as much information as he could, play his assigned part, and get back to Television Centre in Wood Lane to put together a story.

One of the expressionless young women tapped on the glass door. "First BBC coverage, sir. On the number-one monitor."

They filed out into the electronic nerve centre to watch the broadcast on a large screen mounted high on one wall. Peter watched the footage and presentations with a professional eye, clicking his tongue involuntarily at sloppy cuts and marginal hand-held footage. They'd thrown in every second of tape they'd got; not much, since the BBC location crew had succumbed to the same gas as the Queen's party.

Man-in-the-street reaction was the stinger at the end of the newscast. They'd taken crews into the London streets where thousands of people, many in tears, were keeping vigil. Shop ladies wiped eyes on their aprons; bank executives in pin-stripes looked shell-shocked; stunned tourists asked questions no one could answer; they all offered the camera their distress, their concern for the child all Britain loved, their golden-haired Prince. Every copy of the famous fuzzy mouse doll was sold out in the shops; royal souvenirs and mementoes fetched triple their normal prices. No one risked a comment on the benefits to the economy of a royal kidnapping.

"Too bloody good to be a prince for those Taff sods," said a taxi driver.

"Why did they have to spoil everything?" asked one elegant woman. "Everything has been going so splendidly. I detest this hatefulness and destruction."

"What about the terrorists' claims regarding the Welsh language and the jobless rate?" the interviewer had the temerity to persist.

"We never hear a word of Welsh near our cottage on Anglesey. Frankly, what use is it? And if they really wanted to work they'd find jobs."

Peter tried to picture her pouring out hot fat in a fish-and-chip shop like his old mum, but failed. The next clips were from an East London local.

"Bloody yobs," said a dark-skinned man. He sounded Trinidadian.

"Treason, that's what. They want their necks stretched."

"What they want is a hard lesson," said one old regular over his pint. "Only thing the bleeding Paddies understand is killing and maiming. Give 'em a taste of their own medicine."

4

LONDON/JANUARY 12/1700

Nora had mentioned the IRA safe house in Islington with ill-concealed reluctance. What if the other teams needed it? she asked, and fell into a sullen silence. Afraid of losing face, Gwyn thought, but they had more to lose right now than face. He drove the grey plumber's van in a circuitous route through Shoreditch.

Gwyn had mistrusted the doubtful aid of the other main nationalist groups, Etifed and Cadwyn, in the first place, but honoured their old agreement never to act unilaterally. It was one of the compromises. He glanced at Madog. If they knew the other compromises. . . . Driving at least blotted up some of his anxiety and kept his mind from imminent disaster.

Sion ap Huw, crouching forward from the back seat, said querulously, "If Cadwyn had got the transport half right, we wouldn't be driving around London in a stolen van. Do you know what they're going to do to us if they find us?"

"And if Etifed had lined up a second flat instead of sitting on their hands and hoping it would all work out, we wouldn't be driving at all," Elen, the red-haired Cadwyn girl, shot back in her high-nostrilled Anglesey Welsh.

Now that immediate danger was forgotten, the Welsh

were at their favourite game, Gwyn thought with despair: tearing each other to shreds.

Raffael crouched behind Gwyn's left shoulder, watching the street. The January afternoon was darkening early under an overcast sky. Nightfall would give them the advantage of easier movement. Perhaps.

"We're passing too many police," warned Raffael.

"So get out and take the underground," Gwyn snapped back, then regretted betraying his nervous state. "Of course we're passing too many police. Every rozzer in London is hunting for us."

And every hungry reporter. Extra editions screamed hysteria from shop windows and kiosks. People gathered in knots on the pavements talking angrily, a few openly weeping. From the headlines, Gwyn gathered police were blaming the IRA and unnamed Welsh extremists. Just as long as they stayed unnamed. He supposed it would touch off a new rash of "no Welsh need apply" in rooming houses and personnel offices, not that the English needed any special excuse for bigotry. No blacks. No Asians. No Paddies, Taffs, or other home-grown minorities. But maybe it would stir them all, at last, to rise in anger.

They waited out the rush hour behind the hoardings of a strike-emptied building site. After a while, Jean Douglass made a muffled exclamation through her gag. Gwyn turned to see her wide eyes fixed on the child curled up beside her. At last the boy was whimpering awake, his pallid cheeks awash with tears. The nanny held up her hands, bound together with surgical tape, and Gwyn saw tears shining in her eyes. Fair play. They wanted to keep the kid healthy and happy. Gwyn gave Madog the nod to free her hands. A few minutes later the boy was puking weakly onto the floor, filling the van with the penetrating reek of vomit. The sooner they reached the Provo house, the better.

"Those sods at Scotland Yard, stringing us along," moaned Sion. "The longer we hang around London, the more danger we're in. Davies, you'd better get tough with them on the next call.''

"Why don't you shut your whining?'' Nora snapped. Since they had slid out past the police cars at the first flat, she had been fingering her sawed-off shotgun, excluded from their exchange of Welsh.

Silently, Gwyn agreed with her, but he wasn't having his people take orders from the Provo bitch. He had to get rid of Nora before she blew off someone's head to impress the Italian. Not wanting to give Nora the satisfaction of having him ask, he turned to Raffael. "Where from here?'' he asked.

Raffael coolly met his gaze in the rear-view mirror, recognizing the subversion. "Ask Nora. It's her safe house.''

Nora directed him to a main street. "Two streets past the traffic light, left and another left. Number 33.''

But long before the intersection, they saw that the fading daylight ahead was ragged with police roof lights and probing searchlights. Gwyn pulled quickly into an alley littered with cabbage leaves and broken crates. He shut off the headlights.

"Looks like we got a problem, huh?'' said the American brightly.

Gwyn could cheerfully have booted their over-age boy scout through the windscreen, but he bit his tongue.

"Tell you what. I'll go take a look-see,'' Madog proposed in his most exaggerated American accent.

"Take the right passport.'' Gwyn wielded the sarcasm that had reduced first-year Welsh students to tears. Elen giggled.

Madog gave his golden beach-boy grin and slid out of the far door. Gwyn turned off the engine as the American loped away into the London twilight. The heir apparent was crying feebly in the back when he wasn't sicking up his royal bile, and the Douglass woman was sniffling in sympathy. This thing was becoming a farce from the Goon Show, the horse-faced King of England's favourite form of wit. Bad temper bolstered Gwyn while he waited out five minutes in the alley behind the greengrocer's. Then the American silently reappeared and leaped in the passenger door.

"You guys wouldn't believe the number of cops down there. They're all over the safe house; it looks like a termite colony. Nora, I guess they got wind of your friends' hide-out."

"But how?" asked Elen. "Did one of the Provos sell you out, Nora?"

"With encouragement from a cattle prod, perhaps." Raffael shrugged. "It wouldn't be the first time your police have used such methods."

Nora merely nodded, lips compressed, and went on toying with her sixteen-gauge as Gwyn eased the van out of the alley.

No safe house. No shelter. Nowhere to go. They couldn't drive the stolen plumber's van any longer. Sion and Elen had their heads together, whispering. Gwyn drove on blindly, feeling the bleak brick suburbs of Shoreditch closing over him like a tunnel. To be instead in a Welsh lane in summer, green growth embracing overhead in a translucent arch. . . .

"Watch out!" screamed Nora.

He wrenched aside in time to miss the black Datsun. As he passed, he caught a glimpse of the woman driver's stunned face. The people in the back of the van were flung against each other. Gwyn's palms slid sweatily on the steering wheel. More of that, and they might just as well drive straight to New Scotland Yard.

Instead, Gwyn slid the van through alleys and narrow streets, heading towards East London. There would be fewer police, fewer road-blocks, little expectation that the Prince's kidnappers would make for the grim docklands.

It was dark when they pulled into a car park in Spitalfields. There Gwyn dialled the next remote telephone call well after the agreed time. Between concrete slabs he could see an abandoned church and a few drifters turning over rubbish in the street gutters. Their sacks were empty. In recession London, earlier scavengers had claimed the choicest refuse. He leaned forward, pulling his sweat-soaked shirt and leather jacket free of the plastic driver's seat.

"Grenvile here. Good to hear from you. I was worried—" The major was warm, friendly, doing his very best. If he knew of the Islington flat with police swarming over it or the blown IRA safe house, he gave no sign. "But frankly, the prime minister says he must consult his Cabinet before he can come to any sort of terms with you." Grenvile's conciliatory voice paused, and he added helpfully, "A friend of yours wants a chat."

Gwyn jerked the remote device away from his mouth as though he had been burned. Friend? Angrily he identified an attempt at entrapment. They didn't know who he was, who the others were. Not yet, and with luck, not ever. Then a new speaker was on the line.

"Wel, machgen, sut mae'r hwyl?" asked the unmistakable Lancashire voice of the BBC newsman, Peter Holt.

How are things going? He might well ask. Thoughtfully, Gwyn pushed the off button. It was a bluff. Peter Holt could perhaps be considered a friend of the Welsh people in the broadest sense, not Gwyn's friend. Usefulness didn't make a friend. Still, the newsman knew too much. Everything was closing in. He glanced up into Raffael's pale gaze.

"Stalling for time," said Nora quietly, caressing the hacked-down stock of her gun. Even her quiet was a menace.

"Let the two English go and forget it," advised Sion nervously. "You see what it's like out there—the town's rabid. They won't just turn us over, they'll tear us to bloody shreds. It's not worth ninety-nine years in Shrewsbury jail."

"Madog?" Gwyn found himself asking.

Nora swivelled her head, a predator eyeing new prey. The American blinked and lifted his shoulders in silence, looking embarrassed.

Nora spoke first. "We keep the kid. Not the woman."

Jean Douglass made a wild wordless objection, trying to speak despite her taped mouth. She clutched Raffael's sleeve as she pantomimed the child's sickness. They all looked at the kid. He was yellowish pale, whimpering thinly, and hunched over as though he had stomach pains.

"Both of them," Raffael said with finality.

Gwyn frowned. He didn't want the Italian making his decisions. It was a second before the objections started, first from Sion, then from Elen. Gwyn overrode them.

"How?" he demanded, placing the decision between himself and Raffael alone. "We left the flat when the police started searching the building. The safe house is blown. Now they'll be going through hotel registrations and car-hire forms for all of Southern England. It's only a matter of time—"

"Not here," Raffael agreed with Gwyn, and looked around at the others. His gaze fell on Madog, with an expression of amusement. It was the first time he'd addressed the American, or apparently noticed his existence. "Have you any further aces up your sleeve?"

At the silence, Gwyn turned in the seat to see Madog. He wore a strained inward expression. In the American it was probably just wind.

"Yeah," Madog said at last. "I guess so. I guess I've got the safe house to end all safe houses."

Haltingly he described a farm in a North Wales backwater, near Llanfyllin. No phone. Difficult access, though to an American that possibly meant no motorway to the front door. Neighbours who kept to themselves. Sion and Elen debated its remoteness, in the mistaken belief that their consensus counted for something. Nora glanced at Raffael, who pursed his sculpted lips as he considered it.

"You never told me you owned property in Wales!" Gwyn's nerves finally snapped. He yelled at Madog, "You know the problems we face with absentee owners buying up our farms and cottages! You know, so you have no excuse! Do you think you have a right to own everything?

Buying a place you'll never live in. God protect us from help like yours.''

Madog started to speak, shrugged, and kept quiet. It penetrated even his thick skin that there was no excuse, thought Gwyn. No one said anything for a long minute.

"Do you have a better idea?" Raffael asked Gwyn. The Italian looked amused by the outburst.

"No," Gwyn said tersely. "We'll try it."

"Have you gone mad, throwing out all our plans suddenly?" Elen demanded in Welsh. "If we leave London, we're cut off from the entire support structure. We won't be able to negotiate our demands. There'll be no one to pull us out in a crisis."

"This is a crisis," Gwyn told her coolly. As he feared, Elen was starting to get full of herself.

Sion complained, "We haven't planned for more than a few hours of holding the kid. Each of us is going to be missed as soon as the cops start roughing up nationalists, and they'll soon get to people who can tell them—"

"I know that. Now close your mouth."

Leaving London and abandoning the ransom money was bad enough. They'd have to arrange another drop somewhere in Wales. As they argued, Gwyn watched Madog looking at them each in turn. Their American sugar daddy looked alarmed.

Sion appealed to Raffael in English, "It really won't work—"

Nora answered him by thrusting open the van's rear door with her foot and motioning with her sixteen-gauge. "It's going to work fine for us. If it doesn't work for you, then get out."

Sion stared at Nora, rabbit-like, and clamped his mouth shut. For once, Gwyn appreciated her crude violence. Pleased with herself, she tossed back her wild black hair. It was the Provo woman's trade mark, like her hero Carlos's sun-glasses. If the BBC film crew at the Kensington kindergarten had footage on her, she would suddenly have a high profile. Her career would be assured: prestige at home in Crossmaglen and the rest of South Armagh, a welcome back to Colonel Qaddafi's training camp, invitations from the Druze or the Peruvian group with the exotic name. And she would have the approval of Raffael.

Gwyn closed his eyes a moment, shutting out exhaustion and a sense of impending failure.

"We'll never get out on the M40," Nora said flatly. "They'll have road-blocks checking all outbound vehicles. They'll be stopping every old fart on a bicycle, let alone closed vans."

"True," said Raffael. "We're trapped on the north side of the city. There will be a road-block on every bridge. And they will expect us, if we leave London, to drive west."

As Gwyn listened to Raffael, his anger simmered towards full-blown rage at Madog.

A farm near Llanfyllin? Bad enough to have English absentee owners buying up quaint cottages and depriving Welsh families of housing. An American was too much to swallow; no wonder the smiling bastard had never mentioned it. Probably the place contained enough computerized toys to stock an electronics warehouse, was tarted up with a two-car garage and swimming pool, and was named "Madog's Paddock." In neon.

By an act of will, he turned his attention to Raffael's ludicrous plan.

The abandoned wharves of Wapping loomed one by one out of river mist, and the van's exhaust sounded like muffled thunder between narrow brick walls. Gwyn braked between street lights and Madog got out. The others crouched low, hands over the mouths of Jean Douglass and the kid. The American sauntered across empty Wapping High Street and in through the front door of the Thames Division Headquarters. The river police were about to be visited by a fast-talking and persuasive *Los Angeles Times* reporter assigned to maritime features. Of course, if the Thames Division were too busy this evening, its Paris counterpart the Seine patrol might be more helpful tomorrow. . . . Maybe it would work.

As he pulled the van silently away, Gwyn glanced in the rear-view mirror. Through a lit headquarters window, he saw Madog approach a cop with his mock salute. Always had to play things to the hilt, then a little bit further. Disgusted, Gwyn drove on along Wapping High Street, seeking the right-hand turn they now needed.

A few streets east, after two unsuccessful forays, Gwyn found it and wheeled between unlit buildings. He halted the plumber's van on the wet timbered deck of the wharf. It looked abandoned, or at least little used. He shut off the headlights but left on the motor and fog-lights, cats' eyes probing the river mist. For fifteen minutes, they waited.

A diesel's throaty chug-chug announced the boat before its port-side running lights neared the jetty. The van's fog lights picked out a name, *Robert Peel, Metropolitan Police of London, Thames Division,* on the life preservers clipped to the railing. The boat was about thirty feet long and looked fast. For an unpleasant few seconds, Gwyn wondered whether to throw the van into reverse and flee. Then Madog's tanned face appeared briefly at an aft window, and Gwyn motioned them out.

"Wait."

Raffael crouched at the edge of the wharf, examining the raised wooden curb. He pulled at the timber, fighting for balance as the rotten wood suddenly gave way at one end. When he had a few feet pried away, he leaned into the van, slipped it out of gear, and signalled the others to push. It wallowed over the edge, catching noisily on the muffler, and sank into the murky Thames. Sudden waves crashed the *Robert Peel* against the wharf.

The boat was still rocking as Gwyn held it near enough for the others to jump on. Nora and Raffael had pulled black Balaclavas over their heads; the IRA woman kept her shotgun steady on Jean Douglass and tossed a Balaclava to Gwyn. He put it on, though he hated its stifling enclosure.

Gwyn went straight to the cramped wheel-house. There, he came face-to-face with a sweating middle-aged black constable. Behind him stood Madog, holding Raffael's Beretta at arm's length against the policeman's kidneys. It was hard to say which of them looked more unnerved.

"Constable Drake here was kind enough to offer me a tour of his new boat," Madog said, deadpan. "Now I think we better tie up his hands."

Nora produced surgical tape from her shoulder bag and quickly bound his wrists. Elen and Sion explored forward and called out to Nora. With visible relief, Madog handed over the Beretta to Raffael. He took the wheel and steered out into the channel.

"What'll she do, constable?" asked Madog, as though he were still on his journalist's tour.

"Ten knots. But the Thames speed limit is two miles an hour." The black man's voice was pure East London docks. He watched Nora herd Jean Douglass and the Prince past into the cabin and shook his head slowly. "Look, mate, you sure you want to do this?"

Madog pulled out the throttle, pleased with his new toy, and felt around the board until he found what he wanted. "With your lights flashing, no one's going to argue about a little extra speed. This is kind of an emergency."

Constable Drake braced himself against he boat's motion, scowling into the silenced barrel of Raffael's gun. Finally he sighed and sat heavily on the wall bench. Spray flicked the windows as the patrol boat picked up speed. The street lights of Wapping Wall blurred past beyond the fog; Gwyn glimpsed a public house, and recalled their last meal, before dawn. He called Elen to search the galley for food. She came aft, triumphant, with jam, a wedge of Stilton, crackers, and a pot of caviar.

"Caviar! Look what the taxpayer feeds these sods," crowed Sion ap Huw.

"My mate's birthday tomorrow," Drake said defensively. "The three of us chipped in."

"Fascist liar," Sion started in a self-righteous tone.

"So where was your bicycle patrol, anyhow?" Madog demanded ingenuously. "Constable Drake just transferred to Thames Division a couple of months ago. I bet it was the name, huh? Admiral of the fleet and all that stuff."

"Notting Hill." Drake didn't smile. "Four years on the beat. I should've stayed there."

"And missed piracy on the high seas? Sorry, constable." Madog grinned. Holding the wheel with one hand, he leaned over to fish the officer's handkerchief out of his pocket and put it into his bound and unsteady hands. Drake wiped at the sweat standing on his forehead and accepted caviar on a cracker from Elen.

Madog spoke to the constable's reflection in the windscreen, not turning from the wheel. "If a cop pedalled through the South Bronx, he'd last about two minutes. They'd nuke him. Turn him into rat burgers."

Constable Drake smiled feebly around his caviar. Perhaps he'd decided to humour his captors in the interests of survival. By the time they entered Limehouse Reach, Madog had smoothly extracted the man's life story, told in nervous bursts, from adolescent gang fights to late police graduation. Gwyn, impressed against his will, thought of Peter Holt's interviews. Peter, too, always got him to say more than he planned.

"Where do you lot think you're going to?" Drake probed clumsily as they swept north around the Isle of Dogs, setting a bow wave that rocked small boats in their moorings.

Gwyn scanned the cranes and warehouses on the north bank, then cleared fog from the window to watch the river behind. No pursuit was visible, but that didn't mean there was nobody there. The boat was slapping noisily downstream; if a helicopter were hovering overhead without lights, they wouldn't know until too late.

"We will go to Libya." Raffael licked caviar from his fingers, the gun propped on his updrawn knee. Madog looked at him sharply.

"Not in my boat, you won't." Constable Drake's eyes

slid away from the Beretta and the pale eyes within the Balaclava and added lamely, "You can't take a river craft into open water."

"Okay, constable, we won't scratch your new boat," Madog promised, eyeing his jam cracker. "You don't have any peanut butter, huh?"

Gwyn silently cursed the American. Madog Nilsson had bailed them out several times now, which only fed Gwyn's growing malaise about their precarious position. As they sped downstream, he watched the black dockyard silhouettes. After a while the kid woke crying, and the nanny rocked him back to sleep with fearful eyes on Raffael's pistol. Gwyn traced their passage on the river chart above the wheel; they were passing the Royal Docks. There were long stretches of crumbling warehouses and docks ringed in rusty wire fences. Once he saw a wolf-like dog pacing and turning inside the barbed wire.

Gwyn glanced at his watch. After ten o'clock. Thames Division must be after them by now. They couldn't stay on the river.

"Pull in," Gwyn told Madog sharply, striving for some sense of control. The operation was badly astray, and he was the strategist; his brain wouldn't clear. Hell-fire.

"Sure thing."

"Now, Nilsson. That's an order."

"Any minute now," the American said, and started whistling as though he hadn't a care in the world.

Damn his insolence. Gwyn would soon set him straight, but this wasn't the time. He nodded to Raffael, pulled the Browning from the back waistband of his slacks, and took over guarding Drake.

"You don't have to go and shove that thing up my nose." The constable sighed and scrubbed his tied hands across his face. "I ain't going to come the ugly. Not me."

Madog swung left again with the river's northward bend, slid open the port-side window, and stuck his head outside. A cloying stench of excrement flooded into the wheelhouse before he snapped the window shut. Looking pleased, he said, "Beckton sewage works."

Madog turned off the flashing lights, slowed the patrol boat, and steered in towards the north shore. The yellow-green glare of the works' sodium lights illuminated Beckton's piers and brick buildings with daylight clarity. Beyond the works complex Gwyn saw an open car park. Madog touched the *Robert Peel* in at a dark jetty over-shadowed by monstrous sludge barges and shut down the diesel.

Raffael appeared silently, smiling.

Gwyn gave Sion his orders in Welsh, handed him the patrol boat's small tool chest, and watched him stroll off towards the car park.

They sat in the dark wheelhouse for a long quarter hour. Madog tried chatting up the constable again, but he soon fell silent. Constable Drake of Thames Division sweated, hands clasped between his knees. Gwyn, sickly aware of what he must do next, stared out into the sulphurous glow and avoided Raffael's eyes.

Finally a fawn-coloured Bentley ghosted to a halt at the jetty access. Sion ap Huw sat behind the wheel, grinning like a fool. He must have pinched the plant director's car. *Twpsyn*, the idiot.

Raffael and Nora got to their feet, waiting. The Irish-woman's own baptism of fire, her proof of revolutionary devotion, had been to gut-shoot an eighteen-year-old Yorkshire recruit in a Ballymena pub. From that commit-ment there was no retreat.

"Get out," said Gwyn.

"Come on, Gwyn. Forget about Drake," Madog said and grabbed Davies's elbow.

Gwyn shook off his hand and whirled around to face him. "Get the hell out of my way, or it's you, too. Get out!"

Nora smiled nastily but fetched Jean Douglass, swaying on her feet with sickness and exhaustion. The sleeping kid was an anonymous bundle wrapped in a metropolitan police blanket. Elen followed them to the car. Raffael waited until Gwyn motioned Constable Drake into the forward cabin, then went ashore. The boat rocked against the wharf, powerless and unlit.

Gwyn flattened his back against the wheelhouse bulkhead and braced the Browning in a two-handed grip. His hands were shaking badly.

"Sit down."

Drake sat on the narrow bunk, calm now. "Don't do it, mate. You're in enough trouble."

"Then it couldn't be any worse." He pictured Constable Drake doling out caviar on his mate's birthday and polishing the brass work on his new boat. Curse Nilsson for his double-hinged tongue. Easier if this man were an unknown face.

"You're wrong there. It could be a lot worse."

He couldn't let the cop keep him talking. He knew that technique. "It's me or you. Sorry."

"Test, innit? You've got to show them what a hard case you are. We had a test like that at the police academy," Drake supplied, watching him. "We only passed if we didn't go and pull the trigger."

Gwyn raised the barrel and flipped off the safety. The Browning was an antique; it might blast them both to eternity.

"Give yourself a break, mate." Drake winked, damn him.

"Shut up!"

But it was too late. Gwyn glanced outside. No one was watching. He pointed the gun away and hissed, "Fall over after the shot."

He fired into the bunk on the opposite side of the cabin. Drake flung himself back on the bunk, kicking the bulkhead loudly with his heel.

"Good lad," Drake murmured.

"Shut up."

Gwyn quickly gagged the cop with his handkerchief and lurched out of the cabin, sick at his failure but sicker at

the thought of murder in cold blood. Feeling dizzy as
though he, not Drake, were reprieved, he walked up the
jetty and dropped into the front seat of the Bentley. He
reeked with sour sweat. Madog looked down at his own
empty hands, silent. Sion eased the big car forward. Raffael leaned forward from the back seat to touch Gwyn's
arm in acceptance, then shrugged when Gwyn recoiled.

They crossed the bright car park. Elen and Nora were
in the back with Raffael; Madog sat beside Sion. Jean
Douglass and the kid were locked in the boot for now.
Even so, a stolen car full of people tempted fate.

"Is there a watchman?" Madog asked dully.

"Sleeping on the job," Sion joked, soliciting approval.
"I used a gas capsule. We can drive right out."

"Well done." Gwyn found his tongue. "Head north.
Back roads."

MIDLANDS/JANUARY 12/2300

They were somewhere near Coventry, Jean Douglass
thought, when the terrorists began to relax. Believing
they'd got away with their crime, they became less panicky
and more self-important. She held her tongue, terrified of
another sojourn in the car's dark and suffocating boot. At
first, she'd prayed the big luxurious car would be stopped;
but they'd followed winding lanes and back roads without
police road-blocks. BBC news on the car radio mentioned
another IRA bomb in London and an extensive search in
progress throughout the metropolitan area. She sat wedged
in the corner of the back seat, arms around the child. He
had slept most of the way, bless him, half-waking now
and again to whimper and fall back to sleep. She ached,
not so much from their cramped all-night drive, but from
anger at what the criminals had done to her boy. He was
feverish and fretful even in sleep, clinging to her and to
Mungo Mouse. By moonlight, she could just make out the
famous mouse doll's friendly pug face and love-worn fur.
The first Mungo was Jean Douglass's own gift on Pip's

third birthday. Now thousands of British children had copies. Tears stung her eyes as she remembered that sunny day. Perhaps the worst thing was seeing her bright, confident boy reduced to a sick and fearful child.

Six other people were jammed into the car, but the nanny chose not to see the terrorists. Instead, she searched the road ahead for signs of their whereabouts. They traveled on narrow roads through farmland villages. Any names she saw, she tried to burn into her memory—Ditton Priors, Shipton—but the dear Lord knew where they were. Skirting round north of Birmingham? It was impossible to tell in the dark, even without her head pounding and her empty stomach churning from the gas. They were going to Wales, the terrorists made no secret of that, but the road signs didn't yet look Welsh. Her knowledge of Wales was limited, but surely if they had driven due west they would be out of England by now. Jean Douglass stared past the figures around her, into the darkness ahead. Occasionally she glimpsed a brick house or cottage, and the land still seemed flat rather than rolling.

She felt a strange displacement. Back the way they'd come, she could see nothing. It was like leaving everything behind in blackness, all her old life. She was being hurtled through the night, a prisoner. There was no past. There was no present worth mentioning. And what future?

Even if she and the boy survived this peril, she was ruined, and rightly so. When she answered the discreet *Nursing Monthly* advertisement four years ago and was accepted as the Princess of Wales's nanny, she could scarcely credit her good fortune. The Royals valued steadiness, conservatism, discretion, and loyalty; Miss Jean Douglass of Kilmarnock and London had all these. Secretly she sighed over the kirk's straight and narrow path; surely God was more tolerant than some folk allowed. Yet there were absolutes of right and wrong. Now she had committed a terrible, overwhelming wrong, a sin for which there would be no forgiveness in this life. The terrorists, whoever they really were, had carried out the kidnapping, true. But only one person had made it possible, and she was that person.

Last night—twenty-four hours ago now—Sandy had come round to her flat with the photographer who specialized in celebrities. *Paparazzi* got hundreds or even thousands of pounds for the right shot of the right famous face, Sandy said with unconcealed envy. How like her brother to admire fast-money types rather than people who worked steadily towards modest success. The elegant light-haired Italian said it was a great privilege, a splendid co-incidence, to have met the brother of the Queen's own nanny. Now Jean Douglass wondered how much time and trouble Raffael had put into arranging that coincidence. A pint and a little flattery? Poor Sandy, so easily gulled. And poor Jean. She pulled herself straight in her corner. She was no wiser. Her folly would cost her the little boy she loved beyond all else. Jean Douglass prayed silently, hands clasped around Pip's sleeping warmth, for forgiveness. If she had known, if she had any idea. . . .

Fear was getting the better of her. Stop it. Think, Jean! Do something. Study the criminals. If she and Pip escaped or were released, she could be the only means of identifying the kidnappers. She had heard most of the names and could offer descriptions. It was difficult to say more, since most of them were speaking a language she supposed was Welsh. Raffael spoke German to the woman who had struck her, Nora. Only when the two groups had to communicate did they use English.

Gwyn was the ringleader. Jean Douglass puzzled at the familiarity of his face; perhaps she had seen a telly interview of Welsh nationalists, though she rarely sat through any program so idle. She remembered a Scottish Nationalist Party rally in Kilmarnock a few years ago, with unwashed lowland boys strutting around in tatty kilts. She hadn't known whether to laugh or weep. Gwyn was about six feet, light build, brown hair and eyes, sallow complexion, maybe forty years old. He was often impatient. He could be viciously sarcastic, and even in silence he seemed angry. Gwyn disliked Nora, distrusted Raffael, tolerated the others. And feared Madog? Gwyn was the one making ridiculous demands of the prime minister, who, the nanny recognized with both fear and approval, would flatly turn down their nonsense. And he was a murderer. He had shot the black policeman, who tied up was surely no threat.

Madog. Slightly taller, light brown hair, deep tan, late thirties, with a Viking look of a heavy brow over grey eyes. His American accent, the first time he spoke English, had startled Jean Douglass. Surely there were no American terrorists? And who ever heard of an American who spoke tongue-twisting Welsh? Yet Madog's friendliness was appealing, and he always made sure that Pip had his fuzzy Mungo Mouse.

Raffael. Five-ten, slender build, light hair styled carefully, light grey eyes, about thirty, spoke German and English with an Italian accent, smoked Turkish cigarettes. Jean supposed his fairness meant he was from Milan or Florence, somewhere in the north. His manners and his clothes were elegant. At Jean Douglass's flat with Sandy, he'd bubbled over with questions and enthusiasm about the royal family, charming her. Now he seemed cold, exact, even cruel. Uneasily, she kept thinking back to her flat, trying to believe this was the same man.

Nora. Five-four, whippy and nervous, crinkly black hair down to her shoulder blades, dark eyes, an accent that the nanny tentatively identified as Northern Irish. Nora worried Jean Douglass most, not only because of her temper and the quite unnecessary slap in the face. It was her unblinking and depthless eyes. Something was missing behind them. Nora held all the others in contempt—all except Raffael, whose attention she desperately wanted. She constantly stroked her ugly little weapon. Jean Douglass knew some of the others were armed, but only Nora flourished her gun. She could imagine Nora killing people in a panic. Or at her leisure, and enjoying it.

Shawn? Was that his name? Five-eight, chubby, blue

eyes, curly brown hair, rosy complexion, mid-twenties. Despite his pronounced Welsh accent, to the nanny he looked like a miniature John Bull caricature from the nineteenth century. She wondered if it embarrassed him to look so English. Or perhaps it was that so many English looked Welsh?

Ellen? The red-haired girl, who hadn't yet spoken a word of English, was at most twenty. Blue-eyed, five-six, willowy, with a high, light voice. For the most part she spoke when spoken to and seemed awed to be taking part in this appalling venture. She couldn't keep her eyes or hands off Gwyn. Jean Douglass thought she needed some sense shaken into her. But had she herself demonstrated any greater wisdom? What she had done was unspeakable, worse than terrorism. She had betrayed the woman she held in highest esteem, the Queen of England. And she might pay for it with her life, and Pip's.

Jean Douglass felt an ache rise in her throat. Tears swam in her eyes. She blinked, refusing to give way. Weeping would serve no purpose. Instead, she tried to recall everything she could about terrorists and kidnapping. There was the Iranian Embassy siege. The terrorists had wanted some obscure political statement and safe passage to—where? Libya, perhaps, and refuge with that hideous man Qaddafi. They had killed a hostage. Dear Lord. . . .

She disciplined her thoughts. What had finally happened at the embassy? The terrorists had threatened to kill all the hostages, then the SAS had assaulted the embassy in that breath-taking rescue mission. There had been a fire, and the SAS soldiers had thrown the hostages outside. Jean Douglass remembered feeling indignant that the soldiers had tied up the hostages, who might be sympathetic to the terrorists. There was even a name for it, some syndrome or other. Hostages started to see their captors as kind protectors, rather than the monsters they were. Jean Douglass clasped the child more tightly. She was truly frightened, far more than by death, at the prospect of losing enough control of her own mind and soul to embrace that most dreadful evil. *Dear Father in heaven.* She closed her eyes tightly against the welling tears. *Give me enough strength to protect my boy against harm, and myself from the corruption of evil doers. Amen.*

The car rounded a corner sharply, slumping the passengers against each other. Shawn and the girl resumed their conversation in Welsh, with an occasional comment from Gwyn. Shawn was driving, with Madog and Gwyn to his left and Raffael behind. The Irishwoman seemed to be asleep beside him. The child stirred in the nanny's arms at the change of direction, and began to cry weakly.

"Hush, Pipsqueak," Jean Douglass whispered, afraid the terrorists would punish the little boy for noise. "Is your tummy still sick?"

Pip burrowed under her arm, sniffling.

"Hiding like a church mouse instead of a brave explorer mouse? Do you remember Reepicheep?"

The boy nodded. The gallant mouse from Narnia was a favourite bedtime story.

"What would Reepicheep do on an adventure?"

"Be brave," Pip said gravely. "But Reepicheep never got sick."

"Reepicheep was sick once," Jean Douglass improvised. "But it wasn't very interesting, so there's no story about it. Tell me where you're sick."

Jean Douglass listened carefully. Upset stomach, dizziness, hotness, trouble focusing his eyes, aches and pains. Whatever gas they used made an adult ill, as she knew, and would seriously overdose a young child. Was there an antidote? She searched through the residue of her training and could find no answer. A military doctor would know. For now, the best thing he could do was sleep. The nanny wrapped her suit jacket snug around Pip and rocked him as she sang.

Out of the corner of her eye, she saw Ellen suddenly fall silent and turn to stare.

"Do you speak it?" The girl's light voice sounded young and unsteady in English.

"Eileann mo chridhe, eileann Mull." Jean Douglass finished the verse. If it would buy better treatment for her boy, she would be civil. No more than civil. "Not many speak Gaelic now. People learn the old songs, that's all."

Shawn said something in Welsh.

The girl translated. "He says it's the same with us. People in the big choirs sing Welsh, but won't speak a word."

"A shame," the nanny said automatically, as she had often said of Gaelic, and could have bitten her tongue. She would yield no sympathy for these people.

But they just nodded agreement after a glance of curiosity, and a moment later picked up their conversation. Jean Douglass brushed damp hair back from Pip's hot forehead and went on singing of her great-granny's peaceful island of Mull. *Eileann mo chridhe. . . .*

If they thought her a Scottish nationalist, could it buy better treatment? The very thought horrified her. The nanny wrestled with her conscience. Exhausted, she finally decided her Lord would ask her to make no decisions now, as she sped from a fearful day into an unknown night. As her cheek dropped onto the child's fine golden hair, she remembered, *Suffer the little children to come unto me.*

Gwyn drove slowly through the dim streets of Llany-groes, glad of the last hour of pre-dawn darkness. Beside him, Sion was snoring. By daylight, everyone in a small North Wales town would know about a posh car with London license plates before it reached the end of the high street. But he saw no eyes prying from behind curtains, and no one abroad in the narrow streets. He crossed the bridge and followed Madog's directions north to the next village, then west into the Berwyns. They passed a few scattered cottages; the area seemed underpopulated. It had little to attract retired English. After a mile's gentle climb on a single lane of asphalt, Madog pointed right. Gwyn saw only a steep hillside planted with evergreens, but he pulled to the side.

"I can drive us up," Madog offered.

Gwyn put the Bentley into neutral, and they climbed out to change places.

"Looks like it's been dry awhile, so we might get right up to the barn," Madog said. "Better tell the folks back there to hang on. It's not much of a road."

He drove forward until they were abreast of the forestry plantation. Then he turned off the headlights and eased off the asphalt. The running lights showed a pair of ruts leading bumpily up into the deep gloom of the evergreens, which grew in straight ranks without undergrowth or glades. Forestry Commission plantations inexorably covered hill farm after hill farm, their houses and outbuildings weathering to piles of stones in the bracken. In Scotland, sheep had driven the small farmers from the land; in Wales it was black regiments of spruce and fir and pine.

"Grandad went and sold the bottom pasture to the forestry after the war," Madog explained as he negotiated the car over roots and rocks. "I tried to buy it back, but they weren't having any."

"You inherited this place?" Gwyn frowned, unwilling to yield his resentment at Madog's ownership.

"Nope. Bought it from my uncle. He was selling anyway, and I figured it was better than letting some London tax lawyer turn it into a three-ring circus. Caradoc—my old man—thought I lost my marbles."

Rock scraped the rear axle, and Gwyn hoped the American knew what he was doing. If the ruts grew much deeper they'd bog down; the Bentley would be spotted in hours by the farm neighbours, no matter how much they kept to themselves. Soon they climbed around a hill shoulder and above the dark forestry. The track deteriorated into two irregular channels that obviously formed stream beds in wet weather, and they jounced up onto a scoured height of furze and bracken. Snow or heavy frost whitened the north slopes.

"Neighbours," Madog said as they crossed a shallow dip in the hillside. Gwyn saw the pale flank of a whitewashed building. "John Hughes, Cae Isa. He'll let us alone. That's his brother's place over against the far slope."

"What does he do up here?" Gwyn grunted, clinging to the dashboard as they jolted upward again. "He couldn't keep enough sheep to pay."

"Cattle on fodder." Madog hesitated, then his gold tooth flashed in the dimness as he grinned. He added, "He rustles English beef from round Oswestry and Shrewsbury."

Gwyn found himself smiling, too, reluctantly, at the age-old border occupation, and said, "That's why he minds his own business."

Gwyn saw the small hay barn when Madog wheeled the car into a rocky crease of the hillside, once a stone quarry by its appearance. The barn had been built shoulder-high in drystone, but now corrugated in tin covered the upper walls and roof. The American got out, lifted the bar, and eased the double doors wide as the others clambered out. Gwyn got in the driver's seat and parked the car between the bare left wall and a loose stack of hay. Chaff swirled up across the amber running lights and settled. A muddy green Toyota Land Cruiser occupied the other side of the barn. Madog lifted a hay fork down from a roof post and began forking hay over the car. Soon it was covered, a passable haystack with a tarpaulin thrown over the top for good measure.

The others clustered silently outside the barn door, their breath rising tight and white in the freezing air. No one was dressed for the bitter chill. Jean Douglass, with her suit jacket wrapped around the Prince, was shivering in a silk blouse. Nora had her shotgun trained vigilantly on the haggard woman and the child, until Raffael touched the short barrel and gently shook his head. The two nationalists stood apart, gazing deliberately off at the stunted trees as though they'd come on a nature outing. Gwyn looked past them across the bare frosted hillside. Cold. Wind-scoured. Remote. Its bleakness would have suited a medieval hermit. The end of the world, shared by monumentally ill-assorted companions.

The American led them, stumbling on foot, up two stony ruts the Land Cruiser might manage in dry weather. After a steep climb, the track dropped again into a south-facing hollow with bare trees enclosing a whitewashed farm house. There was a small orchard and a stone-paved garth within a low drystone wall. Not large, Gwyn noted, but scrub and sheep-walk at fifteen hundred feet never could have supported luxury. Under the eaves, a bronze wind chime sounded a mournful pentatonic. The farm's name was chipped unevenly on a headstone resurrected as a gatepost. Pen y Cae, the top of the field.

Gwyn looked across the hillside bathed in overcast moonlight. A few flakes of snow scudded along the ground in the thin wind, gathering in the farm's creases and hollows.

5

Peter Holt waited as the BBC team set up for a location shoot in front of the now-famous Kensington kindergarten. Less than twelve hours after the incident, several million viewers around the world had seen the hostage-taking drama unfold. One of the smaller networks, originally frustrated by its second-rank assigned position, had been beyond the range of the gas and had taped the entire episode. Overnight it had sold broadcast rights worth thousands of pounds.

For once, Peter also had benefited from the Welsh connection. A full crew—director, production assistant, cameraman, and sound man—was the measure of his improved status. He glanced at his note cards, then folded them and shoved them in his trench-coat pocket, confident of his material. The director positioned him by the expensive brass-and-glass doors and gave him the count.

"Scotland Yard still has no certain leads on yesterday's violent kidnapping of the heir apparent and his nurse, Jean Douglass," Peter told the video camera. "Thousands of television viewers watched helplessly as the royal party and bystanders were felled by an unknown gas on this site." He paused, knowing that at this point the studio would cut in yesterday's footage.

"The well-organized attack apparently began when two

71

men, dressed as security guards, released gas grenades into the street crowd and inside the kindergarten. Within seconds, terrorists escaped in a hired van with the heir apparent and his nurse. Who hired the van? Scotland Yard is seeking the answer to that question since the discovery of three identical red-and-yellow vans abandoned in various Greater London locations. All were hired over the past fortnight. Questioning of all known Welsh nationalist sympathizers in London has produced little new information. It appears that even the people involved were kept uninformed of the full plan. Police speculate that European-based terrorists were involved, but none has yet been identified.''

Peter eyed the director, but he got no time signal. ''Police are still combing the city for clues to the terrorists' present location, after searching dozens of London houses and flats yesterday within hours of the incident. In one North London flat, positively identified as an IRA safe house, they found weapons and papers—including Welsh-language newspapers and handwritten notes—suggesting that Irish aid to the Welsh terrorists went further than yesterday's car bomb at Grosvenor Square. They turned up no evidence to reveal the terrorists' whereabouts since the kidnapping.''

Peter paused at the director's hand signal and tied it up. A full two minutes. Not bad. For a reporter who was recently in deep disgrace over the same issue, Welsh extremism, not bad at all.

''This is Peter Holt for BBC news.'' The director cued him for a second take. The Corporation was wringing every ounce of worth from his unaccustomed presence here. Not that anyone in Wales would be fooled. ''This is Peter Holt on location in London, for BBC Wales.'' Then to black.

But back at the Television Centre, hunched in front of his own canned image on the news, Peter fretted. Thin, very thin. What Scotland Yard had dribbled made no sense, like their talk of a mock execution of a river police constable down at Beckton. What the hell were they doing at Beckton? The Yard might as well not have put a gag order on such scraps. Useless.

Despite accepting his offer of help, Scotland Yard wasn't telling him everything. Between calls, Grenvile had probed his knowledge of the nationalists—so insistently that Peter found himself growing evasive—but now offered nothing in return. A hostage negotiator's role in life, of course, was to promise friendship, approval, aid, and ransom money, but to deliver nothing. Peter switched the video monitor to replay the kidnapping tape.

The two security guards were only a blur in the upper left screen until the taller of the two threw his gas grenade into the crowd. There was something stubbornly familiar about the second guard. He had glasses and a beard, but those were an easy disguise. Size and stance were harder. Still, since a few blurred frames weren't enough to judge, Peter had said nothing of his nagging suspicions. Nor about the child's nurse. He leaned close as the tape zoomed in on the Queen, then panned the crowd to the Prince and his nanny. The Douglass woman nodded at the two terrorists masquerading as a camera crew, then turned to look at the Queen. After a split second's glance to make sure the royal boss wasn't watching, she led the little boy forward.

What was the message in that glance? Fear? Was the Queen harsh to her employees? Hostility? Sometimes a children's nurse got too involved and started to believe she was her charge's "real" mother. Jealousy?

Just a glance. But what if Douglass was part of the plot? Today's endless phone calls and visits had turned up nothing. The nanny was a staunch monarchist and a starched Presbyterian. Blackmail seemed impossible. The only close relative was a younger brother who professed shock and dismay at his sister's kidnapping. When Peter pressed, Sandy Douglass added sullenly that her ladyship had no time for common types like him these days; he hadn't seen her for months. Miss Douglass had no Irish or Welsh friends. No troubled love life. No political allegiance. Dead end.

Peter couldn't waste any more time on the nurse's personal history. Once terrorists spirited a hostage into hiding, it could take months to winkle them out, especially in this city. The calls from the terrorists came from a London phone that was still unlocated and, to telephone security's embarrassment, apparently non-existent. BBC London was prepared for a long siege.

Peter had been ordered back to Cardiff on the next train. Back to covering the Allt Valley Dam protest and any local Welsh angles he could manufacture on a London kidnapping that would probably be solved, and covered, in London. For him it was over.

Unless. Unless one terrorist manned the London phone and the others had managed to get out of town. Through Beckton? To the continent? How many London safe houses could they have, after all? Or what if they'd slipped through the road-blocks and reached Wales? Peter ruefully dismissed the possibility that the hottest story of his career would follow him onto his own turf. Wishful thinking.

Robert Grenvile watched the BBC news on the television monitor in New Scotland Yard's electronics master control centre. Once again they were waiting, this time for results on the current questioning of the terrorists' young Welsh driver.

Robert cleared his throat surreptitiously. For the few hours a year that he was actually thrown into negotiations, he had perfect command of his voice. The laryngitis was psychosomatic; he knew that without reports from the throat specialist and the psychiatrist. He knew it even before he completed his own military psychology training. Years before any tests, his father's acid "Cat got your tongue?" said it all. And here he was again, reduced to a rasping whisper, trying to maintain equilibrium in a fundamentally hostile environment. At home in Wimbledon, working companionably in the greenhouse with his wife or helping the girls with homework, he was a different man. Kinder, more decent, more caring. It was easier to care about his family, his garden, even about world conditions, in the absence of surveillance monitors and cold-eyed intelligence technicians.

Shock pulled Robert suddenly straight in his chair. On the screen was the opulent Buckingham Palace studio, and the stricken face of the Queen.

"Good evening," she said quietly, her huge blue eyes gleaming with unshed tears. Her make-up was unable to disguise her swollen eyes and the tightness around her mouth. "By now you have all heard of the kidnapping yesterday of our eldest son, the heir apparent to the British throne. Our police and military forces are doing their job admirably, carrying out a thorough search for my son and his governess."

There were scenes of the Prince shaking hands, riding a pony, carrying his famous mouse doll.

"We are most grateful for the compassion and kind wishes many of you have expressed by telephone and by letter. We have only this to say, to the—" she stumbled and recovered "—to the people who are keeping my son. Please, in the name of human kindness, allow him to return safely to his home and family." The Queen looked dangerously near to losing her self-control. "Thank you."

A brief close-up of the lovely familiar face, then back to the newscaster, who announced that the King was returning today from his interrupted Australian visit.

"Major Grenvile, isn't making a television appearance the worst thing the Queen could do?" asked Dr. Chernicki, lifting a stray thread from the cuff of her tweed suit. The American observer had been quiet for hours, occasionally entering some figures on a palm-sized black calculator. Americans and their gadgets. "Doesn't it look like a victory for these gunmen?"

"Not necessarily. An appeal from the royal family could enhance their self-esteem and make them easier to deal

with.'' Perhaps. If only they'd ring again, Robert might
have answers.

Robert saw Fox, the SAS officer, watching, listening,
saying nothing. Like a ferret at a rat hole, waiting to seize
an opportunity. No, that was fanciful. All the same, Special Air Services fuelled its spectacular missions on self-
promotion and sheer ego. Fox was not short a gram of
either quality. Robert reflected on the SAS motto: ''Who
dares wins.'' His own might be summed up as ''Caution
before courage.''

The late news ended with Peter Holt, the BBC Wales
reporter who had offered his assistance yesterday afternoon.

''What about this Holt?'' asked the prime minister's aide
irritably. ''Is he a Commie like these Welsh arse-holes?''

''Labour type. No father, mother's a char or something
of that sort. He's a bloodhound, that boy,'' offered one of
the MI5 juniors who'd been doing his homework. ''Remember the BBC cock-up a few months ago, the story on
coming Welsh terrorism? Peter Holt. His information was
spot on, but some of these media johnnies seem to think
they can release any kind of nonsense they please.''

Robert remembered well the accusations and wringing
of hands that greeted Holt's Welsh-extremists story. Pri-
vately, he favoured a few media shake-ups of the intelligence community. It kept them honest, or at least on their
toes.

''Holt's known for some high-flown illusions about freedom of the press—but if he's a Red he's better at keeping
secrets than we are,'' the junior went on, earning scattered
laughter and a few pained glances.

''I'm more concerned about the terrorists,'' muttered
Robert. ''Who are they? Where are they?''

''What about visual identification or retinal scan from
the videotapes?'' the palace security chief asked his head
technician.

''Too far for retinal analysis,'' the woman answered.
''The guards' and photographers' faces are being trans-

ferred to the enhancer to give portraits that are as clear as possible. Then we can compare them with known Welsh and Provisional IRA suspects.''

A few heads shook. Scotland Yard, like other agencies, suffered an internal rift over the use of surveillance technology. An old guard believed only in personal bodyguards, on-the-ground observation, and, for a situation like this, door-to-door search patterns. It was an attitude that maddened Robert. Everyone knew that the Provos and ETA and Libyans, probably even these Welsh novices, used the finest technology that fibre optics and microchips could offer.

''Which of their demands are face-saving and which are serious?'' Anna Chernicki quietly asked Robert. She seemed to have a gift for the right question at the right time. This one brought discussion back to the real issue, the kidnappers. ''Can we expect them to back down on any of their demands?''

Robert began, ''From what they've said—''

''It seems irrelevant to me,'' said Fox. ''Since we're giving them nothing.''

Robert averted his eyes.

The prime minister's aide seized his opening. ''A billion pounds for Welsh industry? The PM could probably promise that without a qualm, make a show of it on the next budget, and then quietly let it lapse over a few years. A million pounds cash is laughable. What would they do with it? These people have probably never seen a thousand pounds cash. Home rule? They voted that down themselves. This is just a last shriek from the Welsh lunatic fringe.''

Perhaps, Robert conceded silently. Nevertheless, this kidnapping, in a more direct way than he could ever have imagined, touched on his duty to King and country. He fumbled out his handkerchief and blotted his face. His task was viciously simple. Promise the terrorists nothing, give them nothing, but build enough trust that they would willingly hand over their prize, the next Prince of Wales.

One of the Scotland Yard men walked in wearily and threw a sheaf of papers on the nearest desk.

"Well?" asked the palace security chief. "Anything new?"

"Nothing."

PEN Y CAE/JANUARY 13/0900

By morning, the kitchen cooker threw enough warmth to drive the damp from the whitewashed room. Gwyn and Sion sat beside Elen at the kitchen table and Raffael leaned against the wall. Jean Douglass, well groomed despite her sleepless few hours on the parlour sofa, stepped in ahead of Nora's gun. The heir apparent, sprawled in his nurse's arms, whined in a hoarse unchildlike voice about the cold. When Jean sat on one of the kitchen chairs, the boy slapped at her face and broke into thin crying.

Gwyn turned away in disgust and got up to hold his hands over the cooker. It had been freezing cold in the upstairs room, even with Elen's slender warmth.

"They expect us to recognize this brat someday as the Prince of Wales?" Sion muttered and expanded on a favourite topic. "The English murdered Llywelyn, the last true Prince of Wales, in 1282."

Gwyn interrupted sharply, "If we don't grab our future any way we can, you can relegate your history to the archives forever. History is now. We're making it." But he felt less conviction than he would have liked.

And the old insult still rankled. Edward I, asked by the Welsh to name a native-born prince, indulged in a droll practical joke that failed to amuse the Welsh lords. He named his own son, born in the English fortress at Caernarfon, as Prince of Wales.

"Tyrd ataf i, machgen." Elen coaxed the child from Jean Douglass. "Is it always claws and elbows in the morning, like an old crab?"

Elen teased a smile from the child and a nod from the nanny. Elen Parry of Cadwyn dandling an aristocratic

English kid and speaking English? Gwyn frowned. It was a different story last night, when she slid into the cot he'd claimed upstairs. If they were going to be here a day or two, he'd have to set his people straight about fraternizing. His people? Madog and, for the duration, Sion and Elen. Not Raffael or Nora. The sooner he saw their backs, the sooner he'd breathe easy again.

Gwyn heartily wished he'd never accepted their dubious help. He'd have been better on his own. Even going to ground would have been easier; just him and the kid and the nanny. In the Libyan camp Raffael had more or less invited himself into the operation. Qaddafi wanted the European urban guerrillas to support each others' struggles, and even after years as an instructor, Raffael liked to keep his hand in with operations. He'd brought in Nora. Brilliant promise he explained, but she needed more training and especially more discipline. She was inclined to lose control at inopportune times. Maybe that was why none of the hostages she and Raffael had held in Italy had survived: the judge, the car manufacturer, the army general.

Sion and Elen were here as a sop to solidarity with the other Welsh-activist groups. Sion had provided a few weapons through his military black-market contacts. Elen was a nice kid going through adolescent rebellion. In five years she'd be married to a farmer and have two kids, a collie, and a holiday caravan. But she was a hot little piece in bed, and it was in bed he'd agreed that she could join the operation.

Madog was the most sinister compromise. Money talked, and so did technology. Gwyn didn't understand the half of his *lol* jabber about bubble memory computers and infra-red chaff, but so far the American's electronic trinkets had worked. Madog played coy about his supposed American Welsh group; Gwyn had met no other members, seen no correspondence, never heard of it before Madog attended his New York fund-raising lecture. He guessed that Madog acted alone, for his own interests. He feared that Madog acted, not alone, but for a group that was anything but sympathetic to left-leaning national liberation movements. And if Madog represented the CIA, NSA, or some other American alphabet-soup agency, they were all as good as dead.

"He's usually a sweetheart, aren't you, Pip?" Jean leaned to brush fair hair from the boy's forehead. "But feel his brow—"

"Fever," agreed Elen.

Gwyn shook his head, exasperated.

"A cough, too, and sore eyes. He's quite ill. I've never seen him like this. That woman"—Jean nodded towards the sixteen-gauge—"insisted on waking him up."

"And should I let the pair of them slide out of the window instead?" demanded Nora.

"The gas." Elen nodded at Gwyn, confirming the boy's sickness.

Gwyn stared at the stove lids. "Better than starving in the Rhondda ghost towns and on dying farms like Welsh kids. What do you expect us to do about it?"

"Call a doctor," the nanny said coolly. "At once."

"He'll get over it." Gwyn ransacked the cupboard over the cooker for instant coffee but found only unground beans. Another cup of tea, then.

Madog was outside cleaning the door cistern before adding spring water. Gwyn poured the tea, cupped his steaming mug between his hands, and walked through the other cold rooms. The wooden furniture was old, the kind of battered oak that was eagerly snapped up by Londoners fond of rustic discoveries and lacking the cash for Queen Anne. Back kitchen, pantry, and living-room were recently plastered and whitewashed, but faded wallpaper still peeled from the downstairs bedroom walls. Madog was in the process of doing the place up. That cast the kitchen, with its slate floor and no running water, in a new light. Not the type for swimming pools and the latest household wonders, then; instead it was back to quaint Welsh nature.

Upstairs, in the room he had shared with Elen last night, Gwyn looked over a complicated electronic device wired to a car battery. Speaker, transceiver, microphone: an amateur radio set-up. He glanced around the spartan room by daylight. Naked light bulb, scarred oak dresser, mouse-eaten mattress on the cot. American House Beautiful hadn't extended to this room yet. Gwyn crossed the landing to the other room, vindicated by the radio gadgetry. It confirmed his suspicion that the house's simplicity was a posture. Madog was a materialist, like all Americans.

The larger bedroom's dormer window looked south across a snow-dusted flank of the Berwyns. A huge wooden bed half-filled the room, enclosed on three sides and the top, the kind of bed smallholders once used to divide their one-room cottages. A dresser, also time-darkened oak, and a wardrobe. In the far wall, another door opened on a store-room, probably a bedroom back in the days when the Welsh had big families.

Gwyn set his tea on the edge of the dresser and eased the wardrobe door open. A man's suit, three pieces in steel-blue pin-stripes. Fancy that. With a brolly and bowler, he'd look like a director of the Bank of England. Next to the suit, two women's dresses with the label of a Swansea designer. Girls', not women's, Gwyn corrected, eyeing their lacy *décolletage* and casual tartiness.

From the doorway Madog said, "The little lady figured night-life in Llanfyllin was a bit slow."

"And took the next plane back to Seattle?" Gwyn, caught in the act but yielding no admission of guilt, didn't turn from his investigation of the wardrobe.

"Nope. Next bus back to Machynlleth."

"Promise her a ride in daddy's space shuttle next time." Gwyn turned against the dresser and picked up his tea mug.

Madog leaned against the jamb with arms folded over his chest, revealing the gold tooth in his smile. The perfect host. The million-dollar grin was even more impermeable than usual.

"I offered her a talk with the shuttle pilots on the ham set." Madog indicated the next room with a lazy thumb. "But they didn't speak Welsh."

Of course, Madog would court a girl who was Cymry Cymraeg, Welsh-speaking Welsh. In Mexico City he would pick up a Mexican with an Indian face and a Castilian voice. Americans were world-champion collectors of endangered species.

"Isn't that unusual? Civilian radio contact with an orbital flight?"

"Guess I'm just an unusual kind of guy."

Gwyn glowered. Compromise is what you are, and that's unusual only to idealists—if any survive in this ravaged country.

"So it would seem. But unusual in exactly what way, Nilsson?"

"Problem, Gwyn? I wasn't aware that one of my gadgets didn't work, or one of my contacts didn't pan out. Better get it off your chest."

"You're the problem. I don't know enough about you."

"Hey, you know everything worth knowing. Trust me!" he invited with a television comedian's exaggeration, but his eyes didn't smile.

"I think you're CIA."

"You been reading spy books again? Give me a break."

"National Security Agency, then."

"Come off it. I hear those guys spend most of their time arresting each other by mistake."

"Somebody's private army. Right-wing survivalists."

"Thanks a whole lot, Davies. That's a real vote of confidence. I told you I was in the army. That was a long time ago."

"Military intelligence."

"Three strikes and you're out, pal." Madog stooped through the low doorway to the landing. He switched to Welsh, purer than anyone with an American drawl had any right to. "How long do you think we'll need to stay?"

"Today, maybe tomorrow," Gwyn said. "Long enough to make contact again with those sods at Scotland Yard and arrange a drop somewhere."

"We can release the boy somewhere like Manchester. No need to let them know where we are now."

Gwyn shrugged. It hadn't occurred to him that they might still appear to be in London.

"Depends on your wire-tap gadget." He threw it back to Madog. At the bottom of the stairs, Gwyn saw Raffael watching them from the living-room doorway.

"There's the thing," Madog admitted, and went back to English for the Italian's benefit. "I'm not sure about range. We'll soon find out."

"This may take longer than you think," said Raffael. "The police have had time to think, to plan, to grow angry. Yesterday we were kidnappers. Today, whether we choose to be or not, we are terrorists."

Gwyn heard the gleam behind his soft words and glanced quickly from Raffael to Madog and back again. This was the price of having to change plans. Raffael was all right for an hour, not for a day or a week. From the start the Italian made him uneasy. He was too available, too eager to participate. "Solidarity for revolution of the oppressed" had sounded rational in a bare Tripoli conference room. Now it sounded ludicrous. Raffael wanted gold stars from Qaddafi and didn't care who paid the bill.

"And," Raffael added with a show of compassion, "the little boy is quite ill."

Elen materialized in the doorway behind him, flushed pink to the roots of her red hair. She dropped Madog's bucket with a crash before she launched a screed of Welsh at Gwyn.

"Tell that bloody freak with the shotgun if she touches me again I'll—" Elen stopped with her face aflame, at a loss for words. "What does she think I am? Sick in the head like her?"

"Trouble?" asked Raffael smoothly.

Madog spoke up before Gwyn could put words together. "Just ice on the spring, makes it hard to get water. C'mon, Elen, I'll give you a hand." He seized the bucket and steered her through the kitchen with no apparent haste.

But Gwyn saw the grip on Elen's elbow was a hold that, if she struggled, would break her arm.

"How bad is the boy?" Gwyn started towards the kitchen. "Perhaps we should see about a doctor."

"No," corrected Raffael. "We must find some other way."

6

Carrie Powell threw off her wet anorak and stalked through the cottage, shaking melted snow from her short dark hair. Some landed on the grey tiger cat in the chair by the cooker, and he leaped awake with a meow of betrayal.

"Sorry, Pal."

Carrie stooped so he could spring onto her shoulder. The trick had been endearing in a tiny green-eyed kitten. Now ten pounds of cat made a weighty fur collar for a small woman. Pal coiled around her nape, purring, as she tracked muddy steps over the slate floor and slowed to a stop. Her long drive to London had been for nothing after all, and this morning she'd struggled homeward through snow and icy roads in her ageing Mini.

Damn Americans, and especially damn American consulates. It should have been easy: character references, a job in Pittsburgh, a place to live with cousin Mair. What more did they want? Probably looking for Communist or atheist or feminist skeletons in her closet, since the new president's creationist amendment to the constitution, Carrie thought morosely. The important thing was a job. Any job. She'd worked a six-month contract while Llanfyllin's regular district nurse had her baby two years ago; since then, there'd been nothing. Even her ex-husband, once full of an employed teacher's righteousness, was now on the dole. Carrie was thirty, formidably well trained, and since her graduation eight years ago had been gainfully employed for a total of ten months.

Pal dug his claws into her shoulder, his anger a barometer of Carrie's own anger, and relaxed when she sighed and filled the kettle. A nice pot of tea, dear. Carrie slammed the kettle onto the cooker and scowled at the muddy floor. Not that she had anything better to do with her time and skills than wash the floor.

Carrie waited for her elder-and-yarrow mixture to steep. Gran's old concoction was at least free for the gathering, and if it was truly a tonic, so much the better. Was elder tea un-American?

Pal purred and began to groom Carrie's wet black hair as she opened the *Cambrian News*. The Aberystwyth weekly was ranting about hippies, caught stealing mushrooms from a farmer's field again. Hippies had been an extinct species for fifteen years everywhere else; now they called themselves subsistence farmers and flocked to Wales from English middle-class suburbs with government grants. They loomed large in the *News*'s hysterical front-page editorials. Only the obituaries were written in Welsh.

Nothing yet about the royal kidnapping, of course. The *News* would hiss about that next week. Carrie had heard her fill over the car radio on her way back from London on the M4, and as she waited at the two road-blocks where the police took inordinate interest in her mid-Wales license plates. She doubted whether Welsh nationalists had anything to do with the kidnapping. More likely it was an election-year ploy to discredit the Welsh and justify further reductions in economic aid. The poor kid was probably being held captive in a secret-service office until the government could find suitable Welsh scapegoats.

A story on the proposed Allt Valley Dam caught her eye. Undeb Cymru Fydd, Cadwyn, and Etifed announced a protest in Cardiff. That was unusually chummy for the lunatic fringe. But the respectable Plaid Cymru was backing it, too. Without jobs and without inhabitants, the valley's villages might as well be underwater anyway.

Carrie imagined the plotting that would be going on in somebody's seedy Aberystwyth rooming house. The Boys would all be there, heads together in the reek of cigarette smoke and unwashed denim. They could parade their revolutionary fervour, then adjourn to the Nag's Head and drink themselves stupid. The comrades would mutter about creating Welsh "protected heritage communities," never stopping to think their plan was as racist as South Africa's failed black homelands. Living in the past. Carrie had once enraged the Boys by quoting Doris Lessing's opinion that sentiment about the past was for people who didn't know what to do next.

All the over-age graduate students and hack lecturers bemoaning a cause lost seven centuries ago; Gwyn Davies would hold forth on the great intentions of Undeb Cymru Fydd. Always soon, never quite yet. After a few pints he would forget the golden age to come and curse the English squires, who he claimed had driven his ancestors from their farms with falsified English deeds. Pity he didn't stick to dead languages and empty talk; it could have averted tragedy eight years ago. Then she'd been as *lol* silly as any of them. Now she wouldn't be caught dead at a protest, a nationalist meeting, or a useless Undeb subcommittee.

And somewhere in Pittsburgh there must be a decent man whose armpits didn't smell and who wasn't dedicated to putting the Welsh under glass. A football player? A rancher? Even an accountant. He had to be big and blond and randy. Yum. Carrie sighed and winced as Pal's claws dug deep into her nape.

"You're the only problem, love. What are we going to do with you, now Ann can't take you? Everyone's emigrating."

Pal purred on around her neck, a grey cat safe inside on a grey day, satisfied that Carrie would find a way to keep him in table scraps and the only acceptable company:

hers. Carrie wished she shared Pal's gift for living today. Tomorrow would almost certainly be less pleasant.

The phone flung Carrie back into the present and catapulted Pal off her shoulders. He stalked away across the cottage's other room as she picked up the receiver. As usual on a Welsh phone, the caller sounded as though he was standing at the bottom of a well with someone shovelling gravel on his head.

"Who?" Carrie shouted. "Can you talk louder?"

Ten minutes later the elder tea was cooling on the board while Carrie shrugged back into her wet anorak. Pal watched reproachfully from his chair by the cooker, his grey forepaws folded under like an old monk's hands tucked into his sleeves. Carrie's elderly cat had patiently seen her through almost a decade's changes. He had turned up wet and woebegone, clinging to her residence window sill in Aberystwyth, back when she was reading geography and still believed Wales needed geographers. Pal had survived the wardens and regulations until end-of-term and her transfer to nursing in Liverpool. And he survived everything since, marriage and divorce and family quarrels—yes, Mam—and the dole and the slow winding-down of all that Carrie Powell thought was her life.

Things had looked hopeful, once. Carrie was going to get her PhD and teach human and physical geography at Aberystwyth. She had the marks, the drive, and a love of the land: her country, or any country.

Then the world had turned upside-down. First, the Undeb operation that went wrong and thrust her into an ugly trial. Acquittal didn't ease her shame on her family's pain. Then Tad's death left the farm tangled in debts and dreams. Even with the old house and most of the land sold to a Coventry mortician, there wasn't enough to keep Mam and the younger kids. Geography promised no immediate returns. Nursing, on the other hand, meant three years of slogging and then wages she could send home. Or so she had naïvely believed. Carrie Powell, RN, unemployed; specialities, elder tea and odd jobs.

"Back soon, Pal. A sick kid shouldn't take long." And there would be a cash payment from the vacationing German businessman who couldn't reach the Llanfyllin doctor. Sweets for her, a wedge of cheese for Pal. She lifted her medical bag, a glorified first-aid kit with a few of Gran's herbal remedies tucked in for those who distrusted technology. In the Canolbarth, in mid-Wales, people still remembered if your grandmother was a famous bone-setter. "The poor souls won't have much holiday anyway, in a snow-storm."

Pal laid his grey muzzle over folded paws and looked up at her with scholarly regret.

"No, tiger, it's a long drive." But at the door, Carrie turned and sighed. "Will you behave?"

Pal yawned hugely, poured down from his chair, and padded to the door. In the Mini, with a warm neck piece purring over her shoulder, Carrie let out the clutch with its usual clattering thunk. "She won't go much longer, Pal." Crackers, talking to a cat. At least he didn't answer yet.

Gwyn leaned at the upstairs window with his chin on his clasped hands, conscious of falling into his usual class-room stance. Elbows on the podium, chin on fists, a sharp eye for nodding heads at the back of the lecture hall. They all looked about fifteen these days, barely adolescent, a sure sign that he'd spent too long at Aberystwyth. It was three years since he'd even glanced at his work on weak antepenultimate syllables of the inflected-analytic transition. Meic was taking lectures for him this week; thank God he'd made it a week, not a day. Others would cover for him in Cardiff. He might get through without arousing suspicion.

Meanwhile, where in the flaming pits of hell was Sion's inspiration, the one-time district nurse? Someone he'd known in Aberystwyth, he said. Gwyn hoped the damned woman would be less troublesome than Sion. If she would appear, administer an aspirin to keep the Douglass woman happy, and leave as quickly as possible, Gwyn could get on with setting up ransom and unloading the kid. And unloading the IRA arse-hole with her nervous trigger finger, and Raffael who smiled and smoothed and placated more like a visiting diplomat than a Red Brigades expert on hostages. Those two were a mistake, at least the way things were dragging on. But Gwyn didn't want to think about it. Until the danger passed.

Danger. More danger with every hour they kept the darling of the English royal family. Where was Sion's nurse?

It was nearly noon when he heard a car engine down near Madog's hay barn. Minutes later a small dark woman appeared, struggling up the frozen slope. Gwyn went downstairs and nearly collided with Raffael, who leaned in the hall shadows.

"It would, I think, be better for you to keep out of sight," the Italian advised. "Also the others. Miss Jean Douglass and I will make a small performance about our sick child. I am German, she is my English wife."

Across the room, the white-faced nanny nodded. She had combed her blonde hair down. It curled around her heart-shaped face and fell to her shoulders. She wore one of the dresses from Madog's wardrobe upstairs. Even with her lace handkerchief tucked primly into the cleavage revealed by the low-cut dress, Miss Jean Douglass was very attractive. Gwyn wondered uneasily what form of persuasion Raffael or Nora had used to buy her co-operation. He decided it might be best to keep an eye on her safety for the duration. There was no guessing what ticked away behind the Irishwoman's black eyes or Raffael's polished manners.

Feeling like one of his own students sent out for inattention, Gwyn climbed the stairs and sat near the top. After a minute Madog settled silently beside him. Sion and Elen were in the room with the American's radio toys; maybe they could chat up a spaceman. Below, the door slammed and a gust of cold wind hurtled up the stairs. As she came in, the woman was telling Raffael she didn't speak German. Gwyn sharpened his ears to the district nurse's voice. Welsh, doing her best to sound English. A nation of traitors.

A few yards away, Gwyn heard her commiserate about the weather and click her tongue in sympathy for the little boy sleeping in a nest of blankets on the parlour sofa.

"I'll examine him in a moment. Let him sleep for now. First, what can you tell me about his sickness? Has he been in contact with other children with mumps or measles? Is there any history of allergy?"

She was thoroughly professional. Gwyn found himself instead wishing she were a soggy old girl sacked for nipping the medicinal brandy between home visits. This one was altogether too clever and asked disconcerting questions. Now she was asking about recent exposure to poisonous substances.

Their voices at last woke the boy. Gwyn was surprised to hear not the crying of the past day but delighted laughter. The district nurse and the other two joined in.

"Didn't you see him? Did you think he was a fur collar?" the nurse asked. She spoke intelligently to the kid. No baby talk. Gwyn the linguist approved. "Here. Be gentle and he won't claw you."

"What's he called?" asked Pip after a fit of coughing.

"His name's Pal."

Gwyn swore under his breath. *No. Anything but.* Why for God's sake hadn't he asked Sion the woman's name? He knew the man was an idiot.

"See? He's quite friendly."

Ceridwen Powell, and on her shoulder there had always ridden a fierce grey kitten, grandiloquently named after the mythical Cath Paluc—Pal for short. Gwyn plunged into nightmare. Ceridwen Powell would walk barefoot to London for the privilege of selling out the Welsh. Gwyn shook his head clear. Maybe, just maybe, she would exhaust her questions, tell Jean Douglass to make sure the child rested, and never notice the nanny's Scots burr and the boy's childish but quintessentially English tones. She would go her way without ever laying eyes on Sion or Gwyn or any other who could be linked to a recent hostage-taking. Maybe.

Carrie laughed. "He likes you."

Gwyn thought he detected a note of doubt in her voice. Had she recognized the missing heir apparent? Or was his imagination working overtime? Downstairs, the women talked of childhood fevers and the kid chattered to the damned cat. Then a lull opened in the conversation.

"My granny," announced a childish voice in piercingly upper-crust English, "doesn't like cats. She likes corgis. Doesn't she, Miss Douglass?"

Palms shoved into his eyes until he saw crimson Catherine wheels, Gwyn fought a wave of laughter that must be hysteria. Silence took hold of the farmhouse parlour below.

"So much for that idea," said Madog softly.

Gwyn had forgotten the American. Now he saw Madog leaning on the wall behind him, holding a small pistol. The kind of gun a woman would pull out of her garter in some silly espionage flick. Plastic, not metal. Slim barrel, angular grip. Gwyn eyed the latest of Madog's expensive toys; Caradoc Nilsson Aeronautics must handle some unusual custom orders.

"Well," Carrie Powell announced briskly below, after an interminable silence, "there seems nothing to advise but bed rest for a few days. And I really must—"

"No, I fear not," Raffael said easily. "You will unfortunately have to keep us company for a day or so."

"Certainly not! I have an appointment at the American consulate in London tomorrow afternoon. I fully intend to keep it."

Gwyn recognized Carrie's no-quarter voice. He'd last heard it dealing out savage criticism of Undeb Cymru Fydd, and of Gwyn Davies.

"Put your hands on top of your head and turn around," ordered Nora from the downstairs bedroom door.

"Who are you?"

"None of your fucking business. Do as I tell you."

"I see," said Carrie coldly. "So that's the kind of Welsh nationalist who kidnapped the Prince. The Irish kind."

In answer, a thump, and an animal's squall of pain.

Gwyn leaped to his feet but found himself flattened against the staircase wall by Madog's forearm. The American shook his head silently, made his toy gun disappear somewhere, and clumped noisily down the stairs.

"Hey, what's going on around here?" Madog bellowed. "Sounds like you're skinning out a wolverine barehanded."

Gwyn went down after him, recovering his breath. Jean Douglass was backed into a corner with a hand over the child's mouth, too late now. Carrie was standing as instructed, hands on head. Her cat crouched behind for protection, fur bottled in anger. Wide blue eyes and wide green eyes watched black Nora with the same wariness. She saw Gwyn and sighed. Name-calling, an outburst, anything would be better than that sigh.

"Ceridwen?" He couldn't prevent it emerging as a question.

"Gwyn."

She offered the minimal greeting, a compact statue of a woman in a smoky blue skirt and Fair Isle pullover. Gwyn remembered the same outfit from Aberystwyth. His first year teaching. She was first-year geography and Welsh, wet behind the ears from A-levels and a mid-Wales farm, planning to remake Wales single-handed. Why could they never stick with it? The striped kitten had grown into a moon-eyed monster. Carrie looked the same.

"Go very carefully," he told her quietly in Welsh. "The woman's insane."

"You'll have to speak English," she replied. "And my name is Carrie."

"Come along. This isn't a joke."

"Sorry?" She eyed him, then Madog, with equal distaste.

A nation of traitors. Gwyn walked past her to the kitchen

doorway, where Nora had halted. She was creaming herself for an excuse to pull the trigger. Let her try.

"Unfortunately," soothed Raffael again, "you shall have to spend a short time with us, now that you see how things are."

"You'll never get away with it," Carrie answered him in Jean Douglass's words—yesterday? last year?—but looked instead at Gwyn.

"You will finish what you came to do," Raffael suggested pleasantly. "We can afford no sickness in the child."

Madog flashed his golden arse-hole grin. "Hey, Pip, how about a peanut-butter sandwich?"

He took the boy's hand, the one without Mungo Mouse, and strolled into the kitchen oblivious to the stares that followed him.

Gwyn opened his mouth to protest, closed it again, and turned away abruptly. The American had a knack for making him feel redundant on his own operation. It was Gwyn, not Madog, who gave the orders here. And it was Gwyn who should have had the sense to get the boy out of the way of Nora and Raffael. It left Gwyn feeling jangled and useless.

CARDIFF/JANUARY 14/1200

"Free lance, huh?" Al Rees said, making Peter's offer sound like a deliberate insult.

Through the windscreen of Al's car, Peter watched a pair of elderly archivists totter down the front steps of the National Museum. They were wrapped to the teeth against Cardiff's bitterest January in years. Always old people.

"What's wrong with your world-renowned BBC crews, suddenly?"

"You run the camera," said Peter, hoping to avoid another of the photographer's nationalist speeches. "I handle research, interviews, and continuity."

"Don't matter, it's still the same rate." Al named an

exorbitant figure, twice what BBC cameramen pulled down. "Cash."

"Don't talk dull," said Peter. "This isn't the Corporation. This is out of my own pocket. You get paid if you shoot anything we can broadcast."

A Cardiff police cruiser pulled alongside Al's illegally parked car, paused long enough for the driver to wage a greeting, and drove off. Al knew every officer on the beat from Grangetown to Cowbridge.

"What are you on?"

"Officially?" Peter shrugged. "The Allt Valley Dam protest, for what it's worth. With all this hysteria about the royal kidnapping, they'll be lucky if fifty people turn out."

Al worked thoughtfully on his chewing gum, sliding his eyes around the interior of his old Cortina. The newspapers underfoot on the passenger side had known an incarnation as fish-and-chip wrappers. Two windows were broken, the ashtray overflowed, and the car burned more oil than petrol. Al's clothes and flat were in the same condition. Only his camera kit was pristine.

"And unofficially?" Al looked into the lens of his Canon, admiring his smiling image. His dark eyes and year-round sun-tan were inherited from a Hawaiian seaman who stopped in Tiger Bay long enough to enrich South Wales genetically. Al favoured Day-Glo shirts patterned with parrots in palm trees, and a silvered-leather bomber jacket that was his trade mark. His hair was combed carefully over his large ears. "What are you after, *bach?*"

Peter indulged in a last hesitation, then took the plunge. "Welsh angles on the kidnapping. Not necessarily the angles Harry Price is covering." BBC Wales's number-one man, as usual, had cornered the choice assignment.

"And if we sniff out anything good? Can I sell my stills to the *Cardiff Courier?*" The newspaper provided Al's main work, eked out by odd jobs of varying legality.

"To your heart's content—after we broadcast."

"Well, Peter *bach.* " Al used the term of endearment

with no trace of sarcasm. Inscrutable. He hitched his bulk upright in the driver's seat. "Much as I'd like to help you, I have a Plaid Cymru assignment to finish."

"That's volunteer." It was a safe guess, knowing the usual state of Welsh Nationalist Party coffers.

"So's this job of yours, near as I can see."

"Maybe, maybe not." Peter opened the passenger's door. "But I thought you'd see how it affected the survival of Wales as a nation. . . ."

A little rhetoric never hurt. Peter also hoped that Al would tell others that Peter was concerned about the future of Wales. If that information were picked up by the nationalist grape-vine it would help ensure the interviews he wanted. Peter had his well-informed, always confidential, sources. Al had his *clecs*, his bush telegraph.

Peter started to get out of the car.

"Survival of Wales? What do you mean?" Al's hand caught his arm.

"When Welsh terrorists kidnap a member of the English royal family, you can be sure of reprisals. Things could get nasty."

"What do you mean, reprisals?" Al frowned across his steering wheel, knowing the answer but wanting confirmation.

"A round-up of suspects who have nothing whatsoever to do with all this, I would guess, for a start. Just like the seventies when everyone was climbing telly masts, or back in the sixties when the students were spray-bombing English road signs. There's a general election coming up."

"And?"

"The government has to make a show for the English. They have the most votes. There's talk about a second plebiscite on Welsh home rule. There's no way they want to face that one."

"So what?" Rees was unimpressed. "The *Courier* won't print stories or pictures of the arrests. Those arrests just don't happen, as far as anyone admits officially. And don't try telling me BBC will air any footage."

"Unlikely," Peter admitted, remembering his own sharp reprimands for the volatile Welsh-activist stories. "But American telly will. I've got a contact at CBS—the Corporation won't bitch if the Yanks don't air my face. You know how much Americans love to rub British noses in their own problems. The more fascist the Yanks get over there, the more they want to believe the UK's a police state."

"It is," Al said absently. "Listen now, Peter *bach*. This is Thursday, so there's most of two days before the protest. Maybe we can work something out."

Peter waited through the lunch hour, giving the public servants time to return from pricey *cawl* and *bara caws* at *Y Bwthyn Bach* or roast beef at the Royal Hotel. He prowled around the BBC's sprawling studio complex, pausing now and again to gaze out the window towards the sluggish grey River Taff or the equally turbid street traffic of Llantrisant Road, Llandaff.

What new angle was he looking for? Monday's kidnapping still filled the news broadcasts with London-based stories about the frantic search for the Prince and Miss Jean Douglass. Palace spokesmen—since the King and Queen had been discouraged from further appearances—were making television appeals for information and for humane treatment of the heir apparent. The Welsh college student that the London police were holding still claimed to know nothing beyond his own role as get-away driver.

With city police, military police, and thousands of volunteers combing London and surrounding areas, and the terrorists making no new attempts at contact, what could Peter hope to add to the story? He couldn't say, exactly, but he'd know when he found it. The familiar electric tingle would play his spine like a xylophone as it always did when he got onto a hot one. But that was small comfort right now, here in Cardiff, leagues away from the action. Peter returned to hunch over the computer terminal in his windowless cubicle.

When the telephone jangled, he picked it up on the first ring.

"Holt here."

"Couldn't you come up with something a little less officious?" suggested the familiar languid voice. "Unless of course you want to sound officious. You are after all a public servant."

"Elizabeth, I'm waiting for a phone call," Peter lied half-heartedly. "Is it important, or can I ring you back?"

"Not especially important," Elizabeth said coolly. "To you. That much is clear from your punctuality with the support payment. Your daughter feels so terribly let down when you show how little you think of her in this way."

"Why don't you leave Andrea out of it?" Peter suggested, cradling the phone on his shoulder as he picked up a pencil. A few inches of chewed stub. BBC Wales also was economizing, and as usual where least appropriate. Why didn't they cut back on the directors' expense-account lunches? "The kid—God knows how, all things considered—has got enough sense to know the difference between affection and money."

"No doubt that's another slur on my family, but I'm afraid I haven't time to discuss it." Elizabeth's voice dropped half an octave, a misleading promise of warmth and intimacy. It had been alluring, once, that startling purr. Peter supposed it still might be, to the hulking lad in the army-surplus pullover who was her present companion. "When will you have the cheque over here?"

"This evening," Peter told her, cursing himself silently. He hated falling behind and hated even more being reminded of it. It should have been Tuesday night, but Tuesday night he was held over in London, and last night it slipped his mind. He added, with the poisonous courtesy they had adopted, "I won't be disturbing you when I drop it by?"

"Just push it through the letter box," said Elizabeth, equal in polite indifference. "When can we talk over the other expenses? The rising damp in the cellar and the electrician's bill. Oh, and the skylight is leaking again.''

"Soon." Elizabeth and her bloody done-over house in Pontcanna Street, trying to make believe Cardiff was Chelsea. "About Andrea—"

"Doing splendidly," answered Elizabeth briskly. *Now that you're not upsetting the child by dragging in at all hours reeking like a tavern, full of feeble excuses about working late.* There was no need to say it again. It had all been said a year ago. "You can pick her up Friday after school for the weekend. Must go now." She rang off.

Peter scribbled himself a note, then turned back to the computer's video screen and called up his list of political contacts.

Several phone calls later he surveyed his notes, scrawled in his angular hand across curling yellow newsprint sheets.

No comment.

Not yet returned from luncheon.

You'll have to try the London office with that one, I'm sorry to say.

I'm afraid we'd like answers quite as much as you would, Mr. Holt.

Apologies seemed to be the order of the day.

Four Welsh MPs for Glamorgan and Gwent were committed to interviews, three of them English Tories and one a hangdog Labourite. The Labour MP could be depended on to tongue-lash Tories and Welsh Nationalists alike. Peter had managed to include in his requests the hint that he could use Welsh comments on the kidnapping.

Major Grenvile. On impulse, Peter placed a call to the hostage negotiator in London.

"Hello?" A soft voice of indeterminate sex answered, giving no indication of a military police field operation. Yet the connection had the flatness that could indicate a line hooked to tape equipment.

"Peter Holt calling, BBC Wales. I worked with Major Grenvile on Tuesday." He didn't add that it was for one brief, unsuccessful bid to lure the terrorist caller into identifying himself. "Could I speak with him now?" No answer. "Or have him return the call?"

Silence stretched exactly to the point of credibility, long enough for a confused householder to realize the caller's mistake. Or long enough for a military operator to cup a hand over the receiver and quietly throw a question across a London room. Peter knew. He knew many possible reactions to unwelcome journalists' phone calls; it was a hard-earned and ungratifying expertise.

"I'm afraid there's no one of that name here," came the soft response, at last. "I suggest that you try the long-distance operator."

"Right," said Peter agreeably. "Would you tell him I rang? He knows how to reach me."

"I'm sorry. You must have dialled the wrong number."

Without a click, he was back to the buzzing ether of the trunk line. Peter laid the receiver gently back in its cradle and deleted Grenvile from the list on his computer screen. The name silently blinked out of existence.

Peter tapped his teeth with the chewed pencil and prodded the stack of paper on his desk looking for his notes on the Allt Valley dam. He couldn't remember taking them out of his car. Probably still there. Everything else was. He unfolded himself from the swivel chair, grabbed his coat, and headed out through the warren of cubicles to the lift. It was working.

Rain was blowing across the car park. Peter strode past the executives' Jaguars and Saabs to his blue Renault with its driver's door still painted in black primer from the accident. He wouldn't be able to swing the paint job again this month, not if Elizabeth's infernal cellar had rising damp. In a visitor space, some poor devil was hunched against the wet, prying with a penknife at a white Volvo's door lock.

"It only happens when you're in a hurry," he grumbled as Peter went past. He had a holiday tan and a plug in his ear, though he didn't look the type to be sporting a jogger's radio.

Peter found his notes in his glove box, started to close his car door, and thought again. The visitor was still working away at his lock, getting wetter by the minute.

"Want a coat hanger?" Peter called back.

"Got one? Bloody marvellous."

Under a few newspapers in the back seat Peter's summer suit lay wilted in a dry-cleaners' plastic, there since last September. He pulled the top of the plastic open and winkled out the hanger. Procrastination occasionally had its uses.

"Not likely to work but let's try," Peter suggested, straightening the wire. "Not late for an interview, I hope?"

"Just going in to pick up the *Guide* and realized I locked the keys in. Been out of the country. Thanks." The man took the wire and glanced up. "You're Peter Holt, aren't you?"

"Right."

"I've been following your stories on the kidnap. Good stuff."

"Thanks," Peter said, pleased. Too bad McKinley didn't share that view. "Try the other window." The man walked stiffly around the back of the Volvo. Peter followed.

"Terrible situation, pinching the kid. You really think the Provos are involved?"

Peter shrugged, trying to fit the wire between window and frame. "Nobody knows, truth to tell. They're Welsh, but they may have outside help."

"Bloody thugs. Fellow in the next flat thinks he knows one."

Peter thought about that. "You've been in America, have you?" he asked, taking a stab at the tan.

"North, south or central. I suppose that covers it."

"Right." Peter grinned, caught out in his instinctive prying. It made him a good newsman but a rotten acquaintance. He gave up on the left front door and tried the rear. Again, the wire wouldn't fit between window and frame.

Peter grasped the door handle as a last resort and nearly lost his balance when it unexpectedly opened.

"You got it. Bloody marvellous."

"It was open." Peter shrugged. "Most likely you tried every one but that."

"I feel a proper fool." The man looked down ruefully at his soaked jacket. "After all that."

Peter began to fold up the coat hanger. Leave no stone unturned. "You weren't serious about your neighbour?"

"That's what he said. Don't know how serious he was." The man smiled and thrust out a hand. "Teddy Smythe."

"Pleased to meet you." Peter, uncertain whether to push the tip further, was spared the decision.

"Look, Mr. Holt—"

"Peter."

"Come round Saturday evening and I'll introduce you as an old friend. If it was only a joke in poor taste, that'll be that."

"I'd like to." Peter jotted down the address and tucked it into his wallet.

Smythe drove away. After all that, he'd forgotten to get a *Guide*.

Back upstairs in his cubicle, Peter started phoning organizers of the Llanallt march. During a national crisis, the scheduled drowning of two North Wales villages was unlikely to draw more than a few protesters, but it was still the story Peter was assigned to cover. There was always the hope that he could use the interviews to sniff out extremist reaction to the kidnapping for his personal project, the unassigned story on the kidnapping.

"I must say, it doesn't look awfully encouraging," Meleri Lewis told Peter in the cluttered offices of the Cardiff university students' union. No jeans or army surplus for Meleri. Her tortoiseshell glasses, sleek blonde hair, and matronly Jaeger dresses soothed Tory MPs and civil-service drones, as intended. But Peter had also seen Meleri hurling bricks at Welsh Office windows. "Everyone's preoccupied with this ridiculous kidnapping. I just hope we're not the only two people there, Peter.'' She gave him her best madonna smile. It had an undertow remarkably like the Mona Lisa's.

Peter taped her official regrets over the young Prince's kidnapping and rattled back to Llandaff in the venerable Renault. Elizabeth had kept the Triumph. Back in his BBC cubicle, Peter went back to phoning through his list.

Undeb Cymru Fydd. Gwyn Davies was always well informed, articulate, willing to amplify his points in English. Most important, he recognized the symbiotic relationship between the press and the nationalist movement. Peter and Gwyn had evolved a system of reciprocal favours: good copy and footage for Peter, useful publicity for Undeb. But there was no answer at Davies's flat in Aberystwyth. He tried the college's Welsh Department and found himself talking with another lecturer.

"Gwyn Davies? Not here,'' the lecturer announced cheerfully. "If you're calling from Cardiff, you should be able to locate him there.'' The lecturer gave Peter a phone number in Roath and made a hasty farewell.

"Wait a minute!'' Peter flung at him, annoyed. "What's he doing here?''

"Girl-friend. Bloody hell. It's after three, I have a class waiting!''

"Right.'' Peter rang off, bemused. He tried the Roath number twice, but the phone was engaged.

Elen Parry, North Wales press secretary of Cadwyn. Half the Cadwyn executives were still conducting their affairs from inside Shrewsbury jail, serving sentences for an assortment of inept bombings and cottage fires. But Peter couldn't reach Elen in her Coleg Bangor residence.

He tried half a dozen more, without success. Where were they all when he needed them, and when they needed him and the BBC to air their views? Gone underground until the trouble blew over? Or were they involved? Peter frowned at the prison-green walls of his cubby-hole and again dialled the Roath number for Gwyn Davies. Still busy.

Davies might have skipped out on a week's lectures to
visit a girl-friend in Cardiff, yet. . . . Davies had his
contradictions, certainly, Peter had learned over their occasional pint together. As an academic, he was a chilly, self-
righteous purist. As president of Undeb, he was hot-headed
enough for any crazy nationalist scheme, if he could evolve
an intellectual argument for it. Maybe Gwyn was finally
joining the rest of humankind in its crass pursuit of plea-
sures. Still, Peter would expect Davies to emerge from
even the steamiest liaison to make an Undeb statement
about the kidnapping. Love must have smitten him blind,
deaf, and stone stupid.

Peter shoved his tape recorder into his trench-coat
pocket and went out to his car. The right rear tire was
nearly flat again, so he bumped off towards a Llantrisant
Road garage. Slow leaks were the worst. You could get
away with putting them off.

At the nondescript government building tucked away
amid the University of Wales extension service, public servants were already streaming homeward. In the farthest
wing, he stopped at an unmarked door. It was painted the
same ugly green as a thousand other obscure government
offices, including his own. He tapped gently and pushed
inside.

"What the devil do you think you're doing here?"

The small fair-haired man scowled up from his reading—computer printouts of some kind—and tugged his
gold and blue striped tie tight at his open collar as though
caught in *déshabille*. Not a school tie, though it looked
like one; it perfectly complemented his well-cut dark blue
suit.

"Pleasant welcome," Peter said and rested his tape recorder on the back of a new leather armchair, not government issue. "I need advice, Nigel."

Nigel Phipps gazed at his visitor, and Peter became
aware of his comfortable old corduroy jacket, and the elbow patches he hadn't quite got around to, and his hair
hanging over his collar. Nigel, as always, looked lac-

quered and groomed like a mannequin in a Bond Street men's store. Voice to match.

"Advice on . . . ?" Nigel asked, discouragingly.

"How to kidnap the heir to the English throne."

Nigel jerked to his feet and shut the green door. "Now what is it, Holt?" He pointed at the tape recorder. "Is that thing going?"

Peter held up the machine to display its battery indicator, doctored to show no voice level. Surprisingly few people went one step further, lifting the lid to see whether the cassette inside was winding.

"I'm here to find out who kidnapped the young chap and his nanny. And why."

"Wrong office," Nigel said easily. His eyes were deepsea grey and cold. "I'm special assistant to the chief of purchasing for His Majesty's Government in Wales, exclusive of the Welsh Office."

"Right." Peter smiled. "You should order in a door sign to that effect. While I'm here, tell me—have you ever encountered a pleasant chap by the name of Grenvile? Based in London?"

Nigel blinked once and picked up his computer printout. "Purchasing?"

"You could call it that. He introduced himself as the chief hostage negotiator for British military intelligence, internal. MI5, if you prefer. Assigned to talk these kidnappers into being good fellows and letting the Prince go."

"Then you know more about him than I do," Nigel said, rattling his printout open to the next fold. "Sorry I can't help."

"He has strange ideas," mused Peter, ignoring the dapper little man's disinterest and letting himself slide back into his homeliest north-country drawl. "Like press cooperation. He reckons the media should help out government. But what about government helping out the media? It's naught but a one-way street, I see now. The deep freeze is all I've got for my trouble taken."

Nigel stared at Peter over the printout. "Remember

Mogadishu back in seventy-seven?'' Nigel asked. ''That Lufthansa captain keeping West German police informed about the terrorists on board his plane? Commercial radio stations started announcing that he was passing information over the cabin radio to the police. The terrorists listened to the radio stations. All this according to BBC.''

''Amazing what you hear on BBC.''

''The terrorists shot the captain. At least, they held the gun. It was the press who murdered him.''

''Some newsmen are fairly stupid. Some terrorists are fairly clever.'' Peter shrugged. ''Or the heir apparent would be at home right now.''

Nigel curled his lip. ''This lot's not especially smart. They left a trail of debris across half of London and cost the IRA a favourite safe house, what with all the searching and that. Which wasn't secure anyway, of course.'' His voice had lost its crisp edge, a betrayal of the impeccable suit. Peter thought he caught the slightest whiff of Blackpool, but it could be wishful thinking.

''Then disappeared from the face of the earth.''

''Probably by accident,'' Nigel argued.

''Probably. But the question's still who? And why?''

''Ask your nationalist friends,'' Nigel suggested. ''The ones you've been drinking with at the Black Lion.''

Heard it on BBC, again? Peter didn't ask. He knew Phipps's information sources well enough. ''Surprisingly, the local nationalists seem quite shy just now. And don't confuse contacts with friends, Nigel. Gets you in trouble every time.''

''Too bloody right,'' said Nigel and flung his printout onto the desk.

''More wrangling between your people and the local constabulary?''

The service's infighting and manoeuvring for position were notorious, not only with other branches of military intelligence but with every police department they encountered.

Nigel insisted, ''Our job is buying goods and services.''

"Especially services."

"In this hole?" Nigel warmed to a favourite topic. "Did you know there's no word in the gobbledegook they speak here for 'immediately'? 'Right away'?"

"Untrue," said Peter mildly. It still amazed him that Nigel's branch didn't insist on a crash course in the language before posting people to Wales. As a result, the operatives were rumoured to have made some spectacular boners. "Everyone knows the Welsh for 'immediately' is 'next week.' *Ar unwaith.*" At once. Peter smiled broadly.

"Christ, Holt, the noises they make," Nigel confided. "I listen to their fourth channel on telly once in a while, by accident. Flipping round the dial, like. Sounds like someone about to bring up their dinner."

"Most people in Wales speak English now, according to the census. Ninety per cent. Only about thirty per cent speak Welsh."

"Still too bloody many, if you ask me. But I see your layabout nationalist friends are still pushing for more of their lingo in the schools. While they're on about dead languages, why don't they throw in Hebrew?"

Peter nodded, pleased with his spontaneous image of a jackbooted but natty Nigel Phipps spray-painting the Star of David on a smashed storefront. It was easy to picture. Good thing the National Front was a gutter organization, or Nigel would be running it by now. Nigel watched him carefully, drawing his brows together in a single pale bar of concentration.

"Grenvile," Peter reminded.

"Never heard of him." Nigel didn't turn a hair.

"Right." Peter unfolded his lanky frame from the leather chair.

"Holt," said Nigel. "Purchasing, remember? Unless you want a feature on how we keep costs down to save the taxpayers' money, don't come here again." Then, quietly, "And I've warned you once about stories on Welsh extremists. Back off."

"Nineteen eighty-four was a few years ago," Peter

threw over his shoulder as he walked out the unmarked door. "Mind passing that on to your chums in the Bureau of Truth?"

An hour later the piebald Renault's radio was working, for once, as Peter pulled away from the fish-and-chip shop. He turned up the volume when the announcer read the headlines for the evening news.

"Plaid Cymru and other Welsh nationalist organizations have protested this morning's arrests of suspected terrorists. They accuse Cardiff city police and government security services of brutality and denial of human rights in the arrests in Cardiff and Aberystwyth. Several men and women are being held without warrant under the Suppression of Terrorism Act."

Al was wrong. They had announced the arrests. Bringing in the heavy artillery. Peter considered, then swung the car around the next traffic island to head back to Llandaff.

It was starting, a rash of arrests, reprisals, and reactions. And he wanted the story. A few calls, some stock film footage, slide into the editing room when the shop steward wasn't looking, and he could have something for the late news.

As he passed Cardiff Castle, the street lights gleamed on the wet pavement and on the pale hair of a man in a wolfskin coat; he was deep in talk with two shorter men in army-surplus parkas. Long blond hair and exotic pelts. There was no mistaking Yann Morvan, the rock musician who considered himself the cutting edge of Breton activism. Celtic Brittany had its protests and bombs against the French government just as Celtic Wales had against the English government, and they were as thick as thieves. Peter reflected, then decided on a phone call to BBC Wales's music critic. Perhaps Morvan had a concert. Or perhaps all that brought him here was his instinct for trouble.

7

Thursday was market day in Llanygroes. The streets were humming with trade and conversation. Gwyn leaned against a wall near the telephone box in front of the post office, trying to look unobtrusive. In a small mid-Wales town, a stranger drew notice. On their dawn arrival three days ago, the town had been lifeless; now it barely contained its frantic activity. Gwyn, waiting his moment, watched the old men and women idle through the town square from stall to stall chatting with the merchants; a few hardy English were also shopping for their cottage larders.

At last, about mid-morning, a farmer disputed his change at a used-clothing stall. People gathered around, offering him advice and threatening the nervous man behind the trestle table. Gwyn predicted that the dispute would last a few minutes, and he slid into the telephone box.

Madog had tinkered to adapt the remote device for a phone hook-up. The modification meant they could risk a call from the Llanygroes public phone, and they couldn't hold off any longer. All day yesterday they'd been cooped up together watching thin snow drift across the Berwyns, eyeing each other from separate corners, grating on each other's nerves. With luck, Grenvile and his cohorts would be equally distressed by their two days' silence, and they would be anxious to get down to serious negotiation.

Watching the argument grow in the market, Gwyn hooked up the remote as Madog had shown him. Carefully, he pushed the device's metal prongs into the frayed phone cord. If everything worked, the call would be untraceable. If not, a military helicopter could land in the square in ten minutes.

Gwyn took a deep breath and dialled. It had been easier for Sion to call Carrie yesterday, with no need for the remote relay. The untraceable Camden Town number rang once and, after a series of clicks, produced another dial tone, as Madog had hoped. The system seemed to be working. Gwyn counted to three and dialled New Scotland Yard.

"I want Grenvile."

He scarcely spoke the name before a second line buzzed. They probably had recordings of his earlier calls; good thing none of his Aberystwyth lectures were on tape for comparison. Nevertheless, he pulled his handkerchief tight across the receiver and altered his voice as much as possible.

"Good to hear from you." Grenvile came on the line immediately, sounding relieved. "Where are you?"

"Never mind where we are. You'll never find us." The broadcasts on Madog's short-wave radio said the London search was still in full swing. Pen y Cae seemingly lay in one of the Welsh borderland's television blanks, where no signal penetrated. Even the American's technological wonders hadn't overcome that problem. Anyway the telly would doubtless conflict with Madog's pursuit of pastoral bliss.

"The Prince and Miss Douglass—what is their condition? Are they safe and well?"

As safe as they could be in care of Nora and Raffael, both hungering for appeasements to their frustration. As healthy as constant fear for their lives permitted.

"The boy reacted badly to the gas grenade, so we

brought in medical help. He's fine now, and so is Miss Douglass,'' Gwyn answered. "Because of this futile man-hunt of yours, we'll have to change our arrangements about the money drop, and about exchanging the child and his nurse.''

"Of course. Whatever suits you,'' Grenvile said agree-ably. He'd been studying his negotiator's handbook again. "I need a name. What may I call you?''

"Call me—'' Gwyn thought quickly about English ster-eotypes of the Welsh. Arthur, who was a guerrilla captain and not a king. Leave that one alone. Or Merlin, who was a Carlisle poet and not a Welsh ju-ju man. It would do. "Call me Merlin.''

"Merlin. That makes it easier for me, you understand. I'm sure we can come to an agreement.''

"Good try, Grenvile. There's nothing to come to an agreement about, understand? You know what we want. Have you got the million pounds in unmarked small notes?''

"It's sitting beside me in five bank delivery sacks. Where shall we drop it?''

"In a minute.'' Gwyn glanced over his shoulder into Llanygroes square. The argument was still going strong. Now the used-clothing dealer was having his say, gestur-ing angrily with a woollen jumper. "What about the bil-lion pounds for Welsh industry and the creation of a Welsh parliament?''

"They are under debate this very minute at 10 Downing Street,'' Grenvile told him smoothly. "I'm sure you un-derstand it takes time to arrange one of the most sweeping revisions of the British parliamentary system since Magna Carta—''

"Not British,'' Gwyn corrected. "English. The last time Wales had a parliament was the last time she had a Prince of Wales. A Welsh Prince of Wales.''

"Is that what you want, Merlin? A new Prince of Wales?'' Grenvile asked his question without apparent irony.

Gwyn gazed through a missing pane, across the market square full of old people making haste slowly. Long ago in Ireland the English had to kill or exile the aristocracy to prevent rebellion. In Wales they had only to jingle a bag of coins; the Welsh aristocracy rushed into Tudor England seeking wealth and titles. Why fight people when you can buy them? The English always understood commerce. Now little remained in Wales of the old Welsh royal houses. And who cared? The idea of Wales, the spirit of Cymru, survived in her *gwerin,* her common folk. Gwyn wanted to create a just society, give the *gwerin* ownership of their own country, not re-create feudalism. He shivered. The January wind whined through the telephone box.

"What are you trying to do, Grenvile, keep me talking long enough to trace the call? Don't waste your time, or mine. You won't find us." Gwyn hoped it were true.

The negotiator sounded convincingly taken down. "We simply want to do our best to satisfy your demands and to recover the Prince and his nurse. May I speak with Miss Douglass, please?"

"No," Gwyn answered curtly. "We were talking about home rule for Wales. You can do better than 'under debate,' Grenvile. If you want to see the kid again, safe and sound, remember Paul Getty."

After a second's pause, the negotiator said, "I remember Paul Getty. His kidnappers cut off his ear and sent it to a newspaper as proof that he was alive, so his grandfather would pay ransom. Surely you wouldn't mutilate an innocent child."

Gwyn evaded, "Some of my people are all too eager to shed blood. The longer you delay, the more likely they are to do it."

Outside in the Llanygroes market, the short-changed farmer hurled his purchase at the stall keeper and shouted more abuse.

"Sounds like quite an argument," Grenvile pried.

"The telly's on," Gwyn improvised. "Give me a

straight answer. Are we getting a Welsh parliament? And is the prime minister announcing it on national radio and television? We don't believe English promises anymore, not unless they're made in public.''

''You don't seem to realize—''

Gwyn cut across the excuse and switched to Welsh. ''I've had enough of this cack. Are you doing it or not?''

Grenvile didn't answer. Without warning a new voice was on the line, speaking Welsh.

''How can I help you?'' asked a *hwntw,* a South Walian.

Not BBC's Peter Holt, this time. They'd gone to the trouble of lining up a native Welsh-speaker.

''Get Grenvile back. I don't talk to traitors.''

Outside, a few snowflakes eddied across the grey square. The farmer kicked the used-clothing table, and army-surplus trousers and vests slid precariously towards the edge. Any more of that, and the constable would be along to calm things down.

''Yes, Merlin?'' Grenvile sounded troubled.

''I don't have time for nonsense. Here it is, take it or leave it. Before you see the kid again, I want to hear the prime minister on telly and radio announcing Welsh home rule. I want the assembly building in Cardiff opened. When I hear that, I'll call you. Not before. Then we can talk seriously about an exchange.''

''I'll do my utmost,'' Major Grenvile assured. ''I know your requests are an important step. But it's not my decision—''

''I also want to hear that you've stopped detainment of Welsh nationalists without warrant. At least thirty in Wales and others here in London,'' Gwyn said, remembering the fragmentary conversations they'd overheard on Madog's short-wave radio.

''Detainment?'' Grenvile sounded uneasy.

''Your usual *modus operandi,*'' Gwyn interrupted. ''Kick in the door at three in the morning, make sure every house in the street is awakened so word gets around and people lose jobs over it. Any who have jobs. There are many forms of terrorism, Grenvile.''

''No one's been detained—'' The negotiator paused, perhaps listening to information from someone at his end. ''I'll look into it. We haven't agreed on where to drop the banknotes. Do you need anything else? Transport? Supplies? Food?''

''No,'' Gwyn snapped, and then had an inspiration. ''No supplies. Just food. Deliver a month's dried army rations for forty people—'' he thought quickly. What was an open area in London's city core? ''—to the mid-point of the bridle path in St. James Park. Clear everyone out of the area. No helicopters, no distant surveillance, no heat detectors, no hidden microphones. In an hour's time.''

''Merlin.'' Grenvile sounded desperate. ''We must have an open channel. We must know where you are—''

Gwyn pushed the off button on the remote and glanced across the square. People were starting to drift away. He pocketed Madog's gadget and risked a direct call to Aberystwyth. Meic answered at his office.

''Where the hell are you? What are you doing? Have you heard about the arrests—''

''I know,'' Gwyn interrupted. ''There's no time right now. Any messages?''

Owen Thomas in Cardiff, relayed Meic uncertainly, was worried about tomorrow's faltering Allt Valley Dam protest, as though Gwyn didn't have a world-class disaster hanging over his head. And Peter Holt of BBC was calling twice a day. Hell-fire. Had Holt recognized the voice? Was he tying too many loose ends together? Perhaps it was nothing.

Gwyn rang off. Battling a freezing wind all the way, he walked to the car park where he'd left Madog's Land Cruiser. Delivering food to St. James Park should keep Grenvile busy for a while.

Madog's face was a pale blur in an upstairs window when Gwyn started to climb the frozen ruts to Pen y Cae.

By the time he reached the door, the American was waiting in the cramped front hall.

Gwyn set down Madog's two net shopping bags, filled at several stalls and shops to attract the least attention. Corned beef, bread, potatoes, carrots. Not much for eight people. Nine with Carrie Powell. He shrugged off Madog's old anorak and hung it on a hall peg beside his own leather jacket, which could have been conspicuous on Llanygroes.

"How's our food holding up?" Gwyn asked quietly. He and Madog had said nothing yet to the others about the dwindling supplies.

"That depends how much you like beans. We've got a ten-pound sack of navy beans, two pounds of dried fruit, flour, a few other odds and ends." Madog sounded preoccupied. Well, Gwyn reflected, it was his house that was jammed with people who could soon be national villains, or behind bars.

"Three days, with this food?"

"Four days, maybe."

Gwyn regretted the forty kits of dried rations, probably waiting by now in St. James Park. He played with the idea of ordering up more supplies to be dropped at Pen y Cae by helicopter and discarded it. No matter what the zealous Major Grenvile might promise, they would get not food but a squad of Special Air Services goons.

"Long enough." He tried to sound confident. A long siege anywhere, but especially here at remote Pen y Cae, spelled disaster. They would inevitably be traced. "We post a watch from now on," he said. "Just in case someone blunders in on us."

"Okay," Madog said quietly. "Look, Gwyn, we've got to talk about our options."

"Soon." Gwyn frowned. Who the hell did he think he was? The American's contribution was dog-eared dollars and electronic tricks.

"It's your op," Madog said quietly. "I'm not Raffael. I don't want it."

Gwyn shrugged. If that was reassurance, it failed. "I looked in the Seattle phone book, Madog. You and your group don't exist."

"No way." Madog smiled marginally. No gold tooth. "What would we be listed under?"

"Murderers, maybe?" Gwyn suggested with savage sarcasm. "Like me."

"It was a set-up, eight years ago," Madog said. "They framed you."

Gwyn wouldn't be tempted. "You're asking me to believe British intelligence murdered one of their own."

"He was dead anyway. You just sealed his coffin. But you didn't have to take out the river cop."

"What makes you think I did?"

Madog grabbed his shoulder. "Don't shit me."

Gwyn looked deliberately down at his hand, then up at Madog's face. He wanted badly to confess his refusal, but couldn't find words. Madog released him at last. Gwyn wished he could say something. But it was too late for all that. He had become solitary, or maybe he always had been. Not social work but the science of phonemes. Not football but middle distance and marathon. It was too late for regret.

"Just accept what I offer," Madog said finally.

But what do you offer? And what do you ask? Whom do you answer to? The fragmented American left? The naïve American Welsh? Another organization not listed in any city phone directory? How deep does the compromise run? Gwyn knew it was far, far too late to be asking such questions.

A major agency would have pulled Madog out days ago, not let him shelter the fugitives. It made no sense. Was he corrupt and convoluted beyond Gwyn's capacity to imagine? Free lance like Corgi? The Yanks backed the political right in Chile, Angola, Nicaragua, all the rest. Never the left. No sense at all.

"Corgi said much the same thing when I hired him," Gwyn said. "And look at the result—Tywyn."

"I never met Corgi. Never wanted to," Madog said, watching him closely. "Everyone at China Lake knew he was ex-SAS. Did you know how he got a limp?"

"Yes, one of the Provo kids recognized Corgi from his SAS days in Belfast and tried to do him." Gwyn remembered it had inspired a lecture on the proverb, "The enemy of my enemy is my friend."

"Stay away from him." Madog's eyes drifted. "He keeps score."

"I paid him. Even though he screwed up." Even though he willfully murdered three non-combatants against orders. Three children.

"It's a bit weak," Carrie said, handing the tea mug to Jean Douglass.

"Better weak than cold." The Scots nanny stirred her tea slowly. She sat at the kitchen table. Pip was squatting on the floor slates, playing with Pal. "The travel-sickness tablets did help."

"I find them useful for the little ones," Carrie told her. "Just strong enough to give them some rest without upsetting their stomachs. The best we can do under the circumstances."

"He should be seeing a specialist," said Jean Douglass and lowered her voice. "Is it worth making a break? What do you think of our chances?"

Carrie sat forward, elbows on the table. "They're heavily armed. We'd need a good lead. My car's down by the hay barn. We could roll downhill in neutral and start the motor in the forestry—"

She broke off as Nora sauntered into the kitchen with her revolting weapon over her arm. Pip edged toward his nanny at the sight of the Irishwoman. What had she done to frighten the boy?

"Well, now. And what manner of lies would you be telling?" Nora smirked. "You wouldn't be having second thoughts about our operation now, Carrie?"

Carrie eyed the black-haired woman distastefully and said nothing.

Nora turned to Jean Douglass. "Has she been moaning of how innocent she is? Next she'll be wanting you to escape together. And the minute you step out of the house, she'll do you and the kid both."

Jean Douglass was having none of it. "Miss Powell has been very kind to Pip. And as nurses we have things to discuss."

"To be sure," said Nora. She had a singularly nasty smile. "And did her kindness include telling you of the innocent blood on her hands? She likes to kill people. And she's been with us from the start."

"That's a lie," said Carrie, her heart sinking. What had Nora heard?

"It's a lie that you blew a man to hell with a bomb eight years ago?"

Carrie said nothing and looked at her hands on the wooden table. Jean Douglass looked from her to Nora and back again and stood so suddenly that her chair crashed backwards onto the slates.

"Dear God. It's true, isn't it?"

Gwyn halted in the kitchen doorway. Jean Douglass, her face flushed, stood beside an overturned chair with the kid and his inevitable mouse doll clutched in her arms. Carrie sat at the table, face in her hands. The grey cat crouched in a corner with disdainful green eyes fixed on the nanny.

"That woman's not to come near the Prince, do you understand me?" Jean Douglass said in a low, tense voice.

She was as fierce as a lioness defending her young. Gwyn wondered if she really understood, emotionally and rationally, that this was not her chid.

"Okay, Miss Douglass," Madog said. "What's the problem?"

"She's a murderer. She's worse than the rest of you!"

Carrie shook her head.

"We brought Miss Powell here to see to the boy's

health," Gwyn said. "She will examine him if she needs to."

"I won't have him touched by a murderer."

"I'm a prisoner like you, Miss Douglass," said Carrie woodenly.

"To think I was taken in—and by a nurse. My God, you could have poisoned him." She turned to Gwyn. "Keep her away."

Gwyn glanced at Carrie and saw the rose creeping into her face. She always looked most alive when she was angry. He pushed the thought out of mind. It would get worse, cooped up here.

"Carrie's not—" Gwyn began, but Raffael stepped in from the living room to cut him off.

"Miss Powell answers first for the Prince's health," the Italian said with a smile. "She answered second to the success of our mission."

Carrie stared at him. "Don't try to claim I'm part of this stupidity."

"Keep her away," Jean Douglass repeated, immovable. They might as well not have spoken. "If you want any further co-operation."

"Just a minute, you." Carrie faced Raffael. "I don't know what you want, dragging your guns to Wales. I'll hear no more of answering to you, or aiding your crimes. You had no right to bring me here, but as long as I'm here, keep me out of your filthy games!"

Raffael folded his arms, aggrieved, and shook his head gently.

"Quiet yourself," Gwyn told her in Welsh. "If you push these others, there'll be violence."

"Are you pleased with yourself, licking this Irish bitch's arse?" Carrie asked in her flat Canolbarth Welsh.

Gwyn shrugged angrily. It was a minor victory, stinging her at last to speak her mother tongue.

"Carrie!" Nora said with elaborate surprise. "You can't back out now. From the start you talked of nothing but striking a blow for Welsh freedom. You know what happens to those who betray the cause.''

"What cause? Tormenting children?" Carrie demanded. "You make me sick, all of you. Don't try to wipe your cack on me."

The pug barrel of the sixteen-gauge slid down from the Irishwoman's arm.

"Give me the gun, Nora," Gwyn tried.

Elen and Sion appeared in the doorway, and he motioned for them to stay back. The royal nanny was edging toward the pantry door at the far end of the kitchen with Pip. Good. Keep him out of this.

"Right, shoot me," Carrie challenged. Her temper was up, and she had no idea of her danger. Cath Paluc growled, crouching, with his hostile green eyes on Nora. "Shoot everyone who hates your bloody-minded idiocy. People are working seriously towards Welsh home rule, and you've probably set them back a century. Go ahead, shoot. Solve everything with your little phallic substitute.''

Nora slapped Carrie hard across the face. Raffael watched with mild interest, like a patron at an art show. Carrie gasped as her head rocked back and Nora drew her hand away for a second blow. It never arrived. Carrie launched herself at her assailant, landing one fist on the Irishwoman's nose and another over her eye. She had the advantage of rage.

Nora screamed and grabbed Carrie's short dark hair one-handed, flailing with the shotgun. The kitchen spun into a tangle of elbows as they grappled briefly. Raffael smiled in open amusement, perhaps approval, and Madog edged nearer to the two women. Nora jerked free and shoved the gun barrel hard under Carrie's chin.

Gwyn stood frozen, waiting for the blast, and Raffael watched through half-lidded eyes, not quite smiling. Revulsion snapped Gwyn out of inaction. Too late. Madog slid another step sideways, kicked high to send Carrie flying, and hooked an arm around Nora's throat. The shotgun went off with a roar that battered their ears, and plaster and wood splinters showered down from the breached kitchen ceiling.

The dust settled slowly. Gwyn stooped for the gun, kicked into the corner by the cooker. Raffael was crouching over Nora, who was unconscious from whatever treatment Madog had applied.

Carrie had vanished. Gwyn searched around, hating the feel of Nora's deadly toy but unwilling to yield it to her again. He spun into the living-room, coughing at the plaster dust. Carrie stood in Madog's arms, sobbing in gasps. Gwyn turned away with the gun, desolate.

He demanded of Raffael, "Where did you take the nanny?"

Raffael shrugged towards the living-room and turned back to the semi-conscious Nora. But there was no sign of the royal nanny or the boy there, or in the faded downstairs bedroom. Gwyn pounded upstairs and found Madog's room empty. Sion and Elen were huddled in the radio room.

"The kid's gone!" Gwyn, running down again, yelled. "Start searching!"

He was halfway through the front door before he remembered the only other room and whirled back towards the pantry behind the kitchen. Nora was on her feet, groggy, hands at her neck. Madog had given her both thumbs in the carotid, Gwyn realized with half his mind, registering some regret that he'd stopped halfway. Carrie Powell was worth ten Noras. A hundred.

The pantry door was locked from inside. Gwyn put his shoulder to the latch side and forced it open. The room was empty.

"Madog!"

The American appeared at his side, and Carrie on his heels with a tear-streaked face.

"Douglass and the kid." He had no time to say more. Madog pushed past him into the pantry. He was at the small window in two strides. A touch to the latch sent it open and gave them a chilly view of the leafless rowan slope behind the farmhouse. Nothing else. Madog ran for the kitchen and the cobbled yard. Gwyn followed, aware that the others were following. Behind the whitewashed house they fought through a jungle of bramble vines to-wards the far end of the building and the attached stable. Gwyn threw up the crossbar and shoved open the com-plaining double door. Straw dust lifted briefly as they crossed the empty stable to the rickety loft stair. No one was there.

Outside, Madog pointed to the rutted track leading downhill. Gwyn followed the American down towards the hay barn, between bare trees and the shoulder of the hill. About halfway down, they heard the barn's wooden doors squealing on their hinges.

Jean Douglass was trying to swing the heavy doors closed against them when Gwyn reached her. He flung one door awkwardly outward, hampered by the forgotten shot-gun. Then he caught the nurse by the arm. She swung at him, but with the clumsiness of one who's never had to fight. Madog arrived and pinned her arms behind her back. There was no need to do more. The fight had gone out of the nanny, and she looked hopelessly from one to the other. Gwyn found Pip crouching behind Madog's dirty green Land Cruiser, his fuzzy Mungo Mouse held tightly to his chest. Chasing a helpless kid, cornering him in the half-dark with the expression of terror, made Gwyn sick with dismay. He led the boy out by the hand. He was a willing child, even when frightened, watching everything that went on around him with curiosity.

"Are you cross with Miss Douglass?"

"No, Pip." Gwyn looked down, started. "We thought you might be hurt."

"I'm fine, thank you," he said gravely. "Why did Nora shoot the gun?"

"She didn't mean to. It went off by mistake."

"Do you think so? I think she wanted to kill Miss Pow-ell."

Gwyn shook his head, outmaneuvered.

Madog released the royal nanny, and Gwyn let the Prince run to her. She picked him up and they faced their captors warily.

"Did that woman . . . ?" She left it unfinished.

"Carrie's not hurt," Gwyn told her.

"Listen, Miss Douglass," the American said quietly, taking things into his own hands again, uninvited. "Things aren't going too well around here."

"I see that. Who are those dreadful people? Who are they really?" the nurse said angrily, ignoring the tears coursing down her face. Her plummy royal-nanny voice had lost its bloom, and she sounded plain Scottish.

Madog said, "What's important is that Nora's as crazy as a bed bug, and Raffi is big-time trouble. They're very, very dangerous. If you do anything to provoke them, we might not be able to keep you people safe."

Jean Douglass frowned from Madog to Gwyn, puzzled, and absently wiped the back of her hand across her cheeks. "Do you really expect me to believe you care about my safety or Pip's—the Prince's?"

"After that display, I guess it would be a lot to ask." Madog gave her a lopsided smile, not quite the solid gold version.

Jean Douglass snuffled. Gwyn tapped the shotgun absently on his forearm then realized what he was doing and stopped.

"Our plan was to hold you and the Prince for an hour, negotiate our demands, and turn you loose," Gwyn told her. "But now we're stuck here together until we can work something out. I might as well be frank with you, the negotiations aren't going favorably. The military are stalling for time so they can find us."

The nurse was silent a moment. "Why do you tell me this?"

Gwyn shrugged. "The Prince and you are our leverage, obviously. We want to keep you well and reasonably happy so we can get what we want from the prime minister. But we never had any intention of harming you or frightening you. We never expected to keep you longer than an hour. If I'd known more about Raffi and Nora, they wouldn't be here.''

Madog took it from there. ''If you can avoid crossing those two, we'll get you out soon, without harm.''

Jean Douglass nodded wearily. ''I'll do my best.''

Madog smiled. ''Good.''

''In return you can tell me, why are you here?''

In the growing quiet, Pip sniffled. The shed door creaked open a little farther, letting in pale inter daylight. It was still mid-afternoon, though it felt later. Gwyn waited for the American's usual shrug and grin, his stock phrases about preserving the culture and pride of his ancestral country. Instead, there was a long silence.

''Well, ma'am. I'm not quite sure myself, right about now.''

The woman didn't return his smile. She turned to Gwyn. ''And you. What do you really want?''

''Self-government for the Nation of Cymru,'' Gwyn said. He seemed to have said this several thousand times. ''A fraction of the English profits taken from our coal valleys and slate quarries, to do something about unemployment and industry. A Welsh television channel.''

''You have a television channel.''

''We have Sianel Pedwar, Channel Four, but not enough transmitters to send the television signal. The English never came through with the funds. They fear our language will unite us. You see, we don't ask a great deal.''

''Perhaps you believe you're fighting the good fight. But you can't win it, not this way.''

Pip was looking up at them, from one to another. His thumb had crept into his mouth. ''Can we go talk to Pal now?''

''Yes, darling,'' said Jean Douglass. ''Now, Pip, Reepicheep doesn't suck his thumb. Only babies suck their thumbs.''

As they turned to the shed door, Gwyn glimpsed Madog's face. There was no sign of his million-dollar smile.

CARDIFF/JANUARY 16/1400

Peter Holt pulled up his collar and clamped his chattering teeth. At the director's cue, he started his intro to the BBC camera.

"Freezing rain appears to be dampening the spirits of about two hundred people in Cardiff today. They're here to protest the flooding of the Allt Valley in north central Wales for a reservoir." Peter knew the studio would cut to cover of the dreary procession on Castle Street. "One placard reads, 'Keep Llanallt dry,' and it's not a comment on the beverage laws."

Even humor couldn't rescue this soggy event, the non-story of the year. As Peter predicted, most people had stayed at home. Al Rees was watching for a shop doorway, shielding his video camera under his garish silver bomber jacket. He was checking his watch too often, Peter saw from the corner of his eye. The photographer probably regretted his agreement to shoot the other, free-lance story on spec.

"Like most protests, this one consists mostly of standing around in the rain waiting for something to happen," Peter told the camera with as much facile sincerity as he could muster, threatened by frost-bite. "But it seems the Allt Valley Dam in north central Wales will go ahead as scheduled. This is Peter Holt, for BBC Wales."

Within minutes, the BBC director and camerawoman fled for the relative comfort of the Llantrisant Road studios. Al Rees, his hair dripping over his ears, emerged from his shop doorway.

"Pint?" he asked hopefully around a wad of chewing gum.

Peter looked around at the dwindling march. "Sorry, *bach*. We'd better go interview Meleri before she packs it in."

Al was philosophical about minor defeats. "Where?"

They dodged puddles in the broken Castle Street pavement. City of decay. Across Sophia Gardens lay an open space where an old pavilion had collapsed years ago; on the far bank of the Taff lay the Black Friar priory ruins and the bleak old fortress of Cardiff Castle. Sheltered slightly by the walls, they found the student-union president talking to a handful of scruffy post-adolescents.

"All the way down from Coleg Bangor." Meleri beamed at the students and Peter, pleased as though the European Common Market had sent a delegation.

The rally was a dead issue to Peter; BBC had its lacklustre packet. What he really wanted was to get the real story for CBS, the story of the activist groups' reaction to the royal kidnapping and the Welsh arrests. He turned to the least sullen of the North Wales students.

"Have there been arrests in Bangor and Caernarfon?" Peter asked her in Welsh.

"You lot at BBC haven't reported any, have you?" the girl asked snottily. "Still, three of my friends at college have been dragged out of residence in the middle of the night."

"Mr. Holt wants to do a program for CBS in the States, dear," Meleri suggested with bland good cheer. Meleri had once told Peter straight-faced that her political model was England's sole female prime minister, a notorious Celtophobe. "BBC really doesn't have a great deal to do with his question."

The girl tossed back her unwashed hair, chastised. Peter pressed his advantage, nodding to Al to roll video and sound. "Why don't you tell me in a few words what's been going on—"

"Edrychwch!" One of the Bangor students suddenly pointed toward the street, where Cardiff city police were struggling to contain a flood of people from newly arrived buses.

Al counted aloud. "Three—four—six—"

Before the first bus had finished disgorging its full load, twelve others lined Castle Street. Peter whistled under his breath as he revised his opinions. He might have to an update for the evening news. Al needed no prompting. He

shoved his chewing gum between his teeth, shouldered the
video camera, and began taping as several hundred new-
comers milled among the other drenched protesters. They
had more signs. "Save Llanallt & Hafoty." *"Dim gwas-
traff niwcliar.* No Chernobyl in Wales."

Scores of other placards bore angrier messages. *"Dim
heddlu cudd yma.* Keep secret police out," "Stop the arrests!" and "This is not Belfast yet." The signs bore the
chain-links of Cadwyn and the interlaced-sun symbol of
Undeb Cymru Fydd. Peter felt a spreading exultant warmth
as his story unfolded before his eyes.

Rain stopped sluicing into the grass around them, and
tentative pale sunshine glittered on the castle's wet stones.
Meleri slipped towards a knot of organizers with a loud
hailer. Peter watched her walk away, briefly puzzled at her
unusual bulkiness. Then he realized only Meleri would
wear a flak vest under a flowered silk dress. The protesters
began to move toward the Welsh Office.

For the next half hour, he had time to snatch only a few
hasty interviews with Al taping over his shoulder and to
jog onward. A contingent of plain-clothes men with hand
transmitters flanked the marchers and swelled the ranks of
the city police escort. Someone at the front was playing
bagpipes. Bagpipes? When they were only a stone's throw
from the grey Welsh Office, a mob of hecklers ran forward
from Alexandra Gardens to shout insults. A few protesters, all their hopes for the occasion fulfilled, peeled away
from the march to scuffle with the hecklers. Uniformed
police followed them.

Peter barely absorbed the words of Meleri and the other
speakers from the Welsh Office steps. He could edit Al's
videotape later and choose the best material for an American audience. Meleri's interview ran hot, fuelled by the
march's sudden success and plentiful Welsh rhetoric. Surrounded by several hundred angry protesters, Peter hoped
for once that the Welsh would stick to rhetoric instead of
action. He felt very English. Even the Welsh word for the

English conveyed fifteen centuries of enmity. They were still Saxons, *Saeson*.

Meleri beckoned over a stooped man with a unlit pipe in his mouth. Owen Thomas, one of the local Undeb Cymru Fydd people at last. At his shoulder Peter saw wolfskin and long blond hair. Yet according to the BBC rock music critic, no upcoming concerts featured Brittany's wealthiest export to Dublin, Yann Morvan.

Owen Thomas gave a convoluted eyewitness account of one of the late-night arrests; he had an academic's inability to form a simple descriptive sentence. All the while Peter felt Yann's eyes on him, amused or contemptuous. Piqued, when Thomas finished, Peter turned the microphone towards Morvan.

"Do you feel the arrests are unjustified?" he asked the Breton.

His only answer was a broad smile. Morvan had large yellow teeth. They were a match for the wolf coat.

Then Owen Thomas put in, "Yann's just off the plane from the continent. He's not up to date on what's been occurring."

"Not too recently off the plane, since I saw him Thursday," Peter said, slightly bemused at his own pursuit of the irrelevant. Morvan rubbed him the wrong way. "Where on the continent?"

"Vaduz," Morvan said, still showing his canines. "And to answer your next question—picking edelweiss. Learning to ski. Or, if you like, none of your damned business." He spoke English in a flat North American accent.

Vaduz?

"Right." Arse-hole. Peter flicked the auto pause on the mike. "Owen, you said someone snapped Polaroid shots of this arrest without warrant."

Thomas, eager for importance, offered his phone number and promised to meet Peter at his flat with the photos. Tomorrow morning at ten; it left enough time for a preliminary look through the tapes and a call to Cliff in New

York. Al grabbed his arm as they moved towards a knot of protesters and hecklers.

"You crazy or something?" Al hissed. "No one fucks with that guy—"

A police whistle shrilled across the rest of Al's warning. Hecklers started to lob stones and garbage. They were mostly in denim, and Peter reckoned they were gang types or lads on the dole. The shoving match erupted into more serious violence.

Al meticulously taped it all, silently working his gum from cheek to cheek. Peter made a mental note to buy him a case of the vile stuff; he was earning his keep. Plainclothes police sprinted into the melée now, hauling people out. A few went down on the slick roadway, screams lost under the yelling and sirens and loud-hailer directions. Unmarked black vans eased up over the curb, back doors open. Peter scribbled frantically on his wet newsprint, trying to keep count of the arrests.

"Disperse," the loud hailers were ordering now, in the prevailing Irish accent of the Cardiff police force. "Return to your homes. Disperse."

The last squad car rolled off down Museum Avenue as the crowd scattered in sullen disappointment. Over on the corner of Alexandra Gardens, three of the remaining plainclothes cops were dressing down a few of the hecklers. Tough lads, they looked.

"Know those cops?" Peter demanded on impulse.

"Na. They're not regulars." Al hauled out his chewing gum. Holding it between his two fingers, he looked at it distastefully, then flicked it into the gutter. *"Heddlu cudd."*

"So you don't know them—that doesn't make them secret police."

Al shrugged and started away. Peter, tucking his notes into an inside pocket, watched the cops and toughs across the street move away. They stopped among the trees. The branches hid them from view, but Peter saw something exchanged. The cops had handed folded banknotes to the toughs, he could swear.

"Did you . . . ?"

But Al paid no attention. He was busily taping the transaction. Then one of the plain-clothes men looked their way.

"Peter *bach*, I hope you're convinced. Now let's get the hell out of here. This way, round the side."

Mud-splashed and panting, they got into Al's illegally parked Cortina and rattled off towards BBC.

"Did they see us taping?" Peter gasped, still recovering his breath.

"Dunno. But, Christ, if that was what I think it was, we better hope not." It was as close as Al would come to admitting plain knee-knocking terror. He was pale under his permanent Hawaiian tan.

At the curb outside the building, Peter recovered some presence of mind. "Give me the tapes and I'll send you dubs in a couple of hours."

"Good. I want to look it over myself. *Hwyl.*" Al handed over his video cassettes and lurched the mud-spattered Cortina back into the road.

Peter saw a Volvo pull out into traffic after Rees's car. A white Volvo. It reminded him of Teddy Smythe. Tonight. It had almost slipped his mind.

Only the briefest flicker, nothing that could be identified as paper money changing hands. Perhaps an electronic enhancer could isolate something suspicious, but Peter couldn't. If the special police—if they were special police—had indeed seen him and Al taping their activities, it gave a whole new dimension to Peter's already shaky relationship with military intelligence. At last he turned off the videotape monitor and scrubbed both hands over his weary face.

Peter walked downstairs since the lift was out of order. His footfalls resounded through the uncarpeted stairwell and halls. The surly PhD from Manchester who ran the dubbing machines set aside her *Paris Match* and accepted Peter's two videotapes, sniffing at his request for immediate copies. When he returned to his bleak work space, he found the phone's message button glowing and called the switchboard.

"Someone rang for you five minutes ago, Mr. Holt. He'll call you at home tomorrow morning. Gwyn Davies."

"Thanks. What are you doing later, love?" Peter grinned at the squawk of pleased indignation from the grey-coiffed chapel-going switchboard woman and rang off. Bloody hell. He'd forgotten he needed reaction from Davies.

CBS. Peter found Cliff Aslin's number scrawled on the back of a beer mat, waited the usual ten minutes for an overseas operator, and finally got through to New York. The CBS receptionist said Cliff wasn't in weekends—none of the producers were—but she took Peter's message.

Not until Monday would he know whether the Yanks wanted a packet. His luck had deserted him today. Peter collected his dubbed tapes, sent the originals by cab to Al Rees's flat, and shrugged into his wet coat. When he turned to leave, he gave a start of surprise. Leaning in his doorway, dressed down for the occasion in a pigskin jacket, was Nigel Phipps.

"What do you want?" Peter demanded, annoyed by the minor shock.

Phipps, instead of snapping back, asked pleasantly, "Care for a pint?"

With refusal on his tongue, Peter reminded himself that Phipps was occasionally useful.

"Right." He belted the coat and picked up his rally videotapes. "I thought you'd be at the protest today playing reporter. Or whatever your latest cover is."

Phipps scowled but said nothing. Wasted provocation.

Raining again. They detoured through the parking lot long enough for Peter to toss the tapes in the Renault and lock it, then strolled down to the pub. They settled into the Black Lion's snug, Peter yawning.

"Take a holiday, Holt." Only Nigel laughed.

"Thanks. Mind signing for my vacation pay? BBC's rather tight-arsed about it. Of course, I could always get an assignment in Vaduz, where the rock stars holiday."

Vaduz. Spain? Or was it Portugal? What had Yann said? Something about skiing?

"Vaduz?" Phipps looked queasy. "We'd all better hope there's no Welsh interest in Vaduz. Bad enough that the IRA deals there when they can't get Lebanese or Libyan surplus."

Duw, Duw, as Al would say. Peter's luck was present and accounted for, after all. He scrabbled for something intelligent to offer.

"Mostly small stuff." He took a long sip of bitter.

Nigel shrugged, uncomfortable. "Heavier than I like to see on the open market. Liechtenstein's always been liberal with end-use permits. You can say you're buying for the Republic of Antarctica for all they care. The Provos buy bazookas and light artillery there—also their electronic gadgets, all American-service standard. Only the finest."

"Right." Peter feigned impatience. "But what about the new transaction? The big one."

"The helicopter gunship." Nigel eyed him suspiciously. "That's not Welsh. Or IRA. That's Breizh Nevez. New Britanny, the Breton counterpart to the Union of Future Wales."

Peter drained his glass. If he was making Phipps nervous, the feeling was mutual.

"Peter." Phipps sounded unusually diffident. "London asked me to get in touch with you. They're sorry about having to put you off when you called Thursday. It wasn't a secure line."

No more twaddle about wrong numbers, Peter noted with satisfaction. Except it meant they wanted something in return. Something sordid, Peter guessed by Phipps's curdled expression. Almost feeling sorry for the little man, he waited.

"Apparently you lent a hand in London, the day of the kidnapping."

"And?"

"Much appreciated, very much appreciated. All they ask is that you pass on any information that could aid in the investigation. It's been cleared with your superiors in London."

No doubt. After this spring's embarrassment, McKinley would fall over himself to help MI5. And they were really asking no more than Peter had already offered. So why did it give him a chill? He frowned at the telly above the bar.

"They've made contact again," offered Phipps.

"What?" Peter stared.

"Grenvile doesn't think they're in London. They located a phone setup in Camden Town that was relaying calls, apparently from some kind of remote transmitter. Rather advanced electronics."

"Can I confirm that?" Peter reached for his coat.

"Not yet." Nigel squirmed. Even he knew that off-the-record information was no information at all. BBC wasn't the *News of the World*.

Peter didn't bother to comment but turned to the telly. The late news was on. The lead story was a voice-over update with Peter's early afternoon footage of the protest. The next time was intro'd by a familiar logo of barbed wire wrapped around a candle. Amnesty International.

"—protests the alleged unlawful detainment of several known Welsh activists for questioning in connection with Tuesday's kidnapping," the news-reader intoned. "European Parliament spokesmen have also expressed their dismay at an apparent breach of human rights. An earlier objection yesterday in the House of Commons—"

Peter swore. Now he wasn't breaking the story, just following it. Still, he had the videotape for CBS, even for the staid BBC if they finally decided to air an in-depth arrests story on the telly. He wondered how many Cliff Aslins there were in the New York directory. Suddenly he didn't want to wait for Monday.

"Got to go." Belatedly he remembered Phipps, who sat looking miserable, his pint almost untouched.

"What can I tell London?" Phipps hated asking, Peter rejoiced to see.

"Tell them I'll think about it." He got up, threw his coat over one shoulder, and walked out into the wet snow.

In the farthest BBC car park, Peter's car stood at a drunken tilt. The air had escaped his leaking tire. Probably the colder weather. Then he saw the three-inch gash in the side wall and the driver's door hanging open. A quick-search confirmed his fear: no sign of today's rally videotapes.

Peter sprinted for the building and a phone.

8

Cabin fever. A long winter cooped up with uncongenial companions could produce strange results: silent feuds, even murder. On the arctic DEW line, Madog saw cabin fever take five snow-bound months to develop. In the pressure cooker of Pen y Cae, it was taking only days to fall into a routine of boredom and random cruelty.

"This child before the people's court, we have heard, claims to be heir to the English crown, a defunct title which the court cannot consider valid," announced Nora.

Pip watched her solemnly, with no sign of comprehension. He cast occasional wistful glances at his fuzzy Mungo Mouse in the corner, or down at his bound hands.

Nora's charade worried Madog, but he didn't want to intervene unless it became necessary. Any new interference and he'd have Davies down his throat, but their group leader was off for another telephone debate with Grenvile. Maybe he'd decided to skip out. Madog wouldn't blame him. Davies was just starting to figure out that he was in way over his head; they all were.

Nora was pacing the parlour with hands folded behind her back, delivering her peroration. The lawyerish pose, at odds with the Irishwoman's blue jeans and wild hair, was madly misplaced at Pen y Cae. At the heavy oak table near the centre of the room, she had the kid and Jean Douglass sitting with their wrists taped together.

"England has had no monarch since Charles the First was deposed for criminal acts against the state."

Deposed by Cromwell, thought Madog, before he settled down to bashing the Irish into submission. But he stayed quiet and monitored the room from the stair-well doorway.

He touched the narrow wedge of obsidian hanging at his neck just inside the denim shirt. His fingers ran along the delicate scallops chipped along either side of the arrowhead. The museum had conveniently labelled it: projectile point, paleolithic, hand worked in black volcanic glass. Obsidian. A stolen artifact. A deadly artifact, at least to a paleolithic hunter. Not deadly enough to him, however, in the days he recorded one by one by carving notches on his lashed bamboo walls. Then he'd tried it on his own wrists. The Khmer bastards liked that. They took the obsidian away, then, for no reason he could fathom, they kept the chain and gave the amulet back on a length of uncured thong. Madog found he was gripping the obsidian point convulsively. He dropped his hand.

Nora was just amusing herself so far, he thought. The nanny's fear had glazed over. Madog could have told Nora that people who are threatened long enough lose interest. Until the threats become physical.

Sion and Elen sat uncomfortably on either side of the nanny, playing court-room guards. The Welsh nurse, in a straight-backed chair, watched the performance as impassively as the grey cat on her shoulder. Sion cast an uncertain look at Madog, at the wide-eyed kid, and at Nora's back. The IRA woman had pegged Sion and Elen as the operation's proles, her best audience. Raffael spared the proceedings no attention from his perusal of Madog's magazines. Once only, he shook his head in faint exasperation and returned to the *Atlantic Monthly*. Raffael was sipping Madog's vermouth as he turned the pages, the portrait of a Turinese civil servant relaxing after a hard day of pencil-pushing. A terrorist without a press audience, it seemed, was no terrorist at all. Nora was different, even without her sixteen-gauge. Her folded arms looked self-consciously empty without the shotgun, confiscated by Davies and hidden by Madog. The house's sixteenth-century core still had a few useful nooks and crannies.

A rattle of the doorknob froze everyone in place. Davies stepped into the hall shedding snow on the slates. A black wind blasted inside with him, icy and glass-brittle, before he slammed the door. He glanced around, taking in the taped hands of the woman and child, Sion trapped in an expression of self-importance, Elen with enough sense to look disgusted.

"What the bloody hell is going on here?"

"We are conducting a hearing into crimes against the people," Nora told him. "These two are charged—"

"Shut your mouth," ordered the Undeb leader. "And get out of here. Get out of my sight."

Now we're talking, Madog thought. But Nora just folded her arms and lounged against the wall.

Davies walked through the parlour. He lifted Pip to his feet and pulled off the surgical tape. Then Jean Douglass. She murmured thanks as though he'd served her a gin and tonic, then looked embarrassed. Without warning, tears spilled from her eyes and tracked silently down her cheeks. She turned away and the boy came silently to take her hand. He looked afraid now, seeing her weep.

"We'll go home soon, laddie," the nanny told him calmly.

"Don't count on that," muttered Nora, examining her short finger-nails.

Jean Douglass turned to the IRA woman as though she'd never set eyes on her before. Madog was glad he wasn't on the receiving end of that gaze. It was a contract.

"Let's have some tea with milk and honey, Pip." She shot a questioning glance at Madog, and he nodded agreement. Their supplies were dwindling, but it was worth using a little tea to calm things down.

"Are you all right, Carrie?" Davies asked in Welsh.

She ignored him as though he hadn't spoken. Madog stepped in and held out his hand to help her from the chair. Nora watched suspiciously.

"Court's dismissed for today, little lady," Madog told Carrie, who still showed no sign of moving. "You're not hurt?"

"I'm appalled. Bored. Angry. But not hurt." Carrie stood, giving him a long dark-blue stare. "Do you know Pittsburgh well, Madog?"

"Afraid not. I live a few thousand miles west. Why Pittsburgh?"

She shook her head and followed the others to the kitchen. A green-eyed backward gaze was administered by the cat lolling on her shoulder.

"Madog." Davies, paler than the cold snap accounted for, had lingered in the living-room's doorway. In Welsh he said, "The remote device didn't work. Only as far as the Camden Town number."

Madog pursed his lips in a silent whistle. "What happened? Exactly."

"A lot of clicking, then back to the trunk-line tone."

"No one else on the line?"

"Not that I could tell."

"That means they got the Camden Town phone, probably by a house-to-house search. They couldn't trace it electronically. So you didn't get through?"

Davies shook his head. "We can't afford to stay here much longer. This place is steaming like a cauldron."

"Relax, huh?" Madog took Davies by the shoulder and shook him. "They'll never find us. They're Brits—it's not in their union contract."

"English," Davies snarled. "Not British. You don't know the difference, do you? We're British. Britons. The original inhabitants of Celtic Britain two thousand years ago when the Romans invaded."

"Geez, Gwyn, I didn't know you were that old."

But Davies was past humouring and pressed on doggedly. "The English are just transplanted Germans. Invaders."

"Sounds kind of racist to me."

Davies shot him a look of concentrated hatred and started to turn away. Madog tightened his grip on Davies's shoulder.

"That leaves us the transmitter to worry about," he went on. "But you're not going to like the solution."

"I don't like any of it," said Davies abruptly. Maybe the charm of revolutionary life was wearing down. "You'd better tell me."

Madog told him their choices. They could wait and eventually give up or be found. They could use public phones for ordinary direct calls and risk being traced and picked up for questioning. Or they could prepare another phone to relay calls from the remote transmitter.

"Where?" Davies frowned at the bare floor-boards.

"There's the problem," Madog agreed. "If we rigged a phone in Wrexham or Welshpool, the whole area would be crawling with cops in no time. They'll have pulled in every undercover man from trainees to pensioners."

"What about that radio set-up upstairs? It transmits, doesn't it?"

"Loud and clear," Madog told him. "If we use it, we'll be pin-pointed as soon as someone traces the radio beam to its source. All it takes is a direction finder. I don't have a jammer here."

"What if we relayed the call through someone else?" Davies demanded. "Someone in London, or Aberystwyth?"

"We'd still be putting out a beam." Madog hesitated, then motioned Davies upstairs. "Come on, I'd better show you. But let's keep everyone out of harm's way. Nora!"

The IRA woman arrived silently, black eyes narrow with suspicion. Sion was on her heels.

"Problems," Madog told her pleasantly in English, ignoring Davies's smouldering anger at her. "They've got the London phone. We need an alternative."

"The radio?" asked Nora.

"No, but it's going to be useful. Like the news bulletin we heard last night on short wave."

At the upper landing, Madog took the kerosene lamp from its nook, lit it, and trimmed the wick. Electricity was a distant luxury for Pen y Cae; the ham set ran off a car battery. He set the lamp on the dresser behind him, flicked the set's on switch, but made sure the mike was dead. When it warmed up, he tuned across the band and pulled in the usual babble of voices. When he looked up again, Raffael had materialized beside Davies. Both their faces were demonically underlit by the wavering lamplight.

They listened for a few minutes as Madog tuned through Morse code and distance-fractured garble to homely conversations that could be at the next farm. Someone was passing on a weather forecast: blizzard warning. Two men were commiserating over the detainment of a friend in Aberystwyth.

"These could be anyone at all," Madog explained. "Pilots, ships at sea, hams within a few hundred miles. Pick-up's clearest at night because—forget it. What I'm telling you is, if you switch on the mike and start relaying kidnap demands to Scotland Yard, several hundred people at least are going to hear you and will be able to locate you. Got it?"

Davies nodded in silence. Raffael and Nora exchanged terse German. Madog followed it enough to guess Raffael was talking about money and the kid.

"So it means back to the Llanygroes call-box," Madog said. Before Davies could protest, he added, "But there's a way to do it without getting traced."

Madog's plan was so simple Gwyn looked first suspicious, then pleased. It appealed to his romantic notion of the solidarity of the *gwerin*.

Raffael listened, then shook his head slowly. "No. We must get out."

"We could be trapped," Nora snapped.

Gwyn cut them off. "Let's talk about it downstairs. Madog, can we leave the radio on and monitor it? Information on the search is useful when I talk to Grenvile."

Good idea. It would also break them up, keep them tired, occupy some of their energy. Madog showed them how to comb the bands, removed the mike, and left Sion to the first watch.

They were washing up after supper when Sion called down the stairs for Gwyn. Madog drifted in on his heels to find Sion pointing wordlessly at the ham set.

"Danger, danger—"

The voice was barrel-deep and stiff as a sergeant-major's on the parade ground. A military voice, sure to God, but speaking Welsh with a nasal northern accent. The message was a simple warning, a few phrases repeated endlessly. Then there was a crackle of unintelligible response.

"*O Duw,*" said Davies, stunned.

It was repeated again and again.

"Danger, danger. Relay, relay. Ground search in progress. Prepare for police raids. Caerfyrddin, Tregaron, Conwy, north-east hill regions. Danger, danger. Relay, relay. Ground search in progress. Prepare for police raids."

Mesmerized, they listened three times before Nora's sharp demand snapped Davies out of it. Madog hadn't even noticed her come into the room. Dazed, Davies translated.

"But how long's it been going out?"

"That sounded military. Why would they announce their plans? Is it a trick?"

"A leak, maybe. Or a security screw-up. We can't take the chance." Ignoring the other questions, Madog looked around the dimly lit room. "North-east hill regions could mean us. Get the others up here right away. Hide all trace of them down below."

Madog flung himself across to the dresser and hauled it out from the wall. The kerosene lamp rocked precariously until someone took it and slipped off downstairs. Madog

seized a wooden handle with both hands and planted a
foot on the wall beside a small painted door, which liked
to jam when the humidity ran high. It squealed open, and
lamplight glinted on the shotgun inside. Nora darted and
seized it.

"What . . . ?" faltered Sion.

"Hidey-hole. Catholic family." Madog craned around
from his crouch to see the nanny, the kid clutching Mungo
Mouse, the Powell woman, the others standing silent with
shock. "Gwyn, Raffi, I'm going to wait out here and see
if anyone turns up. Keep them together, and quiet." He
pointed at the Welsh nurse. There might be bad blood
between her and Davies, but she seemed to have her wits
about her. "You go through first."

Carrie stood her ground. "Why should I? Especially if
we have a chance of rescue?"

"This is why." Nora, quick to reassert her ownership
of the gun, touched both barrels to the nurse's nape. "Get
in."

Carrie glared angrily at Davies, who looked away. Madog would have to keep an eye on their hostility; it could
be dangerous. Was it mutual or all hers? Davies would
never tell him, that much was sure. She stooped to hands
and knees and crawled into the black space of the priest's
hole, with her blue wool skirt hiked up. She had shapely
legs and a nice round behind. She felt her way along the
wall towards the front of the house. On the other side of
the false wall, about two feet away, was the old stable loft.
With luck, no one would find either entry. With luck. Luck
seemed to play an increasing part in all this, and Madog
didn't like it.

"Why is she going in there?" Pip asked Jean Douglass.

"It's like hide and seek," Madog said. "You have to
be really quiet or we'll catch you too soon."

Pip jumped from foot to foot in excitement. The nanny
pushed him in and crawled in after him, wasting no breath
on protest. Sion, Elen, Davies, and Raffael followed. Madog fumbled a torch out of the dresser drawer, passed it

in, and straightened to find black Nora holding her shotgun on him. He gave her his brightest grin.

"Not you, sweetheart. You're my alibi. You folks in there going to be okay?"

Davies muttered reassurance, and Madog slammed the door and dragged in the dresser back in place.

"Now, let's see what we can raise on short wave."

Nora's shotgun was making his back crawl; he ignored it, and soon the barrel dropped. She was like a red-back crab, Madog figured, she liked to have people notice her threats. Offensively defensive. Was there any tenderness underneath the hard shell? He didn't really want to know. Madog bent his attention to the set, but couldn't locate the sergeant-major. Instead, there was a rush of Welsh-language comment and panicky questions. Faintly, he heard a woman and a different man repeat the warning, with the same request to relay.

"What's that all about?"

"Cymry Cymraeg, the Welsh-speaking Welsh." Madog laughed quietly. "They take care of their own."

"Ah, yes," Nora sneered. "Just like Armagh. Take care to turn you in to the fucking Brits for the price of a pint."

"It's different here." The six counties, even the republic, had had their fill of the bloody-handed IRA. Here there was still some sense of mutual protection. How long would it stay that way? Madog switched off the radio set. "Who are you this week, Nora?"

"Darlene Mary Brownley, born in Sheffield, florist's assistant, unemployed."

"Okay, Darlene Mary. Let's do the rounds."

Madog crossed the landing to the bedroom and stood beside the uncurtained window. The first-quarter moon was lost in a pearl overcast. South and west, across the humped whale-backs of the Berwyns, rose a faint habitation glow from Birmingham. No movement but a haze of snow driven along the high ground; no sound but the rising wind. He remembered the weather warning and wondered whether a blizzard would be a help or a hindrance. Before he could decide, Pen y Cae's silence shattered.

The helicopter manifested itself first as a chattering roar, then as a sweep of glaring searchlights across the muddy farmyard. It lifted over the southern pasture at tree-top level, a long silhouette in midnight green. Madog noted automatically: an Aerospatiale Gazelle, offensive 7.62mm guns on the fuselage side sponsons, terrain-following radar. The call numbers were RAF.

"Holy Mother of God," said Nora.

Madog turned to see her open-mouthed with horror. He pulled the shotgun from her unresisting hands. "Darlene Mary, take off your clothes real fast. You and me are going to bed."

She slid out of them like an eel, her tongue caught between her teeth. Not horror, he realized. Titillation. Madog undressed quickly and shoved the sixteen-gauge beneath his mattress. Under the feather quilt, Nora wrapped herself around him with reptilian grace as the Gazelle hovered roaring over the yard. It wasn't exactly what he had in mind. Hissing contempt, she gave up on Madog and diddled herself furiously. Searchlights briefly probed the room and swept on along the length of the farmhouse. The helicopter lifted over the east slope and roared off down towards John Hughes's Cae Isa. Nora climaxed like an artillery barrage, sinking her teeth hard into his arm. Madog could have guessed she'd also crave blood.

Seconds later a four-wheel drive of some kind pulled up in front, accompanied by the squawk of a walkie-talkie. The knock on the downstairs door was restrained, almost discreet. Madog got up and pulled on a cotton Japanese yukata, tying the sash as he went down the stairs.

"Sorry to bother you, sir," said a kid with a corporal's stripe. He ran his flashlight slowly over Madog from tousled hair to bare feet and flushed furiously.

"Come in," Madog said, none too friendly. He didn't have to fake angry frustration. Nora had done that much for him, at least.

The two men stepped past the door into the cramped hallway. The second man wore civilian clothes. He was sleepy-eyed and silent and carried a notebook.

"Captain Nilsson?" asked the civilian. "Dyfed-Powys police investigation, sir."

"And RAF?" Madog struck a dubious note.

"Yes, sir."

Madog nodded. "Can I help you?"

"Are you alone here, sir?"

The corporal cut off a snicker when the older man half-turned in annoyance.

"No. I'm not alone." Madog permitted himself the surliness. It seemed in keeping. "I have a friend visiting. A young woman," he added, to the boy's mirth.

"And what is the young woman's name, sir?"

"Darlene Brownley."

"Could you—" The round face turned towards the dim parlour, spectacles glinting. "Ah, Miss Brownley."

"Yes. Is there trouble?"

Nora had the sense to tie back that kinky hair of hers, Madog noticed with approval, and she'd wrapped one of his dress shirts around her, covering her to mid-thigh. The corporal's gaze travelled wildly and found safety among the hall coat pegs.

"Where do you live, Miss Brownley?"

Other questions followed. Age, occupation. Darlene Mary, in a voice unacquainted with Crossmaglen, lied fluently and demurely.

"And you, Captain Nilsson?"

"I guess you could call me a remittance man," Madog said with the least pleasant smile he could muster. "When I'm not sitting in on the old man's board meetings, I live the simple country life."

The man in civvies said nothing but scribbled a single word in the notebook; not a polite word, Madog guessed. He wondered how friendly Scotland Yard was with the National Security Agency these days, and hoped Interpol hadn't yet overcome its fussiness about throwing open all file classifications. It would be ironic to be fingered by one of his own data-search programs.

"Want a look around the house?" Madog offered grudgingly.

"If you would."

The search was perfunctory. Madog sweated out every step of it, hoping nothing was out of place, but Davies had been thorough. Crockery shoved in the cupboard, papers and books hastily piled in the parlour, bedclothes straightened in the downstairs bedroom, even the kerosene lamp back in its niche at the top of the stairs. The radio room swam with yellow light as he trimmed the wick.

Beside the dresser, green eyes flared. The grey tiger cat sat pawing at the false wall, chirring, patiently waiting to be reunited with Carrie Powell. Madog calmly picked him up. Pal purred and rubbed against his neck.

"Amateur radio operator, are you? Were you on the air tonight?"

"Not yet. I still haven't got it properly hooked up."

The investigator noted it and went on. He gave the rumpled bed only a glance and Madog breathed easier.

"Next room?" He pointed his pencil stub at the door beside the wardrobe.

"Storage." Madog opened it and handed over the lamp. Bed frame standing on end, broken chair, cardboard boxes. The civilian opened them and lifted the lamp high around the walls for a closer look. Without a word he returned the lamp and went downstairs.

"What's all this about, anyhow?" Madog asked at the door. "You got a criminal on the loose or something?"

"Not precisely, no. A missing person."

"Not—" Darlene Mary was wide-eyed. "You're not looking for the little Prince, are you? All the way up here?"

The civilian considered her lethargically and nodded. "Several locations, in fact. It's just a remote chance, Miss Brownley."

"Poor little chap. Good luck finding him."

Laying it on too thick, Nora. Madog understood that fatal temptation. But the corporal and his special-services companion just nodded.

"That will be all, Captain Nilsson. Sorry to disturb you, Miss Brownley." The civilian gave a twitch of the head in apology and the corporal managed a poker face. Madog watched from the door as the Jeep turned around in the small yard.

"Captain of what?"

Nora stood in the kitchen with hands on her hips. The shirt had fallen open. The Jeep headlights flooded her for a few seconds; too muscular for Madog's taste, and her breasts were mostly brown nipple. The hair at her crotch was straight and rusty brown, so the wild black curls to her shoulderblades were courtesy of a beauty parlour. Vanity. Her IRA group leader would chastise her. Obviously Nora's trained role wasn't seduction. Just destruction.

"U.S. Cavalry."

"Ah, don't waste your lies on me."

Madog grinned and slipped the belt off his robe. Nora caught one end of it and wrapped it hard around his waist. She knelt on the kitchen slates and went to work on him with her pointed tongue. The Jeep finally jounced downhill past the hay barn without stopping and carried on towards Cae Isa. He hoped John wasn't caught printing football-pool tickets or stripping the ear cuts off English steers. Madog pulled Nora to her feet, bent her forward among the tea mugs on the wooden table, and parted her legs. Her acrobatic convulsions brought him off quickly. He disentangled himself, feeling slimy. Sex with Nora was like crawling into an occupied snake's skin, then being excreted.

Across the room Pal waited sphinxlike on a chair, both paws folded under his chin. He led Madog upstairs to the radio room, chirring.

Robert Grenvile, forehead propped on his fingertips, frowned in concentration as he listened yet again to the

tapes he could now repeat in his sleep. Not that they revealed anything new or useful.

A crash penetrated even the foam ear pads. Robert
looked up to see Anna Chernicki, normally cool and self-
contained, leaning dishevelled against the control-room
door she'd slammed behind her. He threw down the head-
set and went to take her arm.

"All right?"

"Yes, thanks. Just let me catch my breath." She
smoothed her jacket. "Have you seen the demonstrators
outside on the steps? They're getting insistent. They decided I was part of the search team and demanded to know
why we hadn't recovered the Prince."

Electronics technicians and search co-ordinators, who
had paused to listen, returned to their tasks at the surveillance screens and computer terminals. The New Scotland
Yard search headquarters maintained the quiet hum and
steady activity of a well-run hive, for all its recent shortage
of tangible results. It was two days since last contact with
the terrorists on Thursday.

"I've watched them on the monitors." Robert glanced
at the nearest phone. "The commissioner decided to
leave them where we could keep an eye on them. But if
they're getting violent, perhaps security should have them
leave."

The request wasn't rightly his to make, Robert knew,
but since Scotland Yard's rumoured reprimand from the
palace, the commissioner had been rather subdued. At the
moment he hunched over a computer with the SAS man,
Fox. Since Special Air Services had volunteered—it was
their policy to volunteer, not wait for a request to take a
mission—to direct further searches, Fox had been more
visible in the control room.

Anna Chernicki shook her sleek head, smiling.
"They're worried about their Prince. Since they can't find
any terrorists to blame, you're next in line. It's just de-
mocracy at work, a bit noisily." She held out a newspa-

per. "Here's something for you, on the lighter side. Front page, lower left."

It was today's *Daily Express*. Robert scanned down to a one-column story headed "Prince of What?"

Last week's royal kidnap was tragic and unnecessary, but has no connection with the real Prince of Wales, said London ophthalmologist Mr. Llywelyn Probert-Vaughan.

"Speaking as one Prince to another, I have the greatest sympathy. No one seems truly safe these days."

Mr. Probert-Vaughan, 57, claims to be the true Prince of Wales. He is a direct descendant of Llywelyn II, the last native Prince of Wales, who died in a 1282 Welsh rebellion against Edward I of England. Mr. Probert-Vaughan is unmarried.

"As Prince of Wales I reserve the right to choose as my successor any legitimate male of our royal house. I did not choose this unfortunate child. He is an English rather than a Welsh prince."

A Buckingham Palace spokesman dismissed Mr. Probert-Vaughan's claim as "genealogically implausible and utterly irrelevant."

"Mad as a hatter." Robert returned the paper.

"An incident like this always brings them out of the woodwork." Anna Chernicki set her briefcase on a desk and captured an auburn tendril escaping from her braided chignon. "What's new today?"

Robert shook his head. Without further calls from the kidnappers, his position was desperate. "Still no contact. Someone tried to relay a call through the Camden Town phone last night, but apparently the device was built with an automatic disconnect. Our people couldn't trace the call."

"And you tried a search?"

"Areas of Wales, Kent, Somerset. We had several reports of unusual activities in places where we thought they could have gone to ground. No luck yet. We have no indication they're still in London, since no one picked up the rations in Hyde Park. Wales was a long shot, just in case these people bolted for home.''

"Let's hope the terrorists are as logical as Major Grenvile," offered a flat voice at Robert's elbow. Fox. "The RAF lads and the police ground teams turned up nothing. Until we locate them, we can't deploy a strike.''

"Strike?'' Robert frowned into the SAS observer's light eyes. Watch the eyes, the handbook said. He had to remind himself now and again that Fox wasn't the enemy. "As long as there's hope of negotiation, the PM will never endanger the hostages with an assault.''

"True.'' Fox smiled without showing his teeth. Tight-lipped. Was that an SAS regulation? "As long as there's hope of negotiation.''

The last thing Robert needed in this information drought was interference from the blood-and-guts, death-before-dishonour SAS. If terrorists and SAS anti-terrorist soldiers were shoved into the same uniforms, handed the same weapons, who could tell them apart? Every year saw another incident of SAS drop-outs turning renegade. Some robbed banks. Rather more joined the private armies of oil kings or banana-republic *presidentes*. A terrifying few turned coldly, efficiently berserk to murder innocent British civilians. Robert shared military intelligence's scepticism about the adventuring SAS. A doggerel rhyme eluded his recall—Kipling, probably—something about letting the wolf in over the threshold. The SAS were a necessary evil. Or were they necessary? In a civilized country, a civilized world, they wouldn't be.

"What now, Major Grenvile?'' Anna Chernicki steered the conversation onto less contested ground.

Robert hesitated but remembered her full security clearance from his branch. It wasn't the clearance category he would have assigned to a University of Maryland professor of political science who was researching European hostage negotiations. Robert suspected she might be other things as well. But the American woman was discreet, had some sensitivity to the jealousies and cross currents of the search operation, and more than once had repelled Fox's skirmishes against Robert's people.

"Now we widen our information net. Do you recall the BBC reporter, Holt? Some of his contacts may be useful. The imperative thing is to locate the terrorists and reestablish negotiations, preferably face-to-face."

"What are your chances with Holt? If we approached an American reporter with any request like that, you'd hear the outcry all the way over here in London."

"He offered his help on Tuesday." To get a story, but with a crisis of this magnitude, there were always ways to encourage further co-operation.

So many questions remained unanswered. Why were there no more calls? What had happened to the kidnappers' high-powered aid from the IRA? Were they an isolated handful of hoodlums without any support structure? Robert suspected that the terrorists had indeed left London. Something had gone wrong, and they'd fled. If they were inexperienced, they might well be cut off from their own network as thoroughly as from Robert. What dangers would that hold for the Prince? He recalled the threatening reference to young Paul Getty, who at seventeen had himself been scarcely more than a child. Childhood was little protection against a terrorist's vengeance or panic. Whatever he did, he must not alarm them or make them angry.

Robert went over his mental list of details that bothered him. The last tape's background noise seemed to be an argument of some kind. Telly, said the Welshman who called himself Merlin. But no program at that hour, on any channel, had contained a fight scene. Electronic surveillance analysis had the tape now and were enhancing the background sound to try for individual words. And Merlin's own words two days ago, *modus operandi*. Military, maybe academic, or possibly just watched too many late-night whodunits.

Dr. Chernicki clutched his arm suddenly. Overhead, a red light began to strobe its warning.

"Major Grenvile, control please," sounded the computer's flatly metallic vocal mode. "Major Grenvile."

Robert made for the glass-walled negotiation booth, his heart racing. He fitted on the head-set and pulled the desktop receiver near.

"Location?" he asked the technician, a discreet fellow who wore post-punk *haute couture* under his lab coat and combed his hair straight back. What was his name? Leung.

"Llandeilo, sir. A town in southwest Wales."

"Grenvile here. Is this Merlin?"

Silence was broken by a man's voice, Welsh, elderly and mortally uncomfortable. "I am the Reverend Iorwerth Morgans of Capel Ebenezer, Llandeilo. I am ringing at the request of an unidentified man who telephoned asking me to relay to you a message concerning the young Prince."

What was this? Robert folded his hands before him on the desk, cool and leisurely as he had not been since the terrorists' last call. Days of torment, now a few minutes of calm.

"Go ahead, please, Reverend Morgans."

The old man made elaborately clear that he didn't know the caller, couldn't recognize the voice, hadn't thought to ask his location, and, in short, was in no way involved with acts of terrorism. Robert reassured him and managed to extract the message.

"The young man said the Prince and Miss Douglass are well. You are to stop immediately all the ground searches, which he has been hearing about on the television. You are to stop arresting Welsh men and women. He says the people you have already arrested have no connection with the kidnapping and you are to release them immediately. He says that when you stop these acts of violence against the nation of Cymru, he will telephone you to make arrangements. That is everything."

"Thank you, sir. We're extremely grateful for your co-operation. Would you like us to assign someone for your protection?''

"Certainly not." The brittle old voice sharpened. "I am seventy-eight years old, and I have not stored up treasures on earth. I take the young man's telephone call as a sign of trust, not danger. And now I will bid you good day."

"Reverend Morgans, please. Was the man speaking Welsh?"

"Yes."

"Were you able to identify his dialect?"

After a pause, Morgans said, "My hearing is rather poor, I am afraid. I do not believe I can be of help."

Robert could read his hesitation, his stiffness. "Reverend Morgans, please, sir. This is a matter of life and death."

Another pause. "Major Grenvile, I am a Welshman. I am an old man but I am not foolish. If I offer my opinion, I may accuse an innocent fellow countryman."

"Sir, we will take your opinion as exactly that. No one will be charged on the basis of your impression of a brief conversation."

"Very well. I took his dialect to be from Dyfed, perhaps from the area around Caerfyrddin."

A southerner. Was he telling the truth this time? Robert thanked the old minister and rang off. Mr. Leung came silently into the booth. The technician handed Robert a computer printout and murmured, "Monitor three."

Monitor three was one of the surveillance screens. It displayed intelligence material relayed from Government Communications Headquarters at Cheltenham, which had recovered from its cataclysmic security scandal a few years back. Robert walked across the sound-absorbing carpet. The screen was cycling mug shots, a few from the prison authority but mostly home snapshots. The Welsh extremists' friendship album.

Robert found it eerie and in some ways pathetic to see faces smiling at the camera, squinting into the sun, holding pets, lovers, or children. Fourteen prime suspects, people with Welsh-extremist connections who couldn't immediately be located for questioning, according to the computer's toneless identification. Students, university lecturers, an infant-school teacher, jobless miners and steelworkers, a bank clerk, a dark-haired girl with a cat in her arms. Mostly young, their faces apparently innocent of malice. Were any of them responsible for a vicious kidnapping? Robert nodded wearily for the technician to kill the display.

Teddy Smythe poured a whisky and apologized. The sparsely furnished flat was a friend's, away on holidays. And the fellow next door hadn't been home for several days. Had his own business, travelled here and there. And besides, Teddy thought the neighbour had probably spoken out of turn. An offhand comment, just a joke. The neighbour was a sarcastic devil at the best of times.

"Right," said Peter, making small golden tidal waves in his glass. It was a long shot, and long shots rarely paid. One Scotch to show no hard feelings, and he was off.

"But I've met the chap he meant."

Peter looked up, reconsidering. Teddy whistled a few bars of an old Welsh song as he capped the bottle on the kitchenette counter, then brought his drink into the sitting-room. He walked slowly toward the long view of the bay, a little too stiffly, balancing the glass carefully as though he'd already put away his limit.

Teddy described the man: tall, thinning hair, glasses, smoked a pipe, sulky-looking bugger. Give him the time of day and he'd toss something back at you in Welsh. Peter nodded and sipped. It was a reasonably accurate description of half the schoolteachers in Cardiff. Or, for that matter, of Owen Thomas.

"Wears a Greens button in his lapel?"

Teddy looked round, startled. "You know him?"

"He's a contact."

"You think he's one of these Welsh nash types?"

Peter thought about it. "Nationalist, yes. Terrorist, no. I know he's not involved. I talked with him two days ago." Unreasonably, he felt he wanted to explain. "I was covering the Allt Valley Dam protest."

"Tell me, Peter, why do these people all want to stand in the way of progress? Block the dams. Tear down the nuclear plants. Prevent nuclear-waste storage. Cling to tiny countries that can't survive as separate entities. Protect dying languages. Why don't they look to the future instead? It's a wonderful future."

Peter mumbled some commiseration and measured the whisky remaining in his glass. It wasn't his business to defend dams or nuclear plants or languages. He wasn't an interest group, he was an information conduit.

Teddy saw his empty glass before he got to his feet.

"No, let me! God, I'm glad of a decent conversation. You don't know until you've monitored five thousand kilometers of pipeline."

Peter, set upon himself occasionally by demons of work and loneliness, hadn't the heart to walk out. He settled back in the chrome-and-leather chair for one more. But Teddy didn't want to talk pipeline technology. He wanted to talk about his holidays.

"First-rate. Worth the long hours, though I can't complain about the salary."

"Sounds ideal."

"I'll bet you could sign on with Shell or Mobil anywhere in the world with your talents, Peter. Promotion, public affairs. Work four months and spend the rest of the year polishing your backhand. Get out of this soggy backwater. Want to try it out? I can probably get you onto a junket. Tour a few well sites, then spend a couple of weeks lazing under a palm tree."

Teddy had the eagerness of a man cut off from friends and family by overseas work. At the bottom of the fourth Scotch, though, Peter dredged down to stubborn rock bottom.

"I know it's a backwater. I know there are plenty of

problems.'' He realized he was approaching his owlish stage and forced a smile. ''That's why I'm here. The problems are the story.''

''I admire your dedication, old man. Hope your firm does.''

''It's not money. What would I do with money?'' Repair Elizabeth's rising damp, for one thing. It didn't seem important right now.

Teddy raised his brows in silence and went to pour them another.

Things remained unsaid when Teddy saw Peter down to his car. An effort at friendship that hadn't somehow jelled? No suggestion of homosexual interest. No doubtful investment proposals. Teddy wanted something. Probably just what he said, decent conversation.

Gwyn had parked the Land Cruiser in the hay barn and was halfway to the house before he realized he was being followed. It couldn't be the call he'd just made to the nonconformist minister—how could they have traced that?

He tensed but stifled his first impulse to hurl himself off the stony track, hit the ground, and roll. Make yourself always a moving target, said the black-bearded Basque instructor at China Lake. But Gwyn's Browning was in the house and he had no real cover on the scrubby hillside. Instead he strolled on, trying to look as though his presence at Madog's house were beyond question. He listened over the crunch of his own footfalls on the sparse snow and decided someone was walking normally, with no attempt at concealment, about fifty paces behind him. As he passed the kitchen window, he saw a slender shadow fade back out of sight. Raffael, on watch. Last night's visit from the spooks had instilled nervous caution.

Madog opened the door before he could knock and bounced outside grinning and waving. Gwyn turned. A rough-looking man in mac, tweed cap, and wellies had halted where the mud met the farmyard cobbles.

''John! *Dewch i mewn!*'' Madog ushered in both of

them. His hand on Gwyn's shoulder was not quite welcome, not quite warning. "Been a long time. I thought they'd got you safe behind bars in Shrewsbury."

"Not yet, *machgen*. I'll live my quiet life a while longer before they trouble me." His Welsh was thick and abbreviated, almost incomprehensible.

Madog's neighbour smiled broadly, revealing gaps where side teeth had been. His shaggy grey hair hung over his eyes, and his face was deep in stubble. He smelled like a cowshed. A hill farmer, and one who thrived in the venerable tradition of rustling English stock.

"John Hughes, Cae Isa." Madog was still grinning like the Cheshire cat. "Gwyn Davies, Coleg Prifysgol Cymru, Aberystwyth."

The farmer looked long and hard at Gwyn, then nodded and pulled his cap a little lower over his eyes in a gesture neatly balanced between Welsh homage to a scholar and all-purpose rudeness. He stumped through the kitchen door, tracking mud onto the slates, and crashed a gallon jar onto the sink board.

"White lightning. That what you Americans call it, Madog?" Hughes laughed until he coughed, then cleared his throat noisily. "What's your friend here been brewing? When he heard me on his heels he nearly leapt out of his hide."

Gwyn shrugged at Madog's amusement. It could have been the bloody *heddlu cudd* dropping in for another chat. He wasn't sure Hughes was an improvement. He urgently needed to talk with Madog. The anonymous relay call to Elen's great-uncle, the crusty old non-conformist minister, was only a stopgap. His sole concern, more desperate every hour, was to re-establish a direct line to Grenvile without risking their discovery at Pen y Cae.

"Pull up a chair, John. I'll critique your creative efforts."

As they settled with glasses of the oily-looking yellow liquid, Gwyn looked around. There was no trace of the others. Raffael must have shepherded them upstairs.

"How is she?" John asked anxiously.

"Smooth. But white lightning is corn liquor. This is applejack."

Was the American going to make a social occasion of it? Their lives could be hanging by a thread. Gwyn tried the stuff, astonished at its kick. Still, it was smooth. He sipped cautiously as the two of them rattled on like old cronies.

Madog had slipped easily from posh Welsh into something close to John's speech pattern. The north-central border dialect was the rarest of all Welsh these days. Most border farmers spoke English, voted English, thought English. Gwyn began to appreciate Madog's warmth for the old brigand. As the strange vowels slid past his ear, he itched for a notebook and tape recorder. If—when—they finished with all this, he'd come back on a research trip.

"I plan to fence the calving pen," John was saying. "Those girls get lively and try to skip back to the flat land."

"And?"

"Fencing is dear these days."

"You want me to pay so you can keep your English heifers snug?" Madog folded his arms, eyebrows raised.

"Chi yw'r berchennog," said John craftily.

Gwyn's ears pricked. Madog was John Hughes's landlord?

Madog snorted and poured another round.

"Where is your home?" John asked Gwyn, who recognized a tactical change of topic.

"I was raised near Dolgellau."

"Thought you sounded from well north of Aberystwyth." The farmer nodded and tried a fresh approach. "Besides, Madog, after that foolishness last night you may not get your rent from me anyway. Those English crawled all around my place, looked in the cowshed and loft and on and on. And the still was sitting brave as you please in the middle of the back kitchen. Strange, they said nothing of it."

Circuitous, thought Gwyn, but not exactly subtle. That was what brought John Hughes uphill with his illegal brew, not the calving pen. He wanted to talk about the raid.

"And they asked questions about you. They saw I had the electricity and the phone and wanted to know if you had them at Pen y Cae. Also they asked if you had house guests. I didn't tell them you were entertaining the district nurse, though I knew her car from when I was laid up with my leg two years ago. Just as well I shut my teeth on it." His blue eyes moved from Madog to Gwyn. "Since it's certain you're not *Miss Ceridwen fach.*"

Gwyn said nothing but topped off their glasses with the apple brandy. His head swam though they'd barely lowered the level in the jug.

"Mister Davies I never saw before—" the farmer cackled and wiped his mouth "—except on the front page of *Y Cymro.* The picture showed him coming out of Abertawe court-house after a trial. Something about blowing up a microwave transmitter."

"Insufficient evidence." Gwyn tossed back the glass, knowing he would regret it.

"And murder."

"Manslaughter. Dismissed."

"Confess, John," Madog said soberly. "Did you come visiting for a little casual blackmail?"

"What kind of thing is that to say? *Madog bach,* you should have stayed with those devils in China."

"Cambodia."

"Whatever." Hughes smiled broadly, exposing gapped gums. "Police crawling around the barn, helicopters dropping on us from nowhere—Madog, it looks to me like you're between the dogs and the wall. You should have told me."

"No, John. It's not your problem."

"It is."

Gwyn watched with a frown. Madog said nothing.

Hughes, unable to provoke more reaction, finally got to the point. "Why I came is, I seem to remember owing you a side of beef. I can bring her up tonight."

Madog was looking out of the window. "How about some potatoes?"

"Twenty-pound sack should do you a while, I guess." John climbed to his feet. "I'll go now and cut down that side. Gareth can bring her up."

"No." Madog stood abruptly. "Keep him out of it."

"Madog, all of us know you're here. Tire tracks, smoke from the chimney, helicopters. Already young Gareth has lied for you when the *heddlu cudd* came round. And his Tad also. Family is family."

"No, John."

John shrugged. "Keep the brew, Madog. I think you'll want it."

"John?" Madog called out from the door. His tenant paused in front of the small hillside orchard opposite. "I'll think about the fence."

9

Peter Holt forced down another mouthful of cheese sandwich as he shuffled through the notes scattered over his unmade bed, then reached for the phone.

"Holt here," he mumbled, expecting Al Rees.

"Pete? Pete?" an American voice roared in his ear. "Christ, you Brits could get better phone service using string and tin cans. Can you hear me?" Cliff Aslin's huge news-reader voice made him sound six-foot-six and tough as nails. In fact, he was small, bald, an orchid-breeder, and tough as nails. Tougher, when it came to his news interests.

Peter swallowed his mouthful. "I couldn't reach you. I thought you weren't in till tomorrow."

"Pete, this *is* tomorrow. I cut my weekend short when I got your message. Look, this is a hot item. Can you fill me in fast? We're getting good files from our bureau in London, and we're calling in our crews from Paris and Frankfurt. But it's starting to look like you're sitting right on top of the volcano. Your Ministry of Defence's latest release from the search headquarters said the terrorists may be in or near Wales."

"Are you certain it wasn't the Home Office?" Peter frowned across his bed-sit, out the dirty window at a fire escape and a brick wall.

"Ministry of Defence for sure. Now, what can you throw me?"

Defence? That could mean the military were taking over the search from Scotland Yard. And the terrorists were in Wales? Peter had to call Grenvile soon.

"A decent video cameraman, for a start. Al Rees works mostly for the papers, but he's willing to free lance. If you use him you get exclusive tapes—and useful contacts."

"Great stuff. What's your situation with BBC?"

"We're just starting to run cautious stories about the disappearance, apparently by arrest, of nationalists. I've got far more. When the Corporation Pooh-Bahs get brave enough to broadcast it, they'll be happy with what I've got."

Peter outlined his footage: interviews with extremist leaders; yesterday's demonstration, complete with hecklers; and reaction from the Cardiff housing estates and pubs.

"What's your own analysis of public sentiment, Pete?"

"There's much more anger and talk today," he said, "both pro and con, since Amnesty International and the European Parliament and some reputable British groups objected to holding these nationalists incommunicado. The Welsh believe in their existence only if an American or a German or someone tells them it's valid."

"Yeah? What are they actually saying?"

"Most people are upset and embarrassed about the kidnapping. Union Jacks hanging in windows, that sort of thing. The government encourages it. There's a general election coming up and the last thing the present government wants is more Welsh Nationalists in the Commons. But I think underneath all that, things are rather explosive."

"What do you mean?"

"Unless they hurt the Prince, I don't think many Welsh would turn in these kidnappers. I mean the real Welsh, whoever they are. Welsh speakers, I suppose." Peter didn't add that by one definition that included him.

"Great, great. Give me all of that, Pete."

Last, Peter mentioned the apparent pay-off by undercover police that he and Al had witnessed.

"No kidding? The cops paid a bunch of hoods to disrupt a political protest? You realize when that gets out, the shit's in the fan?"

"Yup." A few minutes talking to Cliff and Peter always started to sound like a Yank himself. "Things are already touchy in that department. Someone nicked my tapes last night."

"But you said—"

"Hang on, don't get excited. We dubbed new copies from Al's originals. I couriered them to your London bureau this morning. Your people said they'd relay on a four P.M. satellite. They bumped some other leads off that bird and onto the five-thirty. But someone here's a little edgy about the material on those tapes."

Cliff whistled happily. "Great stuff. Make sure you give me some continuity on that and notes for a backgrounder. Any guesses who?"

"Not if I value my health," Peter said lightly, but found he was prickling with cold sweat.

Al and he had talked through to that conclusion last night as they dubbed fresh copies. Al had vaguely promised to take care of things. That failed to reassure Peter, since the photographer had ties not only with the legitimate parliamentary party Plaid Cymru, but also with nationalist groups known for blowing up English-owned summer cottages, telly masts, and government offices. Peter assumed their activities stopped at property damage; he didn't want to find himself in the middle of a guerrilla campaign against police and military.

"Pete, go to it. Tell this guy Rees he's on daily rates as of right now. You're on footage rates, and we pay top dollar for world broadcast. Maybe I can shake down something better. Okay?"

Peter mumbled something, thinking of Elizabeth's

mortgage. He was never much for dickering. Just for getting the story.

"Remember, no one here knows where Wales is, or why anyone would want to kidnap a nice kid like the Prince. Give us lots of background, and we'll throw together some kind of special. Lots of human interest, huh? And good luck, Pete. We lost another guy in San Salvador yesterday. Their government boys thought he was too nosy." Cliff rang off, leaving a profound silence in the untidy flat.

A knock at the door brought Peter out of fugue. He crossed the room quietly and looked through the glass peep-hole he'd installed that morning. Distorted to a full-length view by the fish-eye lens, straddling his aluminum camera case, stood Al Rees in an anonymous blue mac. He'd given up his Hawaiian shirts and silver bomber jacket.

Peter found his trench coat and slipped the latch on the door. Then the phone rang. Al motioned, "Meet you in the car," and thumped off downstairs again.

Aslin again? He grabbed the phone. "Holt here."

"Sorry to be so late returning your call." A man's quiet voice, speaking Welsh. The phone connection was poor, a series of clicks and fade-outs. "You wanted something?"

Gwyn Davies, the elusive president of Undeb Cymru Fydd.

Peter answered in Welsh. "Right. I'd like to get some reaction from you about the kidnapping and about the arrests. BBC is still nervous, but I'm taping a special for CBS in the States. Where are you calling from? Are you still in Cardiff?"

A moment's pause. "Bangor. Congratulations on CBS. If the Americans raise a fist about Wales, we'll benefit. I'd like to help you. What about later in the week?"

"Not much help. The whole thing may have blown over. Can you ring me later at BBC and I'll record from the phone?"

"No." Less abruptly, Davies added, "I'm just leaving for a friend's house."

"Give me the number there."

"He doesn't have a phone. I'll give you a statement now."

"Better than nothing." First things first. He could line up something else later. Peter opened his newsprint pad and pressed the record button on his tape recorder. "Right. What's the Undeb position?"

Davies began, slowly enough for Peter to take notes. They were both old hands at this. His voice sounded strangely flattened; probably the bad line.

"Undeb Cymru Fydd recognizes the seizing of an English child by activists of the liberation movement of the Nation of Cymru."

Peter's eyebrows shot up. Endorsing an act of undisputed terrorism? And Undeb didn't usually steal other groups' thunder. Like all the activist organizations, Union of Future Wales was highly territorial. An alarm bell started to clang.

"The English government's continued insensitivity to the people of Cymru has finally served as a catalyst to a more aggressive Welsh reaction. Undeb Cymru Fydd warns the English government that it is accountable for any harm done to the English child by Welsh freedom fighters. If English mercenaries continue their searches and other acts of aggression in Wales, innocent people may be hurt. The disappearance or detainment of Welsh nationalists shows how morally bankrupt the English government has become."

There was more of the same. Peter jotted until Davies stopped. Then he asked, "Have you any indication who might be responsible for the kidnapping?"

"If I did, would I speculate on it?"

Peter frowned at the evasion. "Does Undeb have any involvement?"

"If that were so, would I be calling you?"

Two evasions. Davies had never been tricky like this

before. It made Peter uneasy. All his alarm bells were shouting now. Davies wouldn't be rash enough for this kind of stunt, surely? He had to find a way to probe. "Look, I know this is volatile—"

Davies cut him off. "I can't talk longer now. I hope you can use the statement."

"When can I record something?"

"I'll call on Wednesday."

"How's the girl-friend?" asked Peter, trying for some of their normal easiness. Gwyn Davies was an old contact, something approaching a friend.

"Married someone else years ago."

For the first time, his voice carried some feeling. Irony? So much for the Aberystwyth colleague's claim that Davies was in Cardiff for romance.

"Right. Call me at BBC on Wednesday—about ten in the morning?"

"Yes. *Da boch.*" The phone connection buzzed and clicked laboriously as he rang off.

Peter held the receiver a moment, then replaced it, unnerved. He checked the tape in his portable recorder, which was hooked to the phone by a suction pick-up. The tape wasn't broadcast quality, but at least it was proof against cries of misquote, a favourite government response to unwelcome revelations. On second thought, remembering last night's theft, he flipped the cassette out of the machine and put it in his pocket.

The flat's door had swung open again in Al's wake. Peter walked out to find four men waiting in the dim corridor.

"Sorry to startle you, old man. Didn't want to shove into your phone conversation."

"Teddy." Peter belted his trench coat, angry to find his heart was pounding time and a half. First Gwyn, now Teddy. He was getting paranoid. "I'm just on my way out on assignment."

"Met your photog down below. Hard luck. Just stepping out for eighteen holes. Thought you might join us.

Short straw goes caddy.'' Teddy turned quickly at a sound on the stairs. Al had come back in and was standing at the bottom.

"Maybe another time." Golf? Teddy could prove to be a right pain in the arse one way or another. Peter nodded to the other three on his way to the stairs. One tall with prematurely grey hair, two shorter, all three as tanned as Teddy. They followed him out. "Thanks for stopping by anyway."

"Remember what I said about the palm tree," Teddy said genially on the pavement as Peter got into Al's car. "Anyone who works Sunday mornings definitely needs a break."

"Right. Thanks for thinking of me. Sorry." Al burned away from the curb before Peter got his door closed.

"I met him the other day," Peter said to Al's careful silence as they rattled through quiet streets. "Locked himself out of his car."

"Yeah. The white Volvo."

"You know him?"

Al looked at him sidelong. "No. Are you sure you do?"

"Right. Spit it up."

"They've been tailing me."

"Get away," Peter said half-heartedly. It wouldn't take much to convince him.

Al handed him a scrap of newsprint scrawled with a license-plate number.

"Everyone wants me to take a holiday," Peter said absently, looking at the slip. First Nigel, now Teddy.

"Yeah? Make sure it's not permanent."

"Think he's undercover?"

"Reeks of it."

Peter nodded. Grenvile was protecting his investment. Clumsy but predictable. He dismissed it.

The rainy streets were almost empty of traffic. As they crossed town Al swore imaginatively at the first few Union Jacks he saw in house windows, then fell silent. Half an hour later, Peter pounded the door of Owen Thomas's flat in Connaught Road. No answer, and it was already quarter past ten. Al Rees leaned against the wall, unwrapping a new stick of gum.

"Try later?"

"I'd like that Polaroid shot of the arrest," Peter said.

"Ivory-tower boy, remember. All those university people have their heads in the clouds," observed Al. "Maybe he forgot."

Peter peered around the dim hallway, which smelled of moth-balls and dead fish. Another doorway faced Owen's. He knocked, and it opened with a speed that suggested a well-used keyhole. A grossly overweight woman with dirty hair looked out.

"I'm looking for Mr. Thomas."

"You and everyone else." Her voice was North London and self-righteous. "They came for him last night. Police. One of them nationalists, was he." It wasn't a question.

Owen Thomas arrested?

"He had something for me." Seeing suspicion grow in her enfolded eyes, he added quickly. "I'm Peter Holt of BBC Wales. You saw the arrest? I'd like to interview you."

"I don't know about that. . . ." Her hand flew to her greasy hair.

"Maybe tomorrow." Waste of time.

Downstairs, Peter found Al propping up the front door jamb. He was scowling across the street at a black post-war Austin with a nationalist bumper sticker and clear plastic taped over the broken passenger window. Peter had sat beside that defunct window as the driver drifted around corners like a Le Mans finalist. No mistaking that wreck. Through the cracked windscreen he saw the usual litter of Undeb Cymru Fydd pamphlets on the seat and floor. A damp parking-violation tag was pinned under one windscreen wiper. Al folded it carefully back to reveal the date. Monday 11 January. The day before the kidnapping. Peter watched as Al pushed in the window plastic and opened the door.

"Owen doesn't need any more parking fines. I'm moving the car."

"You can't just nick it," Peter said, taken aback. "And that's not Owen's."

Al lifted the bonnet, did something with wires behind the block, and quietly closed it again. He slid behind the wheel, straight black hair falling over his face. The Austin's starter chewed away until finally the motor caught.

"Mind taking my camera case? Meet me at my flat in an hour."

Peter reached through the open driver's window and seized the wheel. It gave him at least the illusion of having a grip on something, right now. Al stared back at him with black-eyed, unfathomable gravity.

"Gwyn must have sold Owen his car." Peter glanced away and lifted his hand. "I probably wouldn't even recognize it."

Al nodded. "Someone could get the wrong impression."

"Right." Peter watched the Austin rattle away.

PEN Y CAE/JANUARY 17/2100

All the rest of them were being hunted, Carrie thought, though for different reasons.

Pip was hunted nation-wide because an hysterical England demanded his safety; the Prince was not only his parents' darling, but the country's. Fleet Street, as bursts of talk on the radio indicated, had arbitrarily tagged the royal nanny as a heroine who must be rescued. The terrorists were hunted in revenge. Whatever happened now, they would die if they were captured.

No one was hunting for Carrie. She wondered if anyone had even missed her yet. She had just picked up her dole cheque. Her rent wasn't due for nearly two weeks. Ann, her neighbour, was visiting friends in Welshpool. The immigration officer at the American Consulate had probably dismissed her as unpunctual and demoted her to the bottom of his list. Mam would think nothing much of her failure to ring on Sunday night. No one else would notice her absence. She would have to depend on the English child and the nanny being rescued.

On Carrie's fifth evening at Pen y Cae, she stood in the radio room watching the American's hands move on his dials and gauges as he sought some remaining point of contact with the larger world. Gathering around the radio was becoming ritual. It amplified the events that bound together their lives, and perhaps their deaths, thought Carrie.

Madog began to whistle. Nora had draped herself over his shoulder, but, drawing no response from him, she finally took herself off scowling to pace around the room. Nora didn't take well to being ignored. The others slouched on the cot and chairs, waiting for something to happen.

"Parasite," Nora said, with the usual curl to her lip, pointing to the grey cat purring on Carrie's shoulder. She tapped the shotgun, which she held against her shoulder. Since she'd recovered it from Madog's priest's hole, she hadn't let it out of her sight long enough to forfeit it a second time.

Carrie ignored her. If there were any parasite here, it was Nora, simultaneously feeding on Britain and attacking it. A repressive government only gave her kind, terrorists, a rationale for destruction.

Carrie watched over the American's shoulder. Numbers tracked across gauges, the only lights in the radio room, as the distant voices rose and fell in bursts. Pal stopped purring. She glanced at the cat's ears, lying flat behind slitted eyes. Never willing to let her hysteria drop, Nora had shoved the gun against his head. Madog leaned back in his wooden chair without a word, laid a finger on the barrel, and directed it away. More than Gwyn Davies would do for a living soul.

"Look at the fat thing." Nora was still trying. She blew

her vile cigarette smoke towards Carrie. "We should drown it."

"He's a mouser. He earns his keep," Carrie said clearly and simply for even the Irishwoman to understand. "He hunts mice. Vermin. Parasites on society."

Nora eyed her coldly, looking to see if Madog watched. She'd started that after the police visit last night, after she reappeared on the American's heels half-dressed and wholly pleased with herself. Carrie had seen the sleek Italian look amused and perhaps relieved. Gwyn had looked disgusted. Carrie tried to imagine Nora seducing Gwyn Davies. He was more interested in politics than sex, except when the two coincided. In the glowing eyes and adolescent body of Elen Parry, for example. Elen would sort it out soon enough. Nora had thoroughly annoyed everyone by now, except perhaps Madog. Carrie's curiosity drifted towards their hasty union. What did he see . . . ?

On the cot, Pip curled between Jean Douglass and Elen. The red-haired Cadwyn girl was probing about the Scottish Nationalist Party again, though she seemed better informed than the nanny. The Douglass woman, haggard, answered tersely and encouraged no further conversation. She glanced up to find Carrie's eyes on her and her face hardened. She still chose to believe Carrie was one of the terrorists. The boy clutched Mungo Mouse and watched Pal sadly, forbidden to go near Carrie or her cat.

Outside, the wind hissed around Pen y Cae, salting the old stone house with snow, which now almost covered the ground. Dry snow, said the American this morning, like the arctic. It squeaked when you walked on it, and when it was deep enough you could cut it into blocks for an igloo. The little boy, excited, had wanted to build a snow fort in the yard. Gwyn had vetoed the idea; Carrie had seen no harm, until old John's visit from Cae Isa. Now Sion was on watch downstairs, probably helping himself to their small food supply. Carrie felt more alone than usual, even with Pal once again purring against her neck.

"Listen here," said Madog happily. "They're playing our song."

Gwyn shot him a sullen look. This operation, his grand gesture, was to be taken seriously, and Madog wasn't co-operating. What did he expect from an American? But Gwyn Davies was now quite outside Carrie's comprehension. Why had the arrogant shit drawn her into this mess? Typical of his disdain for the rest of humanity.

Carrie leaned towards the radio as Madog turned up the volume. It was one of the short-wave messages that paused for news broadcasts, relayed informally and with much comment.

"—so now they've thrown the nationalist party leader in jail," a woman said conversationally in learner's Welsh. "It doesn't seem fair the way they punish legitimate political types for their other problems."

"Maybe they think he has the lad locked in his cellar?" a man asked.

The band crackled with laughter, fading under the whine of empty ether as Madog tuned on down the dial. At last he switched off the set.

"The Plaid Cymru president arrested?" Gwyn, propped in the door, frowned around the room. "Grenvile had better put an end to that right now."

Raffael shrugged and steepled his slender fingers. "When you call tomorrow, give him another reminder about the Getty boy."

Gwyn said something under his breath and swung abruptly out onto the landing. Elen silently followed him downstairs. Raffael stood with a courtly gesture to the nanny; it was his turn to guard the hostages overnight. She picked up the sleepy child and clumped down the stairs in her sensible shoes. Carrie kept to her shadowed corner, reluctant to leave. Nora smiled an elaborate welcome at Madog, who only gave her a friendly nod and disappeared into his room across the landing. The Irishwoman watched the closing door with undisguised dismay. Carrie glanced away in time to avoid her eyes, and Nora went downstairs after the others. Carrie sighed and settled cross-legged on the cot. Solitude.

Long after midnight, she slid the dusty curtain back from the window and watched the half-moon sail between clouds. Somewhere outside, a wind chime clanged melodically. Pal crawled down from her shoulder to her folded arms and licked her chin.

"What did we do to deserve this, my dear? Guns pointed at our heads, trouble coming and going? How are we going to get out of this one?"

Pal, tired of her talk, prowled across the dark radio console to the window sill. Carrie idly touched the controls and pushed the button Madog had used to switch the set off. Silently, three midnight-green rectangles lit on the board, and green digital numbers marched across one of them. Carrie peered at the tangle of equipment, perplexed, wondering about the transmitter. She couldn't see a microphone.

She murmured, "Well then, Pal. How do you suppose this might work?"

A cough from the doorway jerked her upright. The American padded up behind her and reached down to the board. Darkness repossessed the room.

"Sorry, little lady," he said. "You just sit here all you like. Didn't know I left this stuff turned on."

On the sill, Pal bottled into a Hallowe'en cat and growled quietly. Madog hesitated at the door on his way out again.

"That's some smart cat you got. Had him a long time?"

Carrie let out her breath. "Nine, ten years."

"Why don't you speak Welsh?" asked Madog unexpectedly, leaning in the dark doorway with his arms folded. He was wearing a long cotton robe patterned in white and blue chain-links. It looked Japanese and much worn.

Carrie narrowed her eyes, trying to work out what he wanted. "What makes you think I can?"

"Gwyn."

"Gwyn—" she started angrily, and stopped. "People like Gwyn are the reason I don't."

"People like what?" He sounded curious and quieter than usual.

"Holier than thou. More Welsh than thou. More dedicated than thou. More anything else you can name. What about the majority of people in this country who don't speak Welsh? Are they less Welsh? Gwyn Davies thinks so."

"Well, now." Madog took up his American drawl. "Straight talk from *Miss Ceridwen fach.*"

"Huh," Carrie sniffed and lifted Pal off the radio. He crouched on the table, watching her from eyes that shone yellow in the dark. As an afterthought she said, "Don't call me that."

"Courtesy of John Hughes, Cae Isa. Why do you hate Gwyn?"

"Ask Gwyn, if he's grown so talkative." She shrugged. "I don't hate him. But he should have known better than to drag me into this mess."

"No." Madog considered her. "That was Sion. Gwyn didn't know it was you until you got here. He was upset."

"I don't believe that for a minute."

"Believe what you like, ma'am. But only in English."

Madog stepped soundlessly into the room, and Carrie stiffened as he reached past her towards the radio table. He pulled paper and pencil from a drawer and scribbled something.

"Here you go. Now sit in the corner with it. Isn't that what they used to do around here when kids talked Welsh in school? Make them sit in the corner with a 'Welsh Not' sign?"

Carrie turned the sheet right side up and read his scrawled "Welsh Not." She looked up, frowning.

"Forget it," said Madog. "Looks to me like they've done a real good job on you already, Miss Powell." He turned for the door again.

"Gran had one of them. In the loft at home."

The American paused. She looked at the sheet, grudging any personal knowledge to this *dieithr,* this meddling foreigner. But he wasn't Welshless, as the word meant.

"What did she think about all that? Being told she couldn't speak Welsh in school and all?"

"She put little frogs in the teacher's well and hung a dead chicken from his apple tree. And she moved things about his house whenever he went out. He decided to go back to England." Carrie smiled a little as she remembered the old tale. Pal chirred and stepped delicately from the table up onto her shoulder. "Childish, really."

"Some might think so," Madog said quietly. "Some might think house-burnings or bombs were a more grown-up way of handling it."

Carrie stared across the dimness, trying to read his expression. Outside, the moon swam into cloud. All she could see was a glimmer at his eyes and the robe's white squares. No gleam from his gold tooth.

"Care to give that back?" asked Madog, as he settled himself on the cot.

Carrie handed over the "Welsh Not" placard.

"Rhaid i ti siarad Cymraeg 'rŵan," he said, you have to speak Welsh now.

"O'r goreu," she agreed. "What do you want to hear? Navel-gazing at the splendours of Welsh history? Melodrama about a dying country?"

"I don't think you believe that."

She didn't answer, only clasped her hands in her lap. Pal rubbed his velvet head against the angle of her jaw and yawned.

"You asked me about Pittsburgh."

"I'm emigrating. My cousin there will sponsor me. As soon as you people come to your senses and let us go free." Carrie leaned forward suddenly, forgetting for a moment that he was her jailer. "Don't you realize you can't win this sort of game? Don't you understand what the authorities will do to you? They're all savages—*heddlu cudd* in Shrewsbury, SAS in Hereford."

"You surprise me, *Miss Ceridwen fach*. I thought you were loyal to the royal family and so on."

"Did you really?" She pulled Pal's tail and he kneaded her arm with his claws retracted. "But if you think I support this lunacy, you're wrong. What do you want?"

"Nothing, really." He stirred restlessly. "You won't like Pittsburgh. Once you get there, move on."

"What would I like?" She was glad of the change of direction.

"Seattle." His teeth flashed with occluded moonlight. "The Pacific northwest."

"Why?"

"Alan Hovhaness lives there, so it must be all right. The composer. Heard of 'Floating World?' 'Mountains and Rivers Without End?' "

Carrie shook her head. "Mountains and rivers without end. That's us."

"Korea, not Wales. I used to listen to him on tape, stuck in—somewhere in the East. I used to wish it were more like that. Temple bells, wind. Seattle's the place. As far west as you can go, next stop Tokyo."

"You're from there."

"And the San Juans. Those are the islands between the U.S. and Canada. Come to think of it, San Juan Island's better than Seattle."

"Tell me." An island sounded more interesting than Pittsburgh, despite kind-hearted cousin Mair's flood of picture postcards. "Are there jobs there?"

"Depends. In the summer there are lots of tourists at Friday Harbor. In the winter people get by on rock cod and pit-lamped venison and a lot of rabbit, and swear about next year's tourists."

"What's special about it?" she challenged. She wanted to be told of a golden island, unlike barren Bardsey with its twenty thousand Welsh saints. She was sick of sexless saints and self-made martyrs.

"Islanders are different. You can walk miles along the beach and see what's washed up from the salmon boats.

Great sunsets. Maybe it's just one of those places. Or maybe it's just home.'' He sounded apologetic, caught rambling.

"Madog from the island in the west," she tried, wondering if he knew the connection.

"Uh-huh. Like naming someone after Kubla Khan. I used to hate my name, until Dad told me about Madog, the Welsh prince who settled America three hundred years before Columbus.''

Of course he would know about Madog the explorer. Americans were crazy for family roots, for a sense of belonging. Why wasn't it enough just to be American? Maybe people needed more than three generations to feel part of a country. Maybe the old Welsh were right; a family was nine generations. Carrie stroked Pal's dense, short fur, wondering how long this interruption would delay her emigration approval. She refused to think it would destroy her chances forever.

"Do the Indians still speak Welsh?''

"The Mandans were the ones who were supposed to be Prince Madog's descendants. They died out from smallpox around 1840. The Europeans wiped out dozens of tribes one way or another.''

"Americans, you mean.''

"Where do you think Americans came from? Most of them. Americans, Europeans, either way, the Indians died.''

"Were they really Welsh?''

He made a sound that could be regret or laughter. "The last one died before anyone was able to prove they didn't speak Welsh. So it didn't spoil a good story.''

Carrie smiled. "A disbeliever? How un-American.''

"Miss Ceridwen fach, we're not all—ah, forget it.''

"Not all boors?'' Carrie suggested, half in apology. "If I didn't know that, I wouldn't be emigrating. Why aren't you there? On your island?''

"Too many boors,'' Madog said. Apology accepted. He also slipped back into English, perhaps without noticing.

"There are plenty of good old boys in the islands. I guess it's like that anywhere people live on their wits and their pride and not much else. They tend to get preoccupied with their own self-reliance."

"What was it like growing up there?" Carrie clung to the voice across the dark room. It was real, a denial of death and terror. It was also a warm, sensual voice.

"I survived, at first. I was a rich kid, a city kid, shipped off to live with my grandparents. I got so good at being like everybody else I even started to think the island was a hole, until I left it. I used to roar around those gravel roads in a '54 Merc without windows. Danny—my buddy—drove a four-by-four with enough chrome on it to blind you. Did it all himself, a few dollars at a time."

"What was he trying to prove?" Carrie guessed he was talking more to himself than to her. As long as he kept talking.

"Same as everyone. That he existed, that he had some value in the world. His old man was a boozer, used to poor-mouth the kids and knock them around."

Carrie nodded and bit her tongue against offering sympathy. Too much alcohol, too much chapel, too much want, there wasn't really much difference.

"Did he prove it?"

"I guess. He was always trying to do the right thing. He did it so good, he went to Vietnam as a lieutenant. His troop fragged him the first week out. If he had been more like his old man, he'd be around today."

"Fragged?" Carrie was puzzled.

"Fragmentation grenade. they blew him up. His own guys." Madog switched back to Welsh. "I'm sorry. This isn't anything you want to know about America."

"Were you there? When they murdered him?"

"It's late, *Miss Ceridwen fach.*"

Madog stood up and shoved his hands into his robe's wide sleeves. Temple bells and wind, Carrie reflected. Mountains and rivers without end. A refuge. They had invaded his refuge, and he had nowhere left to retreat. She saw but didn't understand.

Very quietly, back turned, he added, "If anyone had been there, there's nothing that could have been done to prevent it."

"But you didn't learn. That fragging, that was terrorism. But you didn't learn a damned thing," Carrie objected, irrationally angry. "Here you are now, making love to death."

Madog laughed soundlessly. "Making love to death. I guess that's Nora, all right. So you don't think much of my taste."

"None of my business." Even to herself Carrie sounded like a maiden aunt.

"Too bad." He grinned. "Nora's starting to figure out we're all hostages. Not just the kid and Jean and you, the innocent bystanders. Of course, Nora would say there are no innocents in war."

"Rubbish," said Carrie, rising to her feet.

"Miss Ceridwen fach—"

"Shut up."

"Yes ma'am." His sham obedience was worse than argument. "About me and Nora the Death. Where does that put you and Gwyn Davies?"

Carrie drew in her breath for an answer and Pal dug his claws deep into her shoulder.

"That was a long time ago."

"Good." Madog turned around and walked close enough to clasp her arms. His touch was light. "Carrie."

"Yes." Carrie slipped her hands inside his cotton robe, warming herself at his warmth. A fine gold chain hung around his neck, bearing something that felt like chipped stone.

"An arrowhead. My great-great-grandmother was a Mandan Indian." He said it in an offhand mocking voice, demanding her disbelief. Did that mean it was true? He did it often.

Madog stooped, and Carrie stretched to meet his kiss.

She barely noticed when Pal leaped from her shoulder and ambled off downstairs.

Moonlight lit the feather quilt on Madog's bed and the white folds of the Berwyns outside his south-facing window: peaceful, silent, radiant. Carrie slipped out of her skirt and sweater, grateful for human company. She supposed Madog's love-making would embody all his watchfulness, all his self-mockery, and scarcely cared. But he was gentle, meticulous, carefully paced. A skilful lover, Carrie realized as the edge of the current caught her and swept her into a flood of sensual pleasure. Later, when they lay tangled together in languid satisfaction, they laughed at something she could never afterwards remember, and fell asleep. Before the half-moon slid west beyond the window frame, she awakened him from a troubled dream. He muttered about bamboo, rolled over, and slept like the dead until morning. After a while Pal pushed the door open, slid in, and curled at her feet. Outside the window, the chimes clanged and were still. Temple bells, wind. Carrie lay awake thinking until the cold dawn, hands clasped behind her head, once again a prisoner.

10

The BBC Wales switchboard seized up in a welter of incoming calls. Reporters in other cubicles cursed, trying to reach contacts for a noon deadline. Peter, an old hand, gave it up as a lost cause and ambled out to use a coin box. If he'd wanted, he could have pulled rank for a clear line. These days, Peter Holt's face appeared every evening on the news. Even gormless Harry Price, who revelled in Peter's disgrace this spring, suddenly treated him with unaccustomed caution. Like others who had only themselves to sell, thought Peter, reporters ranked their peers by number of tricks turned.

Leaning against the glassless call-box door, he leafed through the green coil-back school notebook he'd bought yesterday. He'd spent an hour jotting notes and phone numbers from the disorderly sheaf of newsprint he'd accumulated on the kidnapping and protest stories. Most of the scribble he'd discarded, the rest he copied with carnivorous attention. It was one of Peter's ways of sifting through his hunches about a story, sussing out the unspoken and unwritten missing links. This time the process left him with disjointed comments and a list of phone numbers, each one an apparent dead end.

Later he had flipped his video cassettes forward, backward, slow motion, high speed, stop frame, anything to

181

extract pattern from chaos. He concentrated on faces at the London kidnapping. Two fake security guards, two fake photographers, one of whom called out to Miss Jean Douglass. Was his voice slightly accented? Were all four Welsh? IRA? Something else? The faces were legion, suggesting no particular European or new-world country. Palestinian? French? Brazilian? If Grenvile and his people knew, they weren't telling.

Next Peter concentrated on the royal nanny. Over and over again, as he ran the tape back and forth, Douglass lifted her head at the photographer's greeting, "Jeannie!" Then she glanced, calculating some safety margin, at the Queen. How could he find out if the nanny was part of the plot? Her brother was unhelpful. Her friends were few and discreet. Who else could give personal information, something that might establish a motive?

Time to doggedly retrace his steps with a sharper ear. As he dialled the first number, he pictured the grim North London off-licence where the phone was ringing. Peter fidgeted nervously about the phone box, picking flakes of red paint off the walls.

"Sandy? Sure," answered a girl of about fourteen. The connection was poor, but no worse than the traffic noise and wind outside. "Just a tick."

Jean Douglass's brother identified himself hoarsely when he finally took the phone. He sounded half-asleep and thoroughly hung over.

Peter, feeling a fool, tried his long shot. He strained his light voice down an octave and gave himself an indeterminate accent. It was a wild chance, based on the photographer's voice and his hunches about foreign cohorts.

"Sandy, you must help me."

Sandy demanded blearily, "Who is this?"

"You know better than asking," improvised Peter. "Remember a week ago."

A short pause. "Christ. What the hell do *you* want?"

"Queekly," Peter said, hating the amateur theatricals,

but interested in the reaction. "The name of your sister's doctor. We have trouble."

"Christ," mumbled Sandy Douglass again. Not a sparkling early riser, that much was clear. "How the bloody hell should I know?"

"Queekly."

"What's it worth?"

What was this? He'd have to wing it. "Name your figure."

"A thousand, this time."

"Are you mad?" Peter said with some sincerity.

"It's a little different now, isn't it? A raffle? We're not talking about a snapshot, are we?" Sandy sounded more coherent. He was waking up.

"So? Tell me. You have the thousand tomorrow."

"Jamieson. Doctor Ronald Jamieson. What—"

Panicking, Peter snapped his finger onto the crossbar. Immediately, he cursed himself. If he'd persisted, what else could he have discovered?

Sandy Douglass knew something. He had taken money from—whom? Whoever he believed Peter was. The money was for a snapshot. An identifying photo of someone crucial to the plan? The Queen and the heir apparent were too well known to need identification. A snapshot of his sister Jean? it almost made a pattern. Peter leaned in the draughty call-box, looking at his notes.

A thousand this time. It's a little different now. Isn't it. A raffle. We're not talking about a snapshot. Are we.

It must mean something. Peter fought the call-box door open and started back to the office. At the curb ahead idled a battered black Mini with Ceredigion plates and an oval Cymru sticker. The driver had greasy hair to his denim shoulders; a woolly-back. Back-country lad or not, he'd get a twenty-five-pound fine if he lingered there. Peter thought of warning him, then remembered the last time he helped a motorist in distress. Teddy had rung twice this morning; Peter had fortunately convinced the switchboard to intercept his calls. As he walked nearer he met the man's eyes in the cracked side mirror, then uncomfortably went on. Not his problem anyway.

Message notes adorned the phone in Peter's cubicle. Cliff Aslin, wanting to know about more material for the CBS news feature. Al Rees, claiming to have new information. Elizabeth, something about Andrea. Bloody hell, he'd promised to pick the kid up after school Friday. It had slipped his mind completely. He didn't know which was worse, the tongue-lashing he faced from Elizabeth about his responsibilities, or Andy's staunch support. It's okay, Daddy, really. Peter crumpled the notes into a ball and flung them across the flimsy partition. One waste basket for every two reporters, another BBC economy measure.

First, Grenvile. The lines were open. The major took the Scotland Yard phone before Peter had time to flip his notebook open.

"Peter Holt here. I got your message." He didn't add, from Nigel. Who could guess what these people considered confidential? He also didn't mention the genial and persistent Teddy. Peter was starting to share Al Rees's wholesale suspicion of *heddlu cudd,* secret police.

"Excellent. We'd like you in London this afternoon," Grenvile said, with no trace of his recent laryngitis. "Can you make the noon train, with your notes and tapes?"

"No," Peter said on reflex, buying time to think.

"It's cleared with your superiors."

Twice they'd said that, and it annoyed Peter even more the second time. "It's not cleared with me. The biggest story in ten years, and you expect me to drop it for a stroll to London? And who cleared it, McKinley? I don't answer to him. I can still get the sack from the Old Man here in BBC Wales for meddling in something like this."

There were other reasons Peter didn't trust someone like Grenvile to understand, like the breach of an ethical system too rarely discussed or defined, or his own personal horror of becoming part of the news.

"It's extremely—" Grenvile put his hand over the receiver and Peter heard a faint woman's voice in the London background. "Mr. Holt, it's essential."

"What have you people uncovered?"

"Mr. Holt, would you mind calling back from the director's office?"

Did that mean BBC reporters' lines were tapped? No time to worry about it now. He sprinted up the corridor.

Fortunately, the Old Man was in a meeting. Peter ran a gauntlet of hostile secretarial eyes and sat himself gingerly behind the massive desk, a relic salvaged from a Glamorgan court-house. His coil-back notebook looked shabby and forlorn on the oiled oak as he dialled out. Grenvile answered the phone himself again. Getting rather chummy with the press, surely, for a military-intelligence hostage negotiator? But then Grenvile was the operation's head negotiator.

"Right. What can you tell me, Major?" Peter reckoned he might as well brazen it through.

"Anything I tell you is in confidence, you understand. You may get clearance to use some of it afterwards, but now it's for your personal clarification only. If we see it on the air, it's a fabrication. Understood?"

"Understood." It was better than he expected.

"The kidnappers called us," Grenvile said. "Their contact claimed they were calling from London, but we were able to establish from background noise that he was phoning from a Welsh-speaking part of Wales."

"Where?" demanded Peter.

"We're pin-pointing that now. We put out some erroneous information on television, commercial radio, and short wave-but different information on the different media."

"What kind of information?"

"Have you heard the Welsh Nationalist Party president is being detained for questioning?"

"A rumor to that effect." Picked up from Al Rees, who in turn picked it up from his *clecs* grapevine. "But I phoned him. He was in his office this morning saying otherwise.''

"Precisely. He was never arrested, but the news of his arrest was broadcast on short-wave radio. Our kidnappers respond only to the medium-wave and short-wave information. We'll see what they mention next time.''

"So why do you think I can help you?''

"You have good contacts. We're still a long way from locating these people, Mr. Holt. We need every scrap of information we can find.''

"Right." Peter scrubbed his hand over his eyes. Not enough sleep last night, or bad dreams. "Go ahead. I'll tell you what I can." He would cooperate with Grenvile as long as it benefited his story, but not if it would destroy his credibility as a reporter. It was beginning to look like a tightwire act with a long drop.

"Who have you talked to?" Grenvile asked. "Of the nationalists?''

"The usual people." Peter grasped at names. "Meleri Lewis. Owen Thomas, though I heard he was pulled in for questioning. I couldn't reach as many as I hoped.''

"Are they involved?''

"Couldn't say." And wouldn't. Why set an investigation on harmless people who were also good contacts?

"Do you know Ceridwen Powell? Registered nurse? Transmitter bombing a few years ago?''

"I remember the case. Who doesn't? I never met her.''

"What about Sion ap Huw?''

"No answer at his flat in Aberystwyth. I didn't worry about him, Major. Sion's all talk.''

"Let me see—John Hugh Weatherby. Alias Jack Weston. Alias Sion ap Huw. Two years armed service, dishonourable discharge for trafficking cocaine—four years in prison, pre-release to hostel in Aberystwyth, educational privileges.'' Grenvile's voice had the abstracted quality of someone leafing through a file. "For someone who's all talk, Mr. Holt, he has a bad record.''

"Right." But he was still a *twpsyn,* a stupid forlorn shit.

"What about Gwyn Davies?"

"I took a Future Wales statement from him yesterday."

"In Cardiff?"

"He phoned me from Bangor. I'd been trying to reach him in Aberystwyth."

"I see." Grenvile was silent a moment, perhaps making a note. "And you won't come to London."

"It would be somewhat inconvenient." Suddenly, Peter was developing a sense of diplomacy. "Glad to help you from here."

"Excellent."

"Now—" Peter was anxious to press his advantage "—I'm putting together an update for the BBC evening news and a feature for CBS in the States. What can you give me officially?"

Damned little, Peter thought as he scratched shorthand into his notebook. Searchers and investigators were doing their utmost. As soon as the kidnappers were found, face-to-face negotiation would be established. And so on. But it was something, at least, from a man whose very existence had been denied when Peter last rang Scotland Yard.

"Sorry you missed your daughter's weekend visit, Mr. Holt. Working too hard?"

It caught Peter off guard. He hadn't asked what would happen if he didn't co-operate. He didn't have much dirty linen hidden away. He wasn't susceptible to most kinds of pressure. But he was susceptible to threats about Andrea. Innocent little boy in terrorists' hands, royal crisis, national outrage, journalist ethics: they didn't add up to enough reason to let the bastards bring Andrea into this as another hostage. Silent, he clenched the pencil hard enough to give it a green-stick fracture, fighting his need to tell Grenvile where to shove it and how high.

"Right."

"Keep in touch," Grenvile said pleasantly.

Peter rang off, hoping the slam of the receiver carried

all the way to London. He glanced down and realized he was trisecting right-angle triangles on the Old Man's ivory hand-laid desk blotter. Guiltily he launched himself out of the soft armchair. He didn't trust the phones. He'd drop round to the *Cardiff Courier* office to see Al.

In the car park, as he coaxed and choked his old Renault to life, he saw the back-country lad's Mini parked illegally in another numbered stall. The commissionaire would get after him. But as Peter lurched into Llantrisant Road, he saw the woolly-back in the black Mini start after him. *Duw, Duw.* If this was Al Rees's idea, it was definitely time for a talk.

"Let's hear it again." Al cupped both brown hands around a steaming coffee mug in his sister's dockyard café. Bronwen's place was posh compared to the Blackburn fish-and-chip shop where Peter's mum worked. Broni's place had framed jigsaw puzzles on the wall and a juke-box playing Shirley Bassey; the Tiger Bay girl who made good was singing something slow and sultry. "It doesn't make sense."

Peter hunched in the booth, flipping back through his shorthand and phonetic scribble.

"A thousand this time. It's a little different now. Isn't it. A raffle. We're not talking about a snapshot. Are we."

"A raffle?" said Al. "What raffle?"

Peter replayed his memory for tone of voice. Easier if he'd used his suction wire-tap, but he hadn't thought of it. Tone of voice, stress, and inflection. He ran through it again.

"A thousand—*this* time. It's a little *different* now, *isn't* it? A raffle. We're not *talking* about a *snapshot*, are we?"

Al shrugged.

"Maybe it's a name," Peter said suddenly. "A man's name."

"Raffle doesn't sound— What about Raphael?"

"It's a little *different* now, *isn't* it, Raphael?" tried Peter.

As Al finished his coffee, his sister stumped over with refills. Bronwen, all fifteen stone of her in a Day-Glo muumuu, beamed at them and wedged herself behind the counter again. "But Raphael who?"

"He has some kind of accent, anyway. And he sold Sandy a snapshot."

"A photographer," said Al, tapping the aluminum case on the seat beside him.

"My bloody oath," mumbled Peter, and spilled his coffee. Bronwen surged over to the booth clucking in concern, mopped up, and gave him another. "Those photographers in Kensington High Street—a man and a woman."

"Yeah. The man stopped and fixed his scarf, a real clothes-horse. I remember from the ITN tape."

Peter got up. "Broni, love, use your phone?"

At New Scotland Yard one of the technicians called Grenvile to the phone.

"Do you have an ID on the photographers at the kidnapping?" demanded Peter as Bronwen mopped the counter around his elbow.

"We're examining photographs that have been electronically enhanced from the ITN tape. Why?"

"What about Interpol?"

Grenvile hesitated. "When it comes to identifications and persona profiles on terrorists, you must understand that Interpol files are also available to nations that don't share our specific political concerns."

"Libya, for example?"

Grenvile didn't bite. "The commissioner here is working with Interpol, but we don't know what we can expect. We've also found them slow to co-operate on matters of terrorism as opposed to crime. It's the same with all the United Nations agencies these days. Why do you ask, Mr. Holt?"

Peter quickly calculated his information's trading value. That was a negotiator's method, wasn't it? Trade information for information, bodies for bodies? He said, "The

photographer, the man, may speak English with a notice-
able accent. His given or family name may be Raphael.''

After a pause, long enough to hand over a hasty note
for GCHQ at Cheltenham or for Scotland Yard's Technical
Support Branch, Grenvile was back. ''Excellent, Mr. Holt.
Just the sort of thing we hope for.''

''It may be nothing,'' Peter cautioned, and decided it
was time to trade. ''Now, what about a little more detail
on the search operation?''

Al Rees smiled benevolently over his coffee as Peter
scribbled.

ABERYSTWYTH/JANUARY 18/0800

''Dangerous, phoning from Aberystwyth,'' was Gwyn's
only comment as he and Raffael walked down the frozen
ruts to John Hughes's house.

''Yes,'' Raffael agreed. These days, he was notably
neutral. ''But you have used the same phone three times
running, and that is more dangerous.''

Gwyn wrestled John's borrowed Land Rover down the
tracks to the Llanygroes road. The fog-lamps penetrated
only a yard or two into the pre-dawn ground mist. Aberystwyth was two hours' driving even on main roads, but
he would use sheep tracks and lanes barely significant
enough for the Ordnance Survey to map. For the first time
in days, Gwyn felt alive instead of half suffocated. If he
could have planned strategy for the back country, instead
of their panic-stricken flight from London, things would
have been so much easier.

But it was too late to articulate such thoughts in the
conditional, least of all to Raffael. They said nothing more
to each other for miles. The Brigatisto was no longer his
instructor; Gwyn was no longer a student sweating over
maps and negotiation drill in the Libyan barracks. He had
graduated with honours, apart from the final test of Constable Drake, Thames Division. Once, long ago, before a
man died in a transmitter shed, before Corgi's murders,

which were also morally his murders, he would have thought that a victory of courage and decency. Now. . . .

Aber lay congealed in morning fog. Gwyn drove past the residences where Carrie Powell had long ago smuggled her striped kitten in under the warden's nose, past the National Library, past the University College of Wales buildings where Gwyn had worked last week. Near the railway station, deserted on a winter Monday morning, he parked and entered one of the telephone boxes. Raffael followed him in. It was bitterly cold. Their breath coiled towards the top of the phone box and hung there. Across Alexandra Road, a woman silently lifted dustbin lids, one by one, and searched inside. Newspapers and dirty snow drifted in the gutter. Gwyn took Madog's device from his pocket.

"Another third-party call?" asked Raffael.

"Na. Direct to Grenvile."

Raffael nodded approval. It was starting to rub on Gwyn: Raffael's approval, Raffael's pose of instructor. If he was so damned good, why hadn't he thought of better back-ups for the kidnap and contingency plans for having to leave London? Only Gwyn—and the American, he had to admit—had pulled them out of that disaster. If Raffael had done his job, they wouldn't be desperate now. Gwyn clipped Madog's electronic wonder to the telephone cord, trusting its ability to make the call untraceable, and dialled the Scotland Yard number. He was through to Grenvile within seconds.

"Merlin? Where are you?"

"South London—maybe."

"How are the Prince and Miss Douglass?" The Englishman sounded as cool and pleasant as always. They might be discussing a cricket match.

"They're well."

Gwyn recalled Raffael's training sessions in the Libyan camp. The negotiator's standing orders would be to recover information first, then hostages, while yielding only minor concessions. Gwyn still had the upper hand as long as their location was unknown.

He added, "If you want to be sure, offer something in return."

"What can we offer? What do you want?" asked Grenvile.

"Try the truth. There's nothing on the telly about discussion of home rule, or aid to Welsh industry, or improved Welsh broadcasting. You say you're working on our demands, then you throw the nationalist party president in jail."

"Where did you hear that?"

"Telly."

"What channel?"

"BBC Two," Gwyn lied without hesitation.

"Nonsense. You want the truth?" Grenvile sounded weary. "You're not in London. You're in Wales. You either don't have a television receiver—unlikely, in my experience of hostage-takings—or you're in an area without television reception. That means one of very few possible locations. You're getting your information from amateur radio operators, and if you're operating a licenced radio, we can soon pin-point you. That's the truth, Merlin."

"Interesting," Gwyn tried. "But there are rather large gaps in your information."

"Not many. You've been careless. Especially Miss Powell."

"Who?"

"Merlin, you haven't a prayer of getting out on your own. Now let's talk seriously about handing over your hostages."

"If we haven't a prayer, why haven't you found us?" Gwyn strove to keep a cool head. Anger was what the negotiator wanted. "You underestimate our resources."

"You underestimate ours," Grenvile countered sharply. His civility was wearing thin. "We'll know precisely where you are within a day. When we do, we'll bring in heat seekers and dogs and parabolic microphones. We'll know every word you say, what you eat, the condition of your hostages, the number of gunmen. We'll know when you plan to bolt.''

"Threats, Major Grenvile? That's not how to recover your people.''

"I'll tell you how we'll recover our people. Not by talking. When we have the word from Cabinet, a Special Air Services team will go in. You'll be dead or in prison. You'll have achieved nothing, only injured Wales, which you purport to aid. Your name will be a stain on your country.''

"No," said Gwyn, preoccupied with the new tactics. Grenvile had veered far from the handbook approach. "Do your superiors encourage harassment? Lose your grip and you'll get yourself sacked. Just tell me—''

"What the hell do you think I care about that?'' Grenvile snapped, suddenly hoarse. "Carry on and you'll be talking to an SAS negotiator instead. There's one here waiting at my elbow. Is that what you want?''

Grenvile's voice was shaking. He was speaking out of turn, but it sounded like the truth. Gwyn didn't like it. SAS negotiators, SAS hit squads? Yet first they had to find Pen Y Cae.

"Don't threaten me," Gwyn said angrily and risked offering a warning in the same tone of voice. *"Gwrandwch, rŵan. 'Rydan ni mewn peryg. Mae rhywun wedi dod o hyd i ni. Mae 'na beryg orwth ym mhobl i.''*

Suspicious, Raffael seized the phone from Gwyn.

"No more talk," he said into the receiver. His voice was cold, his eyes frozen on Gwyn. "Do what we tell you, or it will be like Tywyn again. You understand?''

Tywyn? Raffael was mad to drag in Corgi's appalling renegade school bombing at Christmas. Gwyn heard Grenvile speak and reached for the receiver.

Raffael suddenly swore in German and dropped the phone as though it had burned his hand. It swung crashing against the metal wall of the box. Gwyn picked it up.

"Raffael?" asked Grenvile.

They had names! They knew. That explained the Italian's rage. What else did they know?

"Merlin," said Gwyn.

"Who was that?" The negotiator sounded mildly curious.

Gwyn ignored the question. "Stop wasting our time. Don't count on finding us. You can't do it. Just see our demands are carried out. When we hear positive news about Welsh home rule, industry, and television, then we'll exchange the hostages. I won't talk to you again, Grenvile, or any other mercenary. Get someone who understands our position and can make it public."

"You can't—" Grenvile cut himself off and regained his calm. His voice levelled out to its normal timbre. "Whom do you want?"

"Get Peter Holt. The BBC reporter."

"I'll contact him. How will we reach you?"

Raffael had recovered his composure. He seized the phone receiver again and slammed it onto the crossbar. Gwyn removed Madog's gadget from the wire and followed him out into the grey January morning.

It was a small and somewhat bare room in a London office building: desk, filing cabinet, and four inhospitable stacking chairs, now occupied.

"Couldn't agree less. I don't think for a minute they'll harm the kid," said Corgi.

"But I thought they were hardened criminals," objected the high-ranking Home Office man in blazer and flannels.

Corgi was wearing a grey suit, though he would have been more comfortable in battle dress and Balaclava. Identity was bad form, especially since one of the clients was flying no colours. If he really thought a Cabinet minister could be incognito in the television era, he was mistaken.

"They're novices," replied Corgi. "They'll be wetting their drawers by now. I'd guess that Nora, the Provo woman who let the cat out of the bag, is the nearest they come to pro. It gives us prep time."

"She's not," said the Home Office man.

"In any case, the kid has brothers," brayed the chap with political aspirations, crossing his pin-striped legs at the ankle. "All's not lost, if you take my meaning. 'They all moved over and one fell out.' "

Corgi blinked. "Speaking for my lads, sir, we'd like to give it a go. Location should be pinned down soon, I gather. We can move in then. Reccy first, then rescue."

"Patently." The Home Office man looked out the window at a phalanx of grey office buildings. "You know SAS will be there."

"Minor difficulty. We always beat the clock."

"Meanwhile Holt's playing footsie with Grenvile and those other arse-holes in Five and claiming ignorance of the coin of the realm. I swear the man knows more than he tells."

"And if he keeps prying, he'll scotch the entire show," observed the fourth man, the cabinet minister who thought he was incognito.

"Silver bullet?" Corgi smiled. "Stake through the heart?"

"No." The man in the blazer exhaled regret. "You'll find something, with the incentive we offer." It was, for him, rather blunt reference to a commercial exchange in the coin of the realm.

"Something discreet." The pol beamed. "So to speak. Discretionary funds. It will be my pleasure."

The man from the Home Office ignored him. "Then the boy. It will have to look good."

Corgi nodded to all of them and took his leave unnoticed among the lunch-time stampede of office workers.

Pen y Cae felt like home only six days after the kidnapping. Gwyn walked towards the house close behind Raffael, keeping his thumb on the safety catch of the Browning. Nora, on watch, opened the door. She met Raffael's eye and slid back into the entry shadows with her shotgun tipped back on her shoulder. Gwyn called after her before the Brigatisto could usurp any further decisions.

"Get the others. We're discussing our options."

"Everyone?"

"Everyone," Gwyn said abruptly.

Nora leaned in the kitchen doorway with her weight thrown onto one hip and her tongue caught between her teeth, tapping her gun barrel into the palm of her hand. Even at China Lake he'd seen how Nora's lust stirred towards power, especially the power of death. Whoever took control, gave an order, drew Nora's unwelcome interest.

She watched him a few seconds longer, then shrugged, "All right."

At gunpoint, Nora ushered in the kid and Jean Douglass. They sat on the parlour sofa. The nanny's heart-shaped face was grey and haggard with strain, and she held Pip tightly on her lap. The boy, freshly washed and combed, watched gravely as the others came in. He was all ears and wide blue eyes. The heir apparent had not yet learned not to learn; he watched everything going on around him. Gwyn smiled at Jean, and her gaze locked on him. Did she think this was an execution? Sion came out with a handful of cold potatoes and Elen followed. Madog took a position at the stair doorway, within reach of Nora's gun hand. Raffael lounged in an armchair, cool and elegant once again. Silently, the cat on her shoulder, Carrie came in wearing one of the *risqué* dresses from Madog's wardrobe, all chintz and ivory lace. The dress suited her, thought it defined a Carrie he didn't know. Gwyn caught himself staring and turned abruptly to the kitchen.

When they settled, Gwyn said, "We have to decide what to do, quickly." He told them Grenvile's threat about locating them and sending SAS hit teams. "If we can stay hidden they'll lose popular support. People will accuse them of bargaining with the boy's life. The longer it takes them to get him back, the worse they'll look."

Sion swallowed a mouthful of potato. "If they do locate us," he said, "that counts for bugger all. They might lose popular support, but we'll never gain any. Not in England, not for Wales."

Gwyn nodded. "But if we hold out, we've got a chance at it. I told Grenvile to get Peter Holt. With BBC and American coverage we'll get a better hearing."

"Peter Holt's English," Sion objected.

So are you, thought Gwyn. "He knows too much, and he's good at putting things together. The *heddlu cudd* know that. Either we get him working for us, or we may find he's working against us."

"What if he refuses?" asked Madog.

"MI5 will lean on him. They'll tell him BBC could reach an unfortunate misunderstanding about his drinking habits or his girl-friend or a kickback he never took," Gwyn answered. "But he'll be willing. He's addicted to news. Down in BBC they call him Jaws, the great white shark."

"What are our choices?" asked Elen nervously. "If they're talking about SAS we're in trouble."

"We can stay on. That's my advice," Gwyn said. "We can leave, taking the hostages. Or we can leave without the hostages."

The nanny, at the edge of his vision, hugged Pip convulsively. Mungo Mouse tumbled to the floor and lay face down. Elen, beside her on the sofa, recovered the fur-worn doll and put it back in the child's arms. The girl's red hair hung down in a curtain, hiding her face. She leaned forward and rested her elbows on her knees so it stayed that way.

"Logistics," said Raffael mildly. He took out one of his Turkish cigarettes and tapped loose tobbacco on his knee. "The boy is valuable. If we leave, we take him with us."

"Why should we leave?" ventured Sion. "Where would we go?"

Raffael deigned to answer. "Where to go—that is the

problem. We could try for Liverpool, then the Continent. Or maybe Ireland.''

"Why can't we just leave Jean and Pip in the house and get away?'' asked Elen.

"They've heard and seen too much,'' said Gwyn. "They'd have the search onto us in minutes.'' Raffael's fault, insisting disguises were unnecessary.

"Let's vote,'' suggested Sion, always egalitarian when he feared a decision. Raffael smiled indulgently.

"In favour of staying?''

Gwyn put up his hand first, followed by Madog. Jean Douglass kept her blue eyes on Gwyn, searching his face for a hope of salvation. The Cadwyn girl sat up straight and put her arm around the nanny. She raised her other hand. Three.

"In favour of leaving?''

Nora raised her free hand. The Italian flourished his unlit cigarette. Sion looked from her to Raffael, then raised his hand. Three. Nora pulled a handful of shotgun shells out of her pocket and tossed them in her palm.

"I say we leave without them. And without her.'' Nora flicked her barrel towards Carrie, who sat on the carpet with legs tucked under her lacy hem, stroking the cat curled by her knee.

Gwyn avoided looking at Carrie. "Grenvile mentioned Miss Powell. He believes she's in this with us.''

"It makes no difference. Sadly, the two fair ladies are worth nothing to us alive. But that is merely a detail.'' Raffael lit his cigarette. The strong smoke drifted towards Gwyn. Raffael was enjoying the exercise. He had enjoyed every exercise at China Lake, watching the novices vacillate between lingering bourgeois guilt and their new revolutionary commitment. Then he would step forward, coolly offering the solution. "So, we have a tie vote. I am responsible for the operation. I break the tie.''

"Remember what you're here for, Raffael.'' Gwyn felt a rush to his face. "Not to give orders.''

Nora turned to examine Gwyn and the sixteen-gauge barrel turned with her.

Madog stood up. "Miss Powell's life isn't up for grabs. She's been working with me in Brittany for several years. Sorry, Carrie. I owe you one set of papers and prints."

"Bullshit." Nora levelled the shotgun at the nurse.

Gwyn turned to Carrie, who offered no reaction but a narrowing of the eyes at Nora. She had always been able to mask her feelings. Even the cat looked coolly back at him. But it was a lie. It had to be a lie.

"Carrie?" Raffael, amused, considered her over his cigarette.

"I wouldn't touch an operation like this. Wouldn't go near it."

"Have you been working with Nilsson?" asked Gwyn.

"Did you really think she was sun-tanning in Morbihan last August? On what she collects from social assistance?" Madog shrugged. "She was with me on an island you never heard of, building electronic devices you wouldn't know how to use."

"Well?" Raffael gestured gracefully, inviting her rebuttal. "Is this true?"

"I was in Brittany," Carrie said flatly. "A friend invited me."

"She's lying!" Nora was outraged or delighted; it was hard to tell the difference.

"Ask Gwyn," said Carrie. "Gwyn knows the truth."

Duw. Gwyn recoiled. She was throwing him her life, and he was never as quick on his feet as Carrie. He looked from Carrie's still face to Nora's medusa stare. What did the Irish arse-hole want to believe?

"She wouldn't touch this. It's true." A pacifist, a nurse, a woman who took in stray cats and birds with broken wings. Not a murderer. Neither friend nor lover to a murderer. Gwyn intercepted a glance from Carrie too close to pity. He studied Madog's threadbare carpet, afraid his eyes would betray him further.

"Don't hand me that cack. One of you's lying."

Madog got up and paced the perimeter of the parlour, tracked by Nora's gun. Drawing fire. Gwyn felt a helpless envy of the spendthrift courage. His own courage was weighed out ounce by ounce and was running short. He remembered the handbook Grenvile followed. Keep them talking. While they're talking they're not shooting. His thoughts moved with underwater slowness when he needed lightning. "If you were committed to a project quietly and unknown for eight years, you might not throw it away even if someone shoved a shotgun up your nose."

"Ah, yes." Nora grimaced. "But whose project? The CIA?"

Gwyn felt sweat start to prickle along his hair-line. Everything in live was to some extent a compromise. Cost and benefit, it all came down to cost and benefit. And how desolate an equation it always turned out to be. Madog turned from the window, hands behind his back.

"I told you, Nora." Madog gave her his golden arsehole smile. "U.S. Cavalry."

"Fuck yourself." Touched a nerve, whatever it was. "I didn't ask you."

"Why didn't we hear anything about you?" demanded Sion. He'd bought it, at least.

"Cells don't intercommunicate," Gwyn snapped. "You know that. And I think we've spent enough time on this irrelevancy."

But Carrie hadn't finished. She stroked her cat and said, "Some of us are serious about the future of Wales."

"Carrie, keep out of it," Gwyn told her. "There's no need."

"You gave me your last order eight years ago. It had to do with a transmitter bombing. A man died." She made Sion and Elen her audience. They watched her wide-eyed. "You never learned. Even watching Ireland fall apart like a diseased whore, death by death, you never learned."

Nora didn't even notice the insult. She was watching Carrie in fascination. She demanded, "Is that true?"

Gwyn swallowed his wrath for Carrie, who called him a murderer and a fool. "It's true."

"Your advice, Miss Powell?" Raffael asked with elaborate courtliness.

Carrie looked around. Dark blue eyes, deep-set and thickly fringed in black lashes. Gwyn wondered if he'd really looked at her since the trial.

"Stay here," said Carrie. "Prepare for an assault. The SAS has its failures, too. You may be able to hold them off and negotiate your demands."

Madog nodded silent agreement.

"So." Raffael smiled as though he'd just collected on the pools. "Just the other woman."

"No. We need her to take care of the kid. And I make the decisions," Gwyn said. Behind his back, under the leather jacket, he closed his fingers on the Browning's grip. He slid the safety off.

Raffael's smile froze, and his hand dropped to the breast of his suede blazer. Inside lay the Beretta.

"You're an adviser," Gwyn said. "I decline your advice. We stay—but nothing says you must. Raffael, Nora. This is a far cry from what we planned in Tripoli. It's out of control. Take one of the cars to Liverpool tonight."

Raffael nodded sagely, then asked Nora something in German. She laughed. Raffael shrugged and turned back to Gwyn. "We may still pull something out of this. It may be they will offer nothing for your Welsh industry or television, but will still give up the cash. We will stay with the group. And the group will leave this place."

Gwyn considered throwing them out. It might result in a shoot-out. He wouldn't risk the child's life, or anyone else's. Even his own. He said again, "We stay."

Feeding on their quarrel, Nora watched them and played with her sixteen-gauge. Madog stood forward from the wall, hands shoved in his back pockets.

"Not wise. I think we go," Raffael chastised, gently instructing a student. "You will understand when you have more experience, Gwyn."

Gwyn's hackles rose at the condescension. "Experience nearly got us all killed in London. What is this, a test match for a new field of operations, with you as revolutionary hero? So you have Qaddafi's blessing—you don't have mine. We do it my way."

Raffael eased to his feet. His hand slid inside his jacket. He said softly, *"Tanto peggio, tanto maglio."*

The worse it is, the better it is. Permanent revolution. Make life intolerable for the proletarians and they'll get angry enough to destroy the ruling class. And form the next oppressive ruling class, to be destroyed in turn by the next wave of freedom fighters with back-shop nail bombs and Libyan-bought arms. A vicious circle. All Gwyn wanted was a sovereign Wales.

"It doesn't work."

Nora watched raptly, shotgun dangling unnoticed at her denim thigh. Across the room, Jean Douglass was sobbing soundlessly on Elen's shoulder. Only the Prince, with Mungo Mouse in his arms, sat on the edge of the sofa and watched unhappily.

"What's all this crap?" Madog walked forward and stopped in the middle of the room, between Raffael and Gwyn. "We've got a place to stay, and I don't see any SAS. Knock it off, huh?"

Raffael looked at him for a long moment, then dropped his hand and shrugged expressively. If they wanted to be fools. . . . Gwyn leaned back on the wall, drained. He turned at a touch on his arm and found Carrie at his shoulder. Like the old days. It didn't make him feel better, or feel anything at all.

11

Merlin broke the connection.

"What do you make of the call, Major Grenvile?" demanded the PM's aide, who had strayed back from the COBRA war room at Whitehall. Starting to push for results, preferably spectacular results, complete with sacrificial victims.

Robert felt rather than saw Harold Stone cross the electronics room to him. Stone, cast in military intelligence's discreet grey-suited mould, had appeared this morning to supervise negotiations. In other words, to supervise Robert. Dr. Chernicki, the palace security people, and, inevitably, Fox, also drifted near. Anna Chernicki was wearing another well-tailored woollen suit. Did Americans in England always favour dress more English than the English would ever wear? On monitor five, one of the big television screens, Peter Holt was narrating a news feature on the last decade of Welsh activism. These days the BBC reporter seemed ever-present.

"Merlin didn't mention money this time." Robert glanced down at his scratch pad. "Usually it's the other way around—they start by demanding release of prisoners and rather vague political changes, then try to settle for cash. Merlin isn't unduly worried about money, but he's adamant about very specific political aims."

"Does that mean these people won't negotiate?" asked the commissioner.

Robert, his head bowed over his notes, struggled to answer. "Not necessarily. But until we find them, we have no way of knowing. And for the present we can't force them to respond."

"What have the searches turned up?" asked the PM's aide. "How close are we to taking them?"

Robert glanced at Harold Stone, who nodded for him to continue. Stone would be a silent participant, then. It made the intrusion slightly less bearable. Robert would be under scrutiny but he would get no backing. Had Fox or one of the others been complaining about his lack of progress? He flipped through his most recent stack of papers and picked out the report he wanted. "We still have nothing like a good lead. Only one or two we should check again, like this report from a Dyfed-Powys police inspector."

"Dyfed-Powys?" the PM's aide asked incredulously. "What the devil is that?"

"South-west Wales and mid-Wales," Robert explained patiently and consulted the report. "The inspector was working with an RAF team Saturday night. One of his notes concerned an isolated cottage near Llanfyllin with an unregistered amateur radio apparatus." Robert forestalled the inevitable next question by going to the wall maps and leafing through to the Wales sheet. "Right about here."

"Saturday night?" Fox leaned forward across Robert's desk. "You've been sitting on this information for three days?"

Robert met his angry light eyes and looked away. Stone offered no aid. "The Dyfed-Powys force called an hour ago. They had decided the place was clean, but passed the information on anyway. The owner's an American named Nilsson. A bit of a ne'er-do-well." Robert glanced at Anna Chernicki, but she was absorbed in her palm-sized black keyboard.

"Run a check with Cheltenham, please," the commissioner murmured to a technician. "What else?"

Robert cleared his throat, unsuccessfully. "Houses in Machynlleth and Bangor are under surveillance, but have turned up nothing suspicious. In general, the searchers noted a good deal of hostility and reticence in answering even simple questions. From the Welsh, that is. English cottage owners were much more helpful."

He glanced around, wishing Stone would offer something. Even public criticism.

Mr. Leung straightened his leather tie and mercifully took over. "We now have electronically enhanced portraits of the photographers and guards at the kidnapping. We did a visual match with the Welsh suspects' photos and the relays from Interpol."

The frames came up on the monitor two in split-screen. Someone had turned down the volume on the BBC, so Peter Holt's long earnest face on the other monitor commented silently between protest and interview sequences.

"Several of our original fourteen are accounted for," Robert contributed in a dry rasp. He fumbled in his jacket for cough-drops, falling back on the pretext that a head cold accounted for his strangled voice. "We've isolated eight men and women who may be among the gunmen. And we have another five portraits from Interpol."

He watched as the faces came up one at a time on the left hand of the screen, enlarged and clearer than in their original snapshots and mug shots. A girl with long red hair, striving to look hard. One prison-numbered mug shot. A bearded man in a pullover. A woman with short black hair, deep blue eyes, a determined chin. A dark-haired man with a narrow angry face. A stocky man wearing a hard hat and overalls. A woman in a factory smock. Then the Interpol shots. Slowly, they cycled on the left screen, then halted.

"Our enhancements from the kidnapping," Mr. Leung announced. "Too far for laser retina scan, unfortunately."

The right half of the screen showed the woman photog-

rapher's face, framed in wild black hair. On the left screen
the images began cycling again and stopped at an Interpol
shot of a crop-haired blonde woman. The two women
looked not even slightly alike. Next the full screen faded
to black, and on each side a mesh of green lines began to
outline a three-dimensional woman's head. Then the two
merged. There was no overlap, only a single schematic.

"Christ," someone breathed. It was often this way when
even highly trained personnel witnessed electronic sor-
cery.

"Noreen Mary Kilpatrick, twenty-three, Provisional
IRA, County Armagh," the technician announced. "Also
travels on Lebanese papers as Gemelia Bishara, and on
West German papers as Elke Hartmann. Last seen in Paris
a fortnight ago."

Next an image of the other photographer, the man with
light brown hair and the scarf flying over his shoulder,
appeared on the right half of the screen. The specialist
cycled through the Interpol shots and stopped at a bearded
man in the chequered burnoose of the PLO. This time,
when the three-dimensional schematics merged, the overlap was somewhat marred by the beards and covered head.

"Raffael Tenorio, thirty-six, Red Brigades, Rome Column. Interpol thinks he may odd-job for Qaddafi in Western Europe. Probably one or more Paris café bombs and
a hostage-taking in West Germany. Also last seen a fortnight ago in Paris, though not with Kilpatrick." A list of
identities followed. Daoud Hamal, Syria. Ricardo Munez,
Peru. Jean-Louis Leclerc, France. Karl Kotowsky, West
Germany.

"Holt, the BBC man, gave us a lead on him," offered
Robert to a suddenly more attentive audience. "I tried the
name Raffael on the man who interrupted Merlin's last call
and got a reaction. He mentioned Tywyn, the school
bombing last month."

"You think these people are responsible for that, too?"
asked the PM's aide.

"It could just be a threat, like mentioning the Getty boy."

"How close a visual match do you need?" asked Fox, subdued for once.

"We consider this conclusive," Mr. Leung answered. "And the next one."

The left-hand shots cycled and stopped. Few observers would note any likeness between the spectacled, full-bearded security guard and the angry-looking dark man. The green web of the schematics rotated, filled in, and merged.

"One of our own, keeping bad company," the technician said. "Gwyn Davies, thirty-seven, president of the activist group Union of Future Wales, lecturer at the University College of Wales in Aberystwyth. No known aliases. He was charged with manslaughter eight years ago. The evidence wouldn't support a conviction. Ran for parliament twice in Dolgellau. Lost by a small margin the second time."

Merlin? Robert considered the contemptuous dark eyes and tried to visualize this as the man who threatened him half an hour ago. Merlin wasn't a murderer. He could swear to it.

"Manslaughter? What were the circumstances?" asked the commissioner, also gazing at the screen.

"A microwave transmitter bombing killed a man working in the control shed at the time. Another of the Welsh suspects was involved, Ceridwen Powell." He cycled up the black-haired woman. "Either careless, or thoroughly cold-blooded."

Or inexperienced, Robert reflected, and at the thought he jerked upright. A glance around the twilit electronics room reassured him that no one had noticed his start of alarm. Sympathy, though always a temporary hazard, was disastrous to a hostage negotiator. His business was to talk Merlin into easy surrender or termination, not to rationalize excuses for terrorism.

"Major Grenvile?"

"Sorry?" Good Lord, he'd been caught day-dreaming.

"Do you have anything on this one?" asked the palace security chief.

The second guard's face filled the left side of the screen, regular-featured, untroubled. The other portraits cycled on the right side. The screen split again this time horizontally, and below the flesh-and-blood faces the schematic traceries formed, overlapped, and cycled on.

Robert shook his head. "Perhaps when we have more from Interpol."

"Other information?" asked the commissioner.

"Only if you count the newsprint rantings of this Llewelyn Probert-Vaughan, who claims he's the true Prince of Wales," Robert said, relieved to offer a lighter note. "He says he'll be delighted to fill in temporarily for the missing Prince."

Scattered laughter broke the grim mood in New Scotland Yard's electronics centre.

"Thoughtful of him," brayed the PM's aide with a tug at his waistcoat. "If people got a taste of a tawdry Taff parvenu on the throne, they'd appreciate the royalty we have. Or don't have, as the case may be."

Faces glazed over, and Robert wished a trapdoor would open under the aide's gleaming brogues.

"Wasn't there Welsh on the new tape?" asked Anna Chernicki. Timely, as usual.

"It sounded like another outburst," Robert said. "Mr. Evans?"

"Sir?" Dan Evans, the bald and beamy South Walian translator, had tufts of hair jutting from his ears like antennae. He presented himself smartly, with the paramilitary precision ingrained at GCHQ Cheltenham. Robert nodded to the technician standing by the tape console. The room filled with Merlin's voice.

"Don't threaten me. *Gwrandwch, rŵan, 'Rydan ni mewn peryg. Mae rhywun wedi dod o hyd i ni. Mae 'na beryg orwth ym mhobl i.*" He sounded angry and nervous, thought Robert, tapping his pencil on the desk. Who could blame him?

Evans looked at Robert, startled. "He says, 'Listen, now. We're in danger. Someone has walked in on us. There's danger from my people.' "

The commissioner leaned forward. *"From* my people? Not *to* my people?"

The technician ran the tape back. Evans listened again. "Yes, sir. Quite certainly it's *from.*"

Robert's pencil snapped in two. There was a long second's silence.

Evans turned to Robert. "I thought Reverend Morgans said his caller had a southern voice? That man's from the north."

"How do you know?" demanded Anna.

"Rwan for 'now.' And his inflection."

Robert frowned and noted it on the profile he was contructing for Merlin. Where was Davies from, north or south?

"Irrelevant," said Fox. "The important thing is his talk of danger. It's essential that we find the terrorists and free the hostages with a single strike."

For God's sake, Robert thought. Could the man deal only in destruction?

"We've got to find them," he said, "certainly. Another sweep of searches, especially in areas that don't receive television transmission—"

"Major Grenvile," intoned the computer's cool electronic voice. "Major Grenvile, telephone."

Merlin? But Merlin said he wouldn't talk to Robert again.

Outside the glass negotiation booth, the SAS observer paced, rhythmically pounding his fist in his palm. Robert, feeling each blow, sat at the desk inside.

"Returning your call," said Peter Holt.

"We've had another call from Merlin," Robert told him. "He says he'll talk only with someone who understands the situation. He wants you."

"What does he have in mind?" Holt sounded cautious, even afraid. Phipps's clumsy work?

"Difficult to say. But I'm afraid you're going to have to come to London after all, Mr. Holt."

"No bloody way. Sorry, Major. I've got a job to do here for the BBC and I'm stringing for CBS. I'm not changing horses in midstream. I'd never work again as a journalist. But I'll help you as best I can."

"You don't seem to realize the Prince's life, and Miss Douglass's, could be lost because of your failure to co-operate."

"Failure to co-operate? Wait a minute, here. Who offered to help in the first place? Major, you're losing touch."

One way or another. Robert drew a deep breath and tried again. "Mr. Holt, this is of the utmost importance. Life and death. We can pay you—"

"Sod you, Major. You lot down in London think of nothing but money. The Welsh are right about that much."

"What can we offer, Mr. Holt?" Robert prayed he sounded less desperate than he felt. The scent of fear draws predators: it was his lifelong observation. Fox the pale-eyed predator, Holt the righteous bloodhound.

Righteous. That was the key. He recalled Holt's military-intelligence file. "I know you feel a responsibility to record events, to inform people of what's happening."

"Right. Record events, not create them." Holt was quieter now.

"Go on."

" 'We can pay you.' You don't have the currency to pay me with, understand?"

Robert kept silent, thinking of predators.

Holt went on. "I want to report what these terrorists are about, but also what you and your jackboot chums are about. Night searches, arrests without warrant, political types disappearing for interrogation." He paused.

"Well?" Robert wanted to hear him out.

"People have a right to know and to make up their own

minds and do what they can about it at the polls or by any other means within the law. No bloody wonder the Welsh got a bellyful and tried this gormless stunt instead. If I help you, I lose my right to comment on it.''

"I see." Another day, Robert might even have applauded Holt's stand. Not today, dealing with a national crisis. As he began to negotiate, his voice steadied. "What if we keep your participation strictly secret? Arrange a phone relay to Cardiff?''

"Maybe." Holt thought for a moment. "In return I want a free hand to film anything. And once it's over—however it turns out—inside information for a book. Exclusive rights. No holds barred.''

Holt was more easily satisfied than Merlin, at least, or Fox. "I can't promise that without higher authority. Perhaps an honorarium—''

"Christ, will you forget money for once! I want the story. That's my offer.''

Rather altruistic, for a man foundering under maintenance payments and rising damp. Robert decided he would find a way. "All right.''

"Done," said Holt. "When can you link me by phone?''

"An hour. Maybe less.''

"Right. I have to make a call you might want to overhear—concerning Miss Douglass. And you can relay the next call from Merlin." Holt rang off.

Jean Douglass? Robert briefly registered shock. Then Fox was leaning across his desk.

"You've wasted enough time," Fox said. "I want a location, and I want your co-operation for search and destroy.''

Anna Chernicki appeared at his shoulder with the commissioner and Harold Stone.

"That could be rash, Colonel," she said quietly. "Merlin clearly opposes this danger he mentions. And there may be others present who can protect the child—'' She hesitated.

Robert glanced at her sharply. What did that mean? He revised his estimation of Dr. Anna Chernicki, professor, University of Maryland. Maybe she was—but what else was she? CIA?

"You seem not to understand." Fox wouldn't look at the American professor; he kept talking to Robert. "Special Air Services requests me to volunteer search and destroy personnel. You're asking me to report that, no, we're going to sit here a while longer discussing philosophy with news reporters while the heir apparent to the British throne may be in mortal danger."

"Search, certainly. The most vital thing now is to establish face-to-face negotiation," Robert answered wearily. "But destroy—whom? We don't know who the gunmen are, or how many. What about this other person Merlin mentions, 'someone who walked in on us?' Do you want an innocent man to die?"

"Dr. Chernicki?" Stone cut off the discussion. It was the first time he'd spoken.

She thought about it. "If you display a military presence in Wales, according to our observers, you'll create widespread hostility. You may also trigger violence from the gunmen."

"Your advice?" prodded Stone.

"Compromise. Just remember, every compromise has its costs as well as its benefits." The American woman smiled faintly. "I advise taking a mobile command unit to Wales. Now, if you'll excuse me, I'll have my equipment sent over from Grosvenor Square."

"Daddy? Are you cross?"

"No, sweetheart, I'm not cross. I'm glad you rang." Peter leaned back in his chair, stretching, with the phone receiver clamped between ear and shoulder. She was a good kid. Knew about deadlines, wanted to be a journalist, God help her. "What'll we do next weekend, Andy? Go to the kids' theatre? Go walking on Gŵyr?"

"Theatre," she said decisively. "Daddy, Mum said I

could call you at work and say your friend came round. He took us for tea."

"Was it the man with the camera?"

"Not Mr. Rees. It was Mr. Smythe. He was funny."

"Glad you had a nice time, sweetie." Right, that about did it for Teddy. He was making himself a first-class nuisance; time for a word with Grenvile about his spook. But there was no point spoiling Andy's fun.

"Daddy, he has a *tattoo* on his arm. He showed me." It didn't take much to scandalize a seven-year-old.

"Lots of men have tattoos, Andy. Some women have them, too. Is it a naked lady?"

Andrea giggled. "No, it's a dog. You know, the kind with little short legs."

"A corgi? Like the King's Mum has?"

"Right. *Arhosa, rwy'n dod,*" she yelled at someone at the other end, probably a school chum. Elizabeth wouldn't learn Welsh, even feared it might spoil Andrea's English. "Got to go, Daddy."

"All right, sweetheart. See you next weekend." Peter rang off. Definitely time for a word. Things were getting out of hand.

PEN Y CAE/JANUARY 18/2000

John Hughes turned his tumbler of applejack between his hands as his waterproof mac dripped on the kitchen floor. On another chair, eyes on the slates and hands clasped between his knees, raw-boned young Gareth sat quietly. Madog watched Davies frowning first at him, then at Gareth. Seeing a family resemblance? It didn't make either of them too happy that John had brought his nephew around; Madog for Gareth's sake, Davies for the others' sakes.

"*Madog bach,* you should see them in the Red Lion tonight, entirely carried away with high talk."

"High talk, John? What kind of high talk?"

Madog poured another round of applejack into the seven

tumblers and mugs. Pen y Cae's back kitchen steamed with a select gathering of the *Cymry Cymraeg*, the Welsh-speakers: Gareth, John, plus the five who understood his cracked Welsh. They gathered close around the scrubbed kitchen table, faces limned in lamplight. Davies made notes whenever John opened his mouth. Carrie was playing prim *Miss Ceridwen fach* the district nurse with a former patient, though Cath Paluc leering from her shoulder spoiled the effect. And she put back the apple dynamite like a pro, Madog noted; she was in for a headache later, unless she had an iron constitution. The others were treating the drink with respect.

"It was the telly started us talking. That BBC lad, Peter Holt, had a special show about the nationalist trouble." John drank his host's health and took up his talk. "They even cancelled *Dallas*."

"What did Holt say?" Davies leaned across the table, forgetting his notes.

"Plenty. I never looked to see that sort of thing on BBC. There was *heddlu cudd*—so Mister Holt said—giving money to rough lads to set upon protesters. There was police down in Cardiff using their little sticks when they arrested nationalists in the middle of the night. There was interviews with ministers of religion and the Plaid Cymru boys and high-nostrilled little men in the university—begging your pardon, Mister Davies—all saying it was against the laws of God and man to treat the Welsh like this. Very eloquent. Even the Englishman Holt talked to them in a kind of Welsh."

"And the boys at the Red Lion liked that?" Madog smiled at John's narrative.

"Young Gareth here and the other lads were hottest. There was nothing I could say, understand, after you borrowed my old Land Rover and ate my side of beef. But Davy Hughes, who calls himself Dafydd ab Hywel these days, and young Gareth who is jobless after the university got through with him—they were flaming like Guy Fawkes at Calan Gaeaf fires."

Madog folded his arms, waiting.

John looked reproachful. "I was getting to it, *machgen*. What they said is, let the *bwganod* spooks come round here again with their helicopters and their questions. If we can burn English vermin out of cottages, we can burn them out of helicopters."

Madog shook his head and glanced at Gareth, who stared at his farm-roughened hands. "And you told them to go home and sleep it off?"

"I did." John fidgeted with his glass until Davies poured it full. "But don't look for them to do that. True, Gareth?"

"True enough." Gareth looked up briefly through a cow-lick of mouse-brown hair. For him, it was a significant speech. Three years of sciences at Coleg Bangor had left Gareth as tongue-tied as ever.

Davies nodded agreement. "Even over here in English Wales, people won't swallow insults forever."

"So you said on the telly, Mister Davies." John savoured a mouthful of moonshine, just long enough to enjoy Davie's shock. "That was a fine snapshot of you outside Abertawe court-house with your hands in manacles, shouting slogans at the crowd from the paddy-wagon door. *Miss Ceridwen fach* also. Eight years ago, I think."

"*O Duw*," muttered Davies.

"And there was your voice saying Undeb Cymru Fydd supports this kidnapping of the little Prince. Then they showed you walking on that hill above Aberystwyth in the summertime, with the sea wind making a right bird's nest of your hair, and the tow all below like she was lying at your feet." John laughed and wiped his hand across his mouth. "Every young girl in the country will be in love with you by morning. What is it, Miss Ceridwen, has the old cat scratched you?"

Carrie dropped Paluc and headed towards the parlour door, but Madog had time to see the pink creeping up her cheeks. Too much applejack. John glanced after her, shaking his grey head. Davies, not amused, set his mouth and angrily scribbled more notes. Elen sat forward on her chair, looking into her cup.

"Well, Madog." The farmer yawned. "Pity you didn't find me home yesterday."

"I didn't call yesterday. I knew you'd be down by Shrewsbury sniffing out heifers at the farm sales."

"And so I was. But someone played the trick on me, if it wasn't you. Things don't walk about by themselves."

Madog explained to the others. "Around here, when neighbors find no one home, they move something in the house. A joke, I guess, but it also lets people know they had visitors. What was moved, John?"

"My herd tally was on the wrong shelf and a slip of paper went from the telephone book."

"What was on it?" Madog pushed his tumbler from fingertip to fingertip across the scrubbed wooden tabletop, worried by the clumsy intrusion into John's house.

"The new vet's number. Now I'll have to phone the operator for it again."

Madog laughed. "That should keep everyone busy for now. Forget it, John, it was probably your sister."

"Na. She might need a vet, the cow, but she knows better than to look at my herd count. It gives her a week's prayer in chapel. Well then, who is this?"

"Pip," said the child dutifully from the doorway. He was recovering some of his confidence, clinging less to his nanny.

Elen picked up the little boy and his stuffed-mouse doll and set them on her blue-jeaned knee. "Where's Miss Douglass?"

Madog watched John's face. It registered no surprise, as he expected. The old farmer beamed until the gaps showed in his side teeth, eyeing the fair boy in red-haired Elen's arms.

"She's asleep. Nora was sitting with me, but she said to come see you. She went upstairs after Miss Powell."

Madog stirred uneasily but before he could suggest anything Davies got to his feet and disappeared into the hall-way.

"Come to me, boy." John shook his rough head, smil-ing.

Pip slid down willingly and went to lean against John's leg. "What's your name?"

"John Hughes. I live on a farm called Cae Isa. Do you know what that means?"

The child shook his head.

"Pen y Cae means the top of the field, you see, Madog being the boss. So Cae Isa means the lower field. Can you say them?"

"Penna-kye. Kye-eesa," Pip repeated. "I like Ma-dog."

"Good lad, Pip." John beamed. "I'll tell you another. I told this to Madog long years ago. *Pwsi meri mew, ple gollaist di dy flew? Wrth gario tân i modryb Siân, drwy'r eira mawr a'r rhew?*"

"It's about a cat," said Pip decisively.

"It is. A little Welsh cat. She loses her fur coat."

Madog shook his head, torn between amusement and exasperation.

"I don't have a cat, but I've got a pony."

"You're a countryman at heart. Maybe the boss will let you come visit my cows sometime." John ruffled the boy's golden hair, then downed the last of his drink. Rolling his tweed cap between his hands, he stood to go. "I'd best get back to look in on my girls. Gareth, we'll go find those chains for your Tad's lorry."

Pip ran to the window and waved at the dark yard as John and Gareth disappeared.

Madog strolled toward the parlour. Out of the corner of his eye, he saw Sion reach along the sideboard and take two potatoes from the bowl. Greed, perhaps, but Madog figured he might also be planning an unscheduled depar-ture.

The nanny was curled under a blanket on the settee. Raffael, reading the *New Statesman*, as usual ignored the others. At the foot of the stairs Madog hesitated, watching Pal lick a grey paw with elaborate disdain for his host. Quick footsteps on the stairs. Nora, her face as bright as Carrie's a few minutes ago, came down at a run and brushed past him towards the kitchen. So they cancelled that old standby *Dallas* on TV, Madog reflected. Pen y Cae had its own soap opera in progress; he only wished he could follow more of it. He padded upstairs and sat quietly in the radio room with the door ajar, listening to the low voices in the bedroom. Soon his patient eavesdropping was rewarded.

"All right?" he heard Davies ask in his mother tongue, stiff and uncompromising as usual. Not stupid. Not ignorant. His concern for the country and the language was real enough, he knew how to manipulate media reaction, he had a gift for rhetoric; but he couldn't seem to bend or give. Permafrost, Madog would have diagnosed in the arctic: the deep, abiding cold that defied human efforts.

Carrie didn't answer Davies's questions, or if she did, it was lost in the sound of Madog's dresser drawer opening. A minute later she said, "You won't find anything. I tried."

"What did Nora want?"

"You wouldn't believe me if I told you."

"When did I ever doubt you? You disbelieved me."

"If you want to be believed, tell the truth."

"You never let go, do you? Like a ferret with a mole."

"Flattering." Carrie laughed quietly. "She wants me to slide out with her tonight, seeing the rest of you aren't worth saving. She's got a radio transmitter to call in a trawler standing off Llŷn."

"Irish?"

"East German."

"Huh." Davies slid the drawer closed. "Are you going?"

"And spend the rest of my days in Libya sharing a bed with Nora the Death? All I want are my emigration papers for America—if that's still possible after your best efforts to foul my character with this mess you call a hostage-taking.''

"We've done our best. It wasn't good enough."

"You should have kept it simpler. No Nora, no Raffael."

"Didn't know you were still interested."

"I'm not. Never again. Now tell me, what are those arse-holes doing here?"

"Qaddafi wants more co-operation between European direct-action groups. Raffael was my hostage-taking instructor at a camp in Libya. Nora worked with him on other operations. She also brought in her Provo chums for the London diversion. That helped considerably."

"Qaddafi? Libya?" Carrie sounded incredulous, a feeling Madog shared. "What the hell do you think you're doing, Davies? IRA's bad enough. Qaddafi doesn't give a damn about Wales. Better to sign your soul straight to the devil. Or maybe you have."

"Carrie."

"Close your mouth, Davies."

"I have a name."

Silence. Then she capitulated. "Gwyn."

"Carrie—"

"What are you doing with this American? He's got secret service written all over him."

"He's useful."

"To you or the English? At least he's interesting."

"I noticed that."

Carrie started to make a retort. Instead she sighed. "What do you know about him?"

"I've checked the directories for Seattle. There's no Madog Nilsson. No Caradoc Nilsson. No Caradoc Nilsson Aeronautics. I sent out a trace through Dublin but no one's heard of him."

"If this Caradoc Nilsson Aeronautics has space-shuttle contracts, it could be a subsidiary, or too fat and powerful to bother with keeping shop. Either way, he might not be listed."

"Or might not exist."

Or might not exist. Madog, listening in the next room, touched the radio controls in the dark and considered his existence. Maybe he was just a computer bug, a gremlin, a pulse lost between the electronic synapses of someone's great board.

Or might not exist. But he remembered islands, and sea otters playing in the tide slick. . . . He remembered Friday Harbor. Worked in the Shell station one summer, pumping gas. Learned to fix most anything in no time flat. Sure, he could remember. I remember therefore I am. But he couldn't remember everything.

Or might not exist. Doubts about his existence came later. His mind slipped off it. He lifted his right hand blindly and groped for the gold chain at his neck, weighed over his breastbone by the leaf-bladed obsidian arrowhead. Danny bought it for him in Pike Street Market the day they went to Seattle to enlist. Probably a fake. Or was it Danny's gift? Hadn't he stolen it from a museum, picked the lock on the glass case and slipped it in his pocket? Sometimes he couldn't remember. Whole sequences of his life were gone without a trace, especially things that had mattered once. Yet at a computer keyboard or work-bench, the memory in his hands would carry him through complex procedures. Sometimes a fragment of real memory surfaced as he worked: a friend, a few words, a job.

Madog's face stung. He laid it on his bent forearm and closed his eyes. Without asking to, without wanting to, he heard the pulsing roar of the Hueys prowling in and the distant mortar fire. Mekong, or was it Sarsar Sdam? He knew he'd been at both places, but he couldn't remember what happened. Didn't want to. He thought there were kids, oh God, though none of them was trusting like Pip. In war there are no innocents. When the Khmer . . .

No. Mountains and rivers. Without end.

"Is he really *Cymry ar Wasgar*, overseas Welsh?" Carrie was asking. "He's too good, too polished. Languages, electronics."

Madog lifted his face again and propped it on his wet
knuckles. Get on with it. Make your peace. The world
takes no notice of your lost time, or anyone's. He thought
he was over this shit, this going to pieces without warning.
Maybe it was like mustard gas, terror killed you soon or
late. Back in the States one of the shrinks had left his file
open on a desk. Knowing Madog's trade, it was a deliberate invitation to scan the diagnoses: depression, schizophrenia, other specialists' terms. Madog had overheard a
more honest assessment from a psych orderly. Nilsson?
His head's fucked. Those Khmer fuckers scrambled his
brains, man. Fuck me, by the time they got him out he
wanted to stay and help them build fucking huts or something.

All these explanations were masks for terror. In psych
files no one was willing simply to write "terror."

Madog slipped towards the welcome blackness. Gripping the obsidian blade, he saw the blood between his
fingers and felt nothing.

"He carries his weight. He's saved my life and yours."
Davies paused. His voice warmed a fraction of a degree.
"I trust him."

"You always were too generous."

"Was I?" Desolation spilled over from that simple past
tense. In a linguist, it was no accident. "Carrie—"

"Na. Forget all that."

Her light footfalls came towards the landing, descended
the stairs, and vanished under talk in the parlour, before
Davies spoke again.

"I can't forget."

The words could have come from Madog's own tongue.
He spread both hands over his face, wishing to God . . .
He wasn't even sure what he wished.

After a while Davies went downstairs. Madog found a
pencil in the table drawer and used its point to tap out an
entry on the miniature keypad of his limited-edition Seiko.
The answers came back rapid-fire. He ignored them,
turned on the radio, and slumped, staring at the digital

numbers in endless procession. All he had to do was flip the lever to send, open transmission, and give Grenvile a radio beam for the direction finder. MI5 would negotiate. SAS would rescue the boy. They'd all be heroes. And what would Madog Nilsson be? Another clapped-out whore with the night terrors.

Instead, he turned the receiver and began listening. The bands were quieter tonight, but the Welsh he heard confirmed John's claim. Open anger about the arrests and harassment, veiled talk of watching police movements, fear at mention of SAS search teams.

"In our Wales," mused one northern voice. "As though she were an enemy." Once Madog thought he wanted that, for Wales to be an enemy. From violent confrontation would come re-creation, a new strength of identity for a desolate small country. Like Raffael's *tanto maglio*. . . . The worse it is, the better it can become. But he couldn't buy that anymore. He just didn't have a better idea yet.

12

"Doctor Jamieson? Hello? Sir, my name is Grenvile. Major Robert Grenvile," said Peter Holt pleasantly into the telephone. Behind the closed door of the borrowed office, he sat tapping pencil on notebook.

"How may I help you, Major?" The physician's voice was cold, suspicious, and very Scots.

Peter fidgeted under the effort of mimicking Grenvile, a toffee-nosed Londoner. Acting John Osborne roles back in his red-brick college's dramatic society had been entertainment; this was desperation. It was for the young Prince, just Andrea's age. It was for Andy herself, if Grenvile was making veiled threats through Teddy's visit. He'd have to remember to take that up with the negotiator.

"I'm calling from New Scotland Yard, headquarters for the national search of which you must be aware. . . . With regard to one of your patients, Miss Jean Douglass." Peter glanced at the big Uher tape recorder on the desk slowly reeling in his words, attached to the phone by its electronic umbilicus.

"I see." Jamieson wasn't giving anything away.

"Naturally we respect the confidentiality of the doctor-patient relationship," Peter ventured. "But this could well be a matter of life and death, not only for Miss Douglass but for all concerned. You follow me?"

223

"I do, Major Grenvile." Could Peter detect even a trace of interest? What if the doctor was a bloody Scottish nationalist?

"In view of this crisis, we'd like to ask your help. In the national interest, and in the interest of Miss Douglass and the child. We need information from Miss Douglass's health and medical records."

Peter waited out Jamieson's long pause. What if the doctor refused? Worse, what if he demanded proof of Grenvile's identity? Not only Peter, but also Grenvile and his cohorts, might never get anything from Jamieson. . . .

"Very well, Major. I'll find the young woman's file."

Peter breathed relief and sat back in the soft leather chair of the executive assistant's office next door to the Old Man's. What Grenvile had told the Old Man Peter didn't know, but he hoped it stayed confidential. Peter had taken heavy-handed ribbing about his "promotion," but he shrugged it off his worn corduroy shoulders. If his benevolent colleagues down in the newsroom got wind that his promotion was not to news planning but to MI5, it would be an understatement to say he was out of business. Ruined, more like. On the street.

"Major Grenvile? I have the file."

Peter slipped back into his theatrically plummy voice. "Excellent, Doctor. What can you tell us of Miss Douglass's medical history? Has she experienced any serious illnesses that might be anticipated to recur?"

Jamieson tersely listed childhood illnesses, a broken ankle from a ski holiday, a formidable battery of test results and inoculations for exotic diseases. Of course, she would have to be supremely healthy to be given responsibility for a royal offspring.

"Is she prone to unusual stress?" Peter furrowed his brow, reaching for other questions to fill in a portrait of the nanny. Something to point to her complicity in the kidnapping. "Any personal problems that could affect her judgement?"

"No. . . ." Jamieson hesitated, but kept quiet.

Peter grasped at straws. "What about her brother? He lives a rather fast life, we've learned."

"Indeed." Jamieson sighed. "You understand, Major, I knew Miss Douglass's mother and father. Fine people. But the younger brother has caused some anxiety. Miss Douglass feels she has failed her parents by not preventing Sandy's gambling. In fact, she has paid his debts and I believe extricated him from other embarrassments. I imagine it could place rather a strain upon her personal finances, as well as on her conscience. I have several times advised her to accept no further responsibility."

"Right!" Peter was excited enough to slip from the Grenvile role. That was it! Sandy's talk of payment for a snapshot. Trying to squeeze more money from the photographer. Just as he extorted money from his conscience-ridden Presbyterian sister. Peter recovered quickly. "Anything else of note, Doctor?"

"Not unless you're interested in Miss Douglass's blood count," said Dr. Jamieson with crusty sarcasm.

"Doctor Jamieson, your co-operation has been invaluable."

He gave the old Scot Grenvile's number at Scotland Yard and gratefully broke the connection. Immediately, Grenvile's voice came on the line.

"What is this about Miss Douglass?"

"Just playing a hunch, Major," said Peter, himself again. "Thought I'd check into whether she might have been involved. Can you send someone round to investigate Sandy Douglass's debts and find out whether he and his sister got together with the photographer just before the incident?"

Grenvile took the North London address. "Anything else?"

"I reckon you'd best cook up some family ties in the north country if I have to impersonate you much more."

Grenvile laughed, to Peter's surprise.

"I'd be flattered. Listen—may I call you Peter? Please drop the major. Call me Robert."

"Call you Mephistopheles, more like. This cloak-and-dagger stuff isn't my cup of tea."

"One would never know it. You've missed your calling."

"Drop the negotiations—Robert. You've already talked me into my downfall." He rang off. Damn it, he'd forgotten to ask about Smythe. Next time.

Peter fitted the tape from the Uher into an already bulging jacket pocket: he needed a briefcase of some kind. "Ask and you shall receive" seemed to be the order of the day. He went out to the secretarial pool to request one and found Al Rees chatting up the pretty blonde.

"Saturday night, then?" Al carefully stuck his wadded chewing gum in the ashtray and got to his feet, hoisting his aluminum camera case. He was still wearing the nondescript blue mac instead of his silver bomber jacket, an indication of his state of nerves. "Taping at the university, Peter? Owen Thomas is out of jail with a very photogenic black eye."

"Let's look at yesterday's tape first." Peter led the way down to the viewing room, past the deliberately incurious eyes of the Old Man's typists. Good. So they'd been warned off.

"Cliff Aslin said the first feature went over like gangbusters, in his words. He wants another interview-and-cover packet with some Welsh interviews, voice-over in English—says it imparts local colour. Have you been following the news reaction?"

Al, unwrapping a fresh stick of Wrigley's, nodded with Hawaiian gravity. "Who hasn't? Screamer headlines about the Welsh revolution. College students on strike. Do-gooders protesting about civil-rights violations."

"Great copy," agreed Peter, looking at the Wrigley's. "Changed brands? Don't let success spoil you."

The photographer snorted, then slid into his strangled Tiger Bay Welsh. "Now then, Peter *bach*. The little man with the black Mini has gone back to Aberystwyth. Not my idea, Undeb's idea. The boys seem to think you know too much.''

''There's the truth,'' muttered Peter.

What else might the boys think? he wondered uneasily. He went into Number Two viewing room, not Number Four, which he normally used, turned on the lights, and locked the door. The room was thoroughly sound-proofed, and he would just have to take the chance it wasn't bugged. Peter set up yesterday's cassette of man-in-the-street and political interviews, plus library cover footage. For a few seconds he watched Gwyn Davies walking on windy Pen Dinas above Aberystwyth, then shook his head in bemusement and pulled up a chair.

''Look now, Al. I've been talking to military intelligence. They've told me a thing or two, on the understanding I keep quiet until afterwards.''

''Lucky boy.'' Al chewed thoughtfully, expressionless.

Peter steeled himself. They didn't quite trust each other—whether the woolly-back in black Mini was Al's idea or not—but each of them valued professional excellence. And survival.

Peter drew a deep breath. ''The head negotiator played me tapes from the terrorist group leader. He calls himself Merlin. I know him by another name.''

''Yeah?'' Al didn't look at the monitor screen, which now showed Davies addressing an Undeb Cymru Fydd crowd at Coleg Harlech. The scene did a special-effects fade to the Swansea court-house. Then to black.

''Al.'' Peter gazed into inpenetrable black eyes. ''Tell me straight now. How would you personally like to see this kidnapping end? For example, I want to see the kid released unhurt. I want a good story while it lasts, and maybe a quick book afterwards. I want people to know what's going on in Wales, not just during this fiasco but in the long term. I also want—Merlin—to get out with his skin on his back. He's a decent enough man, Al, maybe a friend. I think it all must have gone terribly wrong somehow.''

After a long moment, Al said reluctantly, "It did."
Progress. Peter waited.

"What do I want?" Al looked at his hands. The nails
were bitten to the quick. "I want what Merlin wants: a
world-wide audience to see how this country's being destroyed. Not just Wales. What about the jobless in the
Midlands and northern England? I want an end to union-
breaking and nuclear waste dumping and militarism and
police control. I want Merlin out safe. I want CBS credits
and a stack of fifty-pound notes. I want the kid out of our
hair and back where he belongs."

"Looks like we agree, then."

Al shrugged, still waiting.

Peter swallowed, preparing to negotiate. He knew how
Grenvile must feel. "So here's something for your amateur
radio people. The *heddlu cudd* know Merlin and his people are keeping in touch by short wave. MI5 has been feeding false information and charting the reaction."

"Interesting."

"They think the Douglass woman is involved."

Al whistled soundlessly.

"And Special Air Services assault teams are sitting at
their base in Hereford, waiting for the word to slip the
leash." Peter reflected. "Do you know the Powell woman?
Carrie Powell?"

"Retired," said Al. "She'd have no part of this."

"How do you know?"

"After that trial, she went into the speaker's tent at the
National Eisteddod—it's a good audience, and no one talks
of slander—and called Gwyn Davies a murderer, a cow-
ard, a liar, not fit to be considered Welsh. Davies heard
her and wouldn't respond. Accepted it, see? Then she vanished."

"What would it mean if she were involved in this?"

"Gathering of the clans, maybe. Big trouble."

"She's missing. She was in London the day of the kidnapping. Her car was seen next day, near where Merlin's
probably hiding."

"Duw." Al locked eyes with him. "Now, Peter, my Welsh-speaking but English friend, why're you telling me this?"

Speaking English doesn't make you English. Speaking Welsh is different; it makes you a curiosity, maybe Welsh by adoption. Even so, Peter was English, worked for an English corporation, and had slid into bed with English military intelligence. Al had every right to examine his motives.

"I told you the reasons. And something else." Peter's fingers clenched on the chair arm. "When I gave Grenvile some debate about helping the *heddlu cudd,* they mentioned my kid."

"Andy? How is she?"

"Too many uncles. Fine otherwise. Look, Al, those sods don't threaten my kid. Not even once." It didn't really make sense, he realized as he said it.

But it made sense to Al. He nodded. "Sure. Family is family." He looked at the now-blank screen for a while, and added, "Here's something for you. Not for your *heddlu cudd* friends."

"Contacts, not friends," Peter corrected, for perhaps the thousandth time in a chequered career.

"Remember Yann Morvan?"

Peter grunted affirmation. "Breton arse-hole." With a fondness for exotic pelts.

"He's got a helicopter gunship, out of sight on an offshore island. If there's an assault on Merlin's people. . . ."

"God Almighty." Peter stared. "Al."

The photographer was watching him sleepily, pleased with the acid test. It could be true or an invention. Either way, if the information turned up elsewhere, Peter was in trouble. Squeezed from both sides. Bloody hell. He tried anyway.

"Is that going to help Merlin? Or the kid?"

"Ask Morvan," Al said. "No, don't. You'd ask anyone anything, wouldn't you?"

Peter recognized a compliment. "Why not?"

"Just don't. Come on, let's go tape Owen's shiner for the Yanks. Police brutality, see?"

PEN Y CAE/JANUARY 19/0730

Pip wished there were enough snow to lie down and make a snow angel like Miss Douglass told him. Instead, he turned and walked backwards for a few steps, looking at the crooked trail his feet made. Snow was already covering it. Pip looked back at Madog's house, almost tripped on a hole in the road, and kept on downhill. He was shivering. He pulled his jacket tight around himself and Mungo. Pip wished he had fur, even worn-out fuzzy fur like Mungo. It was cold, and it was early in the morning.

Soon he came to the garage. He stopped at the big front doors and tried to lift the piece of wood that held them shut. Even when he pushed with all his might, he couldn't move it; it was too heavy and fitted too tightly. For a minute, Pip leaned against the door. Tears stung inside his nose. He thought everything would be all right once he got into the garage.

If he got into the garage, Nora couldn't pinch him and slap him when no one was looking, and tell him she was going to fix him so he couldn't steal anymore. Pip never stole anything. Miss Douglass said it was unkind to other people, and he had a responsibility, and Jesus would weep. But Nora said he stole food every day from other people's mouths. Raffi was worse. Pip was scared of him, even though all Raffi did was look at him.

Now Pip couldn't hide in the garage after all. But he wasn't going back. Nora would hit him and burn more holes in Mungo's fur with her cigarette. He turned and looked around. There wasn't much to see, just snow going up and down in bumps like a bowl of ice cream. If only Pip knew how they'd gotten here he could walk home, but all he could remember was driving in a car and feeling sick. It was cold. Even Mungo looked cold. He wanted a hot mug of tea with milk and honey, but Miss Douglass was asleep. Maybe Mr. Hughes would give him one, and he could visit the girls in the barn.

Pal might like to visit the girls, too. Should he go back and get Pal? Pal had a nice warm coat. But Mr. Hughes said Welsh cats lost their fur. Pip would remember to look for the zipper next time, like his cousin's pyjama bag. Was Pal all goose bumps inside his fur? Did he have to take it off for the laundry?

Pip wiped his hand across his runny nose like Mr. Hughes did; Miss Douglass made him use a hanky. Where did Mr. Hughes live? Madog's house was Penna-kye, the top of the field, because Madog was boss; Mr. Hughes's house was Kye-eesa, the lower field, so maybe he lived downhill. Pip decided to go see Mr. Hughes. It was an adventure, like Reepicheep.

Without an alarm clock Jean Douglass woke slowly, in stages. At half-past seven, when she reached the blurry margin of consciousness, she realized Pip was not there. Also, the Irish witch was gone from the other side of the bed they shared in the downstairs bedroom. In the kitchen having early tea, Jean decided, and rolled over for another forty winks.

An hour later she awoke clear-headed and got up briskly to wash her face in the bowl Madog had lent her. A skim of ice was floating on the water, and she could see her breath in the dark room. It hadn't been this cold before. She shivered but refused to hurry her washing. When she finished, Jean Douglass brushed down her good woollens, put on the silk blouse that she'd already had to rinse three times, and stepped into her suit. In the cracked mirror propped on the dresser, she looked ready to start a day's work at the palace. Once you started to slide, there was no end to it. Jean Douglass folded her hands briefly, prayed for her boy's rescue and for all the starving children in the world, and walked out to the kitchen.

AIRBORNE COMMAND POST/JANUARY 19/1100

Robert Grenvile leaned forward against his seat-belt, straining to hear over the drone of the helicopter. He pressed his palms hard on his temples in front of the headphones, listening to Peter Holt in Cardiff talk easily with Merlin.

"Certainly I understand your objectives," said Peter in Welsh.

Dan Evans translated at Robert's side, with occasional hesitations. Conversation made simultaneous work especially difficult, the translator had apologized; Mr. Holt's accent didn't help. That was the least of their problems, Robert reflected as the RAF Sea King bucked through an air pocket and levelled again. Robert hated the instability and vulnerability of helicopters. If it came to the worst, at least a fixed-wing craft had a glide path. The glide path of a disabled helicopter was straight down. He glanced out the port, down at the rolling countryside somewhere between the Upper Thames and the Lower Severn, and regretted it.

"Then what are you doing about it?" demanded Merlin.

Robert recognized rhetoric, not query. His ear was finely tuned for nuance; it was his life, his livelihood. Strange, to be merely an observer. Peter Holt was doing better than he hoped, letting Merlin talk out his anger, making the occasional informed comment. It had been a good idea, after all, involving the BBC reporter.

"You know that as well as I do," Evans translated Peter's answer. "Same as I've been doing for four years now. Interviewing, researching, taping. Putting together news packets and features. Selling the odd piece to CBS and other services. In other words, keeping people informed."

"So why are people still wholly ignorant of what's happening here?" A cry of rage and frustration. Still, Merlin was already less touchy than ten minutes ago, or during other calls. "Why doesn't anyone understand what's being done to Wales?"

"To Wales, to Chile, to Afghanistan, to Central America. Among other places," Holt admitted. "Simple. They'd rather watch soap operas than the news. They'd rather read Andy Capp than editorials. As long as it doesn't happen on their own turf. You can talk till you turn blue, but there's no point talking unless people listen."

"Yes." Merlin sounded thoughtful. "So you decide to do something else instead. Something spectacular that people can't ignore."

"Right," Peter said dryly. "But you've buggered it up this time, my boy."

Robert made a note to ask about the constant *machgen*, my boy. Did it convey specific familiarity, or was it just a turn of speech, like "man" in Brixton? How peculiar, to hear people rattling away in a foreign language spoken just an hour's flight west of London, right here in Britain. Perhaps a proposal re Welsh-language requirements for some negotiators? It was slow and uncertain, using a translator. There was also the question of the translator's sympathies, if he were a native. Robert decided to delay any proposal until the operation's outcome.

Merlin challenged angrily, "It's worked so far."

"You can't say it's worked until it over. And you'd best see it's over soon, with no lives lost."

"I'll see it's over soon, with our demands met," Merlin came back sharply. "Keep your lectures, Mister Holt, and get to work on the English government."

A sharp click. Someone had broken the connection.

"Shit," said Peter Holt idly.

"Excellent, Peter," Robert broke in and gave the reporter his instructions for tomorrow morning after things were set up at a temporary headquarters in the borderland. If nothing turned up in that area they would move on to South Wales. Robert got a nod of silent assent from Harold Stone, his personal supervisor. It unnerved him.

"Why did Merlin specially want Peter Holt? You don't

think he's party to any of this?'' asked Anna Chernicki from the far side of the helicopter's rear compartment.

She was squeezed between monitor screens, oscilloscopes, terminals, direction finders, a full range of radios, and other electronic arcana. A Scotland Yard team had worked feverishly through the night installing and testing the surveillance equipment while other teams fitted communications, *vip* seating instead of the standard web seats, and assorted other requirements for the mobile command post.

"Holt speaks Welsh, doesn't he?" Fox put in. "Can we really trust him?"

Shortly, Fox would be dropped at Bradbury Lines, the SAS base near Hereford. Robert briefly embraced the image of literally dropping the studiously hard-bitten SAS lieutenant-colonel, without parachute. Immediately, he felt guilty.

"Yes. And I speak Polish and Russian," Anna said coolly. "What do you think, Robert?"

"No, I don't think Holt's involved." Robert smiled. "I think he's too obsessed with news coverage to give much energy to anything else."

"Including family life, it seems," the PM's pin-striped aide said snidely. "You can take the plebs out of the gutter, but you can't take the gutter out of the plebs."

Anna Chernicki, ignoring him, drew one of her miniaturized devices from her briefcase. At first Robert had taken it for a pocket calculator, but she'd showed him the four-line display window constantly pouring out green digital numbers and text. Now she punched a fast code on the remote terminal's keyboard and bent attentively over her the small display. Fox watched her with barely concealed hostility.

"Override," said a surveillance technician conversationally. The quiet word was enough to swivel all heads. She added, "Monitor one, relay from National Security Agency, Maryland, via *gchq* Cheltenham. Restricted access, emergency waiver. Scrambled."

The relay blasted onto the monitor, and Mr. Leung leaped to adjust the volume. Of course, they were flying almost over Cheltenham right now. When the screen cleared, Robert saw the green-on-black webbing of the visual-identification mode. The left frame faded and resolved to the face of the second, unidentified security guard at the kidnapping. Brown hair worn longish, a pleasant face, grey eyes. The right frame resolved into a recognizable likeness, a blond young man in an armed-forces dress uniform Robert couldn't place, either decorations or insignia. Something obscure. Both faces blinked out, back to the green three-dimensional traceries that moved together and merged perfectly. The young man in uniform reappeared. The right half of the screen gave way to scrolling print.

NAME: Madog Sven Nilsson.

Robert absorbed the information line by line, avoiding Anna Chernicki's eyes as his frustration grew. A hundred years of hate and gun-running from the damnable American Irish; now Britain also had to contend with the American Welsh? The bloody Yanks could never stay out of anyone else's business, officially or unofficially. Robert scrubbed at his face as though he could scour away his fatigue and finally looked at Chernicki. She shook her head slightly as though deploring the same folly.

PERSONAL DATA: Born Seattle, Washington, U.S.A., 9 August 1947. Incomplete BSc (Physics, Computer Sciences) University of Washington. Divorced. Vice-President, Nilsson Aeronautics, RR1. Forster Island.

The monitor scrolled up steadily, line by line. Robert froze suddenly and tore at the papers in his attaché case. There it was, the report from the Dyfed-Powys police. He glanced back up at the screen full of personal data from NSA.

SPECIAL TRAINING: Pilot, medic, translator, electronics instructor, hand-to-hand combat, intelligence.
SECURITY CLEARANCE: Revoked 1975.
DUTY: Volunteered for service Seattle, Washington, June 1967. Captain, United States Army, First Cavalry Division. Tours in Vietnam, Cambodia. Activities classified. Medical discharge 1975.

"The same," confirmed Chernicki.

Robert blinked convulsively, still too startled to wonder why her expression had shifted closer to anger.

PRESENT STATUS: Classified. Reference * code red override *

"Do you have access?"

"No." She was already back at her keyboard. "Not our jurisdiction."

"Then whose jurisdiction is he?"

She didn't answer. A last line lingered on the screen. Leung was cycling the left side through Ordnance Survey maps and Fox was already forward talking to the RAF pilot.

PRESENT LOCATION: Pen y Cae (farm) near Llanygroes, Powys, Wales.

13

Jean Douglass stood in the parlour, insulated by shock, and listened to the terrorists shriek accusations at each other. Gwyn Davies, back from wherever he went every so often, stood in the open doorway scowling.

"When? We don't even know how long he's been gone."

"Are you sure he's not in that crawl space upstairs?"

"Nora, you were on watch."

"I don't watch the brat twenty-four hours a day." Nora shrugged. "It wasn't my turn."

"It was your turn," Gwyn Davies shot back. "If you can't do your part, then get out."

"Have you forgotten something, Nora?" interrupted Raffael. His voice was soft but it made the nanny's skin crawl. "Have you forgotten your commitment to this operation?"

Gwyn Davies ignored him, thank the dear. Jean had for days watched the power struggle between him and the Italian. At first, she wondered how she could make use of it. Soon she realized she could only provoke an explosion far more dangerous than Raffael's take-over bid yesterday, and his threats about Pip.

Jean saw that Madog, as usual, was watching each of them in turn. Finally he said, "Look, this isn't doing us

237

any good. I checked down at Cae Isa—the kid's not with John. He may be wandering around on these open hills in freezing weather. If we want him back safe and sound, we'd better start looking."

"I'll go," said Nora sullenly.

"You'll stay right here," Gwyn Davies told her. "On radio watch, if you can handle that much."

"Go fuck yourself," Nora told him, making no move.

"Upstairs!" Gwyn barked. She narrowed her eyes at him but went.

"You'll waste time sending any of your people," Jean ventured. Would they believe her? A few days ago she would have tried to escape. Now, after a hopeless week of unrelieved terror, she was more concerned with her boy's immediate safety. "Pip will only run away from them. I'll find him."

Gwyn Davies stared after Nora a moment longer, then nodded assent.

Jean let Madog help her into someone's dirty mac, then he put on his anorak. The Powell woman put on her coat and boots and started out the door. Jean held back fearfully—the woman was a killer, as good as self-confessed—but Madog took her arm. She felt safe with the American, misguided as he might be.

"We'll try the hay barn again," said the Powell woman in English as they went out. "It's eleven o'clock now. He's probably been gone a few hours."

"Hypothermia?" Madog asked her. "Could he freeze to death?"

The Powell woman hesitated. "Was he wearing his jacket, Miss Douglass?"

"I—I don't know," said Jean. She had failed Pip yet again, let down her darling by not keeping careful watch. Her failures weighed heavier on her every day. She was so unspeakably weary. Her eyes stung, and she had no strength left to fight the tears.

The Powell woman said something in Welsh. Madog shot her a concerned look and started down the frozen ruts towards the barn. No footprints marred the dry, grainy snow. The wind was lifting it like sand from a dune crest and eddying across the ruts. Even their own footprints were disappearing as they walked.

At the barn, the American crouched by the door and brushed his fingertips over the loose top layer of snow. Underneath, Jean saw a packed and scuffed area. Her heart beat faster. Of course, he would come back to the barn!

"Maybe he tried to get inside," Madog said. He lifted the tightly fitting crossbar. "But I doubt if he could move this."

In the chilly dark shed, with their breath curling overhead, nothing stirred. They checked under and around the Land Cruiser and the two tarpaulin-covered haystacks, which contained the stolen car and, Jean guessed, the Powell woman's car. There was nowhere else for even a small child to hide. Tears rose in her eyes at the dashed hope.

Outside again, Jean watched Madog examine the snow cover downhill from the barn. He shook his head in frustration and scanned the country west; she followed his gaze: barren slopes floured with snow, clumps of rust-brown bracken, dwarfed trees, boggy places in the hollows. If Pip had strayed far. . . . *Dear Merciful Lord, protect thy little child from the forces of evil and the terrors of flight.*

"I'll see if I can pick up a trail across the pastures. Carrie, you and Miss Douglass take the other side?"

"Yes. But Miss Douglass isn't dressed for wading through snow."

"Miss Douglass, do you want to go back?"

"Most certainly not."

"Other side of the road, then. Look along the ditches and fences for torn cloth, lost buttons."

The Powell woman started into the snowy grass. Jean hesitated, looking after Madog, but he was already well downhill, stooping to follow a crease of the pasture. She stumbled after the Welshwoman, her shoes packing with snow and the wind stinging her bare legs. If she ran, tried to escape, it wouldn't help her boy. The thought of Pip, alone and frightened and cold, brought tears to her eyes again. She struggled to keep her grip on reality, on her own soul, and felt it slipping. Jean had remembered the name of the syndrome—the Stockholm Syndrome—and she had resisted it until now. The Powell woman had deceived her for a few minutes, but now she felt not a shred of sympathy for these criminals.

"Stay closer," ordered the Powell woman.

Jean gasped as she plunged knee-deep into icy water hidden under matted reeds. Floundering, she flailed for balance. Before she could fall face-forward into the pool, the other woman steadied her and hauled her onto firmer ground. Jean recoiled from her hand in fear and revulsion. What was she doing stumbling across a snow-covered Welsh hillside with a killer? This nightmare would end, Jean told herself, and give way to the blessed day-spring of hope.

"All right? We should have found boots for you. Come along. Walking will keep your warm. We've got to find the boy."

The nanny faced her, shivering with shock and cold. "What do you care about that? You'd kill us both without a second thought."

The Powell woman shook her head. "Keep moving or you'll freeze."

"No." Jean stood her ground stubbornly, clenching her hands in the mac pockets. "I'll not go a step further till you give your word you'll not harm a hair on the child's head."

"Don't stand there like a lump, my girl. Move your bum."

"Give your word. Swear to God."

"There's one performance I'll spare you," said the Powell woman coldly. "Miss Douglass, the boy could be wandering over a cliff or stumbling into another of these lynchet holes. Don't you care?"

Jean, to her dismay, felt the tears start again and buried her face in her hands. It was too much, too much to bear. The other woman grasped her wrist and shook her roughly.

"No time for hysterics. Move, or I'll leave you here."

"No," sobbed the nanny. "I know you'll shoot him."

"O Duw," muttered the Powell woman. "Look now. I don't kill children. I just want to find the boy and escape with my life from these half-arsed Hitlers. You're not making things any easier."

"I'm not deceived by you." Jean wiped her eyes on the dirty sleeve of the mac. "You're like the rest of them."

"Don't talk *lol.* I told you, I have no part in this." The Powell woman's voice started to work its way up the register. "Madog lied. That Irish bitch was for shooting me, and you, too. Where's your wits? Now move, or we're both dead." The Powell woman shoved her forward and trudged up the snowy slop at her back. "I'm making a break. I think you and Pip should come along."

"Why should I believe you?" Jean realized she was pleading to believe.

"We'll find Pip and pinch John's Land Rover. By the time they start after us, we can be warm and safe in Llanygroes police station."

And put Pip's life at risk? Jean needed time to weigh the woman. Carrie Powell clearly knew these people, but Wales was a small country. Was Madog lying yesterday to save her? She had done naught but deny it. What would Jean have done in her place? The same thing, given the courage. But what about the Irish witch's claim that Carrie Powell had killed a man with a bomb? It shook Jean to the core that she could no longer tell who was lying and who was speaking the truth.

They reached a barbed-wire fence and worked their way along it to the track, always down towards Cae Isa. Madog was beyond sight, probably in the lower pasture. They found no trace of Pip, no shred of cloth, no footprint.

John Hughes met them at the door of his cottage in his overalls and wellies, cap pulled low over his eyes.

"No sign of the lad?" His English was almost incomprehensible.

"Na." Carrie Powell sounded as disheartened as Jean felt. "Let's have a look through your house, John."

His cottage was surprisingly clean, everything on its shelf in the spotless kitchen; the small parlour looked rarely used. They searched in cupboards, under furniture, anywhere a frightened small boy could have crawled to hide himself.

"I tried the cowshed," said John disconsolately.

"Loose hay in the loft?"

"Tried it."

"One more time."

The cowshed was a long three-walled building floored in hay, full of cows and half-grown calves. Their breath steamed out into the cold day, warmly scented with cattle, feed, and manure. Jean saw no loft, but the farmer and the Welshwoman walked purposefully towards the back of the building. The nanny edged between the horns and flanks and rolling eyes and saw a rickety ladder against the back wall. They climbed up one at a time. Once in the small hay loft, they had to stoop. Turning, Jean saw another shadow at their backs. The American had joined them.

"Call his name," said Carrie Powell.

"Pip! Pipsqueak, darling! Are you here?"

There was no answer.

In the small unadorned office in London, Corgi waited for three men to emerge from the early-morning rush of government workers.

The Home Office chap was first, brushing rain from the shoulders of his trench coat. He didn't bother to remove it. Next came the cabinet minister, carrying a briefcase in the hope of looking like another public servant. Last, after a good five minutes, arrived the young man with the expensive pin-stripes and political aspirations.

"Holt's flying around in a Sea King with Five chatting

up this arse-hole Merlin,'' the Home Office accused without preamble.

"Didn't get to him in time," admitted Corgi. "Soon. One way or another."

"Under Five's nose? With the fearless Fox as bodyguard?" The Home Office man exhaled a faint regret. He drew a folded paper from an inner breast pocket. "And didn't your Irish lady friend say the American was a harmless do-gooder?"

Corgi waited. Not the moment to contradict the higher-ups. The cabinet minister cleared his throat. The pol in pin-stripes said, "Well, old chap, don't keep it to yourself. Spoils the fun. Is he a spook?"

The Home Office bureaucrat yielded and passed around his printout. "Courtesy of a charming young fellow in the code room. Most co-operative."

One by one they read, then the Home Office man returned it to his pocket.

"Good," said Corgi, taking the initiative. "We have a location."

"Marvellous," chortled the pol. "I do admire sang-froid."

"The boy," said the man from the Home Office without looking at him. "That's the key. A tragedy. Nice little chap done to death by heartless bastard terrorists."

"The voters will approve," said the minister. "A firm hand on the reins."

"Yes. Only right to bring down the full force of the law to deal with such a travesty," the man in the trench coat agreed, getting to his feet. "But we have work to do. Gentlemen."

The pin-striped pol hurried to hold the door. Corgi lit a cigarette as they left and noted with pleasure that his hands trembled not at all.

The whole plan took his breath away. Devious. Better than devious. Positively Byzantine. Corgi, proud of his nonchalance over such matters, had to confess he was truly astounded. He drew on the cigarette, inhaling deeply.

Amazing employers. A renegade right-wing Tory Cabinet minister, a young man with an unseemly lust for his master's portfolio, and a sport from the Home Office: all three had political ambitions naked enough to make Corgi feel as tender as Bob Geldof, the Irish bleeding heart.

And an amazing contract. Corgi, after dropping an enterprising word about Tywyn in the right ear, had been hired to reccy out the rest of the plan and hop a free ride on it. If everything went as planned, final inventory cooked up by his new employers would read: one kid tragically deceased, one unholy home counties rage against the Welsh, one round of martial law to show the need for a strong law and order government, one coup at the upcoming Tory party convention, and one victory sweep in the next general election. And one troublesome television reporter neutralized by the by.

Bold, very bold indeed. Called for a cool head and a steady hand. But Corgi liked the fee, still had to pinch himself to believe it. A lifetime's earnings, maybe twice that, for one operation. He'd be able to retire to some gentle clime replete with winsome brown maidens. Tahiti was threadbare. Riviera was too near. Grand Cayman? Too many Canadians, he'd die of boredom. Sri Lanka?

Corgi, contemplating a splendid future, exhaled one perfect smoke ring.

In the hay barn there was only the sound of the cattle below stamping and lowing.

"Pip, darling!" Jean called.

Straw rustled suddenly at the dark end of the loft.

"It's only a cat," she said in disappointment.

A marmalade-and-white cat bolted past them and leapt down into the shed. Carrie crouched forward, lifting bundles of hay here and there. The nanny followed, knowing it was no use. Then John grunted and pointed into the shadowed corner. Jean knelt quickly and saw her boy curled around his beloved Mungo Mouse, straw in his hair, sleepy-eyed.

"We had an adventure, like Reepicheep." He sat up. "I came to visit Mr. Hughes."

Jean opened her mouth and closed it as tears swelled her throat. She shook her head wordlessly, lifted her boy in her arms and hugged him tight. *I praise thee, Lord, and all thy works.* Pip yawned behind a fist.

"We missed you up at Pen y Cae, Pip," said the American. "Let's go back and say hello to Miss Elen and your friend Pal. I'll be along in a minute. Just want a word with John."

Pip was asleep on Jean's shoulder, with Mungo clutched next to his heart, before they got to the bottom of the ladder.

"Now!" said Carrie Powell, taking Jean's arm. "We can—"

"Now, Miss Powell?" Beside the ladder, Raffael stood smiling. "Come along. Let us return to our charming country retreat."

PEN Y CAE/JANUARY 20/0600

Wednesday at first light, Gwyn watched John Hughes slog away from the door, leaving a trail of splayed black footprints across the snowy yard.

"Little government men prowling round Cae Isa saying they wanted to check the electricity," John had come to say. What did that mean? Had they located Pen y Cae as Grenvile threatened? Gwyn turned to Madog across the back kitchen, but the American had slipped silently out

"Tea?" asked Jean Douglass, rattling mugs on the draining board.

Gwyn shook his head. He was suspicious of her sudden politeness. Not one of these people could really be trusted. Even the kid ran away as soon as their backs were turned.

Sion. Sion was a weasel; good thing he wasn't clever enough to do much harm. Carrie. Had Madog really been lying about working with her? Elen no longer came silently every night to share Gwyn's cot in the radio room.

Nora was a mad dog. Raffael was the revolution's loyal servant, clawing his way up the corporate ladder to favour with the colonel. If that failed, Raffael would find cold cash an acceptable palliative. And what about Gwyn Davies? Once he had wanted to see the country and the language take root and blossom anew. And he had wanted Carrie. Now at best he seemed destined to lecture in a dead language. What was his own palliative? Revenge?

Madog. He wondered if even Madog knew what loyalty brought him here. Was it obligation to a cynical and bloody-handed organization, or sentiment for a country that was never his?

Elen interrupted his thoughts with a yell from the top of the stairs.

LLANYGROES/JANUARY 20/0800

"Llanygroes." Peter searched the map. "South of Llanfyllin?"

"North," said Al Rees.

"We'll meet them there. The farm is two miles out."

They drove out of Knighton's precariously tilted market square and climbed northwards out of the Teme valley. Peter struggled to unfold the Ordnance Survey map, which aggravated Welsh schizophrenia by dividing the country into north and south sheets. He found the village and shoved the map under a stack of science-fiction paperbacks on the dashboard. The back seat was packed with Al's camera case, his own tape recorders, and a tangle of BBC equipment. In return for helping Grenvile, Peter had received Al Rees, a carload of cameras, and freedom of the press. At least for one member of the press.

Peter yawned. Grenvile's early phone call, and the conversation with Merlin, had ended another long night of staring at the ceiling. He was stumbling into clothes and ringing the photographer before he fully comprehended what he was doing, where they were going. Fragments of Grenvile's explanation retained toe-holds on his memory.

North Wales border. Stake-out. Converging on target. Stress face-to-face negotiation. Alternative strike plan. They were still only words, official double-talk.

"Who's going to be there?"

Once again Al was wearing a shirt with Day-Glo palm trees and his silvered leather bomber jacket, a statement either of aesthetics or of renewed willingness to be conspicuous. Peter had groped out his second-best corduroy suit, the one with elbow patches, and a duffle coat. Ventures into the Welsh back country also demanded the wellies he'd tossed into Al's boot.

"Grenvile," Peter told him. "Probably some of the other people from London. He said Special Air Services generously offered to take over operations, but he sounded less than ecstatic. No love lost between SAS and military intelligence, I reckon."

"SAS and anyone."

Peter shrugged. "They're effective."

"Sometimes," Al snorted. "Remember the time they got lost in the Brecon Beacons? Training recruits or something. They wandered around in a snowstorm until one of their big men froze to death. The Brecon Mountain Rescue people had to bring them out. When they are effective, they're thugs. SAS? Drop the A."

"What's the government supposed to do?" demanded Peter irritably. "Let these people keep the Prince until they finally panic and kill him?"

"You think the kid stands a better chance with your SAS goons?"

"They're just soldiers. Better trained then most."

"Remember Tywyn?" asked Al, leaning into a sharp right-hand turn.

"What about it?"

"*Clecs* says the bombing was done by an ex-SAS man. Does some work for a London security company as a hired gun."

"Hired gun? You're watching too many westerns."

"Peter *bach*, I never watch westerns."

"Too violent, I suppose?" Peter asked sarcastically.

"Too unreal. The good guys always win."

"You're daft. Someone's pulling your leg. It had to be one of the Cadwyn idiots buggering up, or the IRA getting too enthusiastic over a favour to their Celtic cousins."

"Right." Al said nothing more, despite prodding.

Peter flicked on the car radio for the news. University colleges on strike in Cardiff, Swansea, Bangor, Aberystwyth. Five non-conformist ministers on a hunger fast in Caerfyrddin. Yann Morvan giving an Aberystwyth benefit concert for Welsh political prisoners. The bottom story was the self-styled native Prince of Wales, Llywelyn Probert-Vaughan, holding forth in his swanky English voice. Tiresome old fart.

"One's enough, if not too many," he muttered, yawning. Thank Christ Davies was a socialist of sorts. Llywelyn II's ghost could appear with his severed head under his arm, still bloody from the ambush at Cilmeri, and Davies would only belabour him about the innate virtue of the *gwerin*.

"You all right?"

"Better than ever."

"Crazier than ever. Start talking to yourself on telly and see what it gets you. Bad enough that you speak Welsh. Got that radio?"

Peter pulled Al's hand-held two-metre radio from the rubbish under the seat and passed it over. Al switched it on and began flipping through the frequencies as he drove. On the sixth channel, he found a heated Welsh debate over coach-line cancellations and left it open.

Al was again taciturn. "What did BBC say about all this?"

Peter looked out the windscreen. Dirty snow was packed in the corners. "The Old Man liked my dedication. Wondered how I acquired so much information that these government chaps needed my help. Suggested that when all this nonsense was over, we should have a long chat."

"Huh." Al looked sideways from his dark eyes. "Promotion to news editor?"

"Hope so."

"Life as a special agent already dull?"

"Sod off, Rees. I never looked for this."

"Yeah," the photographer ceded, sending Peter one of his inscrutable Hawaiian looks. "That's what we all say."

"Christ!" Peter cut across him, reaching for the volume dial on his two-metre radio. "Listen."

Madog looked around the stunned faces in the radio room. On the second hearing, with translation to English, they were starting to get the idea.

"Break. Break," a woman's homely mid-Wales voice intruded into the Harangue on bus routes. She had already swept the other channels with her cool announcement. "Clear all frequencies, if you please, for emergency calls. Relay all available information on movements of five unmarked Land Rovers, two Fox combat vehicles, three closed vans in Llanygroes region. No insignia, west country plates. Lynx helicopter, no insignia, and two Sea King helicopters, RAF insignia, origin reported as Hereford, repeat Hereford. Clear all frequencies, if you please—"

"Hereford," said Davies. "The SAS base is at Hereford!"

A man's voice interrupted in book Welsh, learner's Welsh. "Clear all frequencies, repeat, clear all frequencies. This is a national security matter. Violators will be traced, de-licenced, and charged."

There was, momentarily, a silence of stunned disbelief. Then it started. Accusations, panic.

"Hereford means SAS!" Elen wailed. "If they send in SAS we're dead!"

"I told you we had to get out!" Nora spat over her shoulder. "We're going to be trapped here and shot down in cold blood!"

Jean Douglass gave a stifled shriek, and Madog turned to see Nora's shotgun at the little boy's head. Beside her stood Raffael with his Beretta drawn. Pip closed his eyes tightly, clutching his mouse doll. Madog got to his feet carefully, balancing on a knife blade. Darkness lay below on either side.

"Can it, Raffi." He forced his mouth to shape words in a laid-back western drawl. "We've got a lot to do around here."

"We must get out. The boy is worth money in Ireland or Europe, I guarantee. He's worth nothing dead. Nor are we."

"Sure. So let's not risk the investment, huh? We can work out the details later."

Raffael finally nodded, and the Beretta's silencer dropped just enough. Before anyone could have second thoughts, Madog seized the gun barrel left-handed and spun him across the room. He yelled as he hit the wall beside the dresser and lost his footing. Before the Brigatisto reached the floor, Davies was covering him with his Browning. By some kind of miracle, Nora restrained her trigger finger. On the cot, Jean Douglass started to cry in deep, choking sobs.

Madog shoved the Beretta into his belt. Raffael, picking himself up carefully, made no objection.

Madog leaned against the radio room wall. It was shaking, or perhaps that was him. He spun at a tug on his belt and looked down. Pip was hanging on to him with one hand and to Mungo Mouse with the other. Madog found a grin and hoisted the kid up for a piggyback. It was over. He did it. He hoped he'd never have to do it again.

Snow blew across Llanygroes market square, blurring the faces and clothes of the twenty-odd men and women circling with placards. Al Rees skidded his Cortina to a stop in front of the boarded-up post office, jumped out, and began pulling camera equipment from the back seat. Peter hauled out his notebooks and small recorder, then Al's battery pack.

"Cover shots, first, interviews later?"

"Get it while it's hot," Al agreed, whistling behind his crooked teeth.

"Who are they?"

Peter knew better than to ask how the protesters happened to be here. Al's unregistered two-metre radio was answer enough. Ten minutes after Grenvile's call this morning, Al's contacts probably knew all they needed. Peter scanned the demonstrators' signs and saw the interlaced-sun symbol of Undeb Cymru Fydd and the chainlinks of Cadwyn. Predictable.

"Local people, probably. A few up from Aberystwyth, since university classes are shut down."

"Merlin's people?"

Al's gaze travelled across the square. Marchers straggled slowly around the snow-limned First World War memorial. Peter could make out its Welsh inscription, starkly outlined in snow, though few local people would understand it now. The usual village patriotism, something about refusing shame and accepting the burden for the sake of fellow countrymen. Then the columns of names: mostly Hugheses, a few Thomases, Williamses, and Parrys.

"*Clecs* says most people didn't know about the protest. Plenty wouldn't support it if they did know."

Peter nodded. That sounded more likely than his last bit of news from the grape-vine, Al's claim about the Tywyn bomb. He wondered about Yann Morvan and the rumoured Huey gunship but Al had set him up so he couldn't confirm it or even mention it.

The demonstrators pulled themselves into better order as Al began taping. A grey-haired woman agreed to an interview. Mair Williams, farmer's wife, local Women's Institute president, local chairman of Undeb Cymru Fydd. No, Undeb and Cadwyn weren't expecting anything in particular today. Yes, everyone was terribly distressed about the Prince's disappearance, but equally disturbed about the reprisals against Welsh activists.

Peter finished the interview and signalled Al to stop rolling.

"Edrycha." Al nudged him and pointed.

Peter glanced at the narrow Llanfyllin road entering the square between tall houses. The protesters also saw and straggled towards the approaching procession of several Land Rovers and large blue vans. Mair Williams lay down in the dirty snow of the Llanfyllin Road, and the others followed her example. The first Land Rover ghosted to a halt. The passenger briefly spoke into a radiophone mike. Then he got out of the Land Rover, a nondescript man wearing a black pullover and black wool trousers. He had a black scarf wound round his head, covering his face below the eyes like a Ninja flick villain. He approached the demonstrators.

"Can I help you to your feet?" he asked in book Welsh.

"No, thank you."

Mair Williams looked up at him over the hand-lettered placard she held against her chest. Peter allowed himself a second's contemplation of the surrealistic exchange, then turned to Al. He was rolling tape, chewing away on his Wrigley's as though the camera's mechanism depended on it.

"We'll have to ask you to move, ma'am," said the man in black.

"Why?" She sounded mildly interested.

"Operational procedures."

"Whose operational procedures, if you please?"

"British government."

The man extended a hand but Mair Williams shook her grey head. the other protesters watched impassively. Finally he nodded, turned away, and leaned into his Land Rover for another radiophone conversation. Within seconds two dozen men, similarly dressed, were in Llanygroes market square. Each of them approached a demonstrator and hoisted the man or woman upright. No one resisted. They used no overt force, noted Peter, and he saw no weapons. The Undeb and Cadwyn people were herded into a silent and watchful group near the snow-moulded doorstep of the Harp public house. The black-garbed soldiers, if they were soldiers, stood easy a few paces distant. Peter waited, impatient to tape a second chat with the Williams woman.

The first man signalled his driver. Three Land Rovers, then three vans, rolled into the square and parked around the memorial statue. When their motors died, Peter heard the snow-muffled chatter of an approaching helicopter. A camouflage-green Sea King descended slowly and touched down on the snow-packed sandstone cobbles. RAF markings were clearly visible on its fuselage. Snow whipped around its long rotors, creating a blizzard in the heart of Llanygroes. Several people crouched and climbed out of the chopper, down into a maelstrom. Peter recognized Major Grenvile but made no move towards him. Let the bastard come to him for a change.

Grenvile stooped forward and walked out of range of the blades. The prime minister's arse-hole aide and the American woman followed. Her auburn hair was braided around her head, and she was wearing a camouflage field jacket over a fawn suede jump suit. The latest fashion in the States, or practicality? She looked bizarre but classy.

"Peter!"

Like the bloody advert for record players. His master's voice. Peter scowled, knowing Al Rees was grinning lazily at him around his wad of gum. Grenvile approached with his right hand extended.

"To the best of these people's knowledge, I'm an honest man," Peter said before the negotiator could start in with more instructions. He ignored the hand. "This is my cameraman, Al Rees."

Grenvile, taken aback, thrust his hand at Al instead. The photographer shook it enthusiastically, smiling broadly.

"Thanks for meeting us here," Grenvile said. "We can go on to the farm now."

They all looked up at the sound of another helicopter. No insignia, flat black fuselage, conspicuous laser and machine-gun mounts. The smaller Lynx chopper banked at speed around the square, then angled in three feet above the roof slates for a stagey landing. The pilot was a stick cowboy, more interested in show than in safety. The American woman shook her head, and Grenvile's face froze to brief hostility. He recovered his nervous aplomb by the time a rust-haired man reached them from the Lynx. It was the eager-beaver sas officer Peter had met at Scotland Yard.

"Get that camera out of here," he shouted at Grenvile, louder than the rotor noise warranted. "And confiscate the tape. This isn't a public event, Grenvile."

"Right," yelled Peter. "I'll be going."

"Stay where you are," Grenvile snapped back. "Mr. Holt has been kind enough to co-operate, Colonel. I've already approved his taping."

"You have no authority to approve anything of the kind." Fox turned to one of the black-clad men who'd followed him out of the helicopter. This one was blond and freckled. "Corporal, bring me that tape."

"Sir."

Al Rees shoved his gum into his cheek, nodded affably, and pulled a video cassette out of the pocket of his silver bomber jacket. "Just changed cassettes."

"Open up the camera," the corporal ordered. He sounded Northern Irish.

Al opened the side, revealing an empty tape slot. The corporal fell back one regulation pace with Al's cassette.

"We tape or we leave," Peter said flatly.

"Then you leave."

"Right." Peter nodded to Al and started away, wondering how they could slip back within taping distance. "Thanks for nothing."

"Wait," began Grenvile. Peter turned.

The professor interrupted. "We're wasting time."

Fox eyed her coldly. "Let us understand this situation, Dr. Chernicki. There is no 'we' here, whatever Washington may have led you to believe. All that's wasting time is

Grenvile's notion that he can talk the terrorists out. They won't come out unless they're dragged out.''

''Dead or alive?'' rasped Grenvile, having trouble with his voice again. ''I know bodies are less trouble, but my orders are to get everyone out of that farmhouse alive. The Prince and Miss Douglass to safety, the gunmen to trial. That's not negotiable, Lieutenant-Colonel, nor is open to further discussion. If you're not satisfied, call COBRA for orders.'' He turned to Peter. ''Carry on taping. Just respect our agreement not to broadcast until after the operation.''

''Right.''

Al nodded as though no exchange had taken place. ''I need more tape. Peter *bach*, lend a hand with the battery pack.''

Peter opened his mouth to say Al already had the battery pack slung under his arm, then thought better. When they reached the car, Al turned away from the group in the middle of the square and pulled a videotape cassette from his back waistband.

''Think I was born yesterday? I always bring a spare tape.''

''What did you give him?'' Peter reached into the boot and shoved the protest cassette under the spare tire. Al pulled their gear from the back seat and locked the car.

''Pirate copy of *Deep Throat*, dubbed in Welsh.''

Peter laughed. ''With any luck, they'll spend all day breaking it down for code.''

Al shook his head and shoved more blank tapes in his pocket. ''Whose side are you on, anyhow? Make up your mind, *bach*.''

Grenvile was waiting for them by the war memorial. ''Are you prepared to talk to Merlin?''

''As ready as I'll ever will be.'' Peter had a queasy thought. ''But not under fire, see? Not if they start any fireworks.''

''Of course not.'' Grenvile bridled at the suggestion.

''Listen, Grenvile.'' Peter remembered what he'd

wanted to ask. "You can call off your bloody spook. He's been making a pest of himself, pumping me about the kidnapping and trying to talk me into getting out of the country. Now he's hanging around my ex-wife and kid."

Grenvile glanced at him, puzzled. "There's no one on you, Peter."

"English. Calls himself Teddy Smythe. Deep sun-tan, fair hair. Drives a white Volvo. Upper-crust voice."

"Peter, that could be anyone."

Peter remembered Andrea's scandalized observation. "He has a tattoo of a dog on his arm. A corgi."

The negotiator motioned over a technician and repeated the description. "Call it in to GCHQ and see if they have anything."

Peter walked around the square with Al while they waited for the technician's reply. They got some cover footage of the protesters deep in talk with a knot of the black-clad men. Second-rate stuff, without any real action. Peter headed back to the Sea King when he saw the technician emerge to hand Grenvile a printout. He talked quietly with Grenvile for a moment, glancing once in Peter's direction.

"Well?"

"Your wife's address," Grenvile said. "And your child's school. We'll send people out, just to be safe."

"Why?" Peter demanded.

"Is this the man?" Grenvile folded the printout in half and held it so Peter could see the top half where a pattern of dots made up a fair likeness of Teddy Smythe.

"Looks like. What the hell do you mean, just to be safe?" Grenvile retrieved the printout and folded it into quarters, not meeting Peter's eyes. "He's ex-military, works for a London security firm as a bodyguard, that sort of thing. We have no idea why he should have involved himself in your affairs. He has a rather mixed reputation."

"Ex-SAS, no doubt," Peter said caustically, remembering Al's nonsense, and scribbled Elizabeth's address on a sheet of his notepad.

Grenvile didn't answer, and Peter glanced up. The negotiator's face was dancing with a nervous tic. Christ. Exactly what Al's *clecs* said.

"Explosives expert?" What else was on that carefully folded sheet?

"Among other things."

"Right." Peter felt sweat break out on his scalp. A mixed reputation for what? Murdering children? And Andrea thought he was funny. A nice man, Daddy. He had to keep his temper, keep cool. "I'm going back to Cardiff." He started away, looking for Al. He'd have to borrow the car.

"Sorry, Peter. That's not possible." Grenvile blinked. "It's in the national interest."

"Screw the national interest. That's my kid you're talking about. Or is it just the other kid that's important?" Peter lost his calm and yelled. "Does a few million pounds make a difference between one kid and another kid? Between their lives?"

Grenvile scrubbed a hand over his face. "You gave your word."

Peter stared at him, too angry to speak.

"We'll take care of it. You have my guarantee. I take personal responsibility. But I can't let you go back to Cardiff." Grenvile glanced across the square and cleared his throat. "It's been suggested already that you're collaborating with these people. That could result in a charge of treason. Both you and your family are better off if you continue to give your help here. That's not a threat, Peter, and it's not blackmail. It's the simple truth."

Peter started another objection, then realized the negotiator was as shaken as he was. He turned back to Grenvile and handed over the address. "Tell them to hurry."

The technician took the slip and ducked into the helicopter.

The RAF crew were climbing back into the Sea King. Fox's black chopper roared suddenly and lifted, churning snow around the market square. Grenvile narrowed his eyes to watch it disappear northwards between slate roofs and slate-grey sky. A cold gust whipped grainy snow from the rooftops.

Dr. Chernicki suddenly whirled around to face the boarded-up post office. Peter heard a sound from the late-night movies, the stutter of automatic rifle fire. Something spat across the snowy cobbles and struck stone chips from the house opposite. The protesters had vanished, leaving the door of the Harp open behind them. Now someone kicked it shut. The black-clad soldiers dived for their vehicles and began to back out into the Llanfyllin Road. There was no cover in Llanygroes market square; even the plinth of the war memorial was too low. Refuse shame, accept the burden. Peter stared around, stunned.

"Get out of here!" The American woman grabbed his arm and pulled him towards the Sea King.

Al kept on taping the Land Rovers' single-file retreat, confident in the protection of his trade-mark silver jacket. Then another burst scattered snow a few yards to his left. He spat out his gum and sprinted for the chopper as Peter ducked inside the hatch.

The chopper lifted before the door slammed shut, rising as rapidly as the Lynx had done. Grenvile, strapped into a seat beside the flight engineer, was already talking into a mike. He reported flatly to someone that they had been fired on and had withdrawn.

"Twll dyn," growled Al in rare anger, brushing snow off his jacket. "The sodding Gog shot at me. I'll have a talk with those boys later."

So much for refusing to co-operate under fire, thought Peter. It was already a thing of the past.

"As we predicted," Dr. Chernicki murmured to Stone, the silent man whom Peter took to be Grenvile's boss. "A military presence provoked immediate violence. You people could create a new Belfast."

They circled the town. On the outskirts, the military vehicles and two grey armoured carriers were regrouping, perhaps for a more cautious entry into Llanygroes.

Five minutes later they dropped to tree-top level where a rutted track left the secondary road and veered uphill through a forestry plantation. Al taped steadily as they flew over evergreens thinning to scrubby pasture; the track wandered on uphill to three whitewashed stone farmhouses within a radius of about a mile. Two Land Rovers and another camouflage-green Sea King were nestled down under the south brow of the hill. Grenvile pointed to the farthest house.

"Pen y Cae."

14

Gwyn saw the black Lynx hover on the south horizon, then drop below the hill shoulder near Cae Isa. He turned from the radio-room window to watch Madog leaning into the black priest's hole, pulling things out. Beside him squatted Pip with Mungo Mouse under one arm, sucking his thumb; the kid had attached himself to Madog after the ugly scene with Nora and Raffael an hour ago. When he wasn't clinging to the American's belt, he was trotting at his heels.

Jean Douglass sat on the cot, weeping steadily into her folded arms, but no one had sympathy to spare for her. Raffael claimed the first Avtomat Kalashnikov that Madog hauled out of his cache but showed no more sign of threatening the boy. The others were silent.

Nothing moved outside the house for a long time. Gwyn heard two more helicopters arriving. Then the rising wind swept away other sounds. Dry granular snow ticked steadily against the windows of Pen y Cae and grew into a white ledge on the outside sills.

"What the devil are they doing down there?" Gwyn knew he spoke from nerves, not curiosity.

"Setting up some kind of headquarters, I guess," answered Madog.

"Can we bluff? Hide the others in the crawl space and pretend there's only you and me?"

"And Nora? The local cops saw her on Saturday night. Here, will you take this downstairs?" Madog handed over a burlap-wrapped shape, too large for a rifle.

Gwyn cradled the package in both arms and went downstairs past Raffael and Nora, who had been talking in rapid German on the landing; he heard his name once and Madog's. They fell silent as he passed and resumed when he reached the bottom. Trading the Prince and his nanny for his ransom demands was no longer his greatest problem. That now took second place to keeping them alive; Raffael and Nora seemed intent on murder.

Gwyn laid the bundle on the kitchen floor beside the cooker and went to the window. He'd sent Elen and Sion to nail boards over the windows, buying an extra twenty seconds' respite if there were an assault on the house. He squinted between the boards, scanning the yard. Snow was drifting up against the trunks of the stunted orchard trees and three starlings were pecking at one desiccated apple still on the branch. Otherwise, there was no movement or life.

He loosened the twine that bound Madog's bundle. It was too late for new secrets. He unwrapped the sacking and sat back on his heels in shock. Madog had handed him a Blowpipe anti-tank device. If they wanted, they could drop a minor inferno on anyone within eyesight of the house. And, given a chance, Raffael might do it. *Tanto maglio, tanto peggio.* Gwyn searched his memory of the Libyan instructor's lesson on the old Blowpipe as he examined the deadly thing lying on the slate floor. If he destroyed the guidance system, the missile would only kill at random, an aerial version of Russian roulette. *O Duw.* He heard footsteps on the stairs, grabbed the thing from the slates, and shoved it far under boxes and boards in the pantry. Madog appeared in the doorway as Gwyn rattled around over the sink for tea.

"Where is it?"

''Back there,'' Gwyn said too sharply. ''Out of harm's way.''

Madog nodded. Out of Nora's and Raffael's way, they both understood. He sat in one of the wooden chairs watching Gwyn.

''Count me out, Gwyn. If there's an assault.''

Gwyn swung around, slopping hot water over his hand. Madog was looking across the dim back kitchen towards the boarded-up window. All the questions he'd never asked. . . .

''This is where you change sides? Are your American bosses waiting down the hill?''

''They're not . . . nothing like that. I should have told you.'' Madog looked uneasy. ''About Cambodia.''

''Cambodia?'' Gwyn found he was staring and deliberately looked down to measure tea-leaves into the cup of water. He spilled most of them.

''They brought me out in a strait-jacket.''

''You were all right in London. And this morning, with Raffi.''

Madog tried for the million-dollar smile and missed by a long way.

Gwyn stirred his tea, watching its slow amber spiral. He searched for something to say and failed. ''What happened?''

''There was a town. Sarsar Sdam.''

''There *was* a town?''

''The Khmer Rouge hit it hard. I was in the area as an observer. They kept me a prisoner.''

Gwyn saw Madog's hesitation, his decision to say no more. Enough had already been said about Khmer Rouge tortures.

''You shouldn't be alive.''

''Yeah.'' Madog laughed, a dry laugh without humour. ''Gwyn—''

''We're all afraid,'' Gwyn said. ''And I have more on my conscience than you.''

"Sure of that? What about Drake? He trusted me. I set him up."

Gwyn hesitated. "What's done is done."

Madog studied his face too long for comfort. "It won't be a long siege, *catlyw*."

Gwyn turned angrily back to the draining board. The American mocked him. The archaic word meant general, war leader. "That's all best forgotten."

"No." Madog got to his feet. "If we forget, who remembers?"

"Why are you here?" Gwyn was unable to reconcile missile launchers with historical romanticism.

"Cymru Fydd. A future for Wales."

Gwyn snorted. "What do your people want? Do you want to stop political action or do you want to keep it going?"

"Regretting the compromise?" asked Madog quietly. "Most of us do, Gwyn."

"Tell me now. I need to know."

"You already know. You asked me. A week ago."

Gwyn flared in anger. "You denied everything I asked?"

"Three strikes and you're out. I never denied the fourth, buddy."

Gwyn racked his brains. What had it been? "U.S. Military intelligence?"

Madog looked across the kitchen. Morning light slanted between the boards on the window and onto the slate floor.

"Whom have you sold us to?"

"I haven't sold you to anyone. And won't."

"Bullshit."

Madog's million-dollar smile flashed in the dim light. "Never heard of double agents? Maybe I sold someone to you. You couldn't win at this game of yours. But maybe you can still win."

"At your game?"

"You got it." Madog turned and walked out of the kitchen.

Riddles. And lies.

Gwyn watched him go out, then followed him upstairs past Raffael and Nora, who were silent now. At the radio-room window Elen finished hammering up what looked like a table leaf and returned to duty at the radio. The cat, on Carrie's shoulder, was carefully grooming her hair. The nanny had cried herself out and sat with Pip and his faithful Mungo Mouse on her lap. Nothing more to be done here; Gwyn fetched the kerosene lamp out of its niche at the top of the stairs, lit it, and trimmed the wick. At the radio, Elen idly turned the dials, skipping from one empty band to the next. The emergency call had worked all too well. Pen y Cae now had no information, no diversion. Only empty air waves and time on their hands. The radio crackled noisily and Elen looked to Madog for help.

"Atmospherics." Madog leaned across her to tune out the static. Instead he pulled in a voice as clear as someone speaking from the next room: the broadly accented Welsh of Peter Holt.

"Merlin? Merlin? I know you have radio apparatus. Do you read me? Can you answer?"

Madog looked at Gwyn, not taking matters into his own hands for once. Maybe it was true about Cambodia, Gwyn thought. Maybe it was just an excuse for the American to keep out of trouble.

"Merlin? Merlin? Can you hear me?"

In silence they listened to Holt repeat his plea a second time and a third time. Gwyn went to stand by Madog's shoulder and gripped the back of his wooden chair.

"I'll talk to him."

Madog pulled the microphone out of the drawer and plugged it in.

"Push this when you want to talk, release it when you're finished."

Merlin here," said Gwyn into the mike.

A long silence followed. Lamplight sketched despair on most of the faces, but wild hope on Jean Douglass's. Outside, the wind rhythmically clapped a loose roof slate.

Otherwise it was quiet enough to hear the hiss of snow against the north-facing window.

"Thank God," said Peter Holt at last. "You all right?"

"What do you suppose?" Gwyn asked angrily. "Get to the point."

Holt paused a moment, probably taking instructions from whatever English overseers he had with him. "You wanted me as a negotiator. They won't allow me to strike bargains with you, only to relay messages."

"So get on with it. Relay your messages."

"Grenvile wants to get off short wave. Things are touchy enough without talking on an open band. Will you let a man bring up a field phone?"

"What are you giving in return?"

A few seconds' silence. "Talk, instead of an immediate assault."

Gwyn glanced at Madog, who nodded agreement.

"Make it quick."

From Madog's room, they watched between the boards over the window. In minutes, a man in black clothes arrived on the double from the direction of Cae Isa, deposited something on the doorstep, and retreated. Sion fetched the field phone and Holt resumed the conversation.

"What do you want?" demanded Gwyn. "Apart from stalling?"

"First, remember this is very serious business indeed."

Gwyn looked around. Everyone in the radio room could hear the conversation, but only the Welsh-speakers could follow it. "Yes. I'm having trouble keeping the child safe."

"Just a minute—never mind. They can't do anything about it now, anyway. How can I help you?"

"Who's out there? Where are they? What are they planning?"

"You know the protocol. I can't tell you anything unless you tell me something."

"What do you want?"

"A chat with Miss Douglass. No trick questions, I just want to know she and the boy are all right."

"Wait."

Gwyn motioned Jean over. She jumped up, spilling Mungo onto the floor, and took the receiver.

"No tricks, mind."

She shook her head, bright-eyes. "Hello? Hello? Mr. Holt? This is Jean Douglass."

"You'll have to prove it, Miss Douglass. Sorry, but I know there are at least two other women in there. What's your brother's address in Glasgow?"

"He lives in London. At 27 Gerald Street."

"Right. How's the Prince?"

"Tired, and he doesn't have much appetite. He's been reasonably well treated until today."

"You'd better explain that."

Jean Douglass bit her lip, and kept quiet.

"Is he all right now?"

"Yes. Will you be able to exchange us—at least, exchange him—for letting these people escape, or something of that sort?"

"I certainly hope so, Miss Douglass. Let me talk to Merlin again."

Gwyn recovered the phone. "Now tell me who's out there. And where."

"Grenvile's here, plus an American woman, a surveillance crew, and a creature from Number 10. There's another lot here. I don't know what they are."

"SAS?"

"Maybe."

"How many?"

"Couldn't say. They're never all together."

"What are they planning?"

"I don't know. I don't think they know. You're out of questions, *nghyfaill*."

"Why call me that?" Gwyn asked coldly.

"You are my friend. I wouldn't be here if you weren't."

"I read the negotiator's handbook, too, Holt."

"Why are you always so hard-arse cynical?"

"Are you asking, or your English bosses?"

Holt's voice gained a decibel and grew more broadly Lancashire. "Just a bloody minute. Get one thing clear right now. I am English. I'm here to see if I can help save the kid's neck and your necks, and let the world know what's happening in this country. Understand?"

"Yes." Maybe Holt was talking straight. But friends? "What do they want? The English?"

"Not English, British. Remember that, Merlin. Scots and English and Irish. Some Welsh."

"Traitors."

"You think everyone with a different political bias is a traitor?"

"Cymry Cymraeg who work against me are traitors. The *gwerin* support me."

"They care about the boy. He's the next Prince of Wales, remember? They take pride in him. He's theirs." Holt paused. "Grenvile wants face-to-face negotiation."

"No." Gwyn was glad of safer ground. "This is as close as he gets."

"They know who you are. They matched the kidnap tape with your trial shots on a computer scan. We may as well drop this 'Merlin.' "

"That's my name for the duration. What else do they know?"

"Give me more information. How many gunmen have you got? Where are people located in the house? Do you have food? Are you in contact with outside groups?"

"We have food."

"They know the Powell woman's involved. They found her car in the shed."

Gwyn started to deny it but realized he would be ripping away Carrie's frail protection from Nora and Raffael. And, in truth, he didn't know her status. If anyone did, it was Madog. He glanced at Carrie and found her impassive. She always had been able to make him believe anything she chose. Even that she loved him, once.

"We're not in contact with outside groups." Even if they had been, better for the *heddlu cudd* not to know.

"They know about the Italian. Is he listening?"

"Not really." But Gwyn saw Madog's attention sharpen.

"I understand. Is he the one causing problems?"

"Half the problems."

"The other half—is that the Irishwoman?"

"It is."

Peter paused a minute. Checking in with his masters again, no doubt. "That leaves only one question. When are you coming out?"

"When the Nation of Cymru has home rule. When Welsh television is fully available to all Welsh speakers. When Welsh industry gets special aid."

"They're talking about it in both houses today."

"Joke hour, is it?" suggested Gwyn savagely.

"You underestimate your effect. Both houses are wrangling over emergency procedures. Amnesty International is addressing the UN security council tomorrow. You know how the UN is about national liberation movements— they'll probably declare you a saint. The European Parliament is hysterical. The Republic is howling about oppression of Celtic minorities. The French are deeply grieved. The Americans are making loud noises about internal colonization. *Pravda* in Moscow is having a field day. They've given Wales more column inches than any British story since the Falklands."

"Huh," said Gwyn. The enemy of my enemy is my friend.

"Come out. Parliament won't be blackmailed into these changes you want, but it's certainly taken notice. You'll be out of prison in a few years. It's not as though you shot the cop."

"A minor distinction." Gwyn bit his tongue hard enough to draw blood. He turned and saw the shock wave travel across Madog's face. Then the American grinned, the solid-gold version, and reached to grip Gwyn's wrist.

"Is Nilsson there?"

Gwyn glanced at Madog, who shrugged and reached for the phone. Instead of Holt's voice, a woman's came through the speaker.

"Captain Nilsson?"

"Right here, ma'am," said Madog in his down-home twang.

"Chernicki, United States Department of State. Would you care to explain to me what is going on? And how you happen to be involved in it?"

"No."

"I beg your pardon, Captain Nilsson?"

"Time to burn the bridges, Doctor?"

Her voice frosted over. "Captain, you're in a highly sensitive position. Your presence adds an international dimension that is causing significant embarrassment."

"The best laid plans of mice and men. You know how it goes."

"It may have escaped your attention that you and your companions are playing out your unfortunate drama to a world audience. Including this conversation. I appeal to you to act accordingly."

"Yes, ma'am." Madog kept his voice just this side of insolence. "What can I do you for?"

A second's silence. "Don't you think you're overplaying your role, Captain?"

"What exactly do you want, little lady?"

"I want you out, Captain Nilsson."

"Are you suggesting you have some kind of authority, ma'am? Files a few years out of date in Maryland?"

"Captain, I'm not interested in debating inter-agency politics with a crisis of this magnitude on our hands."

"I don't figure I can leave right now."

"Are you refusing my appeal, Captain Nilsson? Think twice about your answer. This is for the record."

"Yes. I'm refusing your appeal. I don't much care for it. In fact, I recommend that you rethink your priorities." Madog had dropped his twang. His voice was cool and precise, with an undercurrent that might be Welsh. Gwyn looked closely at the American. Sweat stood out on his face, which was clay-coloured.

"You realize you will face prosecution on your return."

"I very much doubt it. The U.S.A. rarely extradites for alleged acts of a political nature. I'm sure you know that as well as I do, however unhappy this affair is making your undersecretary of state."

"Captain. Disengage."

"When the time's right. That's the nature of the compromise, isn't it?"

"I can do nothing for you if you stay."

"Don't underestimate your considerable capabilities, Doctor." He released the button and handed the receiver back. Gwyn took it and stared at him, confounded.

Holt was abruptly back on the phone. "Can I get in there to tape an interview?"

"No," Gwyn said automatically, but reflected. Coverage could be useful. "Why should I let you inside to spy?"

"This is hot news, fast-breaking news," Holt said. "I want to bring Al in and tape for BBC and CBS and anyone else who's buying."

"I'll lose anonymity."

"You lost it two days ago, Gwyn."

"Live?" Coverage after the fact would be useless.

"We're not linked. Rees and I only have permission to tape as a special agreement. No other media people are here so far. We can fly the tape to London and use it very soon. But not live."

"Let me ask the others."

"I'll get approval from Grenvile's boss."

Gwyn looked around the room and repeated the request in English.

Nora and Raffael sat stonily silent.

Elen said nervously, "If they're alone and unarmed."

Gwyn turned to the radio. "All right. Any double-dealing may cost your life."

"I've already been shot at once today," Holt bitched.

"Your people are all over Llanygroes with automatic rifles."

"Yes." Undeb cells from Wrecsam and Bala? "Tell the English if they bring in more of their storm-troopers they'll have a war on their hands."

"I'll warn them," said Peter Holt dryly. "It's ten-thirty. Interview at eleven?"

"No tricks, Holt."

"Friends, Gwyn. Remember."

Gwyn replaced the receiver. Outside the window, the clouds looked near enough to touch: clotted, grey, threatening. The snow in the farmyard was no longer melting, only blowing into deeper drifts.

PEN Y CAE/JANUARY 20/1045

Peter leaned back exhausted in the negotiator's hot seat. On every side towered the hastily fitted computers and monitor screens of the operation's airborne command post. The equipment and the designated passenger places took every available cubic inch in the rear compartment of the RAF helicopter; Al Rees perched on a monitor, watched vigilantly by a technician from Scotland Yard. Time to move. Peter choked down the last of his coffee from the miniature galley.

"Ready to go?" Al broke out a fresh stick of chewing gum and zipped up his silver bomber jacket.

"Five minutes."

Peter made a point of using English in the present company. He wouldn't risk jeopardizing the interview. This was the story of a lifetime. He'd never wanted anything more in ten years, and it was so near he could reach out and touch it. A reporter's dream. No competition in sight, major news breaking as he taped, world broadcast. So maybe it would be a nine-hour wonder; it was Peter Holt's own nine-hour wonder.

"Mr. Holt."

Peter heard Fox's voice but kept flipping through his

notebook. Anything the lieutenant-colonel had to say, at the moment, was secondary.

"Yes? We're going up to the farmhouse now."

"Wrong, Mr. Holt. There'll be no interview."

Peter looked up. Fox had sauntered over to the Lynx and now leaned into the Sea King's square side hatch, which fortunately faced out of the snow-lashed north wind. The SAS officer had clearly come into his own on field operations. He was wearing the same black trousers and pullover as his men, without insignia, and his face bore the tight-lipped doggedness portrayed on recruiting posters. Peter was unimpressed. Al watched him as though he were a tarantula.

"Too late for that, Colonel," Peter said mildly. "Merlin wants the interview. Change your mind now, and his ugly chums might take it out on the Prince. Besides, Major Grenvile already okayed it."

"Major Grenvile can make all the intelligence decisions he wants," said Fox. "I make the operational decisions. The best thing you and Mr. Rees can do is clear out."

"Something you'd like to clarify, Colonel?" asked Grenvile. He'd stepped from the helicopter out into the snowy pasture.

"We can't upset an extremely delicate situation—and Holt of all people. He's clearly said he's a friend of this terrorist."

"I would have told Merlin the same thing," Grenvile told him, fighting his laryngitis as he fished cough tablets from his pocket. "Especially if there were any chance he'd believe it. Mr. Holt has a long-standing professional relationship with Davies. We have to build trust. Quite acceptable negotiation technique. Mr. Holt can do us an even greater service by seeing conditions inside."

"Under no circumstances—"

"Excuse me, Colonel." The grey man, Harold Stone, stood in the Sea King's hatch. "If you would accompany me a moment?"

Fox held his pale bulldog stare on Peter a second longer,

then turned away. Peter caught Al's eyes. They both gathered their gear hastily. Downhill near one of the unmarked blue vans Fox and Stone exchanged a very few words, heads together. Harold Stone departed in the direction of the command post after a mild nod to Fox. The SAS officer watched him walk away. Peter turned and saw that Grenvile and Al Rees wore like expressions of bemused pleasure.

"Ready to go in?" asked Grenvile. "I'm giving you a pocket transmitter so you can call if necessary. Merlin might not let you near the radio."

He put a hand on Peter's shoulder as they walked up towards the crest of the hill. It was unlike nervous Grenvile. Warning off Fox, Peter reckoned, though he didn't think the lieutenant-colonel needed any further reprimands. He also realized, with unexpected warmth for the man, that Grenvile would give his right arm to be the one going in. With half a dozen SAS troopers, they slogged up to the crown of the rise. Below, beyond a stunted orchard and a small cobbled yard, lay the farmhouse called Pen y Cae. Peter turned and shook Grenvile's hand. The intelligence man squatted down on his heels behind a scrub willow.

"We'll be right here. Call if you want anything."

"Right."

Peter and Al waded through the orchard snow-drifts with hands flat on their heads, recording equipment slapping loose from shoulders straps. When they clambered over a low drystone wall into the farmyard, the door opened silently. Two men in Balaclavas came out and stood either side of the porch, levelling what looked like Soviet assault rifles.

"Identify yourselves," one demanded in Welsh.

"Peter Holt, BBC. Al Rees, independent."

"Enter. Hands on your heads."

He led them into a slate-floored kitchen and motioned them to set cameras and recorders on the scoured wooden table. One covered them while the other went thought their

gear, then frisked them. He found Grenvile's transmitter
in Peter's duffle pocket and tossed it to the first man, who
let his rifle hang on its shoulder strap and quickly took the
transmitter apart. So much for that safeguard. There was
no sign of the other terrorists, or of Miss Douglass and
the Prince.

"All right. You look clean." The first man pulled off
his Balaclava and shook his hair out of his eyes. Gwyn
Davies.

"You get your Wednesday interview after all."

Peter had forgotten. Their phone call Sunday seemed
months in the past. Gwyn's dark eyes were steady on him,
assessing. Peter in turn searched for the academic Gwyn
Davies, full of rhetoric and equivocation. This was a different man: equally cold, but impatient, strung up with
nervous energy like a greyhound, potentially violent.
There were other changes Peter couldn't pin down. He
cued a high-quality audio tape on the Uher and closed the
cover. Al, prowling around the kitchen, stopped at the
window that looked out onto the yard.

"Can we take these boards off? We need more light."

Davies glanced at the other gunman. "Mind covering?"

"Na."

As Al pried at the boards, the other man pulled off his
Balaclava. Peter recognized the American from the kidnap
tape and the photo Grenvile had showed him. Madog Nilsson didn't look like either a fortune-hunter or a flake. He
was a little taller than Davies and more solidly built, grey-
eyed, with mouse-brown hair, strong bones, a sensitive
mouth. He looked likeable, maybe tricky.

"Better," Al said, "Peter, give him your shirt—"

"Just a minute," Davies said angrily.

"—unless you have a clean one somewhere, Gwyn. And
a hairbrush."

"Alan, what the hell do you think you're staging?" Davies folded his arms over the rifle sling, scowling.

"Good, good." Al narrowed his black eyes and canted
his head, eyeing Davies with Hawaiian imperturbability.

"The Ché Guevara of Wales. They won't risk blowing you away, see? I'm getting you out of here alive, *bach*. And the rest of you."

"Al also hid your car." Peter reckoned the photographer wouldn't bother to mention it, but it could build trust. "After Thomas was arrested. It was conspicuous."

"I heard," Davies said. "On the amateur bands. Good work, Alan. You've far exceeded what I asked of you. I'm in your debt."

"Right." Al shoved his gum into his cheek, pleased. "Take off your shirt."

"I'll get something." The American paused long enough to weigh Peter and Al with mild curiosity and faded silently away through the house. He came back with a white dress shirt and a gold-ornamented bristle hairbrush that Peter priced at forty pounds. Davies buttoned on the clean shirt, suffering Al's fast handiwork with the brush. Nilsson watched, looking amused. Peter finished setting up the Uher.

"Now sit here, left elbow on the table, rifle slung over your shoulder. No, that doesn't work. Hold it across your chest, diagonally. That's it. Stay three-quarters to the light, and we'll highlight that profile. Peter, stand in front of the cooker to hold his line of vision. Reaction shots and cover later. Hold it, I want a look in the viewer." Al screwed the videotape camera to its collapsible tripod and squinted. "The girls will beat down the door to join Undeb."

Davies spat angry words at him, too colloquial for Peter. The American grinned, showing perfect white teeth with one gold premolar. But Davies held the pose and gave Peter a nod. The three of them were old hands at transforming nationalism into news footage, at transforming a media event into a heartfelt statement on the future of Wales.

"Welsh first," Davies said. "Then English."

"Right." Peter tossed his notebook onto the table. He wouldn't need it.

"Rolling," said Al and started on his Wrigley's.

"Roll one, take one. Pen Y Cae farm, Powys, Wales. Twenty January. Interview, Gwyn Davies." Peter counted three and went on. "A drama that began in Kensington High Street may end on an isolated Welsh hill farm—"

Peter ad-libbed his to-camera intro without a second's hesitation. How could he hesitate? He'd worked four years for this story and Gwyn Davies was handing it to him gift-wrapped. He worked through his questions, still in Welsh. Davies was careful with his answers, occasionally maintaining silence until the next question.

"When do you plan to release the hostages?"

"When the Nation of Cymru gets its full rights, long promised by the government. For years we've asked cap in hand and had nothing. Now we've been forced to demand."

At first Davies was stiff. Soon he warmed to his best topic, raising his rhetoric to the pitch of poetry. It always caught Peter by the throat, that passionate Welsh *hwyl* that lifted the heart even when the language was unknown. It was one reason Peter had sweated through a Welsh immersion course; maybe it was one reason he was sweating through this, covered by a terrorist with a Soviet rifle. Peter pushed on, full of raw adrenaline. The interview was his own coup.

"Isn't it somewhat unreasonable for Undeb Cymru Fydd to single-handedly declare war on England?"

"We have no quarrel with the English people. They suffer from their government almost as bitterly as we do, especially in remote regions."

Lancashire, for example. Peter restrained a smile. They'd covered this ground many times, usually over a pint in the Nag's Head in Aberystwyth.

"Surely you could have found a legal, peaceable way to get these rights. Don't you believe in the parliamentary system?"

"I ran for parliament twice in Dolgellau, on an Undeb Cymru Fydd ticket. The Tories parachuted in high-powered candidates with expensive campaigns and a fortune in election promises. They tried hard enough to keep the patchwork Welsh Nationalist Party out of the Commons. They tried much harder to keep out Undeb, which follows clear-cut democratic socialist principles.''

Peter dangled a lure. ''Doctor Davies, why did you—''

''Not doctor,'' Davies said quickly. ''I haven't finished my degree.''

Peter ingenuously asked, ''Why not?''

''My funding was cut off when I became a political candidate. I've been carrying on my research, but it's slow work without money. Also . . .''

The pause was just painfully long enough, implying some personal loss. Carrie Powell, Peter surmised.

''Eight years ago I was in prison facing criminal charges after a transmitter bombing. The last thing on my mind was linguistics.''

''What was the charge?''

''Destroying government property. And manslaughter. I was acquitted.''

''Did you kill someone?''

Davies looked up angrily. ''A man died. I didn't kill him.''

''Who did?''

''You tell me who killed him. He was in the transmitter shed. Routine maintenance, the police said. But at three in the morning? He wasn't a Ministry of Communications employee. We committed violence against property, not against persons. But the government wanted more, so it could invoke the Suppression of Terrorism Act and impose heavier control measures in Wales. I believe the man was deliberately placed in the way of a bomb that otherwise would have caused only structural damage.''

The worse it is, the better it is. Did governments practise that theory, too? Great stuff. But Peter said skeptically, ''Sounds far-fetched.''

''So did Watergate and that Iran-Contra connection.''

Good lad. He'd remembered the American audience. ''Can you prove it?''

"Probably, with several hundred thousand pounds and enough years. I think the government's safe."

Peter decided to back off politics. "This kidnapping has stirred up world-wide hostility. If you dropped into a public house in London or Birmingham, you'd probably be lynched. How do you feel about what you've done?"

"It was the only method still open to us. But I think everyone would agree things are now out of hand. We wanted to exchange the Prince for our demands a week ago, but your government has prevented us."

"How?"

"There's been no serious discussion of our demands. The prime minister no doubt thinks it's easier to send in the SAS and shut us up for good. But other people will speak out for the Nation of Cymru. *Do not go gentle into that good night. Rage, rage against the dying of the light.*"

Nice touch, a sprinkling of Dylan Thomas. "How are the Prince and Miss Douglass?"

"They're both in good health, but showing some strain. Miss Douglass is a tower of strength. Pip—the Prince—is a clever and brave boy. I wish we could have met in happier circumstances."

Peter wondered how a television audience would react to that cool observation. Rage? Approval? Davies was working the interview to his own ends. Peter was creating news, just as Davies was shaping the coverage. Each without the other was the sound of one hand clapping.

They repeated the interview in English. Finally Peter gave Al Rees his signal.

"Now," said Al. "Bring the nanny and the kid in here, and we'll have a chat with them."

Peter watched Davies weighing it for image value. Finally he nodded to the American. Jean Douglass and the Prince followed him in a few minutes later.

"Mr. Holt?" The nanny smiled tremulously.

She looked impeccable, her clothes neat and her grooming perfect. If she was showing strain, she hid it well. Why was she treated as a hostage if she was in on this?

Was it a simple cash arrangement, or well-disguised ideological sympathy? Jean Douglass didn't seem like a revolutionary by any standard. She sat in the chair Davies had occupied and took the boy on her knee. He held the famous mouse doll, which the Queen Mother detested and the Queen staunchly defended. The Prince was cheerful, chatting with the American about a cat. Al set them up carefully and began rolling tape.

"Your Royal Highness, how do you feel?" What else, Peter wondered, did you ask a royal hostage in short trousers? "Are you scared to death?" might be slightly tactless.

"It's cold here." He hugged his mouse doll, a thoroughly photogenic kid.

"Do you miss your mother and father?"

"Yes. But Miss Douglass is here, and there's Madog and Mr. Hughes and Pal. Pal's got a zipper in his tummy for his pyjamas."

Peter didn't want to talk about stuffed toys. "What have they given you to eat?"

Davies cut them off after a few basic questions. He'd made his point. The hostages were alive and well.

Davies looked at his watch. Noon. "That's all."

"We're going to tape cover footage outside," Al told him as he changed cassettes. "Hold your fire."

"Where outside?" asked Madog Nilsson.

Al pointed through the partially unboarded window. "Front of the house. Then below, where we can pan from the back of the house across the hills."

Nilsson hesitated, shot a glance at Davies, and said, "I'll show you a good spot from the upstairs window."

Davies took the suggestion. "Tea, Peter?"

"I'd rather go upstairs," Peter said and saw point-blank refusal in Davies's face. At least he'd asked.

The American ushered the photographer upstairs, with the nanny and the boy. Jean Douglass cast a last look over her shoulder, as though a hope of rescue had been torn away.

Peter drank his tea in silence, trying without success to imagine tomorrow, next week, next month. The adrenaline had ebbed, leaving him exhausted. Davies leaned his forehead on his fist, also quiet. Their media event was in the can. For the moment they were off-stage.

"What will happen?" Peter tried, not really expecting an answer.

Davies looked up. "We'll be dead by tomorrow. Except the hostages, if they're lucky."

"Give them up. You've made your point."

"We'll die anyway. Remember the Iranian embassy? The SAS shot the Iraqi gunmen after they surrendered. I don't see any way out alive."

"Glad you're not planning to come out fighting."

"Not much point. The SAS are formidable. I'm assuming that's what's waiting out there. My training in Libya was nothing like that."

"What about the American?"

"Military background, but he won't help."

Davies didn't even sound bitter at the prospect. That was another change in him, Peter realized. It was as though he felt he'd done everything he could and consented to whatever happened now. Depressing.

"Is he a plant? Or is he really one of you?"

"I don't know." Davies thought about it. "Yes, he's a plant. But he's one of us."

Clear as mud, thought Peter. Davies stood abruptly, went to the sink, and poured water from a pitcher. He scrubbed his face and shook water out of his eyes.

"Do something for me."

Peter nodded. Davies, unlike Grenvile, would ask nothing of him that he couldn't give.

"Tell Grenvile that Carrie isn't part of it. She's a prisoner."

"Is it true?"

"Sion brought her in when the kid was sick. I found out too late."

"I'll tell him. And the others?"

"I'll do what I can for them, bargain for their safe conduct."

"What about you? What will you do?"

"I'll get out if I can. Otherwise . . . the English were right eight years ago. A death is sometimes politic."

"Don't talk dull," Peter told him. "Bloody martyrdom. Apart from the uselessness of it, do you know what it could do to this country?"

"Make people think. Stir them to act while Wales still exists as a nation."

"They'd better act fast, then," said Madog Nilsson quietly from the doorway. Al stood behind him, camera on his shoulder, thoughtfully chewing gum.

Peter wondered how long Nilsson had been there listening. He reversed his estimation of the American. Tricky, perhaps likeable. Playing revolutionary on someone else's turf? Improbable. Too much was at stake, as Anna Chernicki had made clear.

Outside, Al taped from two locations, getting wide shots and zoom long shots of Pen y Cae from the front. Then he hefted camera and tripod over his shoulder and started down the frozen ruts towards Hughes's farm, Cae Isa. From nowhere visible, two black-clad and Balaclava'd troopers joined them. Not much to see under four inches of dry snow. They were in the Berwyn Range, Peter supposed. Cover shots would be better in summer. The wind was rising, and it was cold.

"Got enough?" Peter asked finally. Al seemed to be taping three times as much as he could ever use, given the lack of visual interest.

"One more location."

Al tramped off downhill. They were about fifty yards from the small barn where Fox's men had discovered Carrie Powell's Mini and the Bentley stolen a week ago in London. The photographer set up his tripod, took his time scanning around three hundred sixty degrees, and called out to the nearest of their silent SAS companions.

"I need something for scale. Mind walking downhill

slowly towards the barn, then standing by the door? Grenvile says we can shoot anything.''

The trooper glanced at his partner, who nodded. He slung his stubby Heckler and Koch machine-gun behind his back and started out. Al taped as he waded down through the drifts, some of them knee-deep and growing. Peter watched, wishing for once Rees would settle for less meticulous work. He was freezing his arse. Al turned to the other trooper.

''Now you—when you get down there, try to look as though you're talking about something important.''

They did it convincingly, apparently less camera-phobic than usual in the protection of their anonymous head-to-foot black.

''Okay,'' Al shouted cheerfully. ''Take a smoke break. You too, Peter. I've got to change tapes—be about five minutes.''

Peter gratefully joined the Balaclava'd SAS men, feeling as though he'd crashed a masked ball. But one of them handed him a lit Player's companionably enough and complained about Welsh weather in a thick regional accent. The other passed around his compressed-fuel pocket warmer.

Then it struck him. Five minutes? A videotape cassette took perhaps thirty seconds to insert and rapid-reverse. Peter looked around as unobtrusively as he could. No sign of the photographer. He was quiet a moment, trying to ignore his hunch. What had Al seen or heard upstairs in Pen Y Cae besides good camera sites? And did it matter to Peter? No need to agonize over the answers. Peter made the two men in executioner's garb laugh with a mumbled word about freezing it off, pissing in this weather. Then he walked to where Al was last taping. Footprints led straight downhill.

At the back of the barn, close enough to hear their guards' voices, Al was bending over a trampled patch of snow. In its middle lay a package the size of a large book, wrapped in black polypropylene. Peter was close enough to touch him when Al straightened suddenly and spun around. Peter opened his mouth but couldn't say a word. Al had him covered with a hand gun.

"Always have to know everything, don't you, Peter?" asked Al amiably. "Bloody investigative journalists. Only two things I can do with you now. Tie you up or—"

"No." Peter found words, hoping an idea would follow. "You don't have to do that. Al, I'm in deep enough now. I'll go and keep them talking until you finish."

Al looked at him a moment longer over the gun and slowly shoved it in his pocket. "You're with us?"

"Yes, you know that already."

Or dead, thought Peter, but this was no time to split hairs. He looked at the ground, "What is it?"

Al crouched, carefully brushing snow over the package. "Dunno. Madog said put it here." He glanced up. "Better go talk to the ss before they get anxious."

Peter slogged back to the front of the barn, too cold to do anything but shiver deeper into his duffle coat. The worst part was, now he really did have to pee. After a few minutes, Al reappeared.

"Finished."

"Right," said Peter. But finished what?

When they clambered out of the snowy drainage ditch onto the track, Peter saw a group of people approaching from Cae Isa, the tenant farm. Fox was leading four of his sas troopers with the old farmer.

15

"Madog bach, are you there? The English are letting me bring you food and drink. Open your door to me."

Gwyn put his eye to the boarded-over parlour window and saw John Hughes standing in the snowy yard. He had a bundle under his left arm and a bucket in his right hand. He spotted Gwyn and smiled to the gaps in his side teeth. A trick. The Special Air Services were famous for their tricks. But what sort of trick?

"Anyone with him?" asked Madog. Gwyn scanned the orchard and the slope beyond it and shook his head. "Get the field phone. Ask Grenvile."

Madog padded upstairs and came back with the major's phone. Gwyn pushed the button. Peter Holt answered immediately.

"What are they trying to prove, using John Hughes for a whipping boy?" Gwyn demanded. "Is it a pail full of gelignite, or just poisoned milk?"

"They want your co-operation. They wouldn't try anything." Holt sounded subdued and as weary as all of them. "Especially with a civilian volunteer."

"Did you see him volunteer? Or was it blackmail?"

"When he finished cursing Fox, he said he wanted to talk some sense into Nilsson. Seems they're family."

Gwyn glanced at Madog, who looked uneasy. "Very

284

thoughtful of Mr. Hughes. If it's a trick, the hostages will be endangered.''

''It's not a trick.''

Nodding at Madog, Gwyn broke the connection. The American pulled out his little pistol and went to open the door. John Hughes stumped into the kitchen and clattered his pail on the slate floor.

''Fresh this morning. It's a miracle the girls aren't squirting vinegar instead, with these English crawling everywhere.''

Gwyn looked from one to the other. Madog put his arm across John's shoulders; he was taller, leaner, lighter-skinned even with the tan, thirty years younger. But still family.

''Morning, *Miss Ceridwen fach.*'' John took off his tweed cap as Carrie appeared in the kitchen door. ''Mountain snow today and a sharp wind.''

''Best keep the girls in the shed, John. I smell a blizzard by nightfall.''

''Is that true?'' He looked interested. ''Your mam and her mam could smell the weather right good. They were famous through the county.''

Gwyn listened carefully as the two of them rattled away, Carrie in her mid-Wales voice and John in his broader north-eastern accent. He wanted five hours of John Hughes's dialect on tape for the Welsh Department in Aberystwyth. Someday.

''A fine mess we're in.''

''Not 'we,' John. It was kind of you to bring food, but don't let yourself get pulled in. By anyone.'' She glanced at Gwyn.

''Now, Miss Ceridwen, don't set yourself against the man. He's doing a great thing.''

Madog looked at his tenant uncomfortably. Gwyn turned on his heel, unwilling to be savaged by Hughes's sarcasm and Carrie's hostility at the same time. The old farmer's voice halted him.

''Mr. Davies, do you think me a liar?''

Gwyn turned to face him.

"I may be rough-tongued and fond of provoking, but I say what I think, and I think you can triumph, if we settle things quickly. That's why I want to talk with you, Madog."

Madog shook his head. "Carrie's right, John. You're not involved. We're not talking about a few fat English heifers."

"Never mind that. Tarzan of the Apes out there in his black burial suit—Lieutenant-Colonel Fox SAS is his name—and the little major, they want to clear me out and put me up in a grand hotel in Trallwng. I told them not while the girls are milking. So instead I have a bodyguard like that Mussolini. Which means anything I do for you must look innocent."

Madog squeezed his shoulder. "Is there any work in Three-Rocks Field?"

"I can find some. Fencing or ditching."

"John," Carrie warned. Hughes winked at her.

"Find warmer clothes and go up there for two hours. If you see anything suspicious, come down and tell me."

The farmer didn't question it. "Then what?"

"Then go home and have a cup of tea. If these people come around wanting favours, give them excuses."

"Good enough. Now I am going to tell the *bwganod* to get their white Volvo from behind my hay barn. Let them enjoy the blizzard like the rest."

Gwyn frowned. "Who are they? In the Volvo?"

"Spies. They have a telly in the back seat. Watching *Avengers* reruns."

"John," Madog reproached.

"In truth it's all bright colours and makes no kind of picture at all."

"Corgi drives a white Volvo." Gwyn glanced at Madog. "How would he get infra-red equipment, if that's what it is?"

"Friends in high places."

The thought of Corgi sitting behind John's barn with

electronic surveillance equipment chilled Gwyn through. "John, go tell Major Grenvile to get rid of them. Don't talk to them yourself."

"Very well." John Hughes turned to the package on the table. "Here's your food. Sandwiches, raisins, chocolate. I thought you might take a country walk."

"Maybe." Madog flashed his golden smile. "Did the *heddlu cudd* down there touch the food?"

"Na. Snuffed it all over hissing like cats, but there's no drugs or poison."

There was a pause.

"Well, John."

"I'm going. May God keep you and guide you on your journey, my dear. And you, Mr. Davies. Miss Ceridwen, keep your heart up. When we meet again, let's hope it's not in Shrewsbury jail."

Madog laughed. John shook his hand, then Gwyn's, and kissed Carrie on the cheek. He jammed his cap back over his ears, turned up his collar, and stumped outside. Madog kept the door open a sliver to watch him go. As he crunched across the snow, Gwyn heard a sound upstairs. Breaking glass. A trick—

A single gunshot tore the air and echoed back from the wintry orchard. John Hughes spun half around and sprawled face down on the snow. Madog made a sound deep in his throat and started outside. Gwyn caught his shoulder but he tore free and sprinted out to John. On the hillside above the orchard someone stirred but stayed in place. Their murder was done, they would claim it soon enough. Madog turned John over. By the way he knelt motionless, Gwyn knew there would be no meeting in jail or out of it. John Hughes was dead. Madog put his face in his hands a moment, then slowly stood. When he turned, his face was smeared with blood. He was staring at the upstairs window.

"Why did you do it?" he asked so quietly Gwyn strained for the words.

Raffael's voice floated down, disembodied. "We will get away with the boy. No one must stop us."

Raffael? Gwyn stood a moment, sick, shaking inside with anger. He pulled out the Browning, slipped it off safety, cocked it, and turned. Carrie stood in the parlour door, hands grasping the jamb on either side.

"No. No more."

Gwyn shouldered her aside and ran across the parlour to the stairs. In the upstairs bedroom, Raffael stood with the Beretta still aimed out the window. He turned, but not quickly enough. Three rapid shots at Gwyn flew wide, tearing splinters from the dresser. Gwyn aimed for his navel and pulled the trigger. The shot caught Raffael square in the chest and slammed him against the wall. He slid down in a smear of blood and fell over. Downstairs, Grenvile's field phone began to blurt a call signal.

Anna Chernicki waited impatiently in the equipment-crammed helicopter. Grenvile rubbed his face in his hands. Fox, flushed an angry red, paced two steps in one direction, then the other. Al Rees clasped his hands in front of his knees and looked at the corrugated metal floor.

"Can't raise Davies," said Peter uneasily. "He's not answering."

"Hughes was a civilian," said Fox.

"Obviously," Grenvile came back sharply. "As I told you when you dragged him in."

The SAS officer stopped his pacing. "It changes everything. Now we make an assault."

An electronic pulse sounded and a technician murmured in Grenvile's ear. "Telephone relay, sir. From America."

Grenvile took the palm-sized receiver, set it to external speaker, and answered. An angry American voice crashed into the mobile HQ.

"Cliff Aslin, CBS New York. What do you people think you're doing? You ever hear of freedom of the press? You may be able to scare off your limp-wristed Brit reporters, but don't try giving me any bull about restricted operations. So you got a revolution in progress, huh? You guys need a revolution to shake down your god-damned feudal arrogance. Now let me talk to Peter Holt.''

''Break the connection,'' snapped Fox.

Peter scribbled nonsense in his notebook, wishing he were somewhere else.

''No,'' said Anna Chernicki. ''Let me talk to him or he'll keep hounding you.''

Grenvile gratefully handed her the receiver. She identified herself coolly and talked on through Aslin's enraged interruptions.

''I'd like to remind you, Mr. Aslin, that the right to freedom of the press is accompanied by an immense responsibility. Broadcasting information in the middle of a situation like this could cost many lives. Do you want that? And do you think the president wants it?''

Aslin was quieter. ''If your British colleagues handle this in their usual ham-fisted fashion, those lives are already as good as lost. Ask Pete to call me when he can.'' The line clicked and began to drone.

Chernicki dropped the receiver into the technician's hand as though it had scorched her.

The technician murmured again. ''Three press cars are being detained at the turn-off from the Llanygroes Road, sir. The *Daily Express*, the *Western Mail* in Cardiff, and ITN.''

Peter glanced at Al Rees, who shrugged. A media event. But Peter still had the exclusive.

'Send them to the police station in Llanygroes,'' said Grenvile quickly, forestalling debate. ''Tell them they'll be informed of events as they happen.''

''We can mount a strike within the hour,'' Fox resumed. ''Go in through—''

''Not until we exhaust all possible avenues of discussion,'' said Grenvile. His voice was firm and without hesitation.

Peter looked up as the silence stretched. Grenvile and

the SAS man were engaged in a staring match, neither one backing down.

"Call COBRA," Chernicki instructed the technician. "If these gentlemen aren't interested in asking for Cabinet guidance, I am."

"What did he say?" Madog asked as Gwyn set the transmitter carefully on the radio-room desk.

Gwyn glanced from face to face, weighing his companions—voluntary or otherwise—of the past week. Which way would they jump, each of them? The wind was racketing around the roof slates, and even at mid-afternoon it was almost dark. Carrie was right about the weather. She stroked her cat, giving no clue to her thoughts. Madog looked sober; he'd washed John's blood from his face. As she had been since Holt left, Jean Douglass was crying. Pip, in a child's defence against terror, had fallen asleep. Tear tracks also stained Elen's face; for John's fate or her own? Sion was downstairs on watch, if he hadn't slipped away to trade their lives for a lighter sentence. Unusually pensive, Nora watched them one by one.

"It was their ultimatum," Gwyn told them. "Release the prisoners. Then come out one at a time, hands on head. Half an hour to consider it."

Nora said between her teeth, "All in a row on the doorstep like clay pigeons."

"Or what?" asked Madog quietly.

"They're not saying. Send in the SAS, I suppose."

"In Belfast they wait till you surrender, then shoot you where you stand," Nora's rage was slipping.

"Are they bluffing?" asked Elen in a quavering voice.

"No." Gwyn heard his own finality. "We go out, or they come in."

Madog looked around. "We can try another way—a long shot."

They listened as Madog offered his crazy plan. Even Jean stopped her dry sobbing and shook her head hopelessly. Gwyn listened to Madog's confident voice and heard the knowledge of death.

"We'll be killed," objected Elen.

"We'll be killed the other way for certain."

Elen got unsteadily to her feet. "Not me. I'm going out."

"Don't do it," said Nora flatly.

"Prison's better than a bullet."

"You're doing the right thing," Jean Douglass told her staunchly. "God will watch over you."

Gwyn walked downstairs with her. Elen pulled her anorak from a peg in the hall. At the door he kissed her on the mouth.

"Another Cadwyn member in jail for Wales," he said lightly. "Shall we break you out?"

"Just like the old days." Elen gave him a wan smile and walked out.

Gwyn sprinted to the parlour window. He saw Elen walk out into the yard with her hands on her head. She glanced once at John's body lying amid pink snow crystals and looked quickly away. Something made her turn to her right, downhill towards now-untenanted Cae Isa. A voice, shouting something about identification. Elen dropped her hands and reached inside her anorak. Then, suddenly, she flung out her arms as though to break a fall. The automatic rifle fire stuttered across her chest and on into the yard, raising plumes of dry snow. Elen spun back towards the house like a tormented dancer, her red hair swirling wide. Then she crumpled to the ground, went into a shuddering convulsion, and was still. Gwyn stood motionless.

He heard the shrieks before he reached the stairs and sprinted up three steps at a time. On the landing, he saw Madog holding a hysterical Jean Douglass, screaming. So she'd been watching.

"Demerol?" asked Carrie from the radio room. Her medical bag was open on the floor.

"No," said Gwyn. "We'll have to try Madog's plan."

He led the nanny back into the radio room, and Carrie

got her to lie on the cot. Pip was backed into a corner, crying. Nora slapped his face, one side and the other, hard enough to hurt an adult. Gwyn pulled the IRA woman away from the boy. He should shove Nora out the window for a taste of what she deserved. After a few ear-splitting minutes, Douglass sobbed more quietly. Gwyn went to the desk and turned on Grenvile's phone. He also opened the mike on Madog's radio and turned the volume up full. Let everyone hear what happened next.

"Get me Grenvile," he said when Peter Holt answered. The negotiator came on.

"Don't bother explaining," Gwyn told him.

"Yes," said Grenvile flatly, making it impossible to judge his state of mind. "A breach of discipline. Quite unauthorized. We'll all pay for it, Gwyn."

"I'm tired of your lies. If we played by your rules, we'd have killed the hostages and come out shooting."

"For God's sakc, don't do that. May I speak with Miss Douglass?"

"No. She's in shock. You murdered Elen Parry in cold blood as she watched."

"Will she understand a message? Tell her we know about her involvement. She can come out alone with the boy, and no one will harm her."

"She's beyond your promises," Gwyn said coldly. "What involvement?"

Behind him the sobbing resumed. He turned. The nanny lay on her back with her arms flung over her face, wailing something incomprehensible. Gwyn dropped the receiver and bent over the cot.

"Jean, stop." He shook her. "Pip is terrified. You're letting him down."

She sat up, arms still over her face.

"Do you want to go outside? We can't let you take Pip, but you can go alone."

"No! I want to go with you." She worked her mouth and found words. "They'll shoot me; they know what I did."

"What did you do, Jean?" Gwyn sat and put an arm around her, trying to calm the woman when he should be helping Madog with his preparations. "Tell me."

"I—Sandy got five hundred pounds. Raffael gave it to him, from the papers in Rome, for a picture of Pip. Sandy said—my brother said—I should let Raffael shoot Pip. Oh God, not shoot—"

So that was how Raffael got to her, through her brother. Jean started crying again. Gwyn found Carrie's wide eyes and motioned her to watch over Jean. She crossed the room. Pip trotting beside her with Mungo Mouse under his arm.

Grenvile was still on the transmitter.

"Miss Douglass says she doesn't want to come out. She's no part of this, Grenvile. She had no idea what she was doing," Gwyn told him.

"That's two people you tell me had no part in it. You expect me to believe this was all a misunderstanding? How many people am I supposed to believe?"

"Two." Gwyn didn't look at Carrie. He shouldn't have sent the message with Holt. The two-metre band was still broadcasting; he wondered whether people were listening, and what they thought. He had a slipping sense of watching the moment from an undetermined point in space and time.

"Merlin, come out."

"How can we?" Gwyn asked, curious. "You'll shoot us one by one. We might as well die inside. It's warmer."

"No. It won't happen again."

"Nothing has changed for Wales. We haven't achieved any concessions on industry, or television, or home rule. If we surrender, we betray our country."

"You've already done something for Wales. The debate is raging in the house. What's happening in the Cabinet no one yet knows, but we can hope. God knows I want to see your demands met as much as you do."

Gwyn started to scoff but realized the man was telling the truth. It was a fact from the negotiator's handbook, along with the Stockholm Syndrome and the stress and the raw fear. Grenvile really did want the same things, passionately, if only for the next hour.

"Call it a day, Gwyn," urged Grenvile. "Come out, bring your people out. There's nothing more we can do, you or I."

"And nothing more we can say," said Gwyn, with an unexpected tug of regret. "Goodbye, Major."

"Merlin—"

Gwyn slowly switched off the transmitter, then the mike on Madog's radio. Immediately, a voice came through the radio speaker.

"Receive your transmission. Homing. Stand by for pick-up." The Welsh was guttural, heavily accented with another tongue. German? Gwyn couldn't place the voice or the accent, but he had no time to worry about it. The band crackled and went off the air.

Madog flung himself into the room and dropped an arm load of things on the floor. Clothes and a bundle of white sheets.

"All done. We're out of time. Jean, get into these slacks—and you, Carrie. Flak vest?"

"Too heavy," said Carrie.

"Here are your boots. Coats. Socks—use them for mitts. Supplies, Sion?"

Sion ap Huw appeared on the landing with a knapsack. He wore a hangdog look. Gwyn picked up Pip, still half-asleep, and Mungo. He wrapped the boy in a blanket. Cath Paluc sat up on the cot and yawned hugely. Carrie dropped her skirt and pulled on Madog's cords, then rolled up the cuffs. Jean Douglass turned her back and drew on the jeans under her skirt. Nora shook her head, amused.

"Now give the boy a Demerol," Madog told Carrie. "He'll be less frightened if he's asleep."

Jean Douglass, looking dazed, nodded her agreement.

"Too strong," Carrie answered. "A travel-sickness tablet should do it."

Gwyn looked out the window, between the boards. He

couldn't see anything moving out there, but Elen had been killed by shots from the south, down toward Cae Isa. The SAS were probably all over the place by now, their movement covered by the rattle of the slates. They would have sniffers and heat-seeking devices, but if the explosion worked they wouldn't be able to pin-point the location of warm bodies for a crucial few minutes; Madog's orchard was blurred by blowing snow. The wind was out of the north-west. Good. It would blow the smoke and debris down toward Cae Isa, where it could overload the infra-red sensors.

"What's happening?" asked the nanny, steadier since her blurted confession.

"We're going for a walk," Gwyn told her and went to haul open the small door to the priest's hole. "Everyone ready? into the hole. Lie on the floor. Protect your heads with your arms."

Gwyn took a last glance out into the late afternoon. Through the snow, he saw a handful of stealthy black figures among the orchard trees.

The others climbed into the blackness, lit only by the flashlight Gwyn grabbed from the radio table. When the last was in, he followed and pulled the door shut. He swung the light beam around the cramped space. The front wall of the house was naked stone and mortar. Every other surface was time-blacked oak.

"Where is it?"

Madog pointed at the floor toward the black wall, and Gwyn peered for seam lines.

"Are you certain?"

"I had it open last month."

The American pried a knife along the edge of a floor-board. It rose an inch and he dug the blade into the wood to raise it farther. When the board was out, he pulled its two neighbours free. The hole was a yard long and wide enough to squirm through. Gwyn shone the torch down into the hidy-hole. Cobwebs, a flurry of grey that was a mouse, judging by Pal's predatory green-eyed stare. And in the back wall, a wooden door no larger than the one from the radio room. Gwyn breathed again without knowing he'd held his breath.

"We never got around to digging a tunnel." Madog grinned. His gold tooth gleamed wickedly in the faint light. "They stopped burning Catholics at the stake. Okay, everybody down. After the explosion, when I yell, you follow me down that hole and outside. Then we run for it."

"Run where?" asked Carrie.

"A mile south as the crow flies. Gareth's dad's farm. It's a wild chance, but it's our only chance."

They lay on the floor, jammed against each other in the dusty passage. Madog squeezed the plastic rectangle. Gwyn heard a distant boom and several after shocks from the direction of Cae Isa. That was the bomb Alan Rees had planted at the hay barn. Silence. Madog counted under his breath. When he reached fifteen, he touched the detonator again, and the house shuddered and roared like a contained locomotive.

Gwyn buried his head under his arms as another explosion rocked the house to its foundations and something, maybe a roof beam, fell across his back. That was the far wall blasting out, taking the kitchen and upstairs storeroom. Madog couldn't be faulted for precision in explosives placement. They were still alive.

Someone gasped, and Jean Douglass began to pray. Choking dust rose from the floor and walls. Then someone screamed outside, and Gwyn heard the rattle of automatic rifles. Why were they bothering to shoot now? They couldn't have seen anyone.

"Now." Madog's whisper was like a shout in the sudden quiet. He scrambled for the hole and dropped through the floor among the floating spider's webs. "No light. No sound."

He kicked out the small door with one foot and disappeared into a white haze. Nora slithered after him, then the others. Madog took Pip from Gwyn; the boy was now asleep. Outside, they crouched between the stone house foundation and the bramble net, expecting a burst of light and sudden death. They saw nothing but heard a clattering thunder overhead. Helicopter. Gwyn looked up. Paler than the snowstorm, it hovered near the burning roof.

"Heads down or they'll spot us," he hissed. "Everyone take a sheet. Camouflage."

But the helicopter tilted and roared towards the front of the house, spitting fire from its open side doors. Who was under fire?

"Break straight down from the back of the house, away from Cae Isa. If they come after us, scatter. Madog, you stay with Douglass and the kid no matter what," Gwyn said. The American had the best chance of getting himself and the hostages out alive. "Now!"

Gwyn flung himself through the brambles, out into snow-burdened thistles and scrub. He glanced back to make sure the rest were on his heels, then sprinted downhill over the broken ground, over boggy patches and rock outcrops. Fast enough for a hundred-metre gold. Like the messenger from Marathon, he was probably running his best race last.

A shout reached him from behind. He crouched, gasping, to wait for the others. As they came near, the white helicopter swept down on them. Gwyn flung himself on his face in the snow beside a tuft of willows, already feeling the bullets stitch across his back. Nothing happened. He rolled and saw the chopper hovering a scant few yards overhead. It was a Twin Huey. In the square side hatch, beside a floor-mounted machine-gun, stood two man. One, in a Balaclava, manned the gun. The other wore a wolfskin coat. Long blond hair whipped around his head from the rotor wind. Yann Morvan. A strong accent *Homing. Stand by for pick-up.* Gwyn rolled face down in the snow, laughing on the edge of hysteria.

When the Huey touched down, Nora ran past Gwyn toward Madog. She grabbed at the child he was still holding, but Madog twisted away. Nora snarled at him and swarmed up into the helicopter's rear compartment. Yann and his gunner had disappeared forward. Sion followed close behind her. Gwyn got to his feet, but Madog caught his arm.

"Wait!" Madog was gasping for breath, still carrying Pip. "Let them go, Gwyn. Let the *Saeson* follow them. Yann's pilot knows what to do for pursuit."

"Madog!" Morvan's face appeared in the co-pilot's window. *"Hast!"*

Madog waved him off. "No good. Lose them for us!"

Sion scrambled up into the Huey, clumsy with fright. Nora raised her shotgun. Gwyn watched, unable to tear his gaze away, as the IRA woman crouched, steadied the weapon, and fired into Sion's face. Blood exploded in a crimson halo around his head. For a moment he flailed the air, then he fell backwards from the helicopter's hatch and thumped into the snow, as limp as a rag doll. The Huey began to lift.

Jean and Carrie crouched in the snow beside Gwyn. A grey shape bounded downhill towards them. Cath Paluc had given up on the hidey-hole mice and now was enjoying the strange game his mistress was playing.

Nora spotted the cat and leisurely took aim again. Madog pushed the boy's head against his shoulder, in case he could still see. The shotgun blast tore the snow down to bare earth around the grey-striped Pal. Carrie's old cat screamed shrilly and tore off across the snow. Carrie flung herself yelling towards the helicopter. Madog shoved her sprawling on the ground as another blast ripped through the air where she'd stood. Then the Huey swung around in the wind and rose a few feet, spoiling Nora's target practice. Uphill, one of the camouflage-green RAF Sea Kings they'd seen this morning lifted above the burning roof of Pen y Cae. Yann's white Huey gained altitude with dizzying speed and spurted off to the west with the Sea King in pursuit.

Over the lower pasture, the Huey's gunner opened fire on the larger craft. The Sea King lurched sideways in the

air and liquid sprayed from its underbelly. Fuel, Gwyn
realized, and prepared himself for the explosion. But the
Sea King only lost a little speed and altitude, then recovered and went on. The camouflage-green craft didn't return fire; its RAF pilot must think the hostages were aboard
the Huey. The white chopper rounded a distant hillside
almost at ground level, flying below radar. Soon both helicopters were out of sight and sound. It was unimaginably
silent.

"They may draw the chase," Madog said. "Now we
700start walking."

Gwyn looked around. Pal was heading towards the
burning house. Carrie got up and stumbled after her cat.
Gwyn caught her ankle and brought her down.

"You're not going back," he gasped, knocked breath-
less. "He'll be all right."

She fought him elbow and fist as he'd taught her long
ago. Gwyn ducked and spiked her in the solar plexus.
When she folded, crowing for air, he staggered to his feet
and flung her over his shoulder. Maybe Grenvile would
believe she was innocent. He wasn't taking the chance.
Carrie wouldn't die as Elen did.

Madog kneeled in the snow, watching Pen y Cae burn.
He got to his feet with the sheet drawn over his head and
over Pip in his arms. He stooped to lift the knapsack from
Sion's outstretched hand and started to jog south.

PEN Y CAE/JANUARY 20/1800

Peter pushed back his duffle hood and blinked snow out
of his eyes as Al Rees set up the shot. Light was marginal
for taping, but they couldn't wait. Who knew what would
have happened by morning? This was strictly for the record anyway, with Harold Stone's ban on publication or
broadcast and Fox still determined to prevent them altogether from taping.

Behind Peter, masonry and smashed furniture lay spilled
from the standing house walls of Pen y Cae. An hour after

hell had broken loose, smoke was still rising. The scene was reminiscent of grainy stock footage from the blitz, forty-odd years ago, or from Beirut on last night's news. In the trampled yard, now that the wounded were airlifted out, medics were pulling plastic sheets over dead bodies. They already had good cover footage of all that. It was unnerving how quickly they'd grown accustomed to stepping around bodies.

"Rolling."

Al didn't look up. No jokes, no chewing gum. He was still shaken by his role in the terrorists' escape. They were both committed, Al through choice and Peter through self-preservation. But the operation was no longer merely an ideological stalemate. People were dead. Davies's fault, or the assault team's fault? Peter, sick and troubled, found that for once he didn't really want to know.

"Roll three, take one. Pen y Cae farm, Powys, Wales. Twenty January. Terrorist escape story, intro and voice-over."

Al nodded as Peter counted three. More dry snow clung to his eyelashes. He had the microphone in its foam-rubber sock to reduce wind hiss, but it was going to be noisy anyway.

"Six lives were lost today on this remote Welsh farm, when Welsh terrorists, captors of the young heir apparent, made their violent bid for escape.

"Among the dead are two soldiers from a yet-unidentified British regiment. Two British citizens—apparently part of the terrorist ring—and a local resident also died. The body of one terrorist was found in the house. Names have not yet been released.

"Just after four this afternoon, a special military team began an assault on the besieged farmhouse of Pen y Cae. As they breached the terrorists' defences, explosions destroyed part of the house and a small barn two hundred yards away. Hampered by billowing black smoke, blowing snow, and the fear of further explosions, the assault team regrouped. Before it could act, an unidentified helicopter swept down on the farm and opened fire on the soldiers. During the confusion, the terrorists made their break from the burning house, taking with them the Prince and his nurse, Miss Jean Douglass. Military aircraft are now in pursuit of the terrorist helicopter, believed to be heading north into the snowstorm now lashing Wales.''

Peter saw a black figure approaching on his right but didn't turn. Cameras always drew the curious and, in this case, the punitive also. Fox brought out Peter's northern stubborn streak; he would have to shut down their taping at gunpoint.

''Today's escape was unexpected. While an élite anti-terrorist squad gained entry in just over a minute, explosion and fire delayed their search of the house. It was another few minutes before they learned no terrorists remained alive in Pen y Cae.

''Today marked a surprising set-back for a British anti-terrorist group. Britain's most famous anti-terrorist assault was the 1980 rescue of hostages from the London Iranian embassy, by members of the highly efficient but secretive Special Air Services. The black-clad soldiers scaled the embassy walls to enter through second-storey windows after blasting a hole in the building. This afternoon's attempt appeared to depend on similar tactics.''

''Mr. Holt.'' Of course, the voice was Fox's. ''Shut down the camera.''

The studio could edit out the interruption, but perhaps it would be more interesting left in. CBS would love it; they were strong on moment-of-truth journalism. Peter glanced up, noticed that the lieutenant-colonel had been joined by a ''stick'' of four SAS men, and continued his camera presentation.

''Meanwhile, Welsh reaction has been bitter. The terrorists used amateur radio bands to broadcast details of negotiations with the military and of the expected assault. This, and the death of a local farmer in the exchange of gunfire, have aggravated Welsh anger. Peaceable protest marches in Cardiff and Aberystwyth grew violent and are now being forcibly dispersed.''

Al signalled a halt to Peter and stood back from the camera tripod. He looked ashen in a pallid grey light. Peter, without tape, turned to face Fox. He was wearing his tight-lipped look.

''There's no point adding anything further, Mr. Holt. We're going to have to confiscate your equipment.''

''I have Mr. Stone's approval,'' snapped Peter, ''as long as the tape isn't aired until later.''

''Things have changed since this morning. Two of my men failed to beat the clock. The terrorists are at large in a helicopter gunship. We're relocating mobile command as soon as we hear from the RAF pursuit team. The Prince's condition is unknown. I won't permit media parasites to complicate things further.''

''How can tapings for future use complicate anything?'' Peter fell back on being reasonable, but it didn't help to see sweat stand out on Rees's forehead. The earlier tapes were in his aluminum case, the first place anyone would look.

''Corporal,'' began Fox.

Anna Chernicki and the prime minister's aide who habitually dogged her steps joined them.

''No,'' Peter said, and went over the stand protectively in front of Al's camera. ''You can probably find a way to destroy a few strips of magnetic tape. But Rees and I and several dozen others saw your man shoot the woman. She surrendered. Geneva Convention.''

''They thought she was reaching for a weapon. And don't quote the Geneva Convention to me, Holt. This isn't a war.''

''Carry on and it will be.''

''At least a serious insurrection,'' agreed Anna Chernicki. The aide snickered and made a polite show of covering up.

Fox stared at her. ''This isn't Warsaw, or the Pennsylvania coal mines, Dr. Chernicki. No one asked for your advice.''

"Wrong, Colonel.'' She smiled, ignoring two calculated slurs on her background, and turned to Peter. "Come on, I'll walk you back to HQ.''

Al hastily slapped the tripod legs together and shouldered the camera. Peter grinned; he never expected a personal bodyguard from the American State Department.

"Thanks,'' he said as they ploughed downhill through the snow. Andrea would be ecstatic if the blizzard hit Cardiff. Andrea! And Elizabeth. He looked around for Grenvile but couldn't see him. He needed to know what was happening in Cardiff. Al walked briskly ahead, not quite loping to put distance between himself and Fox. He had the tapes shoved inside his silver bomber jacket, giving him a respectably Hawaiian paunch. "You seem to have a warm spot for the media, Doctor.''

"It's called mutual back scratching, Mr. Holt. Sorry to destroy your illusions, if you have any left. I want to ask a favour.''

Come into my parlour, said the spider to the fly. But he was already in Grenvile's parlour.

"Right.''

"What kind of shape is Nilsson in? He didn't sound good on the radio.''

"What?'' Peter stopped in his tracks. "Sorry. I don't understand.''

Anna Chernicki kept walking, and Peter caught up. "Captain Nilsson was with us mopping up in Cambodia. The Reds got him. When we exchanged him out we had to take him off the active roster. Unstable, depressed, personality fragmentation under stress.''

"Right.'' Peter was still lost.

"He was the wrong man for this job. Another agency insisted. So did he. We should have objected more strenuously, given his family ties to this country.''

"Right.'' Job? Agency? She couldn't really be telling

him this. "Aren't you afraid I'll say so in my next broadcast?"

She smiled. "The *New of the World* already suggested something of the kind. You'd be laughed all the way back to the *Blackburn Examiner.*"

Unafraid of minor indiscretions and well-informed about Peter Holt: both reflected her country's casual omnipotence. Suddenly he wished he'd stayed with Fox.

He remembered the question. "Nilsson looked all right. Nothing strange. Davies seemed to rely heavily on him. He took apart Grenvile's little transmitter in about ten seconds."

"Electronic wizard." Chernicki nodded. "That international aerospace business grew out of one Quonset hut behind the Boeing plant at Everett. So you think he's okay."

"Personal interest?"

"Certainly not," she said in her crisp Anglo-American tones. "But there is a possibility that he may do something unpredictable. Our sole concern is for the little boy's safety."

"But—" Peter struggled for his sense of reality. What had Gwyn said about the American? I don't know anymore. "You can't be telling me your government was involved in this from the start. And did nothing to prevent it."

"I am merely an observer."

Chernicki said nothing more. Peter realized he would have to answer his own questions; at most she might affirm or deny. And, heart-breakingly, not a word of this would ever see print.

"Someone learned the plans," he speculated. "Secret service decided to take them in the act. Scotland Yard or MI5 was supposed to nab them immediately, the heroes of the hour." Peter shook his head. "Impossible. They wouldn't gamble with the child's life. Even if they had someone in there who could protect . . . No."

Chernicki wasn't giving him any help. She waited, apparently amused by his guesswork. He could be miles off, or spot on.

"Why *are* you here, observing?" Peter demanded angrily. "Helping out a minor European dependency?"

"I wouldn't be so crude, Mr. Holt." She smiled again, disarming his sarcasm. They were almost at the place the barn used to be, before Al had blown it and the three cars sky-high. "Britain has been a great world power, and we're old friends. And we can't have the keystone of NATO threatened or the whole structure will come tumbling down."

"Right. And if I told anyone this, I'd be laughed back to Blackburn."

"Roight." She echoed his voice at its absent-minded broadest.

Peter shook his head, speechless. Not for long. "What's happening now? Why haven't they moved the mobile command? Where are the terrorists and the SAS helicopters? Who brought in that white chopper, the Huey?"

She started walking again. "I wish I had answers, Mr. Holt. All the gunmen seem to have gotten away by air. With blowing snow like this, any ground traces are covered immediately anyway. It also plays merry hell with our tracking equipment. As for the Huey—have you heard of Breizh Nevez?"

"Bloody hell. Yann Morvan." He recalled Nigel Phipps watching him anxiously, his pint untouched, in the Black Lion. Breizh Nevez, proud new owners of a helicopter gunship with end-clearance papers stamped in Vaduz, Liechtenstein.

"I'm afraid so. We're having some difficulty making your government understand that an alliance of Celtic nationalists could be very troublesome indeed. The Northern Irish, the Scots, the Welsh, and the Bretons in France have just cause to be angry with the governments of Britain and France," she said, to Peter's surprise. "And quite a few of these people have trained in Libya and South Yemen. They're no match for anti-terrorist squads, but they can cause terrible destruction in the attempt. As you've seen. They also have help from established terrorist groups like the Red Brigades, the ETA, and the PLO.''

Peter decided against further questions. The answers made him uneasy.

At operation headquarters, the technicians were packing the helicopter. Mr. Leung stood at the side hatch, head together with another member of the surveillance crew.

''Problems?'' asked Anna Chernicki.

The technician nodded across the snowy pasture. Armed SAS soldiers had thrown a cordon around three cars and a van bearing the insignia of ITN. Harold Stone was down there, surrounded by gesticulating new arrivals. Peter needed no explanation. The press invasion had begun. Willing to hire their own helicopters, willing to test the boundaries of the military ban, they would be almost impossible to keep out. Good. Strength in numbers. And he still had them beaten by days of work, yards of first-class tape.

They were packing up their recording gear when Robert Grenvile ran up to the helicopter. It was the fastest Peter had seen him move. His hair was in disarray and he was out of breath.

''Peter. It's like opening day down there. The prime minister called. It's an election year and people need a lift. The PM wants to give them televised coverage of the terrorists being captured. He doesn't yet realize they may be halfway to Ireland by now. In any case, the press ban's off.''

''Thanks. Can I use a phone? I've got to get our tapes in Cardiff and New York.''

''Holt here,'' he told the Old Man when he answered in Cardiff. ''We have a go-ahead with coverage on the kidnapping story. I've got the tape footage of an interview with the terrorists and Miss Douglass, the anti-terrorist squad assaulting the farmhouse, a helicopter counter-attack from out of the blue sky. You've never seen anything like it. Can you send a helicopter to pick it up in Llany-groes?''

The Old Man cleared his throat ponderously. ''I can't authorize any expenditure of that kind. Bring it back immediately yourself.''

And miss the rest of the story? Peter thought as he rang off. By a miracle, he got straight through to McKinley, the managing executive in London.

''What is it now, Holt?''

Again, Peter made his pitch.

''This is a matter of national security,'' McKinley told him.

''The press ban's off,'' Peter said quickly.

''We'll air the story when we hear that from the government.''

''The place is crawling with reporters and camera crews. ITN's here!'' Peter's voice rose an octave in exasperation, and his vowels stretched like Al's chewing gum. ''Are you serious about news coverage, or not?''

''That's quite enough, Holt. The gentlemen from the SAS have been telling me about your behavior. I might as well tell you now that on the basis of your performance to date, your services will no longer be required by the BBC.''

Peter indulged the briefest satisfaction of his life. ''I've heard better news judgement from a dead canary. If you don't want my tape today, you don't get it tomorrow. Blow it out your arse.''

He rang off, shock already seizing him. Outside, Al Rees shook his head in slow sympathy. *''Duw, Duw.* Let's get on with it, Peter *bach.''*

''Quiet please,'' requested Mr. Leung from Peter's elbow. ''Mr. Stone is talking on the other phone to the prime minister of the Republic of Ireland.''

16

"This fishing boat," said Madog, leaning on the lorry for a breather. It was warm in the stone barn, even with the blizzard prying through chinks and cracks. "Carrie, try to remember. Exactly where on the Llŷn? Was the captain going to come right inshore?"

"Waiting offshore," she said. "West of Nant Gwrtheyrn." Nora had told her after one of John's visits. The information had been accompanied by an offer of transport to Libya. She wished Nora somewhere even closer to hell than Libya. She wiped her forehead and pitched another bale. She didn't want to think about Nora, about their nightmare flight to Tad's farm, about what she left behind, about going on to the coast. She didn't want any part of it.

"You heard Gareth's transistor. Radio Cymru said the helicopter got across the sea. If Nora's in Ireland, the boat won't be there," Gwyn objected.

"We'll have to take a chance." Madog got up and man-handled the plywood over to the farm lorry.

"Stay." Gareth wasn't one for unnecessary words.

"Not safe for any of us," Madog told him. "We can't keep hiding in the milking house to fool the heat seekers. They'll be back with dogs."

"Dyna ni, ynte?" Gareth shrugged and palmed his light brown hair back out of his eyes. "I'll drive. She's a beast."

"Ten years minimum sentence," warned Madog.

"Huh," said Gareth. "Family."

Carrie shut out the argument and concentrated on the hay load. Four bales across, eight bales along, five bales high, plywood over the third layer to make a cramped nest for four fugitives and the child. The load was roped to the flat bed under a tarpaulin.

"Better not Gareth," Madog said quietly. "If you're stopped . . ."

Carrie saw a double-barrelled shotgun tucked neatly under the young farmer's elbow.

"Can't have rats taking over the granary." Gareth looked steadily at his cousin. "Times I forget to take her from the cab."

"Someone could get hurt." Madog took the gun from him and went through into the feed room. He came back without it. For a spy, or whatever he was, Carrie thought he made a fair pacifist.

She went to shake Jean Douglass. Madog lifted Pip, still asleep; when he woke there would be tears over his lost Mungo Mouse and his friend Pal.

Light left them as Gareth stacked the last bales in place, doing his best to leave air passages. Gwyn handed the sleeping child in to Jean Douglass and settled beside her. Then Carrie opposite, the knapsack full of John Hughes's food, and Madog on her right. The small compartment jammed them together like a jigsaw puzzle, with just enough room to stretch their legs if they were careful. Warm, but it wouldn't stay warm long at well below freezing, as it would be according to the Radio Cymru weatherman.

Soon Carrie felt the lorry lurch into gear and crawl out of the barn onto the rutted farm road. Another gear shift and a gravel surface. Gareth was travelling cautiously; it would be a long night. Jean Douglass began to sing softly in a breaking voice, though Pip couldn't hear, her Gaelic song about the beautiful island.

At an asphalt road they picked up speed. Carrie swayed against Madog. He was bent forward with his head on his knees, so tightly tensed he was trembling. She laid her hand on his arm. Nausea? Muscle cramp?

"All right?" Carrie could do nothing. Her medical bag had burned in Pen y Cae. She understood that he sought refuge, sanctuary. Like the music she'd never heard, mountains and rivers without end. Like Pen y Cae. Like his island. She understood that it was almost the only thing she knew about him and that she wanted to know more and that she should put Madog from her mind.

"Yeah." In a moment he straightened and let out his breath. "Small spaces. When I can't get out of them."

Claustrophobia, at least, she could treat. Keep him talking. "Do you know Llŷn? We'll have to find shelter. And how will we call the boat?"

"I've got Holt's transmitter. Don't know their code—but if they're out there they'll be listening. Everyone else for miles will be listening, too, if it's anything like the marine band at home."

Carrie suppressed a yawn. The day was catching up with her. "You promised you'd tell me more about your island."

"Did I tell you about the rabbits? Millions of rabbits. . . ."

His voice settled to a sensual warmth. Carrie slipped down through the layers of it, into a dream of islands in the west. Then Madog was saying her name, quietly, and she swam up out of sleep into dusty blackness. Madog's arm was warm around her. She liked lying in a man's arms, even as chastely as this. There would be a man in America. America.

The lorry growled onward through north central Wales. They were reduced to a crawl; the storm must be worse. No sound from Gwyn, Jean, or Pip. Asleep, probably. Faintly she could hear Gareth Hughes singing to himself in a

rich tenor, one of the sad old ballads. The tiny voice of
Madog's watch told them, "Twenty-three forty-eight."

Passing through the Allt Valley, probably. Carrie pictured the villages and smallholdings. They would log the
hillsides, cut the orchards, trample the kitchen gardens,
flood the sweet-grassed river pastures. Desolation in the
name of prosperity. A phrase surfaced from a forgotten
history text: you create desolation and call it peace.

The skid woke Carrie with a start. All of them lurched
together, and Madog's arm tightened around her. The motor died and the driver's door opened. In the sudden quiet,
they heard footsteps on snow and the sound of a second
car door opening.

"Morning," Gareth said in English. "Something
wrong?"

"Papers, please." An unknown voice.

"Everything's up to date." Gareth yawned. "Gwynedd
police, is it?"

"That's right, Mr. Hughes. What brings you out at this
hour?"

"My uncle's run short, over by Llanllyfin. I wanted to
get away by tea time, but I had chores to finish."

"Still live in Bangor, Mr. Hughes?"

"Sometimes. I help my uncle as he needs me."

Carrie bit her lip, waiting for the fatal question: and
where else do you live? If he said Llanygroes it would give
them away now, and if he lied it would give Gareth away
later. Instead, the officer walked around towards the back
of the lorry.

"I'll take a look at your load."

"Looking for the Prince, are you?"

The policeman grunted non-committally. Carrie felt
Madog's arm lift slowly from around her, and he reached
into the front of his anorak. She caught his wrist, but his
hand was empty. Not the gun. The arrowhead. He bent to
kiss her, and even as she lit again to his touch she remembered Nora. Making love to death. She found his hand
and lifted it to her breast, insisting on life.

Outside, someone fumbled with the tarpaulin ropes.

"I'll get that," said Gareth.

One bale slid from its place, then a second and a third. Carrie straightened and closed her eyes so tightly she saw streaks of fire. A hand closed around her ankle; Gwyn was offering reassurance. Which bales were they moving? Across the back, at the top. If they moved down one layer they would reach the plywood.

"Looks all right. Sorry to cause you the inconvenience, Mr. Hughes."

"I needed a breath of air."

"Drive carefully. The roads are dangerous."

Carrie heard Gareth slam his door and start the motor. The lorry eased forward, uphill.

Over his driver's shoulder Corgi watched the police cruiser pull out from a farm road and ease after the lorry, lights flashing. Routine. His driver needed no instructions. He cut the headlamps and steered onto the shoulder.

Corgi steadied the infra-red scope on the back of the driver's seat and turned his attention to the screen. Under his breath he hummed "All through the night." Against a field of black and midnight blue, the truck was a warm shape etched in reds and yellows, white around the exhaust. The driver stepped out to talk to the policeman, two columns of white blazing with their body heat. He trained the scope on the hay load. Nothing, only the faintest lightening of blue towards the centre. Might be only the residual barn warmth of hay bales cooling from the outside in. Wild-goose chase. Maybe.

The cop and the lorry driver walked to the back of the load and started moving bales. The driver stood aside among an untidy pile of bales on the snowy roadway, and Corgi's patience was rewarded. With the outer bales removed, the heart of the hay load glowed yellow and white on his screen. Indistinct, but large. Several large, warm-blooded animals. And only one species of animal would

consent to crouch hidden, mile after mile, in the dark.
Corgi smiled.

The cop returned to his car, picking his way carefully
on the icy surface. The lorry pulled out, labouring through
its gears.

"Lights," said Corgi, but the driver had anticipated his
thought. Had to be that way, working like clockwork, four
lads together, lives meshed like cogs and wheels. He rolled
down the left rear window as the Volvo eased alongside
the police cruiser.

"Evening, constable."

"Evening, sir."

Corgi put his arm out the open window, offering his
papers, and the cop played his torch over it. He glanced
up and nodded. Just a kid, for God's sake. Pimples.

"Very good, sir. All the way from London today? Cabinet's lost no time on this, has it? We appreciate your
help."

"Hope you still feel that way tomorrow when half the
MoD and Scotland Yard are crawling over North Wales."

The boy laughed. "Oh, it's all right, sir. Finding the
little boy, that's the thing."

"Couldn't agree more." Corgi nodded as his driver
started forward into the night.

Another cop, Madog thought at first, when they slowed
and stopped a quarter-hour later. The voices—Gareth's and
another man's—were up at the front of the truck and hard
to make out. They didn't sound especially angry or excited. Madog heard the doors of the cab slam twice. Did
Gareth have a passenger? Then they drove on, and it
seemed okay for a while. The give-away was turning off
again onto gravel, then rutted snow, on a hilly road.
Something was wrong. It should be asphalt all the way to
Llŷn. Who had Gareth picked up?

He strained his hearing for other clues and thought he
heard the hush of other wheels on snow. A second, lighter
vehicle behind Gareth's truck. They were driving steadily

away from the main road, up and down hills. He had to make sense of it, right now, and he had to be right. Madog found the obsidian blade and felt it along the chopped edge thoughtfully. After a minute he told the others.

The truck finally slowed to a halt on a slight angle. The motor was shut off. The driver's door opened and closed, then the passenger door. Another, quieter car motor shut off. Two car doors opened and closed. Three doors. Shit.

"Get them out," said the unknown man.

"Why? It doesn't make sense," said Gareth. He was pitching his voice to carry, Madog thought, warning them. "The lorry is as safe a way as any."

"Just do it, old man. Discuss logistics later." It was a well-bred English voice. Corgi? Gwyn would know.

"I don't believe Gwyn sent you. Show me some proof." Don't push them, Gareth. "I don't see—"

Something large and heavy slammed into the driver's side of the hay load and slid towards the ground. Gareth.

"Get those bales down," said the Englishman.

"Right. Give us a hand here." Another English voice, sounded like a Yorkshireman. They were untying the tarpaulin. "That's it."

Madog probed under the bottom bale to be sure his gun was where he shoved it. Gwyn's Browning was beside it.

"Remember, no heroics," he said quietly.

"There's no point resisting arrest," Jean Douglass agreed.

"These aren't the good guys, Miss Douglass," Madog murmured. "Heads down. We're asleep."

Bales were being removed from the back of the truck. Back row, second back row. They would be able to see the plywood now. Another row. Under his eyelashes Madog saw faint light, moonlight reflected on snow.

"Well, what have we here?" asked the Yorkshireman. "Sardines in a tin."

Madog made a show of starting awake and nudged Gwyn. Carrie and Jean still had heads on updrawn knees and the child was genuinely sleeping. Four men stood at the back of the truck: one was tall with silver hair, two were dark-haired and shorter, the fourth was a big blond man. They all had Heckler and Koch automatic rifles.

Gareth's truck was parked in a snow-carpeted open space. A white Volvo waited a car's length away to the left. They were in mature oak forest with some evergreens. Picnic tables under four inches of snow. A snow-capped sign, "Welcome to Cwm Emrys. Snowdonia National Park." Looked like they were in the parking lot. No one for miles around. The only sound was running water, a small stream off to his right somewhere, the far side of the parking area.

"So you're the American," said the blond man genially. "You do keep strange company, Mr. Davies."

"Corgi. Thanks for helping out." Gwyn managed to sound cool and efficient, though Madog guessed he'd rather have Corgi's throat between his hands. "Can you set up a diversion so we can get away to Ireland?"

"Trust you don't plan to hop the Holyhead ferry. They'll pinch you for Common Market farm-import violation." Corgi's three wingers laughed.

"No, we have other arrangements," said Gwyn. Madog was afraid he was going to blurt the whole plan about the trawler to Corgi.

"Let's get on with it. The boy first," the silver-haired man suggested to Corgi. But with any luck, money would appeal more than murder to a mercenary.

"A hundred thousand enough?" Madog asked quickly. Why would they want to kill Pip? He'd assumed they intended another kidnap, another ransom bid. And where was Gareth? Alive or dead? At least there hadn't been a gunshot. He began to edge microscopically towards the driver's side of the truck for a look.

Corgi turned to him with interest. "Rather parsimonious of you, Mr. Nilsson, all things considered. Surely you can up your firm's rates to NASA to cover a few discretionary expenditures?"

"Half a million," Madog offered, wondering if he'd

actually trade, or do them just for a laugh. Corgi had a lousy track record for respecting clients' wishes. "Dollars."

"Pounds."

"No way. Shareholders only put up with so much."

"Pity. Can't really pitch in for less." Corgi actually looked regretful. "Competition's offering the round figure. Overhead, you see. My lads here are worth their weight in plutomium."

"I'm easy." Competition? Madog's scalp started to prickle. Gwyn was watching Corgi like a hawk. Madog threw him a warning glance: keep out of this. "How about a leg stretch first?"

Corgi hesitated. "Nothing clever. You first."

Madog got to his feet stiffly, climbed down off the flat bed and clasped his hands on top of his head. It was just about his least favourite posture, though the Khmer gave him plenty of practice. Madog risked a glance towards the front of the truck and saw his cousin. He was sprawled half under the cab and he was stirring. The shortest of Corgi's men frisked Madog meticulously and identified himself as the Yorkshireman by reporting, "He's clean."

Gwyn got down, then Carrie and Jean Douglass. One of their captors frisked Gwyn thoroughly, the women less diligently. They left Pip among the bales. He was sucking his thumb in his sleep.

"So what exactly does this competition want?"

"Let's not upset anyone." He glanced at Jean Douglass.

Who would pay for the little boy's death? It didn't really matter. Corgi would kill Pip as easily as he'd killed three kids at Tywyn.

"Call it a round figure sterling," Madog said, "and I'll throw in Douglass. Won't guarantee you a bonus, but you may get a medal from the King. She's been a naughty girl. You'll come up smelling like roses. We keep the kid."

It was a new twist to Corgi. He considered it.

"He's worth too much," said the Yorkshireman, "one way or the other."

Madog glanced again towards Gareth. Now there was no sign of him under the truck. Or anywhere. If he did something crazy it would cost them their lives. Madog yawned and stretched, then took a few steps farther from the truck.

"Hold it there." The Yorkshireman trained the gun on his chest and his buddies followed suit.

"Sure thing."

From the driver's window of the truck, a shotgun blast roared through the night silence. The Yorkshireman flung out his arms and flew spread-eagled backwards. The silver-haired mercenary crouched with his automatic, but the blast from the second barrel knocked him flying before he could fire. Snow cascaded off the trees all around them.

Now. Madog whirled to Corgi and tackled him low just as he fired, sending bullets spraying over their heads. From behind him, someone fired another single shot. Corgi was fast and strong. He threw Madog off, rolled, and came up running. He sprinted across the parking lot and plunged into deep snow on the far side, under the oak trees and towards the sound of water. Madog dived onto the flat bed far enough to reach his gun and ran after Corgi.

Can't have rats taking over the granary. Gareth always was stubborn.

Carrie saw Madog go after the blond man and turned to the lorry. Jean Douglass stood holding Gwyn's gun in both hands, staring at the man she'd shot. He was rolling on the ground, holding his shoulder. Gwyn had him covered with one of the stubby rifles the four men had carried.

She shook the cobwebs out of her head and went over to the man whose hair had been grey. Now it was matted in blood and tissue. He was hideously dead. The other also lay still, his chest destroyed. She knelt by the third man. He struggled to a sitting position, shivering, with the stunned face and wide pupils of shock. This one would survive if she could stop the bleeding.

"Get something for bandages," she told Jean.

Carrie dressed the man's wound, all she could do without her medical bag. She was treating Gareth's ugly-looking scalp contusion when they heard the gunfire deep in the oak forest. Nothing more happened. They waited a long time. She scrubbed blood from her hands with snow, watched Gwyn lock their captive in the car boot and go in the direction the other two had taken, all with a sense of insulation from what had gone before and what would follow. Shock. It was almost a relief when Jean's terrible calm dissolved into a torrent of tears. Soon she froze again to a deeper silence.

Madog plunged through snow over his knees in places, following the tracks. Corgi had run down beside the stream, sure-footed as an island cougar. SAS material, all right. He didn't even know how far ahead Corgi was until he came to the brink of a small steep rock face. Corgi's tracks crossed and recrossed in confusion there. Madog crouched and looked along the outcrop, then below. Corgi stood flattened to the base, drawing a bead on him. Madog threw himself right, and the single shot grazed his left arm. Corgi had his gun off automatic, saving ammunition. Good. Madog lay still, the snow burning against his face. Playing dead was no way to deal with Corgi. He rolled on his back and shoved his right hand and the gun into his anorak pocket.

Corgi climbed up after a while, cautiously. He'd been careless about Gareth, but it was too much to hope that he'd be careless twice. Madog waited until snow creaked a few feet away and Corgi loomed black against the overcast sky. Then he pulled the trigger, knowing he fired miles wide. He rolled fast and scrambled to his feet. Corgi drilled three shots into the snow where he'd just been. Then nothing more. At the end of his clip, or only near to it? Madog knew his only chance when he saw it. He launched himself at the Englishman. But Corgi was solid on his feet. They grappled for the automatic rifle. Corgi struggled to get the gun high, tried to give himself room to club with it. Empty clip, then, or he'd be trying to fire instead.

Corgi shifted weight suddenly and got an arm around Madog's neck. If Madog could free a hand for his pistol—but Corgi was too strong, too immovable, and soon had him in a steel grip. Painstakingly, like Olympic wrestlers, they tested each other's balance. Corgi's arm crushed the air from Madog's throat, then his lungs.

Opalescence swam in front of his eyes, and he felt the amulet's chain briefly tear at his skin, then snap. Another minute and oxygen starvation would finish him. Slowly, he worked with each breath to give himself a minuscule bit of leeway, and space to breathe. And if he could breathe he could talk.

"Swiss francs. Five million," Madog gasped. Corgi's arm loosened fractionally. "Or a million dollars. Nothing if I'm dead. It's all yours. They took out your pals." Keep talking, and he could get his wind back.

Corgi stood still, considering.

"Not a trace." After a quarter of an hour Gwyn stepped wearily across the car park, now trodden and stained.

"How far did you go?"

"Downstream till their tracks stopped. The snow was trampled. I think they had some sort of struggle there."

"And?" She knew he was holding something back.

Gwyn handed Carrie something small and sharp, not meeting her eyes. "Keep this somewhere safe for Madog."

By touch she knew it was the obsidian arrowhead.

"He's dead," Jean Douglass said in a flat voice.

"Madog can talk his way out of anything. He'll be all right." Gwyn smiled briefly. "Gareth, let's get out of this place. Drop us where Carrie described, so we can try to pick up this trawler. It's our only chance now. Then go to your uncle's farm and stay there."

Carrie cast a last look at the still oak trunks, corrugated with snow, dark against the moonlight. Nothing moved among them. She dropped the arrowhead in her anorak pocket and turned away.

AIRBORNE COMMAND POST/JANUARY 21/0600

Peter jerked awake from an unpleasant dream of falling and found they had lost altitude. He still sat folded into a seat in one of the Sea King's few corners unoccupied by the electronic wunderkind and their sombre technical staff. Al Rees hunched opposite, looking deflated without tapes bulging the front of his bomber jacket. He was tearing a paper film wrapper into confetti. Chernicki was shuffling through papers in another corner, under scrutiny as usual by the PM's aide, who was on the phone.

Cautiously, Peter stretched in his seat, scraping his feet across the metal floor and his elbow against the quilted wall padding. When he leaned towards the nearest window, diffused daylight made him blink. It was morning. All night the airborne command had flown search patterns, touched down occasionally for fuel and ground checks, then lifted off again. Today, only thick cloud was visible. The pilot had once registered a laconic observation that flying conditions were of negative acceptability. The Sea King lurched again, crabbing as the wind caught it broadside. The cloud wisped open and through it Peter glimpsed only more cloud, or perhaps it was snow-covered landscape.

"Not much to see," said Grenvile, who'd come over quietly.

"Where are we?"

"Near Caernarfon, I should think. Still sweeping with radar and turning up nothing. I could ask the pilot exactly where."

"Close enough." Peter yawned in his fist. "I was hoping it might be the Riviera."

Grenvile laughed half-heartedly. "Better luck next time."

"Right."

And next time I have a job, I'll stay away from you lot. But Peter was hard put to maintain his moral indignation over BBC's dismissal. Even if he were covering for the *Blackburn Examiner*—not a bad little rag, truth to tell—he would be exactly where he was now: stomach rumbling from soggy sandwiches and bilious coffee, scribbled notes overflowing half a dozen pockets, unshaven, worried sick, and utterly at home. And his tapes were on their way to London by special courier for transmission to New York.

"Any word from Cardiff?"

Grenvile shook his head. "Two of our people have moved into your ex-wife's house for the duration. Your wife and daughter are fine. There's been no sign of your man with the tattoo."

"Good," Peter said. "Or is it?"

"I think so. Frankly, I can't see him bothering you again." Grenvile looked around. Chernicki was tapping at her keyboard. The PM's aide was still talking. "He may have approached you because he thought you knew the gunmen's location and that he could either get you out of the way or force you to take him there."

"Why?" Peter had tired of official secrets, for once, but asked from habit.

Grenvile looked uncomfortable. "Couldn't say, really. Perhaps he wanted to rescue the Prince himself."

"Or hold the boy for ransom himself?"

The negotiator swallowed. His voice dwindled to a husk. "Just let's hope he's not on assignment. For anyone."

"Prefer free enterprise?" Peter gave up on it, it was all too vile and complicated for this ungodly hour.

Grenvile visibly decided to change the topic. "Thought you'd like to know your stories made top of the news on ITN and CBS and, I gather, nearly every other western television network."

Calculating the effect, Peter regarded him owlishly. CBS meant money. In his last call to the mobile HQ from New York, Cliff Aslin had shouted, "You're working for the good guys now, Pete. We'll buy every inch of your tape."

ITN meant household familiarity and, more important, corporate familiarity for Peter Holt's homely north-country face. He might get another news job. Someday.

"Thanks. What's new? Anything from the helicopters or Harriers?" Peter hated feeling idle. He couldn't tape anything more until they landed. "What about the dogs and trackers?"

"Nothing yet. The camera crews are getting underfoot, especially the Americans who flew in from Frankfurt and Paris. The dogs haven't found anything. But—" Grenvile glanced at the aide. Still on the phone. "Reports are in from the Sea Kings. They say they picked up the white helicopter again on radar, at sea off Anglesey."

"So it was heading for Ireland?" Peter sat forward abruptly.

"But it disappeared. They couldn't find a trace. No wreckage. Nothing on radar, on infra-red, on one-millimetre, or on any other band. Nothing on visual when they overflew the area. They've either got very advanced electronic and chaff jamming, or they're down. And the Prince and Miss Douglass are probably with them, wherever they are."

"What do you reckon, Robert?"

"I reckon—I believe the Huey reached Ireland yesterday and the RAF were following a ghost, a radar blip. They desperately want to see something. They're frustrated. It happens."

"Now what?"

"We'll maintain the search grid until we have ground visibility. Sooner or later we'll either find the Huey or have to admit failure."

"God Almighty. And the terrorists have still got the kid."

"Yes. I'm afraid they've got all the bargaining power in the world now. Just pray they don't sell him to the Provisional IRA or the Libyans. I mean it, Peter. Pray." Grenvile blinked and turned away.

Peter sat back slowly, weighed by his conscience. Dav-

ies's terrorists had escaped partly because of the diver-
sionary bomb at the barn, the bomb Rees planted and
Peter saved his skin by not reporting. If that cheerful kid
with a tatty old mouse doll was drowned in the Irish Sea—
if Andrea—he couldn't even carry the thought to its end.
He better understood Fox's hatred for the demanding,
meddlesome makers and breakers of news. He frowned
up at Rees and saw he was under scrutiny.

"Peter," Al began in Welsh, halting his destruction of
the film packet. Shredded paper lay around his feet. "If
I'd known . . ."

Peter shook his head, preoccupied with his own recrim-
inations.

"Don't blame Gwyn," Al said quietly.

"What?" Peter eyed him incredulously and answered
in English. "Who in hell killed six people?" The aide,
off the phone at last, pricked up his ears in interest. Peter
lowered his voice. "You tell me, Rees. Who in hell should
I blame?"

"That Leung guy let me put the tape on the electronic
enhancer. I saw it all, everything, freeze-frame close-up.
The Italian shot Hughes. He was drawing a bead on the
American when Davies shot him. I saw it clear as your
face. The SAS shot the girl. The white helicopter strafed
the SAS assault. Gwyn didn't do it."

"That's not good enough." Peter was belligerent in his
own need for expiation. "People are dead. Who's to
blame?"

"Saeson," said Al. The English. The all-around Welsh
answer to the world's evils.

"Bullshit," said Peter, in English. "Never take responsibility. Just blame someone else."

*"A cyn ethwyf i yno, i'm bro fy hun, nid oes un car.
Neud adar i'w warafun."*

"I don't understand that." Peter stuck to English.

"And when I came again into my own country, not one
friend remained. Carrion birds detained them." Al raised
his black eyes, brimming with fondly nurtured delusions.

"Written around 670 A.D. It's been going on a long time. Lately you've given up physical genocide for cultural genocide."

"Didn't know you were a scholar of Old Welsh," Peter said sarcastically.

"Lots of things you don't know."

"Shove it." Peter got up, heading towards Chernicki, the pin-striped aide, anyone who didn't hand out that twaddle. Empty threats. History. Sullen racism.

"Major Grenvile," one of the techs murmured as Peter passed. "GCHQ Cheltenham on the line. Stand by."

"Marine-band transmission," said the impersonal machine-generated voice of GCHQ. "From the north coast of the Llŷn Peninsula. Direction finder reading follows."

NANT CERRIG/JANUARY 21/0700

Dawn was a lemon glare behind the peak of Eryri and its snow-shouldered mountain companions. Gwyn looked from the mountains to the sea, lost behind falling snow and fog. A quarter of a mile north, perhaps, he could faintly hear the Irish Sea breaking below the cliffs.

Last night's wind had dropped, leaving snow-drifts deep against stone walls and hillocks. Gwyn tried to recall the terrain of Nant Gwrtheyrn, not far east, where he had once taught Welsh at summer school: cliffs broken by the occasional steep gully, pierced by outcrops, heavily treed. Down at the shore the ground levelled out in places.

White fields lay all around. The road, a gravel tertiary, was an unflawed white ribbon marked off only by the pale mounds of its hedges. Gareth had dropped them there two, three hours ago. Now their straggling tracks had vanished, scoured away and sifted full of snow. Gwyn walked a few paces, staying on the shore side of the snow-bound caravan that had sheltered them. The snow creaked underfoot. When snow creaks it's good for igloos, Madog had told Pip. Madog. Madog had been their safety, or had he? What had happened in the oak forest at Cwm Emrys? Had they joined forces? Met by prior agreement? Madog and Corgi: that would be an alliance forged from nightmare.

Snow and fog lay on the land like a dream. If it were only a dream, he would awaken in Aberystwyth, promise himself yet again to finish his thesis, teach his junior classes. All that was gone now, like a dream. He turned back to the caravan, owned by a retired Sheffield couple to judge by the postcards taped to a wall. They had unwisely left it to the lightest of padlocks. Other caravans and cottages lay within distant eyesight, abandoned to winter or sleep.

Inside the caravan, huddled all through the night without light or heat, Carrie and Jean and the boy slept. It was time to take them down to the shore. Nora's East German trawler might be there, or it might not. They were now out of choices. He shook Carrie, sleeping fully dressed on the fold-down bed, and motioned her outside.

"I want your help."

"What help?" She was sleepy and distrustful.

"Lie low if there's an encounter. Get Jean Douglass and the Prince back where they belong. Tell Grenvile all of you were kidnapped. It'll stand up on a lie detector or under interrogation—and they will certainly interrogate you. Ask Peter Holt for help, he's a friend. Then get your papers and go to America."

"No interrogation will clear me enough for that, Gwyn."

"You'll be all right." Gwyn looked across the white fields into the white ice fog, seeing no distance into their opaque emptiness. "But you're needed here."

"So were you." Carrie searched his face, frowning.

"With any luck he wasn't hurt," Gwyn said awkwardly. It was doubly the hardest thing he'd ever done. "You know he was wearing a flak vest." Carrie shook her head wordlessly. Gwyn wanted to hold her and offer her comfort, but she turned from him. There was nothing more to say.

* * *

When they went back into the caravan, Jean Douglass was bundling Pip warmly. They had no more tablets; perhaps it would be easier on the boy if he believed this an adventure.

"Have you ever gone to the beach in winter, Pip?"

"No." The boy looked at his feet. "Gwyn?"

"You'll have to dress warmly."

"Gwyn?" Pip leaned against Gwyn's leg and looked up with his direct blue eyes. "Is someone going to kill me?"

He was a bright boy, and he wanted to know. Gwyn swallowed any soothing tales he might have offered another child.

"We won't let anyone hurt you. Carrie and Miss Douglass and I will keep you safe, no matter what happens. You know that?"

"Yes." He looked up again. "Where's Madog?"

"Madog went to find a boat."

"Come along, Pip. Tie your shoe lace." The nanny firmly returned things to the commonplace.

"Can I ride on the boat with Madog?"

"We'll see. Where's your blanket?"

Gwyn led them towards the sea, keeping a sharp eye out for other people. He saw only sea-gulls huddled miserably on the snow and a great expanse of grey-white sky and sea and fog. Would a boat risk landing in these conditions? He would have to trust Nora's feral instinct for survival, trust that she had paid or blackmailed well enough to get the trawler here. He wished he had a transmitter. Instead he'd have to hope the boat came within hailing distance.

Dawn was full-blown in the east, away over England, by the time they reached the cliff. Thick fog obscured the water and swirled in wisps almost to the cliff top. Gwyn heard the muffled slap of waves far below. When the fog lifted, a fishing boat could edge inshore to where the deep water came almost within arm's reach of the cliff. They might get away. If the wind didn't rise. If the fog lifted. If there were a boat out there. If Nora was in Ireland.

Snow sifted past Gwyn when he kneeled cautiously at the margin. He saw the route down the cliff and knew Jean Douglass and Pip couldn't manage it. There must be another way. He drew away from the lip, looking back towards the east. If anything, the cliff was steeper there. He signalled Carrie and the nanny on and broke trail through the crusted snow towards a stand of forestry.

In another fifty yards, his guess was rewarded. The land sloped more gently and dropped away in a stream-eroded defile that snaked down into the mist. He thought he saw a footpath flanking the stream, crossing it here and there. They descended carefully from the upper ground and picked their way slipping and stumbling downwards. Soon they were among young evergreens, and the fog curled over their heads like floating wraiths.

They were halfway down the ravine, by Gwyn's estimate, when they heard a helicopter.

"Everybody down," he hissed. "Lie still."

Gwyn lay on his back, straining to see through the mist as the craft combed back and forth at the level of the high ground. If it had infra-red heat seekers, they would be pinned down in a matter of minutes. At last he caught a blurred glimpse of a black, unmarked Lynx, possibly the one that set down at Pen y Cae. As he watched, a second helicopter slid into view. A camouflage-green RAF Sea King, like the one that had pursued Yann Morvan's Huey. Both craft rose inland again, and the fog immediately swallowed their sound.

Gwyn got up. He was sharply aware of the cold snow under him, the small loquacious stream, the aromatic scent of evergreens. They would be harder to spot in the trees. He motioned the others into the forestry and hesitated at the stream margin to decide their best way down to the water.

As he turned back to the mist-combed trees, he felt a bullet spit past his shoulder. It thudded into a small trunk and anointed him with sweet-smelling bark.

17

Robert braced himself by the window looking down, as the Sea King swung high above the cliff. There was nothing much to see: forestry evergreens marching down a snowy hillside, rock outcrops, fog. Visual spotting, in any case, was not going to help in the least. He turned back to the array of electronic equipment. Their applied magic was seriously hampered by these conditions. Trying to deal with fugitives on foot in snow and ice fog was like trying to use electronic countermeasures at the Battle of Hastings.

The radio direction finder emitted a slow steady peep. On its monitor screen, green concentric circles spread from a central point like ripples from the proverbial pebble flung in a pond. A technician touched the controls, and a ghostly irregular line appeared, intersecting the circles. That would be the shore line. The source of radio transmission was moving slowly towards the water; abruptly the circles blinked off the screen. The transmission was ended.

"Major Grenvile." Leung, the sober technician, was starting to look as bedraggled as the rest of them. "Heat detector, sir."

Robert crossed the Sea King's metal floor to the infrared monitor. Harold Stone was already there, silent, frowning as he tapped a silver pencil against his chin.

328

Peter Holt and the Welsh photographer came near, sensibly keeping quiet. The technician adjusted scan and colour range until the screen filled with dark blue and green, splashes of pale blue, grey, red, amber. Those were rock outcrops, vegetation, and water. Several glowing white dots stood out sharply from their background. White depicted heat, and heat probably mean animal life.

"Human?" asked Anna Chernicki from his side.

"I think so, although in this fog we can't get a photo image," murmured Leung. "But look at this."

He typed a command on the monitor's keyboard, and the infra-red pattern gave way to a freeze-frame image of green traceries on black, from the direction finder. It showed the coastline, and a bright green pin-point for the location of the last marine band transmission. Another tapping of keys; the coastline and pin-point were superimposed on the infra-red scan. One of the fiery white dots was moving slowly seaward from the radio pin-point.

"It looks like a man with a radio is moving towards the water," said the technician. "Moving downhill from his last point of broadcast."

"Mr. Leung, is there any indication of a boat or other vehicle at the beach?" asked Harold Stone quietly. "Or any other reason he'd be going to the water?"

"Nothing, sir." The technician adjusted the monitor dials, pulling in a larger frame. "It would show up as a distinct shape, about the same colour as the rock outcrops."

He extended the range further, showing the shore line between two rocky points, and inland about halfway up the hillside. Below and to their left, the tapering grey tadpole shape was Fox's hovering helicopter. On the extended image, the white dots were smaller.

"Look!" Anna Chernicki stabbed an elegant forefinger at the screen. "What's that?"

Another white dot moved slowly on screen at the bottom, towards the first dot. The image flickered and changed. On a smaller segment of coastline, vegetation showed as pointillist dabs that could be individual trees.

"Six o'clock, please."

At the same scale, the glowing white point at centre bottom resolved into three. No, four. But the fourth dot was of less intensity, perhaps smaller, than the other three.

"Could that be—"

Robert pried his gaze from the screen and saw Anna Chernicki's mouth lift in a faint smile. Three and a half warm-blooded creatures. Three adults and a child. Did that mean they were in Ireland? Weren't lost at sea? There was at least a hope.

"They could be almost anything," Leung warned, but even he sounded unconvinced. He was grinning.

Robert cleared his throat. "They could also be Davies, Powell, Jean Douglass and the Prince. Or, of course, local people."

"Number 10 will want to hear about this," brayed the PM's aide excitedly.

Robert glanced away, gathering his patience. Harold Stone politely agreed.

"But who's the other one?" mused Robert.

"Another terrorist?" suggested Peter Holt.

"Perhaps. Or perhaps the dots are all farm animals, strayed down to the water. Three cows and a calf."

"I think," said Anna, "it's time for the colonel's hot-shot pilot to show his stuff. The one at twelve o'clock should be in visual range if they drop the chopper almost down to sea level and skim inland a few yards. At least we'll find out if it's human or animal. Can you get him to do that?"

By radio, Fox agreed immediately. On the monitor, Robert saw the SAS Lynx move quickly up screen and across the shore line. With a crackle, the SAS pilot's dead-pan acknowledgement poured into the operation command post. The Lynx turned inshore again at a crawl and moved eastward. Zero visibility, the pilot reported. When he drew alongside, the dot abruptly fell still on the screen.

Anna frowned. "In fog, anyone on the ground has a tremendous advantage. A single rifle shot can disable one of those light copters."

"What about sending in a team?" asked Peter. Al Rees watched him unhappily.

"Not yet," said Stone. "We'll exhaust our other options first."

The helicopter hovered near the figure for more than a minute, so close their colours lapped on the infra-red image.

"Zero visibility," the pilot reported again, than corrected himself equally calmly. "Man with a light weapon. Under fire. Lifting out."

The grey tadpole shape pulled quickly away from the motionless white dot. As the SAS Lynx neared the airborne HQ, the four figures began to move again, more rapidly. All of them drew together, apparently converging for a rendezvous on the shore line. It demanded action, on the ground, and quickly.

"There's little more we can do with helicopters. They can't hover low against the cliff, and we'd throw our people away by asking them to rappel down under fire," Robert said hoarsely. "The essential thing is to re-establish direct communication."

"Mr. Stone," said a technician. "Telephone. From the Cabinet Office briefing room."

Madog bent the manila cable through the eye of the iron hook, heavy enough to anchor a dinghy, and reached to pick up the splicing awl. Instead he knocked it clattering on the hangar floor under the Huey. An hour's sleep had left him clumsy, stiff and gritty under the eyelids. Getting too old for this kind of crap.

"It's pleasant to watch people work," said Yann in Welsh. He lounged on an uninflated life raft, one of several contingency plans, smoking his throat-destroying Algerian grass. "When they know what they're doing."

"Why don't you fuck off?" Madog suggested. "And

speak English. I'm Chernicki's golden boy right now. Let's keep it that way."

"Sure thing, boss," Yann said in his California twang.

The black marines sergeant looked up, suspicious. Wherever Chernicki had pulled him in from was warmer than North Wales in January; he was shivering in his summer cottons. Sixth Fleet, maybe, taking in the sunshine of Libya. Club Med. He was a helicopter mechanic.

"Okay, sergeant. Think it'll hold?" The rope was another contingency plan.

"Yessir. You just got to hook it on the strut or maybe inside—" He hesitated. "Long as you can climb it. A hoist is easier."

"Yeah. I can climb it. I don't know about this jerk-off. And we don't have a hoist. This is the best we can do on short notice. What time is it?"

"Oh-eight hundred, sir."

"Thanks." Outside it would be dawn.

"Hey, sergeant." Yann offered the joint.

The black man looked at Madog, who shrugged. He took a toke, contemplated it, and visibly decided Yann was okay. "So what are you, anyhow? Civilian contract?"

"That's what they told me in Washington." Yann showed his teeth in a feral grin and glanced at Madog.

"Yeah? Where you pick up this baby? Good old crates, these Hueys. . . ."

Madog spliced in the last strand and listened to the two of them bullshit each other. The marine was crowing about their boarding party three hours ago. No one could play at hurt indignation like an East German skipper caught with a hull full of electronics inside someone else's territorial waters. Madog's thoughts wandered west, so far west it was almost east, to the island. Might as well go there. Even rebuilt, Pen y Cae would be desolate without John. But first he had to settle accounts with Corgi.

Gwyn pulled the others behind an outcrop until the new round of firing stopped. What kind of weapon? It was impossible to be sure of any sound more than a few feet away in the fog. A few minutes ago he heard the scuff of boots on rock, but it could have been anywhere. At least two helicopters were working up in the fog, prowling back and forth. By Gwyn's calculation, he and his people were two-thirds of the distance down from the high ground to the shore line. They had to push on and reach water.

Carrie was on her feet, helping Jean up, when she turned suddenly and clutched Gwyn's arm.

"Helicopter," she mouthed.

Directly overhead, but hovering at considerable altitude. It was doing something, dropping soldiers or deploying a weapon. Gwyn motioned them down on the far side of the rocks again, though there was no real shelter. They were desperately vulnerable to the electronics and fire power of their pursuers, with only the old Browning for defence. Jean began praying soundlessly, holding Pip close to her with a hand over his mouth. Gwyn steadied the gun on the snow-moulded rock and waited.

Through the fog, with dream-like slowness, dropped a line. On the end was a grey plastic rectangle the size of a deck of cares. A gas capsule? But before he could act, the thing crackled and spoke his name.

"Gwyn, this is Robert Grenvile. Detach the transceiver. I have good news."

A trick? Probably. But he trusted Grenvile's tricks more than he trusted whoever was stalking them through the fog. Gwyn edged cautiously forward and lifted the device from its hook. The line snaked silently back up and vanished in mist. The radio was something like the one Peter Holt carried into Pen y Cae, the one they'd lost with Madog. Gwyn crouched back among the rocks and found the transmit button.

"What is it, Grenvile?"

"Let me bring you up to date first. You're in a precarious position. We have you surrounded with special-operation teams. I think you should turn yourselves over— before someone gets hurt. The good news is from the

House of Commons. The opposition leader is sticking to
her guns and insisting on a first reading of an emergency
bill to pump aid into Welsh industry and television, and
another Welsh plebiscite on home rule. Two members have
crossed the House. By evening the opposition may have
coalition of some sort.''

"Prove it.''

"I can't prove it, not by radio. But, Gwyn, have I lied
to you once?''

Gwyn maintained his silence, thinking.

"Is the Prince with you?''

"Yes.''

"I'd like to hear his voice.''

"What'll you give in return?''

"The truth. There's no boat off shore, Gwyn. We're
watching you and the other man on infra-red. We know
every time you take a step. But there's no boat anywhere
near.''

"Where is he?'' Other man? Corgi? Madog?

"Let me hear the boy first.''

Gwyn turned to the others. "Want to talk on the radio,
Pip?''

The boy's face brightened. "Is it Madog?''

"No. It's—a friend of your mam's.'' He held the device
to the boy's mouth. "Quietly. There are people all around
us.''

"Hello?'' Pip was suddenly an uncharacteristically shy.
"Can I talk to my mum?''

"Very soon, I hope. How are you, Pip?''

"Fine, thank you. Mungo and Pal got lost at Madog's
house. Are they with you?''

"Not right this minute. Maybe later on. Goodbye, Pip.''

"Bye.''

Gwyn took the line. "Now where is this man?''

"To your right, as you face the sea. Closing.''

"Listen carefully, Major. When he closes, as you put
it, we may be out of options. I'm not sure who he is.
Someone's hunting us down here. We've been fired at.''

Grenvile said nothing for a moment. "What can we do?"

"Is Peter with you?"

A new voice on the radio. "Holt here."

Gwyn said in Welsh, "Someone is stalking us, as near as I can tell. If it's Corgi, he seems to have a contract to kill the boy. Tell Grenvile that. I didn't want to frighten the boy." He left Madog out of the equation. Probably he was dead in the snow at Cwm Emrys.

"Right."

Grenvile came back on, as calm as though they'd discussed a fishing expedition. Gwyn's heart was knocking under his ribs. Giving voice to terror increased it tenfold.

'I'm giving it to you straight, Gwyn. The special teams are moving towards you with orders to hold fire, but it's an extremely unstable situation. The best thing you can do is move slowly uphill, and we'll try to cut off the other man behind you."

"No," said Gwyn. There was a limit to his trust for Grenvile, regardless of his clean slate for the truth. "Last time we trusted you, you shot Elen Parry in cold blood. Jean Douglass and Ceridwen Powell have nothing to do with this, and I won't turn them over to you for target practice."

"All right." Grenvile changed tack, still unruffled. "Why do you say Corgi?"

"He tried to stop us. Last night near Cwm Emrys. You'd better tell me now, Grenvile. Is he working for you?"

One of Grenvile's long pauses followed; he was probably checking something. "He's not working for us. I suggest extreme caution."

"Thanks." The sarcasm fell flat.

"Gwyn, we've got to get the boy out. If I give my word of honour, my most solemn oath, that the women won't be harmed, will you bring them up?"

"No. Honour didn't help Elen. And you're not getting your hands on me."

"Is that more important than the safety of the women and the boy?"

Gwyn kept silent. He thought he heard a scrape of metal on rock nearby. He stared into the fog. Nothing visible.

Grenvile said at last, "Gwyn, you don't have long. If I come down to meet you, will you start uphill?"

"No. Take care of the other man. Then we can talk."

"We'll do—"

The rest was lost as a bullet spat into the rock a yard away. Gwyn instinctively flung himself backward and rolled to aim the Browning into the fog. It swirled deceptively, promising to reveal a human form and revealing only more grey strands. And then it parted, long enough to show someone crouched at the downhill side of another rock to Gwyn's right, pointing a hand-gun. Gwyn pulled the trigger. The Browning's bullet smacked into the rock, sending up a shower of chips. Missed. The figure vanished back into the mist.

A minute later Jean Douglass screamed.

Robert scanned the infra-red screen and gave instructions into the radio transceiver. Like directing a blind man through a shooting gallery with a barrel of nitroglycerine.

"East again," he told Fox. "Then downhill."

The colonel's white blip moved fractionally to the right and upscreen. The four white dots of his number-one team kept pace; the rest were spread across the hillside behind. Fox insisted on going in himself. More recruiting-poster bravado, but Robert had to admit the man had the experience and courage.

"Down again."

"Still nothing visual," reported Fox.

On the infra-red screen, the hillside was speckled with white-yellow dots. It was unlike a military command-room map; the dots were in no way distinguished one from another. Any of them could be defending the child who was Britain's heir apparent, or attempting to murder him. All of them were warm-blooded creatures, dancing a complex pattern of death and survival.

"Gwyn?" Robert tried again on the other radio.

Davies didn't answer. A few minutes ago his cluster had split apart. Robert directed Fox towards the smaller group, which, he prayed, included the child. He had to make his priority the Prince and worry about the others later.

"Closing," he warned Fox. "Two o'clock." Robert, faintly but clearly over the radio, heard gun-fire. "Colonel?"

Jean screamed when a man darted out of the mist and wrested Pip from her arms. He was gone in an instant.

Without hesitation, Jean scrambled after him. She saw the man retreating ahead of her, back turned, and hurled herself at her child's captor.

The figure turned, crouching, to deflect her attack. Jean had no time to speak, even to pray, before the bullets hit her.

Finally Robert had a reply to his repeated query.

"Coming out," said Fox. "Negative success with target, repeat, negative success. Prepare for casualties."

Carrie crouched beside Gwyn in the scant shelter of the outcrop, face in her hands. The scene was printed behind her eyes. The unknown man with a gun at Pip's head, dragging him into the mist. Jean Douglass stumbling after him.

"If I'd been watching more closely, if I'd gone after them . . ."

"If you'd gone after them you'd be dead," Gwyn said quietly. "Stop, my girl. Keep you wits about you."

Carrie nodded numbly. Gwyn stood and shoved the Browning's clip back in place, staring at the relentless fog on every side. Someone could be five yards away, ready to blast them to oblivion, or nowhere within range. It was impossible to tell.

"What now?" she asked dully.

The Prince was gone. The worst had happened. They could only hope the boy's captor recognized his value alive, and that the gunshots didn't signal Pip's death.

"Now we get Pip back."

Peter watched from the helicopter window as Fox and his men appeared over the lip of the slope and climbed onto high ground. It was a relief to see something with his own eyes, not through the infra-red heat detector's remote sensors. One of Fox's troopers carried a body in his arms, blonde hair streaming over his camouflage jacket. Jean Douglass, who had sold the Prince to terrorists, but whom the terrorists dismissed as innocent. Peter wondered if they would ever sort out the contradiction.

A first-aid lorry jolted over the snowy field, one of the contingent of ground support that had been arriving for the past hour. Medics sprinted out to meet Fox's group. They placed the woman on a stretcher. A cadre of men and women in neutral grey suits swarmed around the SAS men, obscuring them from Peter's view.

"Mr. Holt?" Leung handed him the radio mike. "Please keep it brief. We'll need the line."

"Holt here."

"Peter. I phoned to thank you." A low purring voice, always startling.

"Elizabeth. How are you?" It was a far from casual question after Teddy's stalking.

"Muddling through." She sounded very tired. "Your friends have been marvelous. Someone phoned to say those dreadful men are dead, they found two bodies this morning in a picnic site in Snowdonia. The third is in hospital under guard. I can't say I'm especially sorry. Here's Andrea."

"Daddy! I'm watching you stuff on telly. Mum let me stay home from school. Smashing stuff, it's way better then *Miami Vice.*"

"Thanks, sweetheart." He'd have to talk to Elizabeth

again soon about the television violence. "Got to ring off, Andy."

Peter handed the phone back to the technician and watched people below go about their business. CBS had his footage. All his hunches were spent. The sun was nearly over Snowdon in the east, and the impenetrable sea fog was showing signs of lifting. What was happening below, on the shore, beyond the indifferent surveillance cameras? If he could find a way down there . . .

"These sods think Wales is their personal training ground." Al said in quiet Welsh.

Peter turned and found Al's unreadable gaze on him. Perhaps it was not too late to mend bridges. They did make a good team. Peter crossed the Sea King's rear compartment to sit next to Al.

"For what?"

Al shrugged. "What was *Y Malvinas* for? This is a chance to create a Welsh incident in time for the next election and give the SAS a dress rehearsal. Your government wants to end the mess in Ulster for all time—by more violence, they think. After that, Wales. And they need public support so they can step up nuclear waste dumping here. The worse this looks, the better it is for them."

"Be serious." Peter paused long enough to turn it over. Al's *clecs* had never failed yet. Even the teaser about Morvan's helicopter was spot on. "Think we can get a story on it? Especially the Welsh angle?"

Al nodded slowly, then grinned. "You can bank on it, Peter *bach.* "

Grenvile was on the radio. "I know very well the Prince is still—"

"Bloody hell." Peter furrowed his brow. "We've got to get this on tape. How can we get down there?"

Gwyn listened, then continued downhill. The fog was thinning slightly but still hung over the shore where slow waves were breaking. Here the ground levelled out to a snow-covered flat area overgrown with bramble, willow, and salt-stunted oak. On either side of the open space, rock rose in steep bluffs. No sign of Pip or his captor. Gwyn decided they must be heading for the shore and the boat whose existence Grenvile denied. He crouched beside a bramble snarl and pulled Carrie down beside him.

"They could be anywhere," she whispered. "Should we split now?"

"Go west as far as the cliff, then come back to this rock. I'll go east. When we get Pip, you'll take him up to Grenvile." Gwyn handed her the gun. "Watch out. It kicks right."

"I don't want it."

"Go!"

Carrie started off through the bush, keeping low. Gwyn watched her fade between strands of fog, then turned the other way. In only a few minutes, he reached the limit of the open space. The eastward bluff stepped up from the hidden sea in snowy terraces. Was there a cove on the far side? He climbed carefully, in sight at last of barnacled rocks and sea foam, until a slick vertical face forced him to ascend a few yards. He picked his way across the top, cautious on the icy granite.

A man's voice, very close, was speaking quietly in German.

Gwyn froze. The voice was somewhere above him on the outcrop. He looked carefully upward, but couldn't see over the broken curve of rock. He edged forward. Surprise was on his side. He would climb far enough to circle over his head, drop on him, and send him for a swing in the near-freezing sea water. That would keep him occupied while Gwyn found the kid. He couldn't be too far, if he was alive. At least there hadn't been a shot. Gwyn worked his way cautiously forward, placing one foot at a time on the slick granite, stopping at every step to listen. At last he had gone far enough to get above the man. He climbed on a rough ledge and heard only the wash of waves below. Wait.

A figure dropped, agile as a cat, onto the ledge, aiming

a Heckler and Koch. Corgi shoved the barrel in Gwyn's ribs, forcing him to flatten himself face-in to the granite. He showed his teeth in a mask of blood. Stone chips. So it had been Corgi up in the forestry, and a near miss after all.

"So we meet again, Mr. Davies," said Corgi in that toffee-nosed voice. "Hear you've been getting rather chummy with Bobby Grenvile. Pity he can't help you out of this spot, old man."

"Don't count on it," Gwyn tried. "He's right behind you."

Surprise relaxed Corgi's guard almost imperceptibly, but it was the best chance he would get. Gwyn lunged for him. Corgi was faster. He grabbed Gwyn's hair and smashed his face into the rock. Before he recovered. Corgi struck him behind the ear with the gun butt. Gwyn staggered, clawing for a grip on the granite while the world reeled around him. An elbow pinned him against the cliff so he couldn't fall.

Gwyn felt the gun barrel shoved behind his left knee. He convulsed away from its touch. Not far enough. The gunshot roared against the rock and ripped through his leg like molten steel. He fell onto the ledge, trying to scream. When Gwyn opened his eyes, seconds or hours later, Corgi was gone. Ceridwen.

Carrie knelt with her head on her knees, listening to the roar of her heart and the quiet voice ten feet away. One man was reporting to a superior, apparently by radio, in clipped military jargon. Another was swearing at the weather. She thought there were four of them. She waited, counting the seconds and minutes. Like her, they had taken shelter in the thickly treed crease where the rock bluff rose westward from the sea-level plateau. Glacial action on an igneous core; she compiled land-forms as a catechism of normalcy to get her through the terror. The soldiers were SAS. They would kill her on sight.

After ten minutes, by her uneven count, they headed

down towards the water. They moved silently. Carrie raised her head cautiously and saw nothing but sea mist weaving a tapestry of grey on grey. It was clearer above; the snow-covered rocks were visible in patches. A breath of wind stirred the mist apart. She began to move, still crouching, uphill. If she didn't spot anyone, she would go back to the rock to meet Gwyn. She had crept perhaps thirty yards uphill when she saw the child.

Pip was tied to a young evergreen. His grubby face was stained with tears, but now he was tugging determinedly at the yellow nylon rope that bound his wrists. Another few paces uphill, a fair-haired man crouched pushing bullets into the clip of a small automatic rifle. Carrie recognized the man Madog had run after last night. Corgi. Pip, abandoning his battle with the rope, looked up and saw Carrie.

Quickly, she put a finger to her lips. The little boy grinned in delight. Carrie backed into the undergrowth, wondering how she could draw Corgi down here, yet keep Pip out of harm's way. Difficult.

The granite bluff rose only a few paces behind her. Carrie inched through the bramble and scrub, stopping dead every time a twig or leaf rattled. After interminable effort, she was level with Corgi. He looked around now, restless. Finally, he got to his feet and went towards Pip. Halfway there he halted, perhaps hearing something.

Move, you silly shit. But the man crouched motionless, listening. What now? Carrie looked around for a stone, anything to throw. Nothing. She felt her pockets. A handkerchief. Something light and hard; Madog's obsidian arrowhead. Carrie threw it with all her force at the nearest exposed rock, and heard it tick and clatter twice before it stopped. Corgi spun around, aiming the gun. Then he went to investigate and climbed up on the first shelf of granite.

As Carrie tensed to make her move, the air exploded with shots from Corgi's automatic rifle. Someone farther up the slope returned fire. Corgi, twisting this way and that to peer through the mist, finally saw Carrie. They faced each other, unmoving for the barest second. Carrie, with the Browning off safety and cocked, had one fleeting thought: what was she, a pacifist, doing with a weapon? But it was Pip's life, maybe hers. She raised the gun.

Another barrage of gunshots from above. Corgi threw himself on the broken ground and began to worm his way across the hillside. Soon he was out of sight.

Carrie lowered the unfired pistol, half relieved. No time to waste. She dashed down to Pip and untied him with shaking fingers. Taking his small cold hand, she started uphill.

"Come, Pip. Let's take you back to your mam."

"I want Miss Douglass." He stopped. "And Madog."

"We'll see, my dear." She'd find a way to explain to him later. After a scant dozen steps, she stopped with a gasp.

A man stood in their path a shorter man than Corgi. His eyes were pale blue inside his black Balaclava. He had them covered with a stubby automatic rifle.

"Drop the gun, Miss Powell."

Gwyn writhed in torment. To be free of them all: a man in a microwave shed, three school children, John Hughes, Elen, Sion, Madog, Raffael, the SAS men at Pen y Cae. He spun a a thread of thought and clung to it. If he could roll towards the water it would be over. Deep. Cold. Black. Forever. He lost the thread again.

Once Gwyn thought Madog stood over him, saying something. The side of his face was bruised, and it was hard to understand his words. Beside Madog, flashing his predator's grin, slouched Yann Morvan. Snow was blowing through the long fur of his wolfskin coat. Behind them a knotted rope swayed gently in the fog.

"Bastard got you, huh?" asked Madog. "Let's get out of here fast."

"No." Gwyn shook his head at the ghost.

"*Foll,*" said Yann.

"Na, not crazy." Madog smiled, and his gold tooth

flashed. "Just a purist. He has trouble with compromise. Not like you and me."

Gwyn felt a jab in his thigh.

"Morphine. *Da boch, machgen.*"

"Wait," Gwyn said.

"Make up your mind." Madog looked sad. "Stay or go?"

"You. What do you choose?"

"Me? I don't have to make any choice. I go where I'm sent."

"No. You don't believe that."

No answer. He opened his eyes. Nothing. The hallucination was over. Then Gwyn found he could move gain, carefully, and felt Madog's angular plastic gun in his hand.

NANT CERRIG/JANUARY 21/0930

They let Carrie hold Pip's hand as the party slipped and clambered up the ravine. He was afraid of the black-clad soldiers without faces.

At the top, in the snow-bound field, they handcuffed her. Carrie stared around in shock. Two hours ago the snow swept unbroken from the forestry up through fields to the road. Now rows of military and government vehicles bounded the field, and four large helicopters squatted outside an inflatable hangar with their rotors drooping down around their fuselages. Beyond that, a vast crowd of people and cars and equipment had mushroomed behind a police cordon. Even more distant, along the public road, stood the inevitable ranks of the curious.

Battalions of grey-suited men and women were hastening from the vehicles to surround them. Someone led Pip away. He looked wide-eyed back over his shoulder, uncertain whether to cry. The man who identified himself as Fox stayed close with four of his men. A red-faced man in a grey suit was hurling questions at her in English, but she was too dazed to understand that language. He suddenly fell quiet, and the crowd opened around her.

A blond woman ran towards them across the trampled snow with her plum-coloured coat billowing wide. Her face was pink from the cold and from crying, and in one hand she held a furry toy. Pip ran to her. The Queen snatched up her son and hugged him convulsively. She kissed his dirty face until Pip squirmed to the ground, clutching a new-looking Mungo Mouse. A few people bowed and curtseyed awkwardly; protocol didn't cover kidnappings. From behind, someone jostled Carrie off-balance. She stumbled forward and fell to her knees. Pip looked happy to see his mam, and Carrie smiled at him. For a moment, the tall and beautiful blonde woman considered the dark woman with uncertain curiosity.

Grey suits closed around the Queen and the Prince. One of the black limousines crunched across the snow, swallowed them, and crept silently away. The field was suddenly emptier.

Carrie looked around. No sign of Gwyn, Jean, Madog. Of course. She had to keep reminding herself. She struggled to her feet.

A mild-faced man with greying fair hair approached her. With him was the BBC reporter Peter Holt and a chunky brown man in a silver jacket. Fox and his soldiers fell back, watching closely.

"Miss Powell? Robert Grenvile," the grey man introduced himself. "We're going to have to take you into custody for questioning, and you may face charges. I'll do everything possible. Gwyn explained your situation."

Carrie nodded uncertainly. It was more than she hoped. She'd never been sure whether Gwyn believed Madog's tale.

"Is he here?"

"No. Our first concern was for the Prince. Now we can worry about the rest."

The SAS man, Fox, stepped forward. He had the lower part of his Balaclava pulled down, revealing a thin mouth. His pale eyes gazed first at Carrie, then Grenvile.

"We're going down."

Grenvile frowned. "Not yet, Colonel. My orders are to bring everyone out alive, whatever their part. There'll be a trial."

"I have orders to clean up."

Grenvile said in a strangled voice, "This isn't Ulster, Colonel. Not yet. I know full well what you mean by cleaning up."

Fox nodded to one of the other four men. They turned together and started back towards the ravine.

Grenvile looked after them and demanded of Carrie, "Where's Gwyn?"

Quickly she described his search eastward along the shore. Grenvile sprinted for the helicopter with RAF markings. Carrie stood alone. A man in a camouflage jacket came to take charge of her, casting a look of disgust after Grenvile.

"Who dares wins." Robert remembered the SAS motto and ordered the startled RAF pilot out over the hillside. Between the Americans and SAS he was at his wits' end. It was all he could think to do. He turned to the heat detector. Leung was there ahead of him, with the screen already set up to infra-red scan.

A scatter of white-yellow dots, warm-bodied creatures, was moving steadily upscreen, which meant down to ravine to the sea. A dozen or more others were already scattered around the upper slope, unmoving in their assigned positions. Those would be Fox's men, though they could also include the two unknown and unlocated men. Nothing else, except a single dot in the grey zone of rock outcrops, almost at the water margin. Gwyn. At least he had to risk it being Gwyn. Not Corgi.

Robert's business was to preserve life, not to threaten it. He had days of sweat and insomnia already invested in the life of Gwyn Davies. All the same, he momentarily regretted his lack of any weapon but his wits.

The sea fog was thinning. It clung thickest in a few indentations of the shingle beach and snagged on the granite bluffs. At the window, Robert strained to see through the mist, to identify anything human. Rock and snow and fog. Then the pilot yelled above the rotor noise.

"Can't get in closer. You'll have to go down by hoist."

Robert went forward and looked over the co-pilot's shoulder through the lower windscreen. Below, he saw a man sitting wedged into a cleft of rock. One of the technicians opened the side hatch and prepared the hoist. Robert braced himself for the sea chill and the rotor wind; he should have found a parka. He pulled the padded canvas horse collar over his head and fitted it under his arms, then gave the signal to descend. Halfway down, the cold hit him in a shock wave. When he felt rock under his leather soles, he dropped forward on hands and knees, tearing the trousers of his suit. He pulled off the horse collar. The helicopter lifted up and out.

Gwyn was sitting with his back to the rock cliff, arms folded on his chest. His face was bruised, and blood had soaked through his cord trousers to freeze on one leg. Savages. He looked younger than Robert expected.

"Robert Grenvile." He got to his feet. "Are you all right?"

"No." Gwyn smiled faintly. "You shouldn't have come down here. Corgi will be back for the final lesson. This was just the preamble."

"I had no choice," Robert said quickly. "My military colleagues are on their way to, as they put it, clean up. You understand?"

"Yes."

"I'm not going to let you be a martyr. The SAS don't take time for such refinements. Surrender and I'll get you out alive."

"Why?"

Robert was afraid of that. "There's no time to debate, for God's sake. It's all over."

"Yes."

"Gwyn," Robert tried desperately. "You've made your point. The child is with his mother, Miss Powell is out safely, the House of Commons is moving towards a first reading of the Welsh emergency bill—''

"Promising what?" It was a challenge.

"Promising only to reconsider Welsh home rule and industry and television. All this has shaken the governments rather dreadfully. There may be a non-confidence motion this evening. There's some kind of spat in Cabinet, and two more members are expected to join the opposition. The present government can't take much pressure."

Robert recalled their urgency. "Now will you come?"

"Why go to prison? I'll never walk again."

"Write your thesis. Run for parliament. Do something for your country."

Robert saw a sudden stillness cross Gwyn's face, and his right hand clenched on the gun butt half hidden under his left arm.

"Don't do it, Gwyn."

A pleasant voice behind Robert said, "Hands on your head, and don't move."

The electronic city of the media was already taking shape behind the police cordon: aluminum scaffolding to raise cameras for clear shots, crowds of cameramen, photographers, sound men, assistants, print sub-editors with their portable computers. Peter saw the network logos— BBC, ITN, CBS, NBC, all of the Europeans—and familiar faces. Even gormless Harry Price was here, earning his senior salary for once. Everywhere, reporters scrabbled for a few original words from anyone even peripherally involved with the huge military endeavour.

Soon they would be interviewing each other, Peter reckoned. They would certainly try to interview him, but he knew what his material was worth: a quick book, a nine-hour wonder, a name in the right circles. The hiring circles.

Their presence meant that Peter was rapidly losing his news advantage over them. He caught Al's eye and nodded towards the sea.

Unnoticed they slipped away from the military. Anna Chernicki saw, but she was deep in talk with Harold Stone. They reached the edge of the ravine before anyone tried to halt them.

"Where do you think you're going?" shouted a soldier. "That's off limits."

"Major Grenvile's permission," Peter yelled back and plunged down the footpath. By the time they learned otherwise, it would be too late to do much about it.

Al led the way down at a lope despite the steepness of the grade and the hazard of the SAS and the others below. Peter hissed at him to go slower, but found his own momentum carrying him faster downhill. He concentrated on keeping his footing until Al stopped abruptly. They slithered a few feet and lay still in the snow. Below, half a dozen of the black-clad special-assault soldiers were fanned out across the hillside, searching as they descended.

"Suggestions?" whispered Peter.

"Let me roll some tape," Al mouthed. "Then over to the right. We'll climb down on the rocks and try for wide shots."

"Don't do it, Gwyn," Robert said again, meaning something quite different this time, "Talk."

"Yes, let's talk," suggested the well-bred voice. "About your friends with the helicopter. A lift offshore for myself and our young Prince would be helpful just now. When are they coming back?"

"They're not." Robert saw sweat on Gwyn's chalky face. The hand that held the gun a minute ago was now empty. Robert nodded fractionally. As long as you're talking. "So you had second thoughts about killing the boy."

Robert looked sharply. What was this?

"Rather crudely put, Mr. Davies. But yes, of course, terrible thing even to contemplate. Some clients demand the most unreasonable services. Have to draw the line somewhere, don't you think? I know his parents will be overjoyed to have him back."

"For a fee."

"Cost recovery, Mr. Davies. Expensive operation. More expensive yet when I link up with these East German fishermen. Their electronics and weapons set them back a few *deutschmarks,* and think of the risk. Meter's ticking, so to speak."

"How many people are you working for, Corgi? Not that I thought we had exclusive rights to your services. Are you working for Grenvile?"

Corgi smiled broadly. "As my former co once pointed out, why talk to the horse's arse if you can talk to its head? I have, shall we say, a number of well-placed clients, including some gentlemen with high political ambitions. And of course your charming and well-heeled American companion."

Robert involuntarily closed his eyes. If that were true . . . Gwyn swallowed hard. "I don't believe you."

"You really ought to, old man. You heard the offer he made at our moonlight picnic."

"He paid you off? For what?"

"For his life. Couldn't resist temptation when he reached five million. I must say he places a high value on his skin. He'll reach New York—let me see—around noon."

Gwyn said nothing. Corgi, to Robert's amazement, talked on.

"Told him to clear off. Getting in everyone's way—he really didn't belong here. Trust your boss will rebuke Washington, Bobby. American military intelligence nosing around in England. Disgraceful show."

"How did you find us?" Gwyn shifted his weight slightly, reminding Robert that he couldn't keep this up forever.

"I had a delightful meeting with one of your people in London ten days ago. She was quite chuffed over her arrangement with the trawler captain."

"Nora," Gwyn said bitterly. "She'll be boasting of her exploits in Armagh by now. But how do you know she didn't call off the boat?"

"No opportunity, I'm afraid. BBC radio says an unmarked helicopter dropped a young woman at the RAF base on Anglesey yesterday. Rather churlish of your friends, wouldn't you say?"

"Smart, not churlish. They came to pick up the American, not her. But dumping her probably saved their lives. She's a murdering, treacherous arse-hole."

"Rather harsh, Mr. Davies. But in any case she'll be accepting government hospitality for some time. . . ."

Robert allowed himself a breath of relief. Corgi thoroughly enjoyed the sound of his own voice, thank God. He silently willed endurance to Gwyn.

"O Duw," breathed Al, plastered flat on the snow-covered granite and looking at the scene below. He began to roll tape.

Peter lay frozen, trying not to shiver, and gazed on a scene of raw nightmare. Below them stood Teddy Smythe, covering Gwyn and Grenvile with an automatic weapon. His face was bloody, and he looked thoroughly dangerous. Peter watched helplessly as the story played itself out.

Grenvile stood between them, hands on his head. The mercenary's gun was pointed at his kidneys. The negotiator looked calm, even uninterested, as the other two talked. Peter listened in growing dread as Gwyn questioned and commented, subtly flattering Smythe—Corgi—for his cleverness. How long could he keep that up? Peter tore his eyes away an instant, and glanced at Al. Still taping.

An incredible story. And now it was going to end in terror and blood.

Peter started to worry. What could he do for a stinger? He'd have to use stock footage and recycle tape from earlier in the incident, piece together some sort of satisfactory ending. Maybe some philosophical clips from Gwyn's interview, or the shattered promise of earlier Welsh pacifist activism. Something to give some shred of meaning to Peter's nine-hour wonder and to Gwyn Davies's life and death.

Peter turned his head an inch and froze in shock. Only a few feet to his right lay Fox, flat on his belly. Fox raised a rifle with infinite care and slowly squeezed the trigger. Before the sharp rock echoes died, blood blossomed on Corgi's forehead, and he pitched forward to sprawl across Gwyn's feet. Grenvile lowered his hands, and wiped blood on his suit trousers. In seconds, Fox and two other SAS troopers were down on the ledge.

"Mr. Davies has surrendered himself into my safe keeping," said Grenvile, brisk-voiced as he resumed his negotiation. "He was about to turn over his hand-gun when this man came on us."

Peter, who had heard their earlier talk and knew otherwise, held his breath. Fox kept the short rifle trained on Gwyn.

Gwyn looked at the negotiator a long moment. Then he held out a gun to the SAS officer. When Fox took it, Gwyn leaned back against the rock, eyes closed.

Overhead, Peter could hear the Sea King hovering back and forth, then the slither of rope as the hoist descended slowly through the fog. He watched Grenvile, who was looking thoughtfully out to sea. Al shook his head sadly and checked the tape counter on his camera. Enough for a to-camera extro.

"Looks like you got things all settled without me," said a mild voice, vaguely Welsh, off to Peter's right. "At least I don't have to pay off Corgi. It was looking kind of expensive."

Peter glanced over his shoulder. Wreathed in mist, with a Kalashnikov under his arm and looking rather the worse for wear, was Madog Nilsson.

"Captain," said Grenvile by way of greeting. He looked embarrassed. Well he might, Peter thought. "Excellent work."

Fox nodded stiffly.

Nilsson spoke quietly into a hand-held transmitter. The chatter of the helicopter overhead grew louder as it eased down. A grey-white underbelly showed through the fog. Not the RAF Sea King, but Yann Morvan's Huey. Incredible. Peter was glad to see Al ease his camera up enough to roll tape. Nilsson dropped down onto Gwyn's ledge.

"Hope you're getting good material." Nilsson grinned up at Peter.

"Right," Peter, scrabbling for a question, asked in Welsh, "Yann Morvan. How long have you worked with him?"

"Never met the man in my life." He looked Peter straight in the eye. "Hear he's some kind of Celtic nationalist."

"How did you get here?" Peter demanded.

"Kilpatrick told Miss Powell about the fishboat. And any good old boy can hot-wire a car. I had to get to Caernarfon in a hurry last night."

"Is there really a fishing boat out there?"

"There was. Now in Caernarfon harbour while your authorities question the captain and crew."

"Who do you work for? The CIA?"

Nilsson looked at Grenvile.

"Peter," Grenvile said.

"Right." Peter kept quiet.

"Out of tape," Al said sadly.

Gwyn was with them again, watching.

"You chose," he said to Nilsson in Welsh. "You came back."

"I did," Nilsson agreed. He crouched beside Gwyn on the ledge and said, still in Welsh, "So now you choose. Yann will do what you ask. So will I. Stay and make peace? Or run and make war?"

"Stay."

Nilsson grasped the rope and gave it three sharp pulls. It snaked upward. The Huey lifted and slid farther out to sea. The rotor noise quickly died away northward, close to the water.

Peter gaped. Double agents existed, all right, and British intelligence didn't have a patent on moles and turncoats. But an American playing terrorist and military intelligence at the same time? All to draw a few extremists out of the woodwork so that they could be dealt with summarily? Yet Chernicki's offhand comments and smiling silences yesterday had seemed to indicate that a U.S. government agency had taken part from start to finish. There had certainly been the promise of featuring British intelligence as the heroes of the hour, restoring their lost credibility. But that reading would make the whole incident primarily a media event: the kidnapping of the Prince, Nilsson as his personal bodyguard, the American cousins helping Britain which, as Chernicki glossed it, had been a great world power. Would that alone have attracted the Americans?

What Peter didn't know was the all-important missing link: exactly how cynical were these people, these agencies? What darker ambition, what future leverage on the British government, were they pursuing?

Nilsson got to his feet beside Gwyn, shook hands with Grenvile and gave Fox a lazy salute. "Better call in the medics, Colonel."

Fox returned the salute perfunctorily and turned to one of his troopers. "Get those civilians out of here. And warn that helicopter pilot he can lose his licence for intruding into the airspace of a military operation."

Grenvile and Nilsson had their heads together, but Peter caught only a maddening few words. Something about COBRA, then something about Washington.

"*Duw*," said Al. "World broadcast for sure, Peter *bach*."

Peter nodded, struck dumb by the possibilities. He reckoned there were two ways to handle the story. Brutal kidnapping, brilliant negotiation, SAS heroes, last-ditch terrorist surrender. Fast and flashy. Or he could do the difficult in-depth story that would get him in trouble again with some network, some government office, about this small country that refused to die, gently or any other way. He'd have to give it a moral so he didn't make people think this sort of gormless stunt was acceptable.

Of course Peter knew which it had to be. More trouble. Then to black.

TOP-SPEED THRILLERS WITH UNFORGETTABLE IMPACT FROM AVON BOOKS

TASS IS AUTHORIZED TO ANNOUNCE...   Julian Semyonov
                                       70569-9/$4.50US/$5.95Can
From Russia's bestselling author, the unique spy thriller that tells it from the other point of view.

DEEP LIE   Stuart Woods   70266-5/$4.95US/$5.95Can
The new Soviet-sub superthriller..."Almost too plausible...one of the most readable espionage novels since *The Hunt for the Red October!*"
Atlanta Journal & Constitution

RUN BEFORE THE WIND   Stuart Woods
                                       70507-9/$3.95US/$4.95Can
"The book has everything—love, sex, violence, adventure, beautiful women and power-hungry men, terrorists and intrigue."
The Washington Post

COLD RAIN   Vic Tapner   75483-5/$3.95US/$4.95Can
A stunning thriller of cold-blooded espionage and desperate betrayal!

MAJENDIE'S CAT   Frank Fowlkes   70408-0/$3.95
Swindler against con man compete in a plan to bring the US to its knees and wreak global economy for good!

THE GRAY EAGLES   Duane Unkefer   70279-7/$4.50
Thirty-one years after WW II, the Luftwaffe seeks revenge...and one more chance at glory.

THE FLYING CROSS   Jack D. Hunter
                                       75355-3/$3.95US/$4.95Can
From the author of *The Blue Max*, a riveting, suspense-packed flying adventure in the war-torn skies over Europe.